REDSHIFT RUNNERS

PARALLAX

TONY PEAK

aethonbooks.com

PARALLAX
©2022 TONY PEAK

Also in Redshift Runners

You're about to read: Parallax

Up next: Drying Suns

Then: Termination Vector

Also by Tony Peak from Aethon Books: Eden

Get the Eden Box Set, featuring all three books in the series. 1000+ pages of a far future, alien planet survival adventure perfect for fans of J.N. Chaney, A.G. Riddle, and *Horizon Zero Dawn*.

They hoped to create a paradise. Instead, they created hell.

Phoa was terraformed by nanite swarms for Earth's colonists to create a beautiful, habitable world. But the swarms evolved, overran the planet, and two centuries later, threaten every living thing remaining on it.

Reyes, a scientist from Phoa's last colonial enclave, and Thanata, a bioengineered hunter from a rival tribe, must work together to halt the Green: the massive swarm that absorbs plants, animals—even entire cities. But if the unlikely pair hopes to survive the mutated wilds and the deadly Green, they'll have to learn to understand each other.

Buy this special edition omnibus to experience this complete post-apocalyptic series.

This boxset contains three full-length novels:

Book 1: Eden Descending

Book 2: Eden's Tears

Book 3: Eden's Crown

Get Eden Now!

MEC datafile 2678, Runner Addendum:

The Casimir drive allowed humanity to travel the void using temporary wormholes across spacetime. Its operation required a human pilot, immune to AI hacks—but it gradually eroded the pilot's memories. These stardrives allowed Earth's colonies to spread over the cosmos, from 61 Cygni to Procyon and beyond.

Soon those colonies fought over who owned—or understood—such gateways to the stars. Our species became scattered. Humanity bred itself into varieties that would better survive new worlds and philosophies. After many wars, the Merged Earth Colonies assumed control of the Orion Spur and decided which worlds would eat and starve. Some obeyed, others resisted. Thus the Runners were born.

This group of military aces, space jockeys, and pirates braved blockades and solar flares to help failing colonies and live free of MEC control. Pushing the limits of human spaceflight, many Runners perished in the process. Some forgot who they were and went insane, others were lost to the void, none received praise or honors.

CHAPTER 1

Another body floated past the cracked viewport and Deadeye gave it the finger. It was his ship's captain. The shattered faceplate revealed swollen features caused by a loss of atmospheric pressure. The guy had been a jerk ever since Deadeye took the piloting contract, and now he would probably die with him.

They could have escaped the pirates if he'd let Deadeye make a second jump. Yet the man had been stubborn and arrogant, like most MEC captains—a deadlier combination than torpedoes fitted with nuclear warheads.

While the ship trembled around him, Deadeye searched for a spare thrustpack in the airlock chamber. Of course, there were none because his now-deceased captain had thought it better to give them all to the mercenaries onboard. The mercenaries who should have repelled the pirate boarding party. Now their bodies floated with the captain.

That's what he got for working with MEC. Sure, they controlled most colonies across the Orion Spur, the pay was good, and they seemed to appreciate the skills of an Uzari veteran like himself, but he was expendable. He should have been used to that by now.

He whistled one of the silly romance songs Homesteaders played on their radio streams. It always had helped him think back when he flew dropships in the MEC navy.

Back when he'd had a real name, not just a callsign.

Sure, he could change it. Pick a new moniker from random, or pay an identity broker at the next spaceport to forge a new name for him. He could even pretend it was real and that he hadn't forgotten most of his past due to flying ships through wormholes.

Though he had not lost his will to survive or forgotten to live every moment like it was his last. Even an animal knew it didn't want to die.

He whistled louder as a wrench floated above its smashed toolbox.

The ship's centrifuge had stopped working, and the artificial gravity was gone.

His magnetic soles kept him attached to the deck, but Deadeye had a choice. It was going out there to pry a thrustpack from a dead mercenary or wait for the pirates to find him. He knew he couldn't escape even if he found a thrustpack, but it seemed like a better way to die. He could open his faceplate and get it over with since the hull had been breached with railgun fire, but he wanted to see how far he could make it. That's something a pilot never lost, no matter how many memories faded. Push that envelope.

An "Abandon Ship" alarm sounded over Deadeye's helmet speakers, and the accompanying emergency info scrolled down his faceplate HUD, but he ignored them and pulled the airlock's manual release lever.

It didn't work.

Damn it.

He wasn't surprised. Not much had worked on *Santo Pohl* beforehand, and now that a pirate's railgun round had shredded through its central power router, nothing did. Judging from the limited damage, it must have been a 75mm shot fired by a skilled gunner. As long as the ship's stardrive remained intact and the hull maintained at least 80% structural integrity, the pirates could still make off with their prize. Anything less, and the vessel would come apart when making a jump.

Deadeye checked his boots, smiled in resignation, and kicked out the broken viewport. It gave way easily. Tinted glass shards drifted away into the void. One more kick and the framing caved in, creating a large hole for him to crawl out of.

Get out there. Find a dead merc. Take their thrustpack.

It was better than no plan at all. Pirates usually killed their captives or sold them to Lineage nobles as slaves. Deadeye preferred his chances out there. Maybe he'd use the thrustpack, jet himself into the pirate vessel, and stow aboard. It'd be at least a year before a MEC patrol detected *Santo Pohl*'s radio distress beacon and investigated; the nearest convoy route was a light-year away. Another reason to get moving.

He whistled the song again. .

"We know you're in there," a woman said over his helmet speakers.

Deadeye grunted as he drew himself out of the broken viewport. So they'd taken over *Pohl*'s comm system. Now they'd drive him crazy with chatter—or trace his location since he'd whistled. He tried to mute the channel, but MEC helmets lacked such function. No privacy, just like being in the navy. That's one thing he loved about flying—there was no one to fill his ears with useless information, complaints, or criticisms. It was just him and the void.

"You'd better answer, you hear me?"

The woman sounded annoyed. Then again, he'd never met a happy pirate outside of a spaceport brothel.

He stepped out into the formless dark. One faint yellow running light still functioned on his side of *Santo Pohl*'s hull. The rest was starry darkness. So dark that he shut off his helmet lamp to avoid detection. He pushed off the hull to port, where no lights shone. Without any light source to reflect off his suit, it was as if he didn't exist in the void.

It was a pleasant comfort, drifting alone. For a moment, he imagined traveling to all those stars without consequences or cost. could almost remember his real name. Almost.

That's what flying Casimir drives did to people. It could propel a ship across the light-years via temporary wormholes, but it siphoned the pilot's memories since the pilot had to remain mentally connected to the corresponding navigational system—a failsafe to prevent hackers, military AI, or Prestige bots from taking over the ship.

Humans. Always afraid of someone else taking what they thought was theirs.

The bitter smile hurt his face. Nothing in the universe was free.

"Shit, where is he?" the woman asked over *Pohl*'s comm.

Her accent was provincial—possibly a Cetian, or Luyten.

A rich girl turned pirate?

Deadeye didn't need to wait for his eyes to adjust to the darkness as Uzari possessed genetically-enhanced retinas. It typically took human eyes thirty minutes to adjust to darkness, while his could do so in less than three seconds. Yet such scotopic vision offered little in his current situation since he couldn't spot the dead bodies that had just floated past.

Have to find that thrustpack....

The bitter smile became a grin. There, less than a kilometer away, was the MEC escort corvette from his convoy. Though only two running lights were active, he didn't see any other vessels attached to it. The rectangular fixtures illuminated more bodies.

Shit. The pirates have already boarded and secured it.

Given the speed of the encounter, not enough time had passed for the pirates to gut the corvette's drive systems. Unless they had sabotaged it, the ship could still fly.

His search took on a desperate urgency. He could push off from his vessel and eventually reach the other craft, but the pirates would likely detect him long before he did due to radar. Maybe they'd assume he was another corpse.

It was his only chance.

"Curse it all to the Farmlands, but Jhio's dead," another woman said in a thick Duster drawl over the connection. "MEC got pinpoint lucky with that shot."

"What do you mean, he's dead? Damn it to Vega."

The first woman on the speaker sounded worried now rather than annoyed, and they had neglected to cut away on a different channel so he couldn't eavesdrop on their replies. They were either sloppy, experiencing trouble, or possessed the arrogance of his now-deceased captain.

Whoever had shot *Pohl*'s power router wasn't sloppy.

Deadeye would have laughed but needed to maintain radio silence. If mishap had befallen the pirate ship, then boarding the other corvette looked promising.

Wait.

He spotted a flicker of movement near the busted viewport.

The barest reflection from the yellow running light. An arm. Ah, now the whole body, this looked promising. A mercenary with a bullet through the faceplate. Slowing, turning end over end, the momentum that had sent the corpse into the void was a perpetual force. Deadeye pushed off the hull with his feet in the body's direction.

"He's not in the galley," the first woman said over the comm.

The second voice spoke. "You're sure it's a guy? You've been wrong before there, *capità*. Plenty wrong."

"Yes, Runnie, they're a 'he,' that's the designation in this bucket's manifest. Before you ask, I've already checked the bridge; he's exited the pilot pod. *Fuck.*"

After the second railgun round had pierced *Santo Pohl*, Deadeye had disconnected from the pod. The ship had been dead in the void, and it lacked weapon systems. He wasn't some green ensign, waiting for orders when the choice was obvious. Uzari were bred to fly the best starships, not die in them. While these scum probably planned on selling him, that didn't mean they'd leave him unscathed.

Deadeye held a breath as he neared the mercenary's body. There it was, a thrustpack clipped to the man's suit. Out of habit, Deadeye glanced at the merc's belt and harness, but the prick had lost his gun in the battle.

Deadeye didn't want to shoot anyone, but the recoil could have helped push him toward the escort ship, albeit slowly if there hadn't been a thrustpack on the dead merc.

"Hey, pilot?" the first woman asked. "If you're still alive, you need to answer me, right? We... *heh*, we have a bit of a problem."

Deadeye remained silent.

The woman groaned in frustration. "Listen, you jockey turd, our problem is your problem too if you plan on surviving. You hear me, asshole?"

The second woman snickered. "Ain't catching any fireflies with sour pie."

"Runabout, stow the chatter," the woman said. "Get this heap ready for a jump ASAP. Repair the central router, but don't worry about the centrifuge yet. Get our drones back aboard, the ones these mercs didn't destroy. You reading me over there?"

Runabout sighed. "Sure, yeah, reading you like a yesterday." Runabout sighed.

The pirate conversation, sparkling as it was, wouldn't last forever, and neither would his oxygen supply. He was wearing a skintight MPS, and mechanical pressure suits were only equipped with thirty minutes of breathable air. Surely he wouldn't need that long. Deadeye focused on removing the dead merc's thrustpack.

"Hey, there you are, my precious little turd. About damn time."

The first woman mumbled something but the connection clicked off.

Shit. I'm busted.

Deadeye estimated that he was sixty meters from the corvette. One glance at the ruined MEC cargo vessel and the long, angular pirate craft told him that nothing else had gone wrong, at least on the outside. They'd likely cut the comm so he wouldn't hear. Meaning they were searching for him.

Just one kilometer to that escort corvette, come on now....

He undid the thrustpack's clip. It came free of the corpse, which drifted off to his right on a new, eternal trajectory, coreward. In the direction of the Gum Nebula, if his bearings were correct. He'd studied so many charts that he could recognize certain objects and configurations anywhere. Plus, the navy had drilled so much into him. He might forget his name, but never the routines.

Too bad he couldn't stay out there longer and enjoy a view that not many could, as Uzari didn't get star blindness like other humans.

As he fitted the thrustpack onto his own suit's back clip, Deadeye studied the pirate ship. It was an old frigate, long and thin. Most of it was still sheathed in darkness, but two blue running lights illuminated a name painted vertically along the hull above a dirty airlock: *Miss Cygni*. It had taken no damage from his vantage point—save for a direct hit through the bridge—small caliber railgun fire, from the looks of it. The escort corvette had gotten one shot in, at least. The ship he'd been serving on, *Santo Pohl*, was little more than an oblong box with wide cargo berths. A few bodies floated past *Cygni*'s blue lights, and drifting debris momentarily blotted some stars.

Those mercs had died for nothing. MEC might notify their families in a few years, if ever. Many leaped at a chance to leave their colonies, where opportunities grew sparse. The risk seemed worth it when all they had to look forward to was laboring on farms.

Families. Deadeye didn't have one. No, Uzari did, not in the biological sense. People like him were grown by the corporations. In his case, Uzari Corp. Considering how much other people argued with their relatives, he didn't feel he'd missed out.

Light reflected off something on his upper left. Thirty meters distant, maybe closer. Dull white. Metallic. The contour of a shoulder.

It could be another dead merc. It could be an armored pirate.

Thrustpack exhaust, consisting of pure nitrogen gas, wouldn't give off any illumination. Using the device wouldn't reveal his location, and the same went for their packs. They could be upon him in seconds before he realized it.

Deadeye needed to hurry. Once aboard the corvette, maybe he could work out some deal or even threaten them with its railguns—at least until he activated the engine. A Casimir Mark II would get him to the nearest MEC outpost in roughly two sols: a light-year away. Floating in the black right now, he had no leverage whatsoever.

A grim smile parted his lips as he reached for the thrustpack sync cable. With it attached to his suit, he could maneuver using faceplate commands and eschew the manual side levers. He'd need both hands free to pry into whatever hatch he managed to reach first. There was a multi-tool on his belt, and he knew how to disengage hatch locks from the outside, at least on older vessels. Lucky for him, that corvette looked anything but new.

There.

The sync cable snapped into the socket. He popped his neck, blew out a breath, and—

A lamp shone into his face, blinding him.

While his eyes readjusted, Deadeye activated the thrustpack as something pushed him aside a few meters. The pack quaked on his back, nearly coming free of its clip. Nitrogen gas jetted from it in a powerful gust that sent him away from *Santo Pohl*.

Deadeye tried to compensate by working the manual lever anyway, but the pack feed on his HUD left him cold. The device had been punctured and had released all its gas into the unforgiving vacuum. The jet pushed him away from the coupled starships.

"Hey, will you listen to me now, or do I have to shoot your leg, too?"

It was the first woman. On the left, Cygni's lights reflected off her dull white armor; she appeared twenty meters above him. It looked like a newer MEC panoply, with the chest insignia and shoulder logos reprogrammed to show a red, winking woman's face. No doubt activated just now to intimidate him. She aimed a pistol.

Deadeye spread his arms and shrugged.

"I'll reach Cygnus by the time you get off another round. You know, you could've blown up the pack with that stunt."

"I'm a good shot," she said. "Good enough to take your ass out right now."

The starships grew smaller as he continued drifting away from them. He glanced at the corvette and sighed. Its running lights dwindled to the size of stars themselves, blending with billions of others.

"So much for needing my help," he said, feigning disinterest.

"Shut up; I have a proposal," she said. "Our pilot was killed in action, right? He was an Uzari like you. I checked *Pohl*'s manifest, so don't deny it. We need to jump three lights years before anyone else appears. You can do it easier than Runnie or me—and with a lesser chance of entering a fugue coma."

"A pirate captain that can't fly her ship? I almost feel sorry for you."

"Ha, you mother...."

The woman grunted. "Okay, I'm about to stop being nice, so listen. You help us; we let you live. I might even drop you off at a cozy little spaceport."

Deadeye bumped into something, turned, and grabbed the arms of another dead merc. The woman's helmet lamp was still on, illuminating a face frozen with terror.

"The longer you take to reply, MEC boy, the longer it will take for us to collect you," the woman said. "We need to leave with all three vessels. My pilot's dead, which only leaves Runabout and me to fly them. You get all that, MEC boy?"

"If you read the manifest, then you know my name."

He took the dead woman's hands and danced about. He whistled the Homesteader song again. Bumping into her had slowed his momentum, changing his trajectory, and her body provided leverage to turn himself around. He felt around her back, but there was no thrustpack.

"Sure, okay, Deadeye," the woman said. "Damn it, stop dancing with that merc icicle and talk to me. We have a deal, or not?"

Deadeye continued to dance with the dead merc, but his ploy had failed. No thrustpack, not enough momentum to reach the corvette before she stopped him, and the woman was indeed an excellent shot. That left him one recourse.

"I prefer to know the name of whomever I'm signing a contract with," he said.

"Ha! All proper and tight-assed already, I see. This isn't a contract, Deadie boy. This is you helping us, or we leave you out here."

Deadeye shrugged. "Then tell Runabout I said hi. No contract, no deal. I have standards; I don't just fly for anyone."

The woman snorted. "Standards? You were flying for MEC, transporting goods to Lineage fops who aren't starving. You've got a lot of nerve; I have all the advantages—"

"And I can fly *Cygni*, which you need an Uzari like me for the nav system," Deadeye said, still turning in a slow circle with the dead woman. "We have a contract?"

"Fucking spacer cryoshit in a can—fine, you have a contract. Here, I've sent it to your feed. Sign it, or I'll shoot you for real this time."

She produced a longer pistol.

"Okay...."

Deadeye released the corpse and examined the words scrolling down his faceplate. He signed the contract with a single nod. It wasn't the typical pirate drivel but a professional business arrangement with rights, profit shares, and a code of conduct. Their ranking system mirrored the one used by the MEC navy.

He snickered. "Captain Talon? Did you give yourself that callsign, or—"

Something darted from Talon and wrapped itself around his right ankle. A cable. Its smart mesh tightened into steely fibers. The other end was attached to her long pistol.

"Hang on, Deadie boy."

She activated her thrustpack, jetting them to *Miss Cygni*.

"You ask any stupid questions; you attack us, you try to fly anywhere than I tell you, hell, if you so much as bring mites onto my ship, you're dead. Got that?"

"Sure thing."

He saluted the dead merc, glad he wasn't joining her.

CHAPTER 2

___

THE AIRLOCK DOOR SLID SHUT BEHIND HIM, BUT TALON PRESSED Deadeye to the deck with her boot. He remained there, meaning *Miss Cygni*'s centrifuge maintained gravity. He guessed 0.6Gs. The round structure hadn't been visible outside; such systems were internal on old warships.

"Right, now, this is the pilot you found? He's skinnier than a lightning rod."

The woman standing over Deadeye in *Miss Cygni*'s airlock chamber wore a green Homesteader MPS, complete with a matching helmet and tinted faceplate. The outfit was caked with the dirt of a hundred worlds, and yellow graffiti dotted the helmet.

"Heh, like there were any other skinny MEC boys to choose from."

Talon retracted the mesh cable from Deadeye's ankle and aimed the ballistic pistol at him.

"Runabout, this is Deadie boy. You have the pilot pod ready?"

"It's Deadeye."

He tried to sit up from the deck. "Can I—?"

"No." Talon kept the pistol on him. "Runnie, the pod?"

Runabout crossed her arms and nudged Talon with an elbow. "Jhio needs burial."

"Not now," Talon said, still watching Deadeye. "We need to jump. I'll fly the transport; you take the corvette. Little MEC boy here gets *Cygni* with a gun drone making sure he doesn't fly elsewhere. We'll rendezvous with the others at—"

"Jhio died, *capità*." Runabout's rustic drawl broke with a sob "Pieces

9

of him were all over the pod, the bridge... see that there, I barely got that viewport sealed over, and you're acting like he's a bit of salvage we can just—"

"He got his burial, the Runner way." Talon squeezed Runabout's arm. "He was my friend, too. I'll miss him. But he knew the risks. We'll do a memorial later. Right now, we have to jump. You with me?"

Runabout stared at Deadeye; then her arms fell to her sides. "With you."

"Good." Talon untinted her faceplate. "Now, Deadie, I'm saving air here, so keep that helmet on. You can link up with the pod's life support shortly."

Her face was young, but her grey eyes were far too old. No hair was visible, due to the comm cap covering her crown and ears, but her eyebrows were dark brown. Turning her head revealed a tiny mole on her left cheek and a scar behind her jawline.

"You're going to fly *Santo Pohl* after ripping it apart?" Deadeye chuckled. "You must be desperate."

"You wouldn't understand." Talon nodded to Runabout. "The corvette ready?"

"We lost a right many drones," Runabout said. "Ain't going to replace those easily. Ain't going to fly that corvette easily, either. We ain't Uzari or Zyn."

"We'll follow *Miss Cygni* through the wormhole, so the nav system shouldn't fuck with our heads too much."

Talon gestured at Deadeye with the gun. "Go on, get up."

Deadeye stood, keeping his hands raised. "Got the UNS ready?"

"Never took it offline," Runabout said. "Pod's clean now, but you ain't got a seat since it was... well, got you a sleeping bag inside it now."

Talon nodded out the airlock. "You'd better get going. Lucky for us, they drew the corvette up close, and must have hoped to prevent us from boarding the cargo vessel. These mercs they hire now aren't too bright."

"Right then, be waiting for your signal. Deadeye, fly true, or you'll get a haunting." Runabout donned a thrustpack and waited for them to leave the chamber.

Deadeye kept his hands up as Talon escorted him down a slim corridor. "Do you have coordinates already set? You said you were in a hurry, after all."

Talon followed behind, still aiming the pistol at him. "Move."

Deadeye snorted. "The bullet would go right through this little old maid you want me to fly."

"I have a patch kit." Talon motioned him on. "Runnie, we're good up here. Head for the corvette."

"*A les estrelles*," Runabout said over the radio.

Deadeye felt rather than heard the airlock open and close. "What's that mean?"

"To the stars. It's something they say out in the Dust Systems."

"Weird," he said. "Like her suit and your MEC armor. Where did you—"

"Keep moving," Talon said.

Deadeye didn't see anyone else aboard as they passed crew berths, two cargo bays filled with damaged combat drones, and a rec room that looked even grungier than the airlock: dirty jumpsuits, beer cans, half-eaten food in the same round magnetic bowls he'd used in the navy. Once they neared the bridge egress, his boots clipped with each step, their mag soles gripping the deck.

Miss Cygni lacked a forward centrifuge but had the power couplings for it on either side of the rec room. The pirates had likely sacrificed the extra artificial gravity for maneuverability and a smaller target. Three bots floated past them, their torch tips cooling to dull blue from recent use.

"Nice ship," he said. "I've seen better billets, though—"

"If you talk trash about my girl, I'll space you," she said.

"So, how badly did MEC hit you guys?"

Deadeye glanced at the long, dark slag marks that ran along the starboard wall and the swaths of metal welded over their corresponding punctures. Damage from railgun rounds, maybe 57mm. A few more degrees and the deadly projectiles would have plowed straight through the ship to its engine. But the damage had been quickly repaired, these people weren't amateurs.

"Your friends on that corvette dusted us with rail rounds. It took out our pilot, and the crew berths on Deck 2 had to be sealed off, but our repair bots managed to seal the rest. It's flyable."

"Ah." Deadeye nodded as if everything were perfectly normal. "You have a small crew, or did *Pohl's* mercs give as good as they got?"

"Jhio was our only casualty," Talon said. "But I'll need new combat drones now."

A pirate outfit that operated without gunners or a human boarding crew. They were either crazy or highly skilled. Probably both.

"I suppose that's your next raid, a MEC drone supply vessel?"

"You don't need to know anything; just fly my damn ship."

Talon pushed Deadeye into the bridge. The movement caused his soles to unclip from the deck, and he floated across the small space. It was little more than a closet with two seats, a newer MEC computer terminal, and the pilot pod. The viewport had been blown out, and a sheet of ablative shielding had been welded over it. Dark stains clung to the walls.

"This is so small that it would kill us if I farted in here."

Deadeye stopped his momentum by catching himself on the side of the pod. It was a half-spherical shape, with a sleeping bag inside where a reclining seat used to be. The usual IV canisters and feed tubes were present, containing the nutrients his body would need while flying. An array of screens lined the tiny cubicle, along with safety restraints and a UNS interface jack.

Though some spacers claimed Uzari flew starships with their minds, that wasn't true. The jack gave him a neural connection to the Uzari Navigational System, an electroencephalography app that allowed a pilot to parse data without the need of a screen or manual controls. It freed up his hands and eyes, allowing precision control in dangerous situations, such as taking evasive action in battle—or navigating a wormhole. It was a direct connection, immune to hacking or AI tampering, such as a Prestige attack.

Out of habit, he felt the back of his head where the jack connection was, below the helmet rim. The jack was implanted right above the atlas vertebra at birth, growing along with the rest of his body at the base of his skull. It could not be removed, not even with the best surgical procedures, having grown into his central nervous system. It was a simpler installation for other humans but riskier to use.

"You trust me to do this?" Deadeye asked. "Why? You're just pirates."

Talon glared at the freshly-welded viewport, the dark stains on the wall where Jhio's blood had splashed. Her jaw firmed, and her left eye ticked.

"Because someone has to do it. And you don't want to die out here, right?"

Deadeye locked eyes with her for a moment, then sat in the pod, strapped himself in, and inserted the jack into his neck.

Talon let out a breath and nodded. "Good, now if you're done talking—"

"Oh, *merda!*" Runabout cried over the radio. "We have three bogeys inbound to our coordinates. Hear me over there, right? Three ships!"

"Friends of yours?" Deadeye asked.

"Fuck no." Talon rushed from the bridge and continued talking over the radio. "Deadie boy, fly to the coordinates I've already loaded on *Cygni.* Runabout and I will follow through your wormhole—"

"You have any idea how dangerous that is?"

Deadeye blinked as the UNS data scrolled down the lower left of his vision. *Miss Cygni*'s systems were at his mercy. Everything, from the contraband drones and guns in the cargo hold to the jump log, which showed voyages all over the Spur, from the inner worlds of the Golden Band to the outer reaches of the Dust Systems and beyond. Pirates didn't typically travel so widely.

He could jump anywhere, and leave Talon and her foolish plan behind.

An object floated into view on his right. One of the repair bots, fitted with a small barrel that wasn't a torch: Talon's insurance that he'd honor the contract.

"Hi there, buddy." Deadeye smiled at the bot and accessed the ship's radar screen. "Hi there, buddy."

Sure enough, three blips were closing in on their position. Given that those radio waves traveled at the speed of light, as did the rebounded waves that provided the ships' location, and that the ships had been sighted so quickly.

"They're too damn close for comfort," he said. "Two hundred and fifty kilometers now, less than a light-second. Their transponders read as MEC military. Talon, you in *Pohl* yet?"

"Almost there," Talon said. "Runnie, how's that corvette's railgun?"

"Tell me you're joking," Runabout said. "I ain't a gunner; you know that!"

"So I guess that handiwork on *Santo Pohl* was yours, Talon?"

Deadeye brought *Cygni*'s fusion engines fully online.

"Not bad shooting. That takes training."

"No time for biographies," Talon muttered a few curses. "I'm in *Pohl*'s bridge. Holy shit, Deadie, you actually used this pod? It looks like a crushed beer can."

"Only the best from MEC."

Deadeye studied the diagram in the lower right-hand corner of his sight, where a UNS overlay showed a hologram of *Miss Cygni*. The frigate's docking claw was still attached to *Santo Pohl*. It would take at least ten seconds to disengage. Another thirty seconds to steer clear of the other craft, then at least twenty seconds to make the jump. Casimir drives came online much faster than the ones ancient humans had colonized the Spur with, but the MEC ships would be upon them before then. One minute wasn't going to be enough.

He could hail the MEC vessels. Their transponders advertised them as corvettes. More than enough to rip *Cygni* and the two stolen craft apart. He could refuse to jump and watch the pirates get destroyed unless the bot beside his pod killed him first.

"Deadie boy, you ready? Disengage the claw!"

Something in Talon's voice... the look in her eyes when she'd been on *Cygni*'s bridge... he'd not seen that in a long time. Determination, maybe even honor. A typical pirate would only care about profit. Or at least that's what he had been told to believe.

His finger lingered over the distress beacon button—then he disengaged the claw.

"Runabout?"

Deadeye fired *Cygni*'s portside thrusters and maneuvered away from *Pohl*.

"Fire the railgun at me. Make sure you miss."

"What?" Talon and Runabout shouted.

"Then, when those corvettes ignore you and come after me—rake them with a burst. We'll make the jump afterward."

Deadeye connected his helmet to the H2O and oxygen canisters. The nutrient ones were fitted with lines that snapped into two sockets on his MPS' sides—no point in escaping, only to die of thirst or asphyxiation afterward.

"Hell no, you're not shooting at my girl," Talon said.

"It's our only chance," Deadeye said as he checked the nav coordinates Talon had preloaded. They were currently in the GJ 3379 system; seventeen light-years from Earth.

Their destination was three light-years away, as she'd stated earlier: Ross 47, a red dwarf known for its deadly solar flares. A desperate escape route.

"A hundred k's closing right on me!" Runabout cried.

Deadeye glanced at the trio of blips on the overlay while *Miss Cygni*'s Casimir drive prepped for the jump. The device used exotic hadrons in a process he didn't fully understand, but it generated and stabilized a temporary wormhole long enough for a starship to travel through. Talon and Runabout planned to follow him into it. It was an insane ploy since the safest method was for each vessel to generate its own wormhole.

If the wormhole collapsed while a ship was still inside, it would be reduced to atoms, scattered only the void knew where.

Insane or not, he wanted to see if it worked.

"Runnie, you hurt my ship, and I swear, I'll make you take that damn helmet off in a crowded Sadisto locker room!" Talon yelled.

The blips were less than five thousand 5, kilometers away now. Easy targets for missiles, if *Miss Cygni* had any. But the craft possessed just one

75mm railgun, and it swiveled in a 180°, forward-facing arc on the ship's bow. His stern, the rear of the ship, faced the incoming corvettes so that he couldn't fire at them.

"Runabout, shoot and miss; you can do this."

He thought about Homesteader farmers.

"Like dusting tater bugs, you want to spray around the plant, not directly on it."

"How did you know...?" Runabout said, then laughed. "Ha! Here it comes, then!"

"Shit, they're two ks away; let's go!" Talon cried.

Deadeye watched the distance count down on the overlay. "Now!"

The captured corvette blasted a sweeping fusillade above *Miss Cygni*'s hull. Deadeye sucked in a breath, hoping Runabout would save enough rounds from spraying the incoming MEC patrol. The ship's radar showed the projectiles as a cloud of dots that passed over *Cygni* like angry bees.

Bees. Where did he remember that from?

"Make the jump!" Talon cried. "I can see the bastards in my scopes now!"

Deadeye fired *Cygni*'s rear thrusters to fool the patrol into thinking he would flee or reorient himself and fire at them. On his overlay, *Santo Pohl* was lined up on his portside stern. Runabout's corvette remained in place —facing the first ship in the patrol. They were closing in, not utilizing missiles or railguns. They wanted prisoners.

Before he could urge Runabout to fire again, she did so. Radar showed him a second cloud enfilading the incoming corvette. The MEC vessels reoriented themselves to engage the captured corvette, giving him the needed time. But he shook in the pod, recalling when Talon had fired on his ship less than an hour ago. The captain's shouts for evasive action, the alarms. That MEC crew was experiencing the same trauma now. Probably more mercs, dying cheaply for cheaper pay, far from home.

His breathing grew ragged. Sweat lined the interior of his gloves and slid down his palms onto his wrists. The UNS overlay showed his heart rate increasing.

How often had he survived those situations? How many crews had he killed?

His eyelids fluttered. Ross 47. Three light-years. Bees, tater bugs....

A voice pierced the muted reverie, yelling for him to make the jump.

Deadeye activated *Miss Cygni*'s wormhole sequence. The Casimir drive hummed, a reaction he felt as it vibrated the entire ship. He licked his lips, awaiting the familiar plunge into darkness, the flash of light and disorientation. He stopped himself from touching the jack in the back of his neck. His gateway to another reality.

Would he remember all of this afterward? Would he—

Miss Cygni stopped shaking. The Casimir drive shut off.

Deadeye stirred inside the pod, then coughed. His throat was dry. Too dry.

Jump... three light-years....

His mind snapped to attention, and he checked the IV canisters around him. They were empty, except the glucose one. The H_2O canister contained mere droplets. The waste pump, attached to his crotch, was empty. He'd not filled it, or its contents had already been sent to *Cygni's* environmental recyclers.

Did we make it? Goddamn it, did we....

Deadeye sucked in quick breaths until his HUD revealed the truth.

Miss Cygni had traveled three light-years via a temporary wormhole.

Three and a half light-years with a Casimir Mark II meant he'd been in the pod for eight sols. More than a week.

"Anybody—"

He coughed again, unable to finish the question.

The UNS feed displayed his location: twenty-two astronomical units from Ross 47. A little over three billion kilometers from the red dwarf, so they should be safe in the event of a solar flare. Well, safe for a short while, anyway. As his eyes scrolled down, so too did the UNS feed scroll by, showing him the state of *Miss Cygni* and all objects within two hundred thousand kilometers. The ship was in good shape, and two others were less than a kilometer behind his stern: a cargo transport and a corvette.

The wormhole had transported them all. He wanted to laugh.

Flying through a wormhole via the UNS was like piloting through blurred, starry darkness in a fugue state. It was all subconscious reaction, utilizing his training and mental connection to the nav system. Like a dream, he rarely recalled afterward but experienced snippets from in random waking moments.

Deadeye managed to suck a few water drops from the H_2O canister line attached to his helmet. Enough to allow speech, though his voice remained gravelly.

"Anybody... anybody hear me?"

He tried multiple frequencies. No answer.

Breaking radio silence over that many frequencies was dangerous, now that he was a criminal, but Talon must have trusted the location, or she'd not have selected it for a jump. Still, any other ship a few AU distant would hear him within minutes.

"Anybody?"

"I'm here," Talon said on the radio. "Phew, goddamn, that was some jump. I'll have a migraine for a week. I'm leaving this MEC tin can as soon as you bring *Miss Cygni* about. Make it quick."

Deadeye flinched as sweat pooled in his left eye, running off his forehead.

"This pod setup is terrible. I'm almost dehydrated over here. You've got the life support temperature set too high. Plus, the nutrient canisters would barely have fed a child."

"Want me to order you some breakfast, too, Deadie boy? Thought you were an Uzari, you know, the types who're bred to survive supernovas and spacer impotence."

"Leave him be, *capità*. Jhio said the same stuff. Don't you go denying it."

Deadeye grinned as he pried the IV lines off his suit.

"Hi, Runabout."

"Hiya." Runabout sounded happy to hear from him. "Nice flying back there. Even nicer plan, plenty of guts, and craziness. Talon said so, too, but now she ain't telling."

"Okay, you got me. You did good back there, both of you."

Talon grunted as if she were stretching.

"Well, come on, Deadie boy, get *Cygni* over here. I want a shower, and a meal before the rest show up. Or a solar flare."

The mention of food made Deadeye's stomach rumble. "The rest?"

"The Redshift Runners," Talon said it like he was supposed to know who they were. "Not pirates, like you keep saying."

"You attacked a convoy and stole the vessels and cargo. Sounds like pirates."

He winced as he crawled from the pod and stretched. At least there was no gravity; he'd have fallen on his face; he felt so weak.

"Plus, you forced me at gunpoint to perform the best tricks this side of the Golden Band, things most spacers only dream of doing."

Runabout chuckled, but Talon was as silent as a derelict. Either she was ignoring him or was thinking. It was bluster on his part, but Deadeye needed to sell himself once again. He couldn't work for MEC now; he'd be flagged as MIA, presumed dead. If he turned up at one of their outposts, they'd arrest him, thinking him a pirate anyway.

And he needed to fly for someone. He had to pilot a ship, any ship.

Anything that took him deeper into the void, where, in those wormholes, he might remember himself.

"Even through all that bullshit, I can tell you want a second contract." Talon sounded amused. "But the Runners don't hire mercs. This was a one-off, Deadie."

The armed bot hovered closer to his head. Since he assumed it had a camera trained on him, with Talon watching, he grinned.

"You think I'm still a merc?"

Deadeye sat back in the pod and fired *Cygni*'s starboard thrusters, orienting it in *Santo Pohl*'s direction.

"I want to be a Runner. Judging from how that escape played out, you need me. You can trust me. I can fly anything."

"Heh, how about flying a little faster over there? I'm not using a MEC toilet."

"You held it for eight sols?"

Deadeye fired a few more thrusters in short bursts until he was parallel with *Santo Pohl*'s airlock. The docking claw was already prepped.

"Just get over here, will you? If you want to join us... sure, I'll have to convince the others, and that'll go easier if I don't smell like a sweaty spacesuit."

"Can we begin with you telling your floating buddy here to back off?" he asked.

"No," Talon said. "You leave Icara alone. She's doing a fine job."

"She won't follow me into a shower or anything, will she?"

"Only if we need the credits for the voyeur feeds." Talon snorted. "Damn. Would you sit tight for a moment? You're not the center of the universe or anything."

Deadeye started to ask for more details until a single blip appeared on the UNS radar. Sixty thousand kilometers away. In cosmological terms, so close one could touch it. Someone had been waiting for them, possibly for sols. Doing that in a flare system was very risky, meaning that whatever Talon and her friends hoped to get from the MEC cargo, it must be special. Her comment about food for Lineage fops came to mind.

A male voice spoke over the radio. "Hullo out there, this is Wizard on *Valkyrie*; come in."

"*Valkyrie*, this is Talon. Perfect timing, Wiz. All the crew together?"

"Yeah, but that's not Jhio we heard on the radio," Wizard said. "Big trouble?"

Deadeye tensed as he extended *Cygni*'s docking claw to *Santo Pohl*. The question about a crew sounded strange until he used *Cygni*'s scopes to examine *Valkyrie*. It was a carrier transport, a pre-MEC model. It could likely hold several corvettes, maybe even a cruiser or two. Whoever these Runners were, they meant business.

Out of respect, he kept silent. He was a stranger, and they'd be suspicious of him until he proved himself further. That, and Icara hovered centimeters from his head.

"Everything's under control, we got both MEC ships, but we lost Jhio," Talon said. "I'll tell you more when we're aboard *Valkyrie*. We... might have a new pilot."

CHAPTER 3

———————

Valkyrie's cargo bay was large enough to hold a small space station, but the Runners had filled it with crates, barrels, parcels, capsules, pods, and cartons Runabout led Deadeye through the labyrinth, with Talon behind him. He knew without looking that her hand was on her holstered pistol.

He was a stranger, a possible threat, so he understood. Maybe he'd need to pour on the charm. At least Icara flew a full meter above him now, so he wasn't as concerned that he'd get a free craniotomy.

They walked without helmets with the carrier's life support on, except for Runabout. *Valkyrie's* air had the stink of chlorine filtration, so he took shallow breaths. He preferred pure tank oxygen, having used the odorless gas while flying.

"Your contract mentioned rankings, like those in the MEC navy," Deadeye said. "Does that make me an ensign? If I'm accepted, of course."

"Something like that," Talon said. "It's more about command structure than benefits since we all get equal shares of any spoils we find. Runnie here is our bosun. I'm captain of this outfit, Strike Group *Valkyrie.* As I said, we're not...well, we're not typical pirates, all right?"

"Right," Deadeye said.

"Heh, try to contain your excitement," Talon said. "We don't order the ensigns to clean the waste pumps. Unless Runnie needs you to."

"So, Runabout, you never take the helmet off or untint the visor?"

He sidestepped a crate filled with servo motors and other bot parts.

"Not even in the shower?"

"You talking silliness, of course, 'cause I'm the cleanest spacer this end of the Spur."

Runabout still wore her stained MPS and helmet and under *Valkyrie*'s centrifuge-produced gravity, walked with a graceful gait befitting a dancer rather than a farmer.

"I've never met a Homesteader like you before," he said. "That graffiti on your helmet, are those marriage terms? That's why you stay covered because you're...?"

"Saving myself?" Runabout gave a wry laugh. "Ain't that bad. Keeps prying eyes off me and the mites, too. Don't much care for germs in the spaceports, either, right? And me getting married? *Ha*, no time soon, that's a right fact."

Deadeye smiled at Runabout's carefree tone. Most Homesteaders were focused on having as many children as possible, and settling every world from the Golden Band, which surrounded ancient Earth at twelve light-years, to the Dust Systems, which was everything else out to twenty light-years. But Homesteaders carried out their manifest destiny with cultish zeal, settling hellish worlds with little supplies or driving other colonists off the good ones. Maybe Runabout had left all of that behind for whatever the Runners offered.

"What about you, Deadie boy?" Talon asked. "You've got the stiff, no-bullshit walk of an NCO, but your eyes remind me of a drugged Sadisto in withdrawal."

He smirked. "You're saying your friends won't like or trust me. I get it."

A tall, bald, dark-skinned man appeared. "Do you?" A tall, dark-skinned man with a mustache and goatee appeared.

He wore a pocketed yellow jumpsuit without sleeves since both arms were tentacles beneath the elbow. The veiny appendages wriggled with the nervous energy common to all Zyn, another corporate, genetic offshoot like Deadeye. Zyn had lower body temperatures and pliable bones that suffered less under variable gravities. They'd been developed for deep-space missions by the Zyn-Tro Corporation, a now-defunct entity swallowed by the economic wars across the Spur. They'd been engineered without hair follicles, since Zyn-Tro considered hair an extravagance that spacers didn't need.

"Easy, Wiz."

Talon stepped past Deadeye and tapped the Zyn on the shoulder. "This is Deadeye, an Uzari. He was piloting the MEC cargo ship, but I convinced him to fly back with us so that we wouldn't leave any vessel behind. He signed with the Runners."

Wizard's brown lowered. "You're fucking kidding me."

"Hi," Deadeye said. "Nice to me to you. I'm—"

"Talking too much."

Wizard snatched a piece of scrap from a nearby crate and crushed it into a metallic ball.

Runabout leaned on her hip and wagged a finger at Wizard. "No, you don't; you keep still and behave. Deadie—I mean Deadeye—he saved us, flew us all through a wormhole like Dame Nyx herself."

Wizard glared at Deadeye. "He's got spacer scum written all over his face."

"It's on his ass, too, but we don't have time for you to look right now, do we?"

Talon tugged off her comm cap, unleashing a dark brown ponytail and long bangs. She pushed the bangs back and gave Wizard an exasperated look.

"Jhio's dead, and this flyboy is better than I like to admit. He flew us here, didn't radio anyone, didn't tamper with my girl *Cygni*, and hasn't even flirted with Runabout yet. He wants in."

"A Runner, huh?" Wizard looked Deadeye up and down. "Skinny as fuck, too. Then again, all you Uzari are. It's not my call, Talon, but I say no. Just my instincts."

Runabout nudged Wizard with her rump. "I say yes."

"Tease." Wizard smiled and offered Runabout a can of beer.

She waved it aside.

"Where are the others?" Talon peered between the stacks of containers. "We need to offload the MEC cargo to *Valkyrie*, decide which ship we keep, and jump to Hartwell."

Wizard glanced at Deadeye again, then beckoned them to follow. "In the rec room. Epsi's been vaping in my ship again; you need to talk to her. And we're running low on hadrons for *Annie Argent* and *Corsair*. They can't jump farther than a couple of light-years, hell, maybe not even that. You listening?"

Deadeye caught Talon staring out the bay's long viewport, where *Santo Pohl* was visible. Whatever the cargo was, she must want it. MEC had hired him to fly without imparting anything; he had no idea what he'd been transporting across the void.

Talon blinked, then flicked her ponytail over her shoulder. "How can I not? You gripe worse than a spaceport plumber."

They left the cargo bay, walked briskly down two narrow corridors, and entered a circular chamber lit with indirect lamps. It contained a few couches, chairs, drink coolers, a fridge, a magnetic chess table, and even a holo billiard mat hovering in midair.

"Hey, if it isn't my favorite buncha fuckups," a grey-haired man in dark orange fatigues said.

He flicked one of the holo balls across the billiard mat without looking at it.

"Ross 47 is a flare star, remember? I'm tired of waking each sleep cycle, wondering if my ass will get irradiated to a crisp."

"Hiya to you too, Fluxo."

Runabout grabbed the beer from Wizard and threw it.

The man caught the beer, opened it, and took a long drink. "Hi yourself, garden gnome. And it's Fluxman. Nice to see you, too. Find a suitor this time?"

Runabout gouged Fluxman in the ribs and flopped into a chair. "Dame's tits, no. Did you, huh? Or you still flogging it to that little sex doll we spaced at Altair?"

Fluxman finished the beer and smirked. "I don't kiss and tell."

A woman with short blonde hair in a blue MPS walked over from the fridge and ogled Deadeye.

"My, Talon, please tell me this is the cargo? I call first dibs."

Deadeye arched an eyebrow and smiled. "Hello there."

Talon pushed past the woman and deactivated the billiard table. "No, Epsi, he's a Runner prospect. Vote him in; then you can get laid. Where's Perseus?"

Wizard, Fluxman, and Epsi fell silent.

Runabout hung her head. Talon's shoulders slumped, then she straightened.

"His ship didn't make the rendezvous," Epsi said. "We waited and waited some more. Wizard took *Argent* and searched the system when we detected some gravitational lensing like a Casimir leaves behind, but there was nothing. Not even debris."

Deadeye had heard it before. Wormhole travel was dangerous. Even a well-maintained Casimir Mark II drive had a wormhole collapse rate of 2.2%.

"Goddamn it," Talon whispered.

Wizard grunted. "The other Runner carriers are losing pilots, too. MEC is on to us, I'm telling you, and the Lineage, they aren't paying the rates they used to. The Freelancer outfits on this end of the Spur are charging more for food and hadrons."

Talon gave a forced smile. "We're not in this for the money, remember?"

"We still gotta eat," Fluxman said.

"Speaking of that." Talon snapped her fingers and brought up a hologram from her mobile. "Here's what that MEC convoy was carrying. I mean, look at it."

Even Deadeye leaned forward with the others, just as curious as they were.

"See that?"

Talon pointed at several packed modules and seed crates on the holo and grinned.

There are eight full hydroponics labs in that tin can. Six tons of seeds, too, for beans, corn, potatoes, squash, rice, apples, cranberries—a few others, too."

The others didn't share Talon's enthusiasm, save for Runabout, who gave a whoop. Deadeye knew how important those things were. Eight labs could provide crops for eight colonies. Homesteaders would kill for such a haul, and MEC kept such facilities top secret since their worlds suffered food shortages.

Talon's grin faded as she eyed the other Runners' somber looks.

"Really? This is what the Runners are about; this is why we fly out there."

"Jhio died for some seeds?" Fluxman tossed the empty beer can into a bin. "Oh, yes, lemme strap in *Corsair* right now and risk my life for some damned seeds."

"Jhio knew the risks." Talon glowered at Fluxman.

Fluxman went to the fridge and got another beer. "Yeah? Then where's his body? Was there anything left to send out the airlock for that stupid little ritual we always do?" Fluxman went to the fridge and got another beer.

"She wants to replace Jhio with this Uzari scamp," Wizard said.

"I certainly vote yes." Epsi smiled.

"It doesn't matter; he won't live long either, like the rest of us." Fluxman stared at the unopened beer can, lip curled down in disgust. "Sure, let the poor bastard join."

"The fuck is wrong with all of you?" Talon stalked around the rec room, meeting every person's eyes as she passed.

"The Runners are what keeps some of those worlds alive out there; we're all those people have. They expect us to help them."

Wizard shuffled a few chess pieces with his tentacles. "Hey, we know that. But we're always dying for tools, seeds, or damned generators for people who don't know us. We don't even know ourselves. Fluxman keeps forgetting where his cabin—"

"Fuck off." Fluxman slammed the beer back into the fridge. "Fuck off."

"He's right; you're forgetting things more," Epsi said.

Fluxman balled his fists and stomped toward Wizard. "I said to—"

"Knock it off!" Talon yelled. "We're all affected by the drives, the nav system. That's... that's why Deadeye is a good fit for us. Like Jhio, he can handle the longer jumps, and he's less likely to forget, got me? Got me, Deadie?"

The pleading look in Talon's eyes, to back her up, took Deadeye unawares. The same woman had been ready to shoot him a few sols ago, and now, after her actions were being criticized by her companions, she hoped he would bolster her claims.

This was what he'd wanted. Like them, he needed the Runners for his own reasons. Seeds, tools... it didn't matter why he would die out there. As long as he could fly, that's all he needed.

"I got you, Talon." Deadeye faced the rest of them. "You don't want to trek out there for seeds, or whatever the target is, I will."

Wizard snorted and rolled his eyes.

"I'm no coward, you asshole," Fluxman said.

"No one here is, or you'd already be dead," Deadeye said. "But as Talon said, I can fly the missions you don't want. I've got nothing to lose. I'm just another Uzari, a navy man; somebody MEC used and replaced. I can't go back to MEC, I'll already be flagged as KIA, and if I show up, they'll consider me a pirate anyway for not staying with the convoy. They don't accept contracts from former pirate prisoners, either. If I'm going to die flying, it might as well be for people who need the things I can do."

Talon's jaw firmed. "A vote then, right now. I say yes. We need him."

"Yes," Runabout said.

"No." Wizard's tentacles knotted together. "No."

"Sure." Epsi shrugged and smiled.

"Yeah," Fluxman said. "Why not? Saves me from dying for a plow bot."

"So I'm... Ensign Deadeye now?" Deadeye tilted his head. "Which ship do I get?"

Fluxman shared a glance with Wizard. "You hearing this guy? Damn."

"*Princess* has extra room." Epsi grinned at Deadeye until Runabout elbowed her.

"You'll fly whatever I need you to for the mission," Talon said. "You being an Uzari and all, well, you'll be making lots of jumps for us, and since you're a veteran, combat escort, too. As I said, I'm the captain, Runnie is our bosun and backup pilot, Wiz is our key jump pilot and engineer, Epsi is a yeoman and auxiliary pilot, and Fluxman is the best mechanic spinward of the Golden Band—and he's a good pilot, too."

"No gunners?" Deadeye asked.

"Everyone here knows how to use basic weapon systems," Talon said. "Railguns, missiles, torpedoes, deploying countermeasures like ECM cubes, or combat drones. We link all those systems together, the Duster way."

"While flying?" Deadeye sniffed. "You must be some serious badasses, or you're crazy. That's a lot to focus on simultaneously, even for an Uzari."

"Spacers operate that way out here," Wizard said. "Jack of all trades."

"No, you're just a jack-off," Fluxman smirked at Wizard, who smiled and gave him the finger.

"The Runners lack the resources and personnel that MEC wastes out here," Talon said. "Every pilot, every vessel, has to be maximized."

"Yes, we're badasses," Epsi said.

Deadeye pointed at Icara floating above him. "And how long will this little lady be my best friend?"

"Forever and forever." Runabout chuckled.

"Until we know you aren't gonna kill us," Fluxman said.

"As long as I think it's necessary," Talon smirked. "Icara watched Fluxman for a month until I got tired of him mooning my poor girl. I had to erase her drive afterward."

Fluxman shrugged. "Gotta please the audience."

Epsi laughed. "Welcome to the crew."

Before Deadeye could thank them, Talon spoke. "Now, let's get that cargo loaded. We can use the corvette's railgun, but the rest of the ship is too old, and we don't have space here on *Valkyrie* for both MEC vessels. We'll take its hadrons. The cargo ship has more tonnage; it can help us fly goods to those whoever needs it—and lots of space for upgrades, too. I say we stow it in the hangar."

The other Runners nodded or muttered, leaving to carry out Talon's request. She paused, then gave Deadeye a cautious look, like she might be regretting her decision. He'd heard old stories about Earth's pirates and how they'd forced captured physicians or carpenters into their outfits to tend their crews and wooden vessels. Nothing had changed over the centuries, only now it was pilots and engineers.

"You get to the bridge, Deadie boy. You ever flown a carrier?"

"Maybe, I'm not sure," he said. "So Icara will be watching over me, even though the rest of you will be awake and capable of stopping me if I do something stupid?"

"You're on probation until I trust you. Unless you prove me wrong."

He shrugged. "I just made a jump, but I'll do it."

Talon snorted as she walked away. "My big-talking Deadie is tired? You can rest at Hartwell. The bridge is down the corridor on your left and up the lift. And take a quick shower; you have spacer stink."

The crew's welcome had been lukewarm, but at least there wasn't any silly initiation. He could live with Icara following him, and who knew, he might make it with Epsi; she was rather cute. It was a far better situation than dying for an employer who didn't care about him. Flying a carrier felt like the icing on the cake.

Cake. He remembered eating something like that.

Before leaving the rec room, he studied the chessboard and where Wizard had moved the pieces. A perpetual game, that's what a spacer's life was. Always one move away from checkmate.

Deadeye moved the black king on the chessboard, smiled, and left.

"You want me to jump nine light-years?" Deadeye eased into the pilot pod on *Valkyrie*'s bridge. "That shower wasn't that damn energizing."

"Yeah, so? At least you smell better. And you're supposed to be Mister Hotshit Uzari, remember?"

Talon buckled into the captain's chair beside the pod. She rubbed her gloved hands together and stared out the viewport into nothingness.

He started to argue, then chuckled. "So you're going to sit beside me for twenty-one sols? Hope that seat doubles as a potty."

"I'll be here for a few hours, hadron brain, then I'll head to my cabin."

She'd changed into a dark red jumpsuit, and her hair shone from a fresh shower. At least these pirates weren't stingy with water. In the navy, he'd been allowed one shower between jumps—and that was if the officers had already enjoyed one.

"So you all get a nice little vacation while I stay connected to the UNS? Shit. You Runners need a union or something."

Talon tapped her console nervously. "You and that sarcasm. But, *heh*, I wish. We'll repair our ships and refit *Santo Pohl* for Runner use. In a way, you've got the easy peasy lemonade part."

"Lemonade?" He raised his brows. "What's that?"

"I don't know what it is; something Runnie claims is better than Cetian wine."

"Then what's bothering you?" He attached the IV lines to his MPS.

"All these questions you keep spouting, that's what." She typed something into the console with quick keystrokes. "Okay, coordinates are set. Got it on your UNS?"

Deadeye jacked into the pod, and a split second later, the UNS feed popped into his vision. *Valkyrie*'s version of the app featured light blue text that he found too bright.

"We're going to Luyten's Star? Back near the Golden Band, eh? Hmm."

Talon typed some more than caught him looking at her. "What now?"

"Nothing. Well... who usually flies this carrier other than Wizard? Did Jhio?"

"Wizard mostly. Zyn are as good as you Uzari when it comes to, you know, the UNS thing. I still have a headache from that three light-year jump, and I bet Runnie does too, that cheerful little sap. But the encephalogram in the med bay says we're okay."

"She seems sweet."

He checked the oxygen mask and H2O canister. Though *Valkyrie*'s life support would remain active during the voyage, pilots still wore oxygen masks if they grew too fatigued. He waved at Icara as she hovered past.

Talon smiled sadly as she finished typing. "Hell yes, she is. She's too trusting sometimes, too easy with people. Can you believe she's two years older than me? *Heh*."

"I don't know how old I am anymore."

He brought *Valkyrie*'s Casimir drive online. An older model, it powered up a few seconds slower than the one on *Miss Cygni*.

"Epsi said the med scanner rated you as twenty-eight. That's good. I was worried, um, since there's some grey in your hair. I thought you were a little older."

Deadeye laughed. "I'm alive, and that's all that counts out here. That and flying."

She smirked. "Oh yeah, you're a Hot-shit Uzari. Hey... you ready?"

The undertone in her voice hinted that she felt guilty for asking him to make a second, longer jump after having made the previous one. Uzari or not, exhaustion could set in. Most pilots who tried flying longer than thirty consecutive sols died in their pods. Plus a Casimir Mark II shut off if one jumped more than 60 light-years at once, due to increased hadron consumption. Space travel wasn't as easy as the voyages in sword and laser vids.

He couldn't recall the first time he'd used an Uzari pod. The same corporation that had bred people like him had also produced the best pilot pods. The cerebral strain of piloting through a wormhole slowly drained the pilot's memories. Most MEC pilots lasted five years at best, perhaps six. An Uzari or Zyn, maybe fifteen.

"Yes." He glanced at her. "I know you're testing me, but let this be the last time. I never bullshit when it comes to my skills."

"You make this jump;, you're fine by me, right?"

"*Right.*"

Deadeye lied since Talon looked like she might chew through her lower lip. Jhio's death could be affecting her more than she wanted to show, but he sensed it was other issues. Her fellow Runners, the cargo, he wasn't sure. But he didn't need her losing confidence in his abilities at the onset.

A star chart overlaid his vision, and it repeated on the pod's screens, which enclosed around him to provide extra assistance. It was an unnecessary failsafe. Deadeye had logged into the UNS so many times, that he had the stars memorized. It was the one thing he could never forget. People, places, events, heartaches, and triumphs came and went with the light-years, but destinations unavailable to pre-FTL civilizations were forever burned into his mind. He didn't even question why anymore.

Luyten's Star was a red dwarf, nine light-years away. A few hundred years ago, it would've taken the old Kapteyn ships nine years to make the journey. The crew would have entered cryostasis. How people had managed that, Deadeye couldn't imagine.

"Here." Below the elbow, Talon stuck the last IV line into his right forearm. "I can't have you starving and weak after a few sols."

"Read me a bedtime story, too?"

"Oh, shut the fuck up."

She tried to cover her smile. "See you soon, right?"

"Yep. See you soon."

Deadeye initiated the jump.

Chapter 4

A light blue planet blockaded by battleships and cruisers. A wide debris field in the engagement area, like a giant swarm of bees on the radar screen....

"Don't make the... can't, it's Parallax...."

The words rang in his brain, echoed in his ears until he realized he'd spoken them. Deadeye trembled so much that the IV tubes rattled against his arms. Every blink made the UNS feed refresh in his eyesight. As he glanced side to side, the feed scrolled more numbers at him, so much that he wanted to claw his eyes out.

Teeth gritted, he started to reach for the jack in his neck.

Yank the bastard out....

No. Have to keep it in. Have to reach that red star, nine light-years.

He'd get them there, nine centuries, nine lifetimes, whatever it took, those marines...

"Goddamn it," he breathed, then retched.

Nothing came up but bile.

An alarm beeped. Dulcet and trite.

Deadeye worked his jaw and pinched the bridge of his nose. His fingers were numb. The UNS overlay in his vision blurred, then came back into focus. He shifted on the pod seat, which had fully reclined. Empty IV lines brushed against his thighs.

A second later, he tried to stand, fought a bout of weakness, and raised the chair to a sitting position. He rechecked the overlay, then compared it to the star positions on *Valkyrie*'s console screens.

They had just entered the Luyten system. Twenty-one sols of his life, gone.

Deadeye started to speak, but his tongue stuck to the top of his mouth like glue. He stretched his jaw until it popped, worked his facial muscles, and glanced around.

Talon sat asleep in the captain's seat, now wearing a tight black MPS with a matching hoodie. There was a sweet yet bitter scent on the bridge, and he guessed it was a fragrance she wore. Eyeliner and lipstick, too?

They must have a business transaction coming. Or she had a date.

Icara hovered right in his face, and he tried to swat her away, but she glided aside.

He tried to speak again, but a coarse rasp escaped his throat.

Talon's eyes fluttered open, and she sat up. "We there?"

"Yes." The word finally exited Deadeye's mouth. "0.09 AU from the star."

In other systems, that would have been too close to the sun, but given Luyten's low luminosity, they were well within its habitable zone.

Several blips on the UNS radar made him frown. An impulse rose deep inside him. Buried by the light-years, but now instilling quiet anger.

"Good, I'll go wake the others."

She yawned and looked at him. "What's wrong?"

"That."

He pointed at one of the screens. "AOS, five bogeys."

Five blips were closing in on two larger ones—fifty-four kilometers from *Valkyrie*. Acquisition of signal had come quickly, meaning the carrier could be in danger, too.

"How close are we to Hartwell Station?" she asked warily.

"One hundred and fifty kilometers. It's pirates, Talon. Their transponders are scrambled."

"We have an appointment," she said without conviction. "We shouldn't... oh shit, that's our contract for the seeds and labs we took... but those are likely Harpy vessels."

"Then we need to safeguard that contract," he said.

A distress call came from the two larger vessels. Homesteaders, pleading for aid.

"We can't help them," she said. "We can't fight the Harpies. You got me?"

Deadeye cycled through *Valkyrie*'s inventory and systems until he loaded its missile batteries. Its railguns had been stripped, probably for the Runners' smaller craft, but the old carrier still possessed a cache of forty two missiles. Explosive tips, nuclear powered.

"The hell are you doing?" Talon rushed to his side. "Deadie, that's not our fight; I didn't give you the order!"

He tracked the engagement in his UNS feed while bringing *Valkyrie*'s missiles online.

"You said the Redshift Runners help people. These aren't MEC vessels those assholes are targeting. Their transponders are reading as Homesteaders. They're unarmed, with families. You said you guys aren't pirates. Were you lying to me?"

"No, but the Runners don't need a damn war with one of the most vicious pirate factions. Those are Harpy ships; they trade blood for blood. Deadie?"

"Then why try to feed those people, only to let them die?" he asked.

People on the light blue planet in his memory, dying....

"Stop it, you got me?" she asked.

Valkyrie's targeting system popped up in his feed. A reticule appeared over each of the five smaller blips. His anger became a cold, calculated set of decisions. Maybe it was his old naval training. Maybe he'd seen too many helpless people die out there.

"You got me?" she repeated, louder.

Deadeye. The flicker of memory passed through his mind. That's the name the MEC navy had given him because he never missed. Only now, seeing those reticules, with over three dozen rockets of death at his command, did he remember that.

"Damn it, are you listening? I'll haul you right out of that fucking pod—"

"Unidentified vessels, this is *Valkyrie*," Deadeye said, his voice still raspy. "Disengage from that Homesteader craft, or I open fire. My only warning."

He ignored the pistol that Talon now held to his head, and ignored the other Runners hurrying into the bridge to see what the ruckus was. Ignored the screams in his mind, a recollection of people dying over the radio, distant kills in an even more distant war.

The pirates didn't respond.

"I swear by the void...."

The gun shook in Talon's hand, the barrel touching his right temple. But her eyes were on the console screens. The others watched in silence.

It was crazy, sure. But so was watching people die in the void. The distance didn't shield him from the horrors they would face or what he had to do.

Deadeye pressed the fire button.

Fifteen missiles crossed the emptiness that separated people from homes, the barrier between mortality and ambition. The black velvet sea they traversed at the very cost of their lives, their identities. The void Deadeye loved and hated.

"Why so many, hotshot?" Fluxman asked. "They only got ten seconds of fuel."

"Shut up, let him make them space dust," Runabout said.

The rockets streaked toward their targets at three thousand meters per second.

"Deadie... you just fucked us all." Talon holstered the pistol.

"You didn't order this shit, Talon?" Wizard asked.

"No." Talon's reply was colder than frozen steel.

"There goes the Hartwell spas, then," Epsi muttered.

Five seconds out, two of the pirate vessels released countermeasures. Anti-missile rockets, Deadeye guessed. Eight of *Valkyrie*'s missiles vanished off the radar.

Two seconds later, three pirate vessels disappeared from the screen. Another changed orientation every half-second, possibly spinning out of control from impact damage. The last vessel was blasting away from the two Homesteader craft.

"Yeah, you cooked their asses right; you sure did!" Runabout shouted.

"Well, that was a thing," Wizard said.

"Not bad, I gotta admit," Fluxman said. "We gonna get lunch now?"

Epsi muttered about closed spas and lost massages as she left the bridge.

Talon grabbed Deadeye by the collar as she straddled the pod. Before she could speak, a voice came over the radio.

"*Valkyrie*, this is *Queen Ursula* of the Homesteader Pact. By the Dame herself, we owe you a mighty big thank you!"

"That's great to hear, *Queen Ursula*," Deadeye said, staring into Talon's eyes as her fingers tightened on his collar. "Do you need further assistance? Anyone wounded?"

"Aye, there's a few busted heads in here, but we'll manage them right nice from here on out. The Pact will honor it if you ever need anything, and then some, right?"

"Right." Deadeye maintained the stare down with Talon. "*Valkyrie* out."

A few seconds passed.

"Yeah." Wizard's tentacles popped the IVs from Deadeye's suit. "We'll just be out here, then. Come on, Fluxman, swallow whatever stupid joke you had."

Runabout patted Talon's shoulder on her way out. "He did good; ain't no sense in arguing. I'll make sure we've got all the goodies loaded on *Cygni*."

Even Icara hovered away since he wasn't threatening the crew or the ship.

Only after everyone had left the bridge did Talon speak, and then in a fierce, shaking whisper.

"You ever fucking do that again, I swear I'll space you naked with your lungs full of oxygen, so you'll suffer extra. I gave you an order, a direct order—"

He gently pried her fingers from his collar; the anger had drained her.

"Those Homesteaders are alive," he said. "Alive, Talon, because I acted. That's what the navy taught me to do. They know the Runners did that. Your contract is secure. But you want to build a reputation and get more contracts? This is how you do it."

"Those pirate assholes got what they deserved, but I'm the captain here! The fucking navy teach you about, *ha*, chain of command, yeah? The others won't say it, but you destroyed those little shitcans too close to the Homesteader's vessels. There are families on those ships. The debris might have damaged their hulls, might have—"

"I'm not apologizing," he said.

She pushed herself out of the pod and kicked the IV lines at him.

"Get up."

He raised a hand and waited, looking at her expectantly. Again, he was risking such bluster, but if he was going to fly for these people, they needed to understand him.

"What the... you've got a lot of nerve."

She grabbed his hand and helped him from the pod; her strength had returned.

"Isn't that why I'm here?"

He coughed, swayed, then tripped over the IVs.

She caught him. "Ugh. I should throw you off my ship, you know that?"

"We taking *Miss Cygni* to the station?"

"I'm flying her myself this time, hear me? You're in no condition to pilot a garbage trawler. Shit, you're not even coming; you should be in your bunk. Or the brig."

He laughed. "I have a bunk? See, you're not kicking me out."

She gave him an incredulous look. "You're one cocky bastard, know that?"

"If you're not cocky, you're not a pilot."

She started to reply, then her mobile beeped. Upon checking it, she sighed.

"What now?" he asked.

"My contact in Hartwell wants to meet the pilot who punked those pirates."

Miss Cygni closed with a rectangular outpost in orbit above a barren, yellow-brown planet dubbed Luyten B, a name dating from the pre-colonial era. The system's distant sun emitted a fierce, pink-white glow, reflecting off the outpost's metallic hull. Its name came in over the bridge screens and some basic spectrometer readings for energy and radiation content: Hartwell Station.

Though the cabin temperature rose by half a degree, they were in no danger. *Cygni* had a light blue hull, which reflected some of the sunlight and its heat. He'd heard that ancient starships had to be painted white for such a feature, back when they'd been built planetside without the benefit of industrial shipyard printers.

Deadeye sat beside Talon on the bridge, who occupied the pilot pod. He kept glancing at her: how she sat in the seat, her light touch on the manuals, the UNS adapter around her head connected to the EEG jack. That must feel weird, not possessing an installed jack port of her own. There was steady professionalism in her technique. Again, he wondered where she had learned it.

"Never seen a woman fly a ship before, Deadie boy?" Talon fired a few lateral thrusters to orient *Cygni* with Hartwell's docking platform.

"Still don't hold a candle to my skills, and that's a fact," Runabout said.

"Talk is cheap," Epsi said. "I would have already docked."

"Can we land already?"

Fluxman fidgeted with his orange fatigues, usually worn by magistrates on MEC's settled worlds. Maybe it was a trophy, or the man had been a law officer before joining the Runners.

"I know we all want to get drunk, laid, and paid, but I handle my girl with class, okay?" Talon engaged the docking claw and leaned back in the pod seat. "There."

"Hartwell Station looks even worse now, damn."

Wizard blew a raspberry over the radio, having stayed on *Valkyrie* while they met Talon's contact.

"The Vega Freelancers still run this place, too, and they charge too much."

"But those credits keep them quiet," Talon said.

Wizard snorted. "The worst place to sell contraband this side of the Spur. Especially if it's stolen MEC cargo."

"And we brought the pilot who flew the transport, gotta love it," Fluxman said.

"We didn't steal anything." Talon tugged down the hoodie's cowl, revealing pigtails rather than a single ponytail. "That ship was carrying hydroponic supplies for—"

Wizard yawned loudly over the connection. "Stealing."

Talon laughed, placed her mag soles on the deck, and stood. "I promise you'll get to come next time. Text me if anything enters the system that even classifies as a MEC vessel, transponder or not. Okay, everyone, get out; this show won't start itself."

"Way ahead of you." Deadeye slowly rose from the seat.

Though the energy drinks Fluxman had provided granted some boost, it still took an effort to get his soles onto the deck.

Talon watched him.

"I've got this," he said.

Talon motioned for the others to go ahead while she took his arm. "Right. You always have to brag, bullshit, and lie about everything?"

"I'm just warming up my talents for your big bad contact. Nobody talks to pilots directly unless they're desperate."

He shooed Icara away as she buzzed past his ear.

"That's our middle name, so don't knock those instincts. Maybe your little war game out there impressed someone. Someone with deep pockets."

He sniffed. "What is that smell, anyway? Your, *er*, fragrance."

"I don't wear perfumes, cryobrain. It's butterscotch, my favorite coffee."

"I've never heard of it. Is it some rare bean variety in the Band? It's nice."

Talon broke eye contact. "Nothing, just a drink from my homeworld."

He let her help him from the bridge, down the corridor, and the airlock. Or, at least he told himself he was letting her help him. In truth, he wanted to pass out.

"That reminds me...what do Runners get paid?" Deadeye asked.

Epsi overhead that, rolled her eyes, and laughed.

Talon looked him up and down. "Heh, sure, if I put any credits in your pockets, you'd fall right now."

He smiled. "So there is a salary."

"Ha, get off my damn ship already."

She helped him from the airlock and onto the dock. A collapsible, sealed mesh tunnel connected *Miss Cygni*'s airlock door to the dock and the enclosed platform beyond it. Though the tunnel possessed a breathable atmosphere, it was barely heated, and their breaths came out in icy puffs. After a few seconds of weightlessness, the stability of 0.8Gs allowed their boots to touch the platform.

"They still ain't fixed the centrifuges on this here floating knick-knack," Runabout said, still in her MPS and helmet. "Last time we visited, it was a right pleasant 1.1Gs."

"All I care about is if it's strong enough to keep beer in my belly," Fluxman said.

Epsi checked her mobile. "Hey now, the nail guy is back on Deck 12. So getting my cuticles looked at this time."

"You bunch of spoiled hangar rats," Talon said.

"The first thing I want is a nice, new MPS. Like you've got there, Talon." Deadeye made a point not to let his eyes linger on her.

"You obey orders this time; I'll see what I can do, right?"

She walked him across the enclosed platform with brisk confidence, the pistol still holstered at her side. She had a trim athleticism that only came from someone who exercised regularly in heavier gravities and took plenty of supplements.

Rich girl turned rogue.

He paused for a moment to allow his body's equilibrium to normalize. "Deal."

"Hurry up; I was hoping to enter Hartwell with style."

Though Talon tapped her hip with impatience, she waited on him, which didn't alleviate his embarrassment. In the past, or at least what he recalled, he'd remained on whatever vessel he'd been assigned to while the crew left for shore leave.

It hit him that he might never have set foot on an actual planet.

Deadeye shrugged. "Better be nice, Cap'n, or I'll find a new employer in Hartwell. Someone who can appreciate my skills."

"Cap'n?" Talon asked. "Really?"

"He's talking shit already." Epsi smiled and rolled her eyes again.

"You're not the only pilot prostituting themselves there," Talon said.

"I'm hurt, Talon," Deadeye said. "Seriously."

Runabout snickered. Fluxman burped.

"Cryoshit, you're insufferable." Talon frowned, straightened his collar, and faced the others. "Let's stay alert. We're the only Runner crew smaller than a MEC pay debit."

"And if things go wrong in there?" Fluxman nodded at the door.

"Like last time?" Epsi mumbled.

"I'm allowed my gun since I'm *Valkyrie*'s commander," Talon said. "Stow it, I don't like that new rule, either, but there it is. If something happens, tell them...."

She hesitated, looked at Deadeye, and continued.

"Tell them you're from *Valkyrie*, and we just punked five Harpy vessels. That should be good enough. Hey, remember, they want what we got, not trouble. Fluxman, don't get drunk this time. Epsi, no hookers back on the ship, not even for an hour. Runabout... shit, just tell the suitors no, got it?

"Good luck with that," Wizard said over the radio. "But our new pilot has earned us some rep already, so smart advice there. No one's trying to dock on our platform, and that's mad respect on this end of the Spur."

Deadeye spread his hands. "You're welcome?"

"Yeah, you're my fucking hero." Talon led the others inside.

Deadeye grinned until they all entered the station, then he leaned over the door rail and vomited. Two jumps, back to back, had taken more out of him than he liked to admit, but he wouldn't let anyone inside Hartwell see it. He had to be indefatigable and indispensable to Talon and the others—or die trying.

But no one had called him a hero for a long time.

He coughed, spat, forced a smile, and walked in. Icara trailed after him.

Chapter 5

Hartwell Station was filled with merchants, privateers, mercenaries, peddlers, scavengers, and whoever else had been rejected by the Spur's major powers. Banners, placards, flashing holo signs, and drone advertisers clamored for attention as soon as they entered the main cargo bay. Before *Miss Cygni* had finished docking, drones had flown around the ship, flashing discount deals in bright glowing letters.

It wasn't Deadeye's kind of place, there were too many people about, too many stares directed his way. He missed the piloting pod.

Runabout, Fluxman, and Epsi cleared security and waited on the other side of a holo barrier. Talon stood beside him as two guards completed their security scan of them, but she kept looking at him as if something bothered her.

"I did comb my hair, right?"

He grinned. "Or is it something else?"

"You smile, Deadie. A lot."

Deadeye shrugged. "It makes everything go well. Like making two jumps in a row, raiding convoys, aiming guns at people's heads...."

Talon frowned at one guard who lowered his wand too close to her thigh. "My crew doesn't kill anyone unless we have to. The mercs on that ship you were flying for? They refused to stand down. Other people need that cargo more than rich assholes."

"I'm not judging," he said. "But I'm having difficulty believing all this philanthropic grandstanding at the point of a gun... Cap'n."

"Follow me, and you'll see why we do this. You might get paid, too.

Besides, people like you don't even remember the bullshit you say after a few jumps."

"We remember people who smile."

"Typical man." Talon rolled her eyes. "You always this chipper?"

"Might as well be."

He continued smiling as the guards did a second scan, this time of Icara.

"You never know when you'll die out here."

Talon sighed. "Oh, come the fuck on, how many scans do they need?"

The guards shared an annoyed glance and kept scanning. MEC spaceports utilized automated scanners or drones, but everyone else preferred human-initiated searches due to a distrust of hackers and xenophobia towards Prestige AI.

Runabout leaned on her hip. "Here now, why're they taking so long?"

"Your captain isn't smiling," Deadeye said.

Talon cocked her head, smiled, and flipped him off.

The guards finished, gave them the go-ahead, and the holo barrier cleared.

"See? I know what I'm doing."

Talon blew on her finger like a pistol, then strode on through like she owned the entire station.

Epsi tapped Deadeye on the shoulder. "Don't antagonize her, newbie. I want to enjoy myself this time."

Deadeye chuckled. "Hey, I'm all for—"

Fluxman shouldered past Deadeye. "Yeah, don't screw this up for the rest of us. Come on, Epsi. We gotta pick up rations and power cells."

Epsi gave Deadeye an apologetic look that bore some warning, then followed Fluxman into the crowded corridors leading out of the cargo bay. A fresh rumble in his stomach made Deadeye want to sit down, but he fought it off. No time to get sick.

"Pshaw, don't let them get you all flustered." Runabout tugged his sleeve.

"I'm good."

He kept pace with Talon and Runabout, but he still felt nauseous.

"So is this the Runner HQ? Do I get to meet your grand admiral or whatever?"

"Us Runners, we ain't got a leader; we're sorta like Freelancers," Runabout said.

"Then how do you keep all of your pilots and captains in line?" he asked.

"Heh, we don't, but Runners have a rep to maintain," Talon said.

"You screw that up, and others won't deal with you. Word travels fast, even out here."

"I'll bet." Deadeye avoided eye contact with two spacers wearing stolen MEC armor.

Though he wasn't loyal to his former employer, he still recalled the pride the armor had instilled in people. It was hard to let that go; the navy's training ensured it. Perhaps it was indoctrination or brainwashing, but that part of his life was the last time he'd ever felt proud of himself as far as he recalled, anyway.

A few spacers cheered them as they passed for shooting the Harpy vessels. Deadeye winked and waved, but Talon elbowed him.

"We don't have a headquarters, either," Talon said. "And we don't pick feuds, like bragging about punking some Harpies. That's how we stay alive."

He grinned. "That, and my piloting." He grinned.

"You're definitely a navy guy since Duster pilots aren't anywhere near as arrogant," Talon said. "You've proved yourself; now stop selling the flyboy crap."

He glanced at Icara. "What about my babysitter?" He glanced at Icara.

"She's my eyes when we're in port," Talon said. "You'll learn to appreciate her."

He nodded, not telling her that he needed to puke again. Hisboasting usually distracted people from seeing his faults. Usually.

Hartwell Station was filled with humans from all over the Spur, seeking employment, goods, information, or entertainment.

In their makeshift suits and zealous smiles, Homesteaders waved in recognition at Runabout; she received five marriage proposals in as many meters. A band of Sadistos in blood-red skinsuits urged Deadeye to obey his pain because that was the way of the universe . Their body odor nearly took his breath; Sadistos were infamous for never bathing. Ritual scars and tattoos covered their faces.

One spacer walked around selling a handful of data chits, claiming she had the coordinates to the Tombs, an ancient colony fleet lost long ago. Another man traded in so-called artifacts from the Ring: colorful gadgets cobbled from worn parts that might fool superstitious travelers, but no Duster would fall for it. Talon always spoke to such types, though, as if she were interested in antiques but always came away disappointed.

Bands of Freelancers regarded him, and his shipmates with measured, reserved glances and one group wearing a raptor insignia shot them murderous glares—Harpies. A shrine to Dame Nyx attracted superstitious spacers. The goddess embodied the darkness out there, promising to see travelers home if they but asked her blessing. The tall, lovely idol of an androgynous figure in diaphanous robes, surrounded by actual candles, was too much for Deadeye's secular tastes, but Runabout crossed her heart and caressed the statue's bare feet before moving on.

"Why the feet?" Deadeye asked as they walked on.

"Because the Dame's feet are always grounded and stable, you thin little heathen." Runabout pinched his thigh and chuckled. "I'd be right smooching them if not for this here helmet."

"Is that why you have a foot fetish?" Talon kept an eye on the Harpies, a hand on her holstered pistol. "Now I know who leaves those toe and tinsel vids on the holo."

"Pretty feet always lead to prettier joys if their garden is all ripe and clean." Runabout gestured at her crotch.

"There's nothing clean in here, but it's sure as hell ripe," Deadeye said.

The stink of human sweat, bad breath, and occasional flatulence mixed with aromas of pepper casseroles, milk cakes, vape smoke, and the sweet stench of Starrio, a simulant inhalant common among spacers Deadeye just wanted to smell the air in his oxygen tank again.

"Stop flirting," Talon muttered to Runabout.

"Ain't doing a thing but walking." Runabout sauntered past a scavenger crew that whistled and whooped at her.

"Walk sloppier, then." Talon gave the scavengers a dirty look. "Doesn't that shit bother you? You're a woman, not a piece of meat."

Runabout waved at the scavengers before they entered another corridor. "Easy peasy for you to say since nobody looked at me before this helmet. It's nice to be a pretty, bright star when you're right, smack dab in a cluster of hotter ones. But the best part? I can right walk away, ain't got to accept their offers. Unlike back home."

"You don't need their approval; that's all I'm saying," Talon said.

"She's right; you're beautiful."

Deadeye squeezed past a gyro vendor and a melatonin huckster, declaring their wares to be the best in the Dust Systems.

"Hah, you ain't never seen my face, you slick talker," Runabout said.

He smiled. "I hear it in your voice, in your *manner*. You radiate life."

"Listen to this sweet babbler, *capità*! Tongue dancing more than lovers in a *sardana*. Right then, what's Talon here radiate?"

"Hopefully credits?" Deadeye walked faster.

"Thanks," Talon said.

A few prostitutes tried to entice him as he walked past their parlors, but he simply smiled and followed Talon. He hadn't gotten laid in at least four jumps, and he didn't have the funds anyway. Sex and other needs, physiological or psychological, were bartered in such places. Like he'd been bartering himself since the navy... discharged him? Or had he quit? MEC's database on *Santo Pohl* had marked him as simply a 'skilled veteran,' nothing more.

It doesn't matter now.

Several spacers cursed at a large screen outside a street bar, and Talon stopped.

"Wait," Talon said. "I want to see this."

Deadeye checked the vid's timestamp. "This is from Sirius, five point seventy-six light-years away. So it's already two weeks old if they used the standard couriers."

"*Shh,*" Talon said.

The vid was a MEC news report. It conveyed what amounted to propaganda, detailing how another colony in the Sirius system had been the recipient of a food surplus due to farming yields in the surrounding star systems. Deadeye no longer felt pride in his old MEC uniform as the report went on, explaining how MEC had decreed that under-performing colonies had willingly donated their food. The smarmy attitude of the attractive, young, blonde new anchor made him wince. The accompanying footage of starving colonists watching their food get loaded onto a transport while being scrutinized by marines made him nauseous. The other people watching murmured and frowned.

"Buncha assholes," one spacer said. "On one end o' the Spur, we got the Boundary and the bots keeping us out, and on the other end, the damned Arcturus Ring and the great big 'ol nothing out there. Meanwhile, we Dusters starve."

"There are worlds in the Ring, but nobody's got the resources to settle 'emwith," the bartender said. "Too far away, and too many Ringers that will kill you for a hadron. And the Boundary? You serious? The Prestige would tear your lil' shippy apart—if you could even navigate that crazy mess."

Deadeye and his comrades edged away from the screen, but Talon glowered at it as if she wanted to reach across the light-years and choke the MEC news anchor.

"You know who runs that fucking colony at Sirius?" Talon smiled with grim contempt. "Lineage noble houses, that's who. MEC gives them whatever they want since the nobles control manufacturing and the best miner facilities. MEC gives them the people to work them since everyone's still scared shitless that the Prestige will show up and hack the bots they should be using."

"I thought the Prestige remained within the Boundary?" Deadeye asked though that wasn't his real question.

Hadn't I flown against that automated craft before?

"More MEC propaganda," Talon said. "The truth is, they fought a war against the Prestige, suffered heavily, and managed not to piss them off again. Meanwhile, there are overcrowded colonies where there's not enough food or housing, and MEC tries to police migrations with guns rather than diplomacy."

"My people ain't learned the lesson either; they keep on sending poor families out to settle every speck of rock out there," Runabout said. "Then MEC comes in, all pissy and powerful, and takes over the settlements that make it."

"Is that where those hydroponic labs are going?" he whispered in Talon's ear.

"They'd better be." Talon hurried from the bar, where the crowd booed the report.

One person brushed past him, but Deadeye wheeled about and caught them by the arm. A young man. His face registered shock, then anger, but Deadeye raised his brows, smiled, and let the would-be pickpocket go. Prostitution was supposed to be the oldest profession, but thievery came close. Not that Deadeye had anything worth taking. He was still wearing the grey MPS from *Santo Pohl*, though he'd deprogrammed the MEC logos off his shoulder pads. He needed a shave, a hot meal. Maybe a....

Deadeye fought dizziness and leaned against the corridor wall. The maintenance drones flew around him as the last few people departed Scobee Station. The new decks and modules gave the place a shiny look, like something from a Merged Earth Colonies virtual brochure. The last colonists to Gliese 752 had boarded, and he needed to report to his commanding officer before he got reprimanded for carousing with the Pulsarettes again. The last time he'd gotten drunk with one of their girls, he'd....

A hand grabbed his elbow.

Deadeye started to punch, but a firm hand jabbed him in the right armpit. Numbness erupted down his right arm, and he sucked in a breath. He coughed and blinked at his attacker. It was Talon, eying him with annoyed concern.

"What?" he mumbled.

Hartwell Station was crowded once more. There were no maintenance drones. No Pulsarettes dancing and cavorting; they'd all died or retired many years ago. Maybe lifetimes ago. Hartwell was again dirty, smelly, with modules built right atop each other rather than Scobee's orderly design. Instead of a colony ship docked and bound for Gliese, several Freelancer vessels, angular and grungy, waited at the docks.

"You're not well." Talon steadied him while Runabout looked around.

"It's jump sickness. I'll be fine."

Talon gave him a doubtful look, then pulled him along. "We're already late. Come on before you fall. You're lucky the station's gravity didn't—"

"I make my own luck."

He trailed after her through the crowd.

"Is that there some silly Uzari proverb?" Runabout asked.

"Uzari doesn't have those, either," Deadeye said. "As far as I know."

"Good," Talon said. "I don't want another Cepheid missionary on my ship."

He laughed as they passed through a small hydroponics garden where spacers could relax and enjoy greenery usually found planetside.

"You don't seem like the religious type."

"*Heh*, I'm not," Talon said. "We were transporting him to Leonis for a nice payout. He preached to us the entire trip. The bastard even had a recorded holo of himself to continue the sermon while he slept. I've heard about the Holy Variance so much I could fly into a sun."

Deadeye nodded. Talking helped ground him in the moment, not in whatever memory of what had been. It also kept his comrades from asking questions.

"I was almost married by a Cepheid once," he said.

Talon balked, then laughed. "Really? How did that go?"

"There was this woman who raised tuna in an aquaculture commune. The place stank like you wouldn't believe. Anyway, our cruiser was out of hadrons and had to leave, so I would marry her so my crew could... I could...."

Talon's brow creased. "What was her name? What happened?"

Deadeye blew air out his lips. "I... hell, I don't remember now. Sorry."

Sympathy blossomed in Talon's gaze for an instant, then her typical aloofness returned. He was thankful for the drone that flew between them, flashing capacitor ads.

"So you might be all merry married, all contracted and such?" Runabout snickered. "No Runabout for you, then. Ain't having it with a married man."

"Um, didn't know I was on the menu," Deadeye said.

"Well, you're not," Talon said quickly.

He nodded and kept smiling at the merchants they passed. Though Talon was right, and they needed to focus on their contact, it was still amazing he had recalled that much about possible matrimony—a rare thing among the stars. But the most important elements of that story were gone now. How many more jumps until he couldn't remember any of it?

"Shit. Go this way." Talon nodded down another corridor as six people wearing raptor logos clomped toward them.

"Those *gilipolles* ain't looking friendly," Runabout said.

"What's that mean?"

Deadeye followed the two women into the corridor, which was darker and crowded with more spacers.

"It means assholes," Runabout said. "Reckon, I forget you ain't from New Catalonia. I wish I could forget I was."

"Ah, the asteroid settlement near Sirius," Deadeye recalled it from his star chart knowledge. "You didn't like it there?"

"Would be in a pretty fancy dress right now, a *pubilla* with my own farm," Runabout said. "Not the life for me, ain't no way. Out here, I can be whatever I want."

"Quiet." Talon tugged Deadeye and Runabout behind a stall selling starship waste disposal systems.

The stench of bleach, disinfectant, and biocides took his breath.

While they hid, the Harpies stalked on past. Several of them wore brass knuckles or clasped at blades sheathed to their belts. So much for Hartwell security.

Talon's mobile showed a live feed linked to Icara's camera; the little drone kept the Harpies in her sights until they were well into the next corridor.

"See, Deadie?" Talon whispered in his ear. "Now we've got more enemies, on top of MEC. Everything has a price out here, even your hotshit heroism."

"I'd do it again," he whispered back.

Talon tugged him and Runabout with her into the corridor. "I know. Hey, I was wrong; you saved people and our contract. But don't let it go to your head, right?"

Fluxman and Epsi appeared in the next cargo bay, a smaller chamber than the first one. It was quieter, with fewer vendors and even fewer guards. Deadeye picked up on the tension among the gathered smugglers and tried to stay alert. It felt strange, seeking danger without the aid of the UNS or nav screens.

With more than a bit of swagger, Talon walked into the bay. Epsi and Fluxman fell in behind them. Runabout's usual bouncing gait stiffened.

"Friends of yours?" Deadeye whispered.

"Nobody's friends out here, only acquaintances," Talon said.

One of the smugglers, dressed in a faux leather jacket and matching cap, greeted them with a single wave. Talon led the group to him, where others played backgammon on a holo board. They paused their game and watched.

"You the guy from *Hidalgo?*" Talon asked.

"You the gal from *Valkyrie?*" The smuggler crossed his arms.

"If the void will have us," Talon said.

It was an obvious Runner code phrase.

The smuggler let out a breath and sat at the backgammon table. "Shit. You're an hour past due. You get the entire haul?"

"Yes, but we lost our pilot." Talon thumbed at Deadeye. "We found a new one, right? So don't look so worried. I'm still going to make that rendezvous with the others."

The players at the table shared cautious glances.

"Here now, start telling us what's happening," Runabout said. "We all Runners here, or a bunch of hangar scamps?"

Fluxman grunted. "The Vega Freelancers sold us less than our usual supply quota. Gotta say, that's not good. Not this far out from the Golden Band."

The smuggler crumpled his cap in one hand and downed a whiskey shot. "The Lineage has started cooperating more with MEC. They're calling the Runners pirates, too. Or that we're revolutionaries who need to be spaced."

"That's nothing new." Epsi took one of the shot glasses from the table and drank the alcohol. "What's the news out there? You heard from the other crews?"

"Yes... and no."

The smuggler set his empty shot glass on the table. "We managed to avoid a famine at Ross 128, but one of our carriers got punked by a MEC patrol at Procyon. They took the ship, arrested the pilots, and scrapped the smaller craft. Contacts are ratting us out. Fewer people are paying us."

"Is this your way of saying that we're getting less for this mission?" Talon asked. "I've already sent the signal to my ship to deposit the crates in the bay we rented. And my pilot just saved those Homesteaders' asses out there."

The smuggler spread his hands. "You think it's any better for my crew? Plus, we can't keep pilots. The Casimirs either fry their minds or they get all cocky and jump forty light-years for the fuck of it. Maybe this Runner thing isn't worth it."

"I'm in this for the long stretch, you hear me?" Talon sighed and shook her head. "Anything else? What about you wanting to meet my pilot who punked those pirates?"

"We heard about what you did, saving those Homesteaders," the smuggler said. "The Harpies are pissed, but they always are. They've gotten too goddamn brave around Hartwell here lately. Who managed that stunt?"

Valkyrie's crew all looked at Deadeye.

The smuggler stood. "You an Uzari? Wanted to say thanks. The people on those ships weren't strangers, or more crazy settlers headed for void knows where. *Hidalgo* is on the other side of the system, and our ship... anyway, thanks. You're getting my share and what we can still pay for the convoy job."

Deadeye nodded to the smuggler as the man handed over a credit case. Physical, encrypted currency was still the norm across the Spur, and judging from the case's weight, he'd been given at least thirty thousand credits.

"Wait."

Talon handed the man a keycard to unlock the bay where they'd stored the labs and seeds.

"Your share? What's up?"

"He's leaving with those settlers, that's what," Runabout said.

"Sure am," the smuggler gave a sad smile. "I did one last run, so my family might have fresh food to eat, wherever we end up. But I can't do this anymore. I forgot my daughter's name a few sols ago. I'm making one more jump, and then...."

"Then you'll always remember her," Deadeye said. "Good luck to you."

He knew it was an empty sentiment as both their memories would surely continue to erode.

The smuggler nodded. "And to you. Remember, being a Runner is like this backgammon game. You only win if you get everybody home."

The man and his comrades left. There was one black piece left on the board. Deadeye rolled the dice but frowned. It wasn't enough for him to move the piece to safety and thus win the game.

"Not everybody gets to go home. Wherever that's supposed to be."

Talon nudged his arm. "Come on, Deadie, lose the long face; you're killing me. Let's divvy up these credits and land another job."

He watched the smugglers leave the bay. Wondering whom he'd forgotten while soaring between the stars.

Deadeye enjoyed another cup of orange juice while he and his shipmates sat in a food court on Hartwell's upper levels. The vast chamber housed a variety of food vendors, selling everything from Cetian tomato soup to Eridanian cantaloupes. Still, he loved the juice's sweet, acidic taste, its vivid yellow color. It was familiar yet new.

Fluxman downed another beer and belched.

"Thirty thousand? That little shit from *Hidalgo* shorted us twenty thousand credits."

"More because some of that is the smuggler's share to Deadeye," Epsi said, smiling sweetly at Deadeye. "Give me a loan, pretty please? I'll make it worth your while."

"And just how much was that dandy little share?"

Runabout sipped limeade through a straw from beneath her helmet rim. "Dame and dark, this ain't nowhere near real lemonade."

"Five thousand was that bastard's share."

Talon flipped the credit case open on the booth table and doled out the funds. "Thirty means we each get five thousand."

Deadeye finished the juice. "That's cutting into my own normal share—"

"You're new, and you disobeyed a direct order earlier." Talon sat back, arms crossed.

"You're damn lucky I'm letting that slide, Mister Hot-shit. The Redshift Runners are a team. You're former navy, so you should know. No rules means no survival."

Deadeye eyed the empty cup as if more juice would magically appear. "You're quoting MEC naval slogans at me now? That's rich."

"I wish the hell we were." Epsi accepted her credits and finished her beer. "I wish the hell we were."

"None of us joined for the money, got me?" Talon looked each of them in the eye.

Deadeye stared at his credits, then pushed them back to Talon. "All I need is food, some new clothes, a new MPS, and maybe a few good books. Give the rest to the crew."

Epsi and Fluxman reached for the extra funds, but Talon laid her hand atop the rectangular chips.

Runabout made a "dun duh dum" sound and snickered.

"I'm buying you all better equipment with this," Talon said. "Give the dirty looks a rest, right? You're not drinking and whoring this stash up. Deadie boy... good on you."

Fluxman burped again. "Here's to flyboy, then." Fluxman burped again.

Talon pushed the case over to Runabout. "Miss Frugal here, you get everything else we need. Grab Deadie the stuff he mentioned. And make sure you pay off the Freelancers so they'll keep their mouths shut. We didn't pay them enough last time."

"What will you be doing?" Epsi asked.

Talon checked her mobile, then stood and beckoned to Deadeye. "Getting our next job. It'll be a good one, right? We'll meet up back at *Cygni* in an hour."

Runabout stood with the others. "Hey now, Deadeye, I can guess your size, but whatcha like to read? Some of them spacer romances? I love me some of those."

"Um... anything on the Spur's colonies. Especially the Golden Band systems."

"How droll," Epsi said. "Give me a thrill 'n chill explorer series any sol. Maybe you should come and let me read you some of mine, hmm?"

Smiling, Deadeye started to answer, but Talon waved a hand.

"Okay, now come on."

Talon tugged him from the food court as the others left.

"Why me? I'm the new pilot."

Talon put her hoodie cowl back on. "Because you're a better liar than they are." Talon put her hoodie cowl back on.

"Oh.Thanks?"

He didn't ask why she had interrupted the casual flirting that Epsi kept throwing his way, but she was the captain. Maybe she thought he had space herpes or Struve syphilis. Perhaps she wanted him for herself. As if he could land a provincial gal.

They rode an elevator to Hartwell's comm deck, where dispatch ships arrived and departed, bearing messages that needed to be relayed quickly. Since news traveled on radio waves, it could take years for important warnings to reach outlying worlds across the Spur. Decades, even. A courier operating a Casimir Mark II B drive, with a 0.004 multiplier, only took sols or weeks. Yet as he and Talon walked across the deck, seeing those pilots left him cold.

Many were thin Uzari like him or a few Zyn, their tentacles drooping from exhaustion. There were even a few Aquarii, a MEC-sponsored genetic strain of humanity with larger eyes and delicate bone structure.

Men and women staggered to drone stretchers or knelt outside their tiny scout ship's airlock, trying to acclimate themselves to Hartwell's gravity and trying to remember that they weren't in the UNS pod any longer. He knew that feeling. Like waking from a dream: starving, thirsty, wondering if those around them were close friends or mere acquaintances since one remembered them less and less. Retrograde amnesia or dementia would claim most of them—those who didn't die from cerebral hemorrhage or in combat.

"You expecting a message?" Deadeye swallowed, nausea returning.

"The comm deck is always the best place to find Runner prospects, and I got a text on a good one." Talon paused. "Hey, you okay?"

"Sure, I—"

"You're a good liar, but I see it, right? You can tell me when the jumps make you ill. I'm not going to toss you here and leave, got it? No matter how salty I talk to you. Or how much you piss me off."

He smirked. "Are you *Valkyrie*'s doctor, too?"

"I'm whatever I need to be out there."

She steadied him as he bumped into an empty stretcher floating past them.

"Suck it up; I need you to pay attention."

Before arguing, she led him into a comm booth where a weary pilot had deposited public domain holo cards instead of encrypted ones intended for a specific party. Which meant the sender hoped for a response from anyone—a desperate act. Talon shut the booth door and sat beside him on the small seat. He tried to sit straight. Icara hovered outside, alert and inconspicuous.

"Keep up, okay? Lots of people out there hire Runners for all sorts of things. They'll send messages to places like this, and we Runner captains accept jobs few other crews will bother with. I have alerts with Hartwell's network that texts me whenever something like this hits the comm deck."

Seeing people like him suffering after a jump lowered his typical bluster levels. He felt vulnerable there beside her, and the words spilled out.

"Hey... sorry, I disobeyed an order like that. I was in the moment and—"

"It's fine, those people are alive, and we completed the contract. But don't do it again. You have no idea how hard it is to keep people in line in this outfit."

Though she said nothing else about it, Talon's shoulders relaxed. He breathed easier, too, watching her load up the terminal.

"The sender is from Ross 614? There's nothing there. It's a red dwarf flare star."

Talon leaned forward as the holo message played. "Shh." Talon leaned forward as the holo message played.

"You shush me a lot."

She smirked. "You blabber a lot. Now listen."

The head and shoulders of an older woman appeared. She wore a Lalande Corp uniform, a colony transport service.

"Please, anyone receiving this, this is Captain Sakomoto of *Happy Maui*. Flares have damaged our drive in this system. I deployed our one dispatch scout to deliver this message to the nearest outpost. Please help; we have over a hundred passengers, including children. We lack cryogenic facilities, so please come quickly. Sakomoto out."

The holo flickered and vanished.

Deadeye rubbed his temples and raised his brows. "Hmm. Short and sweet. Doesn't Lalande transport passengers for the fee of indentured service?"

"Another reason to help those people."

Talon copied the message's attached coordinates to her mobile and stood.

"Hot damn. This is perfect."

He followed her from the booth. "I missed the part about what she's paying."

"You're telling the rest that we're getting forty thousand for this job. I need you to go along with me on this, Deadie."

As they hurried back to the elevator, he avoided looking at the courier pilots. Eventually, that might be him if this Runner thing didn't work out. He wanted to fly, but something about those spacers' disposable quality bothered him. Like they were a medium rather than people.

"Why lie?" He yanked his arm close as the elevator door banged shut.

"They'll get their money." Talon looked at her mobile. Not at him.

"You're a poor liar, too. Why take the job at all? Is it something else?"

Talon shrugged. "This from the guy who gave away his share? Trust me."

"At least I didn't lie about where it came from."

She flicked him a cool look. "It's not about the money; you got that?"

"Hey, I got it."

Talon pushed her cowl back. "It's just... this is important. You with me? This is going to lead to something bigger; you wait. The others they won't understand yet. I needed to tell you, because they won't get suspicious if you back me up on it."

"We're trusting each other a hell of a lot," he said. "We don't know each other."

Talon blew out a breath. "If that's a pickup line, it's fucking terrible."

He pretended to study his glove. "Epsi would have liked it."

"*Ha*, shut up. Besides, I trust my instincts. You trusted me enough to join. Right?"

He smiled, and she finally returned it. "Sure, Cap'n."

The elevator jerked to a stop, the door opened, and Talon exited it in fast strides. Deadeye barely kept up, wondering why she'd been so defensive.

What did she want on that Lalande ship?

CHAPTER 6

FLUXMAN KICKED A SUPPLY CRATE IN *VALKYRIE*'S CARGO BAY.

"What is this, a charity outfit? First, that piece of shit shorts us on credits back at Hartwell, and now, we gotta rescue some colonists who were stupid enough to sign on with Lalande?"

Talon tugged off her hoodie as she paced in an open area between the crates and other containers. Her halter top revealed golden swirls of water and flame tattooed on her arms, neck, and stomach.

"You want out, that it? We can send you back to Hartwell right now with a deserter ribbon. Nobody's here that doesn't want to be."

Epsi shrugged. "You never know, Fluxman, Lalande might pay a reward. They wouldn't want any bad publicity."

"What about all the people out there starving, or the colonies where kids are breathing cheap cycler air so they'll get cancer?" Fluxman jabbed a finger at Talon. "That's what we oughta be taking care of; that's why I joined. Fuck those corp types."

Deadeye sat on the crate Fluxman had kicked. "There are children on *Happy Maui*." Deadeye sat on the crate Fluxman had kicked.

"You our fucking moral compass now?" Fluxman snorted. "Y'all hear this guy?"

Runabout tiptoed between them and handed Deadeye a small package. "Hiya, I hope I did right by your tastes and all. Hartwell ain't exactly the Dame's library."

"Thank you." Deadeye opened the package.

It contained two holo cards detailing early Terran settlement in the Orion Spur and an actual, physical book about Sagittarii cultists seeking a way back to Earth. He flipped through the pages; it seemed more like fiction, or even religious drivel than a true account of Spur history. As he put them back into the package, he caught Talon studying him and the books. She looked away.

Wizard joined the group, one tentacle wrapped around a steaming cup of tea.

"So, what did I miss? Fluxman bitching about the next job again? Runabout finally getting married to a big sexy Zyn with a black tea fetish?"

"Oh, you silly flirt." Runabout handed Wizard a package, too. "Found you this."

Fluxman stalked out of the bay. "Great, let's all unwarp presents like it's Cepheid New Year." Fluxman stalked out of the bay.

Talon started to speak, but Epsi tapped her shoulder. "Easy, he's pissed because he couldn't get drunk again. He'll be up for it by the time we get there. How far?"

"Four light-years." Talon took Wizard's tea and sipped it. "Shit, Wizard, you know I hate those grapefruit sweeteners."

"Then get your own." Wizard laughed and reclaimed his beverage. He opened the package. "Hey, Runabout, you found one!"

"Another little charm?" Epsi groaned. "You're so superstitious."

Wizard held up a small red figurine of a smiling, corpulent person sitting atop lotus blossoms.

"This will give me luck on the next flight. Four light-years? I've got you all covered. This kicks ass, Runabout."

"What is it?" Deadeye stood and tucked the books under his arm.

"It's a Red Buddha." Wizard frowned. "You don't know that is, do you? It's Zen, one of the old Earth beliefs, about being here now. When I'm in the pod, I don't waste time worrying about what I might forget or if my ship will make the jump. I focus on the right here and fucking now, and I always come through the wormhole."

Deadeye turned to Talon. "I'm not flying this jump?"

"Nope." Talon balled up the hoodie and tossed it into an empty crate. "I need you rested and fresh for this little fun fest at Ross 614. You'll be on point in *Miss Cygni*."

Wizard shared a curious glance with Runabout.

"*Ha*, you're letting him fly your girl again? An ensign?" Epsi raised an eyebrow. "My, my, Deadeye, you did make an impression."

"Stow it." Talon tugged Deadeye's sleeve. "Here, I'll show you to your cabin. Runabout already put your new clothes in there."

Minutes later, on B Deck, Deadeye examined the 2-meter by 2-meter cabin, complete with bunk, holoprojector, a tiny closet, an even tinier shower, and a bathroom. It smelled of disinfectant and old spacer's boots. The ceiling lamp flickered twice, and two satchels stuffed with clothes waited in the corner.

"Shit, I told Runnie to ditch Jhio's stuff."

Talon hauled the satchels into the corridor and gave him an apologetic look. "Yeah, this was Jhio's cabin. But hey, there's your new MPS and some clothes Runnie bought at Hartwell. Not too bad, huh?"

He smiled. "Room service?"

"Yeah, right. You get some rest; the galley will have something at 1700 hours."

She offered a tight smile, glanced at his book package, and headed for the door.

He held up the package. "You like books?" He held up the package. "Sometimes."

She paused in the corridor. "My cabin is next on the right, and everyone else has theirs on C Deck. Now get some sleep."

The door slid shut. Deadeye sat on the bunk, bewildered yet grateful. A cabin beside hers... and her obvious interest in the books Runabout acquired for him. For a moment, silly, adolescent fantasies played out in his mind; the sort dreamt up by lonely people near others. But Talon needed him to fly her ships. Nothing more.

The beehive was silent. Its occupants lay in piles about their home, wings still shiny, thoraxes and antennae still glistening with honey. Deadeye gingerly picked one off the deck, his insulated glove shielding him from the radiation that had eradicated the hive. He'd promised her that she'd have honey cakes and syrup on her next birthday....

His throat was dry. "Why are you going there?" His throat was dry.

No one answered.

"Why are..." Deadeye fired the ship's thrusters, but it didn't matter.

She was gone, like the bees, like the goddamn water treatment plant, like everything else in the colony. He rubbed his eyes, but all he could see were UNS charts, coordinates, useless little minutiae that told him nothing about where she might have gone or where he was.

"Parallax," he whispered as if the word would open some magic portal from a Homesteader fairytale. "I can't jump...."

The enemy missiles closed in. He loosed countermeasures, fired the thrusters....

"Get away from them!" he cried. "We already killed them... their AOS...."

Deadeye tried to yank the UNS jack from his neck, but it wasn't there. He glanced at the IVs inserted into his limbs, but they were gone, too. He scrabbled about on a hard surface as a blue-white orb exploded above him.

"Hey, calm down!"

That voice. Familiar, yet so far away. Deadeye shielded his eyes from the merciless supernova above him. Any second, it would burn away his skin.

Hands clasped his wrists. He fought, kicked, and flung someone to a bunk on his right.

They slapped his face. "Calm the fuck down!" They slapped his face.

Deadeye coughed and shrank back. He was on the floor of his cabin; a sweaty sheet knotted up beneath him. The ceiling lamp's cool, blue-white light did nothing to warm him. He shivered, chill bumps popping along his clammy skin.

Talon straddled him, holding his wrists again, bangs hanging in her eyes. "Deadie? Calm down; it's fine. I'm not going to hurt you, right? Hey, can you—"

"I hear you."

He closed his eyes and released a breath he'd not realized he was holding. A metallic taste preceded a warm trickle down his chin.

"Void dammit." Talon grabbed the edge of the sheet and wiped his mouth. "Not even been here for one sol, and you've already made me bloody you up."

He blinked until the light didn't hurt, then furrowed his brow at her. "Why are you here? In your underwear."

"I heard you next door, that's why. It's 02:00 , for void's sake. You were shouting, punching the deck, all sorts of craziness."

She released his wrists and got up.

Deadeye crawled to the bunk and sat on it. "Sorry."

"Do you always sleep on the deck like that?"

He shrugged. "Just not a bunk kinda guy."

Getting his bearings, he stared around the cabin. His new MPS hung in the closet. The orange juice cans Runabout had brought earlier still sat on the projector.

The book about Sagittarii cultists was open.

She crossed her arms. "Will you be okay?"

"Playing doctor again? Look, I'm fine. It was a nightmare, don't you ever have those? Or do you make a habit of sneaking into people's rooms and reading their books while they sleep?"

"What the hell are you talking about?" Talon backed toward the door.

He pointed with a trembling finger. "That book—"

She rolled her eyes and left. He shook his head and started to mutter things about a shitty attitude, but she returned with a pill and a beer.

"Take this. No, take it; it's melatonin, and drink this whole can. The alcohol might help you sleep. Deadie... c'mon, I'm not leaving until you do."

He glared up at her and finally accepted the pill and beer.

"How long have you had PTSD?" she asked in a low voice.

"Don't know." He shrugged again, guzzling the bitter, frothy drink. "Deadie..."

"You expect me to remember that, an Uzari pilot?"

He laughed, crushed the can, and flung it across the cabin. "There, doc. Happy now?"

Talon rubbed her arm, looked around the cabin, then back at him. He spread his hands and raised his brows. She shook her head and walked out. The door slid shut.

Of course, it was PTSD. But remembering? What a joke. He got off the bunk and lay back on the deck. Stared at the open book. Maybe he was imagining things.

Maybe she was lying.

"I need my pod," he mumbled, unable to keep his eyes open.

Ross 614 was a red dwarf binary system and just outside the boundaries of the Golden Band. Less than fourteen light-years from Earth; prime MEC territory. Deadeye had scrolled through the holo books Runabout got him, and Ross 614 was the subject of weird spacer legends. Disappearing fleets, ghost ships, quasar dragons, and other superstitious nonsense. To him, the reality was harsh and frightening enough out there without imagining more woes within it.

The eight sols spent on *Valkyrie* with the others had passed too quickly. Fluxman always beat him at billiards, Runabout forced him to sing one of her shanties, and Epsi flirted but never committed to anything. After more than one sleep cycle he suspected Talon had crept back into his cabin, but the book was never left open again. She'd not said much to him, but he'd resorted to brewing her coffee, trying to make amends. Pilots weren't accustomed to apologizing because most of them never thought they were wrong. He'd been wrong far too often but still lacked the words to express that.

At least Talon always drank the coffee. She didn't like anyone else's.

Now he sat in *Miss Cygni*'s piloting pod, jacked in, the UNS feed displaying spectrographic data on the twin suns. "Okay, Cap'n, I'm six AU out from those red babies and seventy five thousand kilometers from *Valkyrie*. Still not picking up *Happy Maui* on scopes or radar."

"Deadie, this is *Valkyrie*; keep looking," Talon said.

Wizard was sleeping after making the four light-year jump from Luyten's, so she'd commandeered the cruiser. He sensed she wanted to be out there in her frigate with the rest of them.

"*Annie Argent* talking ain't nothing here but ass dust from MEC convoys," Runabout said. "That Lalande ship is likely cooked more than my *àvia*'s scallops."

"Your grandmother would have kept searching," Talon said. "I'm still receiving the downlink from their distress beacon. Fluxman, you got anything in that tin can?"

"*Corsair* here, sure, I've got boils on my ass from sitting in this pod for so long," Fluxman said. "But a buncha helpless colonists? Nah, the garden gnome is right; this system is emptier than my credit account."

Epsi whistled over the radio connection. "*Ha-ha*, pay up, you moon lubbers. There she is, sixty-eight thousand kilometers from my position here in *Princess*."

Deadeye checked his radar; *Princess* was twelve thousand from his position, making Epsi the furthest from *Valkyrie* among their group. He fired his starboard thrusters in a short, high-speed burn and headed for her bearing. After a few seconds, *Happy Maui* flickered into existence on his feed—along with four other blips.

"Son of a bitch," Deadeye muttered.

"Say again, *Cygni*?" Talon asked.

"I've got AOS on four vessels, inbound for *Happy Maui*, and their transponders are reading as MEC military," he said. "Forty-three kilometers out from the transport, closing fast."

"How the hell didn't we see them earlier?" Fluxman asked.

"Probably the flares in this system, screwing with our instruments," Epsi said. "What's the matter, people? Are you afraid of some MEC pushovers? My railgun is ready."

"They might have missiles, and we don't?" Deadeye adjusted his trajectory. "This isn't a coincidence. This is a trap, Cap'n, and we sprang it."

"We're still boarding with *Happy Maui* and taking any survivors," Talon said. "Got that, everyone? Fly like you mean it."

"Easy for you to say, *Valkyrie* has all the firepower," Fluxman said.

"Burnt scallops, coming up hot, then!" Runabout laughed.

"And I'm bringing the BBQ sauce," Epsi said.

Deadeye ignored the rest of their chatter as he sped for *Happy Maui*. The MEC craft fell into formation, around six kilometers distant from each other, so one ship's countermeasures could protect the other three while engaging hostiles. And all he had was the one 75mm railgun. Pirates didn't expect resistance and rarely utilized heavier armaments.

He checked the ammo on his UNS feed: "193 sabot rounds."

Since his weapon fired ten rounds per minute, tops, he was in good shape—if he were fighting merchants.

"*Valkyrie*, you getting any transmissions from *Happy Maui*?" he asked, already guessing the answer.

"Negative," Talon said. "MEC might be jamming them. Deadeye, dock with them anyway, we came here for a rescue, and Lalande always pays."

"Shit, those are corvettes," Fluxman said. "This is suicide."

Epsi chuckled. "Got any better ways to die?" Epsi chuckled.

With *Valkyrie*, The Runners outgunned the MEC patrol, but it would take precious seconds for the carrier to shift the balance. Until then, it was their lightly-armed, outdated vessels versus warships. As *Miss Cygni* closed with the unresponsive transport, Deadeye kept his doubts to himself—until the corvettes opened fire.

Chapter 7

"Evasive!" Deadeye shouted as he blasted toward the nearest corvette.

Unless he closed the distance with the patrol, he was an easy target for their missiles. If he came within less than five hundred meters, the MEC ships risked damaging themselves with any loosed salvos as long as he didn't crash into them.

"He gotta death wish?" Fluxman asked.

"He's fucking insane," Epsi said. "*Ha!* I love it."

Deadeye maneuvered *Miss Cygni* in a straight trajectory, then jetted his starboard thrusters for a split-second burn. The UNS feed displayed his proximity to the corvette: twelve kilometers, then three kilometers... then six hundred and fifty meters. Lower and lower until he could read the other vessel's airlock safety signs through his scopes. One hundred and twenty-six meters. He kept going.

"Come on, now, he's got the right idea!" Runabout yelled.

"*Cygni*, pull back!" Talon cried over the radio. "You're going to—"

Nothing existed outside of Deadeye's pod. Numbers continued scrolling in his vision. Yaw 339°, pitch 22°, roll 348°, and decreasing. He held *Cygni*'s manuals in loose grips, calm, not tensing up. The railgun's aiming reticule settled on the corvette's bridge. Without hesitation, he fired. One round, then two. Another tap on the thrusters, and he was barreling away from the corvette. Yaw 12°, roll 28°. No time to even see how much damage he'd done. Just another maneuver, another jet from the thrusters, and *Miss Cygni* was oriented behind the corvette. Deadeye tapped the fire button three times.

One round pierced the corvette's hull below its power router, while the other two rounds dashed across the darkness and sheared through the closest corvette a kilometer distant. The MEC crews had been caught off-guard, expecting the Runners to flee or maintain their distance. The advantage would last but a second.

He started to fire again, but *Cygni*'s heatsinks prevented him from dissipating the energy so the frigate's systems wouldn't overheat. He cursed, eager to finish the kill.

More voices came over the radio, perhaps orders, maybe warnings or cheers, but Deadeye had no time for them. In that moment, he was *Miss Cygni*, each tight burn, every burst of thruster gas, each crush of g-forces inside the bridge, every hum of the engine all melded into his conscious-ness as he performed hairline maneuvers. Everything else seemed to tran-spire slowly while he operated in real-time.

Like when he'd gunned down that cruiser over Epsilon Eridani—or enfilading that rebel convoy trying to escape the massacre on Struve III. Distance from a target tended to alleviate the guilt of killing another human being. People were simply numbers in a feed or percentages on a casualty list afterward. But he'd heard those rebels on the radio; he'd gritted his teeth while those people screamed as the shrapnel cleaved through them—

"I'm hit!" Epsi's angry cry drew him from those memories.

Deadeye didn't waste time with questions; he assessed the situation with his instruments. Epsi had attempted the same ploy he'd just made, a mad dash straight at the MEC ships. It had almost worked, but one had strafed her with railgun rounds. The high-velocity projectiles had torn into *Princess* and disabled its lateral thrusters. Epsi could move forward or backward but lacked the capability to reorient herself.

One corvette placed itself in *Princess*'s forward path, preventing Epsi from leaving the engagement. If she thrust backward, she'd remain in their line of fire for too many dangerous seconds.

"Got you covered, all nice n' tight!"

Runabout brought *Annie Argent* alongside *Princess*'s portside hull, shielding Epsi from the other two corvettes—while exposing her own craft.

The compact arrangement of starships less than two hundred meters from one another alleviated the threat of MEC missiles but granted brutal, close-range gun bouts. Railgun fire zipped back and forth, punc-turing holes in hulls, shattering bulkheads, or crushing airlocks. Debris, tools, and even a few MEC mercs flew from the decompressed chambers and thudded into an opponent's hull.

Deadeye jetted to within fifty meters of the corvette blocking Epsi and peppered it with railgun fire. A hit behind the bridge, a glancing strike near its rear thrusters, then a direct hit on its forward railgun. He cursed as his weapon took precious seconds to reload. The goddamn heatsinks were too slow. By then, the other two corvettes had deployed anti-ship drones, which possessed thrusters and 30mm miniguns.

Ineffective versus larger ships, but deadly against the smaller, unarmored Runner craft. If one breached an airlock and boarded, the occupants were as good as dead. He was helpless, strapped into his pod, as were his comrades—unless he deployed *Cygni*'s combat drones. Right before he activated them, Talon hailed him on the radio.

"Deadie, I need you to dock with *Happy Maui*; your drones can help those colonists get onboard. Remember why we're here."

"Oh, I'm remembering all right."

Fluxman flew *Corsair* past one of the corvettes and exchanged a railgun salvo that left gaping holes in both craft. Or at least that's what the UNS reported, based on radar and scopes—there was no direct visual. For all Deadeye knew, *Corsair* might be floating scrap already.

Deadeye turned the manuals while jetting a starboard thruster. "I can target their routers; I can disable these bastards." Deadeye turned the manuals while jetting a starboard thruster.

The targeting reticule neared the corvette.

"The others are taking MEC heat so you can get the job done, you hear me?" Talon asked. "Get those colonists!"

Deadeye's thumb hovered over the fire button, then he cursed and jetted his forward and port thrusters. The maneuver barreled him away from the MEC vessels and toward *Happy Maui*, six kilometers distant. Since he was docking, Deadeye had to slow *Miss Cygni* to a fraction of its speed, using 30% of his gas thruster fuel to do so.

"Shit, the drones are at my starboard airlock!" Epsi shouted.

"Coming 'round with the cure, don't you be fretting," Roundabout said.

"Fuck, there went my forward thruster," Fluxman said. "Great. Fucking great."

"Gonna piss yourself, too?" Runabout laughed. "Get in there, Fluxo! Epsi darling ain't wanting this drone date to ring her airlock bell."

"I'm sealing off *Princess*'s bridge!" Epsi yelled.

Deadeye knew he could save them, knew his skills could turn those MEC vessels to scrap, but Talon was right: his newfound friends were taking all that punishment so he could save the colonists. Besides, the UNS showed *Valkyrie* finally nearing the engagement; it could have loosed missiles minutes ago, but with the Runner ships so close to the MEC ones, it wasn't an option. Talon would have to display her gunnery skills again, and he was a little sad he wouldn't get to see it.

"*Happy Maui*, this is *Miss Cygni* of the Redshift Runners; I'm here to lend support," Deadeye said. "Do you read over?"

Two seconds passed. The UNS feeds jumbled in his eyesight, the fates of his comrades now a mere collection of numbers and holographic diagrams. An impersonal yet voyeuristic perspective on the frailty of human life. Talon issued more orders, and more fusillades passed between the ships; one MEC corvette drew away but blew apart. Epsi had gone silent, and Runabout was ramming *Annie Argent* into the drones while Fluxman tried to orient himself and return fire.

"*Cygni*, this is Captain Sakamoto of *Happy Maui*," a woman finally said. "The Merged Earth Colonies have already pledged their intention to aid us."

"If they'd wanted to help you, they'd have already flown you out of this backwater," Deadeye said. "My friends are risking their lives right now, so you might survive. We'll take you to the nearest outpost. Now let me dock."

Sakamoto sounded tired. "The Merged Earth Colonies have—"

"Used you for bait, so they don't give a damn about you," he said with a passion he'd not realized he felt. "We jumped four light-years, captain. You can be on my ship in four minutes, ready to leave this place. Or you can starve out here. Your choice."

The UNS showed another MEC vessel breaking away from the battle, probably to fire its missiles. *Valkyrie* beat them to it and released its own deadly volley. On his radar, several blips darted for the corvette, and a second later, the MEC warship was gone.

"Still want to wait for MEC's help?" Deadeye asked.

Seconds passed. He started to hail Sakamoto again.

"What becomes of *Happy Maui*?" Sakamoto finally asked.

"We're not pirates, captain," he lied. "But we expect Lalande to pay a reward for our trouble, bravery, and the damages we've suffered."

"Saving people must be an expensive business," Sakamoto said.

He grinned at the sarcasm in her voice, even as he watched the battle radar with bated breath.

"It sure is, captain. But aren't people the most valuable thing in the universe? Particularly, your people?"

"Fine, docking approved." Sakamoto paused on the line. "I expect my passengers and crew to be well-treated, pilot...?"

"Deadeye," he said. "Docking claw extended. I also have some drones ready to assist with your, uh, evacuation and all."

"I'm sure. Sakamoto out."

Deadeye sighed and leaned back in the pod as Runabout's joyous squeal rattled his earbuds. He smiled again, then tried to wipe the sweat off his face. His faceplate blocked his hand, and he laughed at having forgotten such a minor detail. Then the radar showed that the other two MEC vessels had jumped from the system.

"Holy cryoshit, I thought I would get spaced," Epsi said. "Thanks."

"You did good, Runnie," Talon said. "Real good."

"Yeah, you're welcome," Fluxman said.

"Ha, you too, Fluxo," Talon said. "Can you still fly that tin can?"

"Hell no, I'm dead in the void," Fluxman said. "Lalande better gimme a blowjob for all this shit."

Before Deadeye could join the conversation, Talon sent him a message on an encrypted connection. "Deadie boy, let the drones do their thing, then get back to *Valkyrie*. We're leaving *Happy Maui* for MEC. Hear me over there?"

"I don't get a little pat on the head, too?" He chuckled.

"You and that navy ego." Talon snorted. "Okay, you did kick some ass out there, right? But you could have told me you were going to try that. I almost fired my goddamn missiles up your rear thrusters. Finger on the button and everything."

"Guess I'm special after all. That means I get a raise, right? Or am I a lieutenant now, with a nice beret and all?"

"No, my glamourous little fucko, it does not." Talon laughed, then a serious edge entered her voice. "Make sure those bots finish; they know what to get. Got me?"

"Got you as always, Cap'n."

He blew out a breath and rubbed his eyes

I'll never get her motivations.

Once the passengers were onboard, Deadeye sealed them in the passenger berth. The bots spent half an hour on *Happy Maui*, during which time he had to keep reassuring Sakamoto, via *Miss Cygni*'s intercom, that everything was fine. Yet she kept sending the bridge messages, demanding to know what was happening. He finally muted the passenger berth comm and lost himself in the UNS.

Staring at the holographic stars, studying common trajectories through the Golden Band and the inner edge of the Dust Systems, even out to the Arcturus Ring, which was anything more than twenty light-years ~~LY~~ out. Some old-fashioned spacers liked to call it all Terran Space, but most simply referred to it as the Spur. Shorter and simpler, like most people's lives who braved it.

The encrypted channel came on again. "They finished yet, Deadie?"

"Almost... I think."

He sat up in the pod. "How's everyone? Can you even get those ships back on *Valkyrie*? *Corsair* took a serious ass-beating."

"Yeah, we just got that heap back into the hangar, but *Princess* is the real problem," Talon said. "We might have to leave it behind; just salvage the engine, hadrons, railgun, and the pod. Epsi's pissed, but she'll be okay. How's my girl?"

"*Cygni* is good." Deadeye crossed his arms and smirked. "It's a nice name; it suits your ship. But do you know why so many vessels are named after women?"

"I sense a stupid, machismo-filled joke coming," Talon muttered. "Why?"

"Because men love to get into one but don't know what to do with her afterward," Deadeye said.

Talon laughed. "Isn't that a self-own?"

He smooched his fingertip. "Oh, that's between *Cygni* and me." He smooched his fingertip.

She laughed harder. "Okay, but make sure she's clean when you fly her back to *Valkyrie*. You've been waiting to use that joke for a while, right?"

He shrugged, even though Talon couldn't see it.

"Maybe. Where did you get her? She's not as old as I first thought. Back when I was ogling her while floating outside *Santo Pohl*, waiting to be shot by a crazy pirate captain."

"*Heh*, I stole her from a MEC shipyard, a few light-years from the Ross Boundary," Talon said. "It wasn't easy, right? Big thin frigate and all. The pilot who helped me flew for the Runners a few weeks before UNS sickness overtook him. That's when I hired Jhio. How're my bots?"

Her obvious change of subject wasn't lost on him. "They're almost finished. I'm reading what they're adding to the cargo manifest."

"And?" Talon's question was too nonchalant.

"*Happy Maui* sports a newer Casimir drive model, newer than anything our outfit has."

Deadeye scrolled down the parts list in the manifest.

"A more powerful reactor, experimental Casimir gates, and a classification of hadrons I've only heard about. Back when I was in the navy, only the admiral's ship got this treatment."

"Looks like we got lucky, huh, Deadie boy?"

"You like calling me that, don't you?"

"Sure do. And I need you to keep this under wraps from the others. Like, keep that jockey boy mouth shut. I have a big project, something special that'll make us all richer than the Lineages' top houses, right? But I need time."

"You got it... Cap'n. But what do I get for all this secrecy?"

"Extended shore leave? Extra chocolate rations? Hey, maybe five minutes with one of Fluxman's sex dolls?"

"Oh, you're hilarious," Deadeye said.

"You won't be disappointed. Return to the carrier before 15:00, so we can jump back to Hartwell and drop those people off. *Valkyrie* out."

Happy Maui had eighty-six passengers and crew, and though *Valkyrie* boasted plenty of available cargo space, it didn't have enough life support for that many people for more than two weeks. Or beds. As for food and drink, they'd have to make do with preserved noodles and recycled water. Deadeye kept the bridge sealedin case Sakamoto got any ideas, and he watched the colonists on *Cygni*'s various internal cameras. The people wore white-grey Lalande fatigues and seemed grateful to be rescued. A few kids play-fought as space pirates, not realizing how dire their situation had been.

He smiled sadly. He had a few memories of childhood: growing up on a space station, learning different navigational systems and standards, the other Uzari kids in their sleek olive-green jumpsuits... the rest was all temporal haze and mental fog.

The current situation felt familiar—transporting colonists—but Deadeye couldn't wrest that memory from the emptiness plaguing his mind.

Moreover, he couldn't stop thinking that the entire mission had been an excuse for Talon to acquire the newer engine parts. Her initial excitement about the lead, back on Hartwell Station, confirmed his suspicion.

"What do you think?" he asked Icara, who floated nearby in her customary position. "Maybe the Cap'n will trust me now, and you can take a vacation?"

"You realize I still have Icara connected to my mobile, right?" Talon asked.

"Shit."

He smiled sheepishly at Icara's camera eye. "You read lips, too?"

"Only when it's flyboy bullshit."

She snickered and cut the connection.

Deadeye had docked back in Valkyrie's hangar within the hour, and he swaggered over the deck toward the others. Runabout leaned on her hip and cheered while Epsi gave him a naval salute. Fluxman grunted and opened a can of beer. Acting like a bragging idiot might help conceal that he and Talon were keeping things from them. He still wondered why she had confided in him, the newest pilot, but right now, he'd enjoy being the hotshot of the moment.

"*Ooo*, that was some tipsy-turvy, crazy flying you did out there."

Runabout nudged him with her rump as he passed. "The Dame herself would take notice, y'all."

"While we took every damn bit of that MEC heat."

Fluxman finished the beer in one swig. "Good shooting, though. You liberate any hottie colonists?"

"I just want to liberate them from their credits," Epsi said.

Wizard, who'd recently woken, stared at them all while leaning against a crate. "You guys serious? MEC laid an ambush for us, and we jumped at it. Two of our ships were damaged all to shit. Next time, they'll be more prepared."

"Oh, did we wake you from your beauty sleep?" Epsi grinned. "Meh, let them come. This is why we're in this outfit. Sticking it to MEC."

"I watched *Valkyrie*'s recording of the battle," Wizard said. "That was a clusterfuck, and you almost got turned to space dust. We're not Stein rebels or some silly shit like that—we're Runners. I didn't join up to take on the MEC military, not like this."

Talon walked into the hangar, back in her red jumpsuit. "*Happy Maui*'s colonists are secure in Bays 8 and 12. They have enough air, food, and water, and there are potties in there, but some are already complaining about how 'cold' we keep it on this ship. I have the hatches locked, so there's no chance of them snooping around."

"*Ugh*, colonials," Fluxman mumbled.

"Better than dying on their ship, right?" Talon smiled. "But great work, everyone. You turned that shit show around. We'll take a sleep cycle, then jump back to Hartwell. Deadie, you're in the pilot pod this time. And you're off probation, no more Icara."

"Are you sure that's a good idea?" Wizard asked. "Look at him. More full of himself than a Lineage baron who's eaten all the pastries."

"I trust him," Talon said.

"Ah, the rewards for saving your asses out there," Deadeye said.

The glares sent his way made him chuckle.

"But you can have my share of whatever Lalande is paying us,"

Deadeye said. "As I said, all I need is food, a book now and then, and a ship to fly."

"You really are crazy," Wizard said. "And I mean, void-touched crazy."

"Suits me; save my ass anytime you want," Fluxman said and headed for the rec room.

"Oh, I'll spend those credits while I think about you, yessir," Epsi said. "Maybe you can join me? I'll buy you a pretty pink MPS."

"Make it hot pink," Deadeye said.

"Oh my."

Epsi winked and sauntered off.

"You got a true grit believer in this one, *capità*. He's a keeper." Runabout patted Deadeye's shoulder and followed the rest into the rec room.

Once the others were out of earshot, Talon drew close and lowered her voice.

"When they're asleep, the bots will offload all that stuff from *Cygni* into Bay 4. I'll need your help if any of the others wake up during all that. Runabout sleepwalks sometimes, and Fluxman always has to have a beer in the middle of his cycle."

"So what do I do, sing Homesteader shanties to distract them? Juggle?"

"Use this."

Talon reached into a nearby crate and handed him a deflated, vinyl object the color of human flesh.

"You're fucking kidding me," he said.

"Finally, some salty language out of you," Talon said. "Fluxman always keeps a few extra onboard. Have it ready, and if they come looking this way, you... create a distraction. They're nosier than a Lineage tax collector, so nothing less will work."

Deadeye held the empty sex doll like it was a dead snake. "They still make them like this, the inflatable kind? Wait, has Fluxman already used it? Voidshit, Talon. Nope, no way I'm having it on with this thing."

"You pretend, cryobrain, you don't actually have to...you know." Talon regarded him with barely restrained amusement. "Maybe nobody will wake up, right?"

As she started to leave, he blocked her path. "So why am I doing this again?"

She raised her brows. "You gave up your share. Why worry about payment now?"

"Cap'n. I'm not a joke."

"No, you sure as hell aren't." Talon kissed him.

Deadeye blinked, then smiled. "Yeah... we're good."

A moment of silence passed as they looked at each other.

Talon finally smirked. "Keep that to yourself, too. You got me?"

"I got you."

He watched her walk from the hangar, not caring about the sex doll in his hand.

CHAPTER 8

It was 01:29 when Deadeye heard someone coming down the corridor outside the hangar. Talon still hadn't finished moving all of *Happy Maui*'s parts from *Miss Cygni*, and he wanted to lie down. He was supposed to pilot a jump in a few hours.

"What the fuck are you doing with my girl?" Fluxman asked.

Deadeye winced, put on his best lying smile, and turned around. "Just having some fun, Fluxo, it gets lonely out here—"

"You don't get to call me that."

Fluxman pointed at the half-inflated sex doll on the floor.

"Now, you gonna tell me what the hell you're doing with her?"

"Well, nothing at the moment." Deadeye winked.

"Huh."

Fluxman flicked a finger against the beer can in his hand. "She's not even fully inflated? Now that's disrespectful. This some kinda weird-ass Uzari kink?"

Deadeye shrugged. "This is my first time."

Fluxman stared at him, then burst out laughing. "Holy shit. You need to get laid that bad, there's always Epsi and Wizard; he likes men or women. I've hit him up a few times, not gonna lie. Runabout's a tease, but you touch her, I'll kill you. She's a sweetie."

"I'm shy," Deadeye said.

"Cryoshit, I've seen how Talon looks at you." Fluxman sipped from his beer can. "Doesn't matter anyway. Hell, keep the doll; she chafes."

As Fluxman entered the hangar, Deadeye casually strolled into his path.

"So, how did you get your callsign?"

"You're not gonna let me drink in peace, are you?"

Deadeye just looked at him blankly.

Fluxman sighed. "I flew for a little pirate outfit once, the Burners."

"Never heard of them," Deadeye said.

"Good, 'cause they were assholes. They're all dead now, probably still floating spinward near the Ring. Anyway, I was their mechanic and used magnets to unlock hatches on the vessels we boarded. They called me Fluxman, a stupid little play on magnetic fluctuations and all that crap."

As Fluxman tried to walk around him, Deadeye tapped his shoulder.

"Hey... what's the deal with those magistrate fatigues you wear? Are they a trophy?"

"They're mine, you toilet cob."

Fluxman took a deep swig and wiped his mouth. "So? What about them?"

"You were a MEC magistrate? What happened?"

Fluxman's brows furrowed with annoyance. "What happened to you, navy man? You cooked those MEC assholes fast enough out there earlier. I'd say you got a vendetta against your former comrades, eh? You tell me that, I'll answer your nosy question."

The comment caused a cold ball of guilt to form in Deadeye's gut. He'd attacked those corvettes to save his new shipmates, but there was no denying Fluxman's accusation. Only, Deadeye couldn't recall why he'd been discharged.

"I'm not sure, really," Deadeye said. "I remember bits and pieces, but not...."

Fluxman grunted. "Spacer's excuse. We never remember until we want to."

"I lit up those corvettes to help you guys," Deadeye said. "I didn't enjoy it."

"I enjoyed being a magistrate." Fluxman studied his beer, nibbling on his lower lip. "Liked helping people. The planet I got stationed on was... uh, the name was...."

The familiar vacant look in Fluxman's eyes, the following confusion, and resulting frustration, Deadeye knew it all too well. The fate of one who piloted through wormholes while jacked into the UNS. And being a non-modified human, the effect would be worse on the other man. Fluxman started to walk away, then he wheeled around and thrust his finger in Deadeye's face.

"Yeah, I remember how they starved those kids... how MEC forbid us to unlock the hydroponics storage until they got their own precious asses outta there. I remember... *fuck*, it was bad; I don't have to justify this to you! They died, I buried them, all those kids and all MEC left me with was that damn uniform, they left me with...."

Deadeye remained silent. He knew how much a pilot needed to vent.

"I never forgave those motherfuckers after that," Fluxman said. "I might not remember all the details, but I know it was wrong, taking that food for someone else. Those people looked up to me, expected me to... anyway. What do you care now? What does anybody care?"

Deadeye still said nothing. Words mattered little against such horrors.

Fluxman wiped his eyes, drained the beer can, and threw it into the hangar. It clattered beneath *Annie Argent*, the noise echoing across the ample space.

"Now, every time MEC sees me? I'm in that uniform. 'Cause I know they'll remember, even if I can't."

Fluxman flashed a defiant smile, nodded, and left.

Minutes later, Deadeye spotted Talon sneaking from the hangar. She gave him a little wave and hurried down the corridor. Though he was tired, he'd been hoping for another kiss or two. Hell, perhaps Fluxman was right; he just needed to get laid, to unload stress in the oldest way humans knew how. Spacers were more promiscuous than a spaceport prostitute, partly because their lives were short.

Partly because space was colder in more ways than one.

He stashed the sex doll in a hangar crate and smiled. "Maybe next time, girl."

Eight sols later, at Hartwell Station, Deadeye watched the Lalande colonists disembark from *Miss Cygni*, with Talon at the controls. While the others talked and joked, he focused on the families who exhibited relief and gratitude. A few turned and waved back at *Cygni* on the other side of the joined airlocks. Sakamoto had connected them to Hartwell's Lalande representative—little more than a holo AI, this far from the Golden Band—and the Runners were now seventy thousand credits richer.

"You feel stupid yet, Deadeye?" Wizard laughed. "All this money and you're still poor as fuck. No offense, but damn, you're still broke after all that. How's it feel?"

"I'm rich with satisfaction," Deadeye said, rubbing his temples.

He was still groggy from the jump. He'd not slept on *Valkyrie* as

Talon had wished but insisted on accompanying them to the station. At least the red and grey MPS Runabout had gotten him fit well.

Talon tapped her fingers on *Cygni*'s manuals as the last colonists exited the airlock. "Yeah, Wiz? What will you spend all that on? More Red Buddhas?"

"I'm saving to rebuild the Zyn Institute in the Sirius system," Wizard said. "There's more like me out there that need help after Zyn-Tro left us hanging."

It was the same with the Uzari. The corporations had bred altered humans, sold them to MEC or whomever, and then abandoned the projects when they were no longer profitable. MEC produced its own Uzari pilots now, and the Zyn had been greeted with xenophobic bigotry after Zyn-Tro ceased their production. Many wouldn't hire them. It was even worse for the Aquarii. Many were exploited as slaves, and the rest were sent to the Arcturus Ring on one-way missions to resupply far-flung outposts—with their employers knowing they'd not be healthy enough to fly back.

"Listen to the biggie philanthropist," Epsi said.

She looked at her mobile while applying more lipstick. "A few more hauls like this, and I can retire to Azure Shoals or some other posh spot in the Golden Band. I'll even let you ruffians come to visit."

"I just spend mine," Fluxman said. "Long as it comes outta MEC's pockets."

Talon nudged Runabout, who sat closest to the pilot pod. "And you, Runnie? Go on, Deadie boy hasn't heard your trite little scheme."

Runabout crossed her legs and leaned on her armrest. "Why, I reckon I'll keep on sending funds to my kin out in the Dust Systems, oh, and those right cute zoo projects the Thule Freelancers keep putting on every world with the teeniest wee bit of air and water."

"Zoo projects?" Wizard snorted. "We don't need more animals breeding across the Spur; we have enough already. Look at Deadeye here. Hornier than a Cetian steer."

"Moo," Deadeye said.

The others snickered.

"*Hah*, you funny bunch of twats."

Talon maneuvered *Cygni* to another docking platform on one of Hartwell's higher—and wealthier—levels. The rest of the crew grew quiet and shared inquisitive glances. Deadeye waited, knowing Talon always had another job, another contract, up her sleeve. She hadn't said much to him since exiting the jump, but she'd asked him to make her an extra cup of coffee before they left.

Wizard finally spoke. "So, we leave *Valkyrie* on autopilot two AU from Hartwell, and now we're going to traipse into the rich farts' part of the station? We could still get hit by the Harpies, you know."

"That's why I left *Valkyrie* out there, right?" Talon smirked. "Besides, I have a contract from a nobleman, and the Harpies won't touch us while we're docked up here."

"Thought you despised the Lineage as much as I do?" Epsi twirled her lipstick across her fingers.

"I do, but I like their money." Talon activated *Cygni*'s docking claw. "Deadie and I will negotiate terms while you all enjoy whatever expensive trifles they sell here."

Epsi grabbed Runabout's arm. "You're getting that massage this time."

"Okay, okay, I'm sick of hearing you prattle and fuss over it," Runabout said.

Fluxman unbuckled from his seat. "Good enough for me. See you in two."

"Wait."

Wizard shook his head. "Captain, Deadeye looks tired. Plus, he's new. Why's he your majordomo all of a sudden? Other than the obvious reasons."

"What reasons are those?" Talon's question was laced with venom.

The others shared another look and exited the bridge. Wizard stood and crossed his arms, locking stares with Talon. Deadeye wanted to leave the bridge, too, but she laid a hand on his arm.

Talon adjusted her gunbelt. "Well?" Talon adjusted her gunbelt.

"I've been here longer than the rest, so I can see what's going on," Wizard said. "And it's cool, it's fine, he's cute. You do you. But we're in the crew, too. We deserve to be in on the deal, not just the cut afterward."

Talon cocked her head and delivered a blistering, humorless smile. "For the record, Deadie here is going because he knows the MEC navy, and that's related to what I got going on with this noblemen, right?"

A second passed. Wizard's nostrils flared. Talon's left eye twitched.

Wizard waved both tentacles under his chin. "Okay, then. No problem."

"So trust me, all right?" she asked. "When have I ever done you wrong?"

"You shit in my toilet that time when you had the pod runs," Wizard said. "Stunk up my cabin for what, six or seven sols?"

Talon laughed and clapped him on the shoulder. "It was four sols, you Starrio junkie. Get off my ship, go and have a good time in there. See you at 14:00."

After Wizard left, Deadeye cleared his throat. "I don't want to cause any problems. Was that true that you need me for some MEC naval info?"

"Is it true that you need some sleep?" Talon handed him an energy drink. "I wasn't lying to him, it's a naval issue, but I needed an excuse to have you with me."

"Aww, you're sweet, Cap'n."

"Oh, I can be bitter, too, like this, ensign: only an Uzari can make the jump this guy wants, and it's not going to be a short one."

"How long?"

Deadeye followed her out of the bridge.

"That depends on what we manage to negotiate out of him," she said.

"You're serious?"

She rolled her eyes. "You don't have to act so shocked with every surprise I dump on you, you know. Is that too much to ask?"

"If I didn't react like that, you'd be disappointed."

He stumbled into *Cygni*'s airlock chamber but raised a hand when she turned to help.

"I'm fine."

"Good, that's my Deadie. Stay sharp."

As soon as the inner airlock slid open, Deadeye felt out of place. The walls and floors were cleaner than an admiral's office, and the air smelled of brisk, expensive cologne. Corridors branched off to several doors. Private suites, each guarded by Vega Freelancers. Talon slid a keycard at one door.

"Rich clients, Cap'n?"

"Rich and unforgiving. No matter what I say, back me up in there, okay?"

They entered a tight module lined with more sealed cabin doors. People in shiny blue livery and segmented jumpsuits guarded it. Deadeye groaned mentally. The noble houses of the Lineage always made their hired thugs dress like that. The guards' bored stares clashed with the snobbish attitude of the butler who waved Talon over.

"You are late, captain," the butler said in a provincial accent.

"Please deliver our apologies to Lord Kattral," Talon said. "Will he see us?"

The butler regarded them with a wrinkled nose like they were walking turds.

"This way, please. You must leave your sidearm out here with the sentries."

After Talon turned over her pistol, the butler led them into one of the cabins.

Lord Kattral's chamber was decorated with the typical Lineage paintings and banners celebrating aristocratic ancestors. His heraldic device was a blue scepter. Unaltered bloodlines were of paramount importance since they considered themselves the only true humans in the Spur. The nobles didn't practice open warfare against MEC, but they kept a stranglehold on trade and manufacturing across the Golden Band and parts of the Dust Systems. They were known for centuries-long feuds and far shorter tempers—but in Deadeye's experience, everyone always forgave the rich, as long as they received part of the cut.

Talon strode to a middle-aged man sitting at a table playing holo cards. She waited, hands-on-hips, not even acknowledging the armed guards that scowled at her proximity to their employer. Kattral likewise ignored her, tapping cards one by one in the Barnard version of solitaire, where the top cards randomly morphed to a different suit every few seconds. After a long minute, Kattral spoke.

"I have it on good confidence that a MEC convoy will be delivering a special cargo to their outpost at Sextans 292."

Kattral's voice was measured and cultured, even more so than Talon's. He flashed a kind, fatherly smile, but his eyes were as devoid of emotion as a fish's.

"It will only be there for thirty-one sols, their time before it departs for a more secure location. Do you possess the capabilities to carry out such a task?"

"Of course, m'lord."

Talon's cordial tone almost made Deadeye do a double-take.

"My best pilot may be able to make that voyage in less time. He's former MEC navy."

Deadeye had no idea how he could lessen that time. LHS 292 was at least twelve light-years from their current location—a journey of twenty-seven sols, using a Casimir Mark II. Most pilots couldn't make such a long-distance trek in a single jump. It would tax his mind and body to the fullest. That was nearly a month in the pod.

Kattral didn't look at Deadeye. "An Uzari mongrel? I assumed the Runners had eliminated that element from their ranks. What does he know?"

The urge to grind his fist into the asshole's jaw swelled in Deadeye's chest, but he kept a neutral expression. "LHS 292... wait a second."

Talon tensed but maintained a polite smile while Kattral tapped more cards.

Deadeye thought of the star chart the UNS had all but burned into his brain. LHS 292 was indeed a MEC naval outpost, but there should be one closer based on their defensive protocols. Arc point to arc point, a few light-years to the next arc.

"Gliese 251," Deadeye said. "There's a MEC depot there. If that convoy travels through this sector, they'll likely refuel there before jumping to Sextans. It's only nine light-years away."

Kattral paused in his game. "What did the mongrel suggest?"

Once again, Deadeye controlled the impulse to lash out. The presence of armed guards aided him in that private endeavor while Talon repeated what Deadeye had said.

"Excellent—as long as your crew can reach that location in time."

Kattral studied his cards with narrowed eyes. "You must depart with the utmost speed if that is to happen. Your time window decays even as we speak."

"And the agreed-upon amount... m'lord?"

She kept up that effortless, fake smile.

"Doubled, should you deliver the cargo," Lord Kattral said.

CHAPTER 9

PARALLAX. THE WORD CAME TO HIS LIPS, MOUTHED LIKE A NAME forgotten by someone else. Deadeye's gloved palm lay against the dropship viewport, where the light blue world shone outside. The other vessels were in position, in orbit, ready to attack.

His eyes opened. The dim yellow lights of *Valkyrie*'s bridge dispelled the scene in his mind. Memory, dream, fantasy—he had no idea where one began, and the other ended.

Deadeye still gripped the manuals as he exited the fugue state that all UNS pilots entered during a jump. There was little actual maneuvering required while traveling through a wormhole; the path through spacetime usually facilitated a smooth journey across the light-years. It was a primal, subconscious need since holding the physical controls tricked the human mind into thinking it had conventional control over the voyage. It was the pilot's mental ability to navigate the wormhole in the UNS itself, rather than any flight actions such as course correction via *Valkyrie*'s thrusters.

After all, he was flying the ship with his mind, like superstitious spacers claimed. But more than once, he'd exited a jump into a volatile situation in the navy. Having the manuals in hand saved his life, ship, and crew.

"The hell?"

He studied the chart in his UNS feed. *Valkyrie* had exited the jump seventeen AU from their destination in the Gliese 251 system. Roughly twenty-six billion kilometers. Frantic, he checked the ship's chronometer and the compensated itinerary since time passed differently for those who slipped through wormholes. They still had one sol until the MEC convoy reached the naval outpost that orbited the red dwarf.

Deadeye double-checked the jump data. It was as Talon had entered it before they'd left Luyten's Star, where Hartwell Station was located. There'd been no mistake.

"You look like someone pooped in your helmet."

Talon walked around the pod and smiled down at him. An oil-stained jumpsuit and smudged cheeks gave her a mechanic's air. Tools hung from her utility belt.

He sat up in the pod and accepted a water bottle from her. The liquid washed away the dry foulness in his mouth. Six sols in the pod. He wanted to vomit.

"You didn't tell me... we'd exit early."

He drank again, and his nausea subsided.

She sat on the pod's lip. "I had us exit the jump a light sol out before their radar has time to detect us. I need you to fly with the rest of us for this mission. You know the MEC navy better than the rest. So I want you in your bunk, getting some sleep, right? No coffee, either."

Though she was pushing him hard with such a strategy, he smiled. "You look like you've been busy."

"Wiz and Fluxman helped me get *Princess* back into flying shape," she said. "I wish I had another Zyn with his mechanical skills. Wiz's tentacles can reach into areas that even my repair bots couldn't, and with Fluxman directing us, we finished in half the time. That old sailor knows every ship's make and model from the last thirty years. So, are you excited? On this mission you'll be in *Santo Pohl*, playing decoy. No fancy flying; I need you to fool those bastards long enough for us to get the cargo and get out."

"Wiz? Oh yeah, sorry."

Deadeye didn't look at her as he pulled the IV lines from his suit sockets. For a second, he'd forgotten who Wizard was. Too many jumps in too short a time.

"I promise you, all this will be worth, got me?"

Talon rose and hurried out, her voice echoing back to him. "Have dinner with me before you sleep, okay?"

Wincing, he pried the last IV out. "Sure thing."

Dinner? Hmm. Maybe Fluxman would save him some potatoes this time.

Half an hour later, he joined her in the rec room. The others were absent. It was 22:45 . The scent of buttered potatoes, soy succotash, vegetable soup, and brownies made his stomach rumble. His MPS clashed with the t-shirt and pants she wore. The scent of cocoa butter soap high-lighted her showered state, free of cheek smudges. She studied him, leisurely drinking from a water bottle.

"Everyone in their bunk already?" He sat opposite her at a small table.

"Nice, isn't it? They're tired, anyway."

She slid a cup of orange juice over to him and nodded at the serving bowls heaped with steaming food.

"It's reheated leftovers, but I know you're starving after that jump. Go on, eat up."

Deadeye obliged, devouring the potatoes and succotash in big bites. Onions, peppers, and garlic gave the succotash an explosion of flavor he'd not had in some time, and the potatoes stuck to his gut better than any naval fare had in his career. The soup was a little bland, with more spinach than tomatoes, but he finished it in a few spoonfuls. By the time Talon offered him a brownie, he was stuffed.

"Nope, Deadie, you're eating this too. Fluxo made them special for all of us."

"That guy can cook?"

He sampled the soft, moist dessert, its chocolate flavor lingering in his mouth afterward.

"Damn, that's good."

She left the table and fidgeted with the chessboard. "You play?"

"Sort of."

He joined her in an in-progress game. Black was losing, with four pawns, one bishop, and the queen taken.

My sort of odds.

He nudged one of the knights. "Check."

"*Hah,* this isn't a space battle; you can't just pop in like that."

"We did that all the time in the navy."

He sipped his juice. "The trick was to have good enough reconnais-sance beforehand to avoid exiting the wormhole into an enemy ship. Some managed it; some didn't."

Talon brushed past him as she examined the board from all angles. "And you?"

"I always made my target trajectory."

He pushed a rook to threaten her queen. "By the time I was on their AOS, I was already launching torpedoes."

"You're baiting me."

She moved the queen to take the rook and smirked.

"You were in my cabin again; I smelled your soap."

He looked up from the board. "You want to tell me why?"

"Maybe I had fun with Fluxo's doll."

She took his other bishop.

"Checkmate."

He started to turn the black king over, then met her eyes.

"What's the deal with that book?"

"I knew some Sagittarii once."

Talon flicked one of her captured pawns, knocking his king over.

"There might be clues to one of their stashes in that little book, all right?"

"You could just ask to borrow it."

He placed the pieces back into position.

"I'm not good at asking."

Her thigh brushed his as she helped him reset the board.

"But you're persuasive... Cap'n."

She looked everywhere but at him. "Don't call me that. Not right now."

"Sorry. But hey—thanks for all this. The food, the game. The company."

Talon finished her water and toyed with the empty bottle. "It's nothing."

"It is; you don't give yourself enough credit—"

"You want to sleep with me?" she asked.

He downed the juice, not taking his eyes off her.

"Yes."

As soon as they entered her cabin, her lips were on his. He forgot about eating too much, the jumps siphoning his energy and memories, and his inability to recall most of the past. The need to be touched and experience the mutual desire for physical contact ignited a fire in him that refused to be contained. They embraced so tight it hurt, kissed so hungrily she bit his lip. She laughed, then cupped his face.

"Deadie, I told Epsi you're mine, I told Runnie, I told them to...."

"I got you."

He knelt and slowly pulled down her pants, and her underwear.

Quivering with release, she gripped his hair and moaned.

At 07:00, he walked with Talon into *Valkyrie*'s hangar. They kept passing a cup of coffee back and forth until it was empty. Fitted in their piloting MPSs, they'd not showered after waking, lacking the time. Suit or not, he still smelled her soap on himself, but at least the outfit covered the hickeys Talon had left on his neck.

The others gave them sly looks, but Talon dismissed it with a business-like demeanor as she briskly approached *Miss Cygni*.

"Here's the plan. I'll be in my girl *Cygni* while Deadie flies decoy in *Pohl*. Runnie, I want you in *Annie Argent*, Fluxo in *Corsair*, Epsi in *Princess*, and Wiz here on *Valkyrie*, ready to jump out of this system as soon as we make it back."

"Sounds great, then what?"

Epsi looked from Talon to Deadeye and winked knowingly at him. He pretended not to notice.

Talon brought up a small holo from her mobile. It displayed the MEC outpost and their planned flight paths.

"Deadie takes *Pohl* in, smooth as silk, claims he's being chased by us since we'll be on their radar. Soon as they let him in, we pounce, get the cargo, and get the hell out, right? Like we did that time at Ross 47."

Fluxman grunted. "Those Lineage ships didn't have this many guns and rockets."

"Quit griping; we've got this." Epsi elbowed him. "Who's point?"

"Me," Talon said. "We'll start in "V" formation, right? Then we'll break off into a swarm with countermeasures deployed to fool their missiles. Hit their ships where it hurts, so there's no pursuit. Power routers, bridges, thrusters—the usual."

"An outpost like that will have shredders," Deadeye said.

Shredders were minigun-like weapons fired in close-range naval engagements and thus rarely used. However, they were deadly deterrents to boarding actions, spitting out six thousand rounds per minute. Armored vessels might endure such a barrage, but not unarmored Runner craft.

"Not if your keen little eye gets 'em first."

Runabout pointed at Talon. "Gonna strafe on that first run? You're the best gunner and all."

"Yep," Talon said. "I'll be getting the cargo afterward while you all cover me. Deadie, you join in; hit them close with the railgun since you'll be right on their dock. Then we blast back to *Valkyrie* and jump to Luyten's. Everybody good?"

"I can do this with my eyes closed." Epsi strolled over to *Princess*.

"Heh, we're right with you, *capità*." Runabout ran to *Annie Argent*.

Fluxman entered *Corsair* without a word, and Wizard simply nodded and left for *Valkyrie*'s bridge. Talon gave Deadeye a quick grin, then rushed to *Miss Cygni*.

"Back to it, then."

Deadeye clambered into *Santo Pohl*, trying to get over that he didn't remember entering the ship before. Its unfamiliarity ate at his morale.

How soon until I can't remember Valkyrie's corridors and cabins?

How much longer until he forgot who Talon was?

Minutes later, as he left the hangar in *Santo Pohl*, he cast those thoughts away by focusing on the UNS's readings. ETA to the MEC outpost was sixteen hours, using their ships' light-speed drives. Flying through the void that's all that mattered. That's why he was with the Runners; as an Uzari, it was the very reason he'd been created.

Yet he kept glancing at *Miss Cygni* on his radar all the same.

CHAPTER 10

"Shit, we're on their radar by now," Talon said. "Let's do this."

Deadeye flew in the lead since he was pretending to be pursued by the other Runners. His comrades maintained a four--kilometer distance behind him, making it appear that they were right on him. They messaged him first before he could radio the outpost since *Santo Pohl*'s transponder still broadcast as a MEC cargo ship.

"*Santo Pohl*, this is Outpost Nguyen Delta. We have detected four unidentified vessels closing in on your position. Why have you ignored communication protocols?"

They were asking why he hadn't already contacted them. Deadeye maintained course, the UNS displaying a schematic of Nguyen Delta. It was a small outpost, five levels in height, with an enclosed hangar containing the targeted convoy ship. He was still forty kilometers from Nguyen, far too close for their comfort. With the Runner ships traveling at light-speed up until the final minute, it gave MEC far less time to detect them.

"These pirates have been jamming comms, and my power router keeps going in and out after they strafed me," Deadeye said. "Request to dock with Nguyen Delta."

"Request denied. Stay your course, *Santo Pohl*; Nguyen Delta will initiate a missile strike. Stand by."

Deadeye cut the connection and cursed under his breath. Since when did MEC outposts sport missile batteries? He recalled what the smuggler from *Hidalgo* had said weeks earlier: that MEC and the Lineage were taking a firmer stance on Runner activity. Piracy was still rampant on this end of the Spur, so he should have expected such changes. But now *Valkyrie*'s pilots would need to adopt a different plan and fast.

"The outpost is targeting the rest of you with missiles instead of letting me dock,"

Deadeye said over their encrypted frequency. "The ruse won't work; we'll have to rush them, all guns blazing."

"Fuck that; you're gonna get us killed," Fluxman said.

"We'll die if we maintain this course," Deadeye said. "Too late to leave now."

Before anyone added their opinion, he caught the salvo's launch on the UNS. Twenty blips. Four missiles for each of his fellow pilots. Now less than twenty-eight kilometers from the outpost, it would take the missiles nine seconds to reach them.

"Goddamnit," Talon said. "Countermeasures, everybody!"

"Then what?" Epsi asked. "We can't take them on—"

"No choice now." Deadeye knew that the outpost would target him as soon as he opened fire, but he would risk it. *Santo Pohl*'s railgun loosed rounds at 12 kilometers a second—much slower than fusion-powered missiles but still a threat to structures built to maintain a pressurized atmosphere and little else.

The targeting reticule appeared in his vision. It was a constant companion, pinpointing where he planned to wreak destruction and death. A little black hole all to itself, where people thought they could solve their problems or forget their own.

He'd already forgotten his, so it no longer mattered—such an easy lie.

Deadeye blasted close to Nguyen Delta and opened fire. ten kilometers from the outpost, then five . Closing fast, risking a collision unless he slowed down. Missile warning on the UNS feed. Thrust to port, then back to starboard, then to port again. Yaw went to 276°, pitch 300°. *Santo Pohl* lacked countermeasures, so he had to out-maneuver the incoming missiles—and the only way to do that was to fly so far that their fuel ran out. Then the missiles would simply travel on the last trajectory their targeting sensors had selected. Dangerous if his ship remained still, which it didn't. More thruster power, then swerving about toward the outpost again. The missiles darted harmlessly into the void. G-forces brought about by *Pohl*'s tight, powerful thrusts pressed Deadeye into his seat, the manuals mere sticks in his numb hands.

The UNS feed blurred.

Should have rested longer after that jump....

Deadeye blinked and regained control of himself, of the ship. Thirteen kilometers to the outpost after his evasion, with no missile warning. He opened up with the railgun again. Though he was still flying ahead of the rounds he'd fired seconds earlier, it helped create more action on MEC's radar. More variables for them to worry about.

"Deadie, you okay?" Talon asked. "You did a few hard spins there."

"I... damn it."

Deadeye thrust to port again as another missile came his way. "I'm fine. Do you have that cargo yet?"

"Ha, smartass." Talon laughed. "We outran those first few missiles, but we need to swarm the outpost now, got it? You're closest; target those shredders and whatever other guns they have. Hurry, I'm fourteen kilometers out!"

"Ain't gonna matter much if MEC cuts loose again," Runabout said. "One of them little fireflies exploded close, gave me a nasty hull breach on my starboard aft."

"I'm on it, targeting the outpost now," Epsi said. "*Ooo, this is going to hurt.*"

"*Ugh*, my railgun's jammed," Fluxman said. "Fuck it all to the void."

"Fluxman, run interference for the rest of us then, like one of Runabout's Homesteader jigs," Deadeye said. "I'm too close for them to try missiles on me now."

"Deadie, watch those guns," Talon said. "Shit, I said to watch out!"

Santo Pohl shook, but Deadeye ignored the red warning text scrolling down his feed. Two breaches beneath *Pohl*'s bow, neither of them vital. The reticule appeared in his sight again; now, Nguyen Delta was nine kilometers away. So MEC had been firing at him for the last several seconds and calculated where his subsequent trajectory would be.

"Come on, Mister Hotshit, take those guns out!" Talon cried.

"Deadeye, a round just cleaved off my starboard auxiliary thruster," Epsi said. "You waiting for an invitation?"

The others voiced concerns, but he remained focused on the reticule. Six point five kilometers, then four. Had to get close, and make sure his shots connected. The familiarity of targeting enemy batteries flooded his mind; the stress of eliminating an opponent before they destroyed him or his shipmates, the maddening wait for the railgun to reload, the silent hell that enveloped his reality while waiting for a kill confirmation. And at any moment, expecting an enemy round to pierce his hull, splatter him all over the bridge, or ignite his fusion core: so many ways to die and so little time to live.

Deadeye squeezed the trigger three times. The first shot took out one of the outpost's railgun batteries. The second tore through the rear thruster array of a docked escort vessel. The third atomized one of the shredders, but he veered too close to the hangar, and a second shredder peppered him with thousands of 20mm rounds. Though *Pohl* had no atmosphere at the moment and thus no sound, he still felt the impacts in a series of fierce vibrations right behind the bridge hatch. They'd almost got him.

He jetted the forward thrusters, thus stopping his momentum, then fired the portside thrusters, turning his Yaw orientation to starboard for 125°. The maneuver lined up his railgun with the enclosed hangar where their main target waited.

One round from his railgun smashed the shredder—but not before the merciless device sprayed *Pohl*'s bridge with hundreds of rounds. The recently-repaired viewport gave way. There was no sound, just a scattering of shrapnel, ripped seats, savaged terminals, and the remnants of the IV canisters on his right side. Those miscellanea existed a second before the void claimed them in a rush of depressurization.

Equipped in a sealed helmet and MPS, Deadeye was unaffected, but the remaining IV lines shook like short-lived snakes on his left side.

The railgun reloaded as his thumb twitched over the trigger. Its heatsink absorbed energy slower than the one on *Miss Cygni*. Fluxman was taking fire from the other side of the outpost, Epsi whooped as she destroyed a battery, Runabout evaded more missiles, but Talon had gone silent. No time to hail her. Couldn't distract any of them, for a moment wasted often meant death.

Two more seconds to reload. Deadeye swallowed and kept his eyes fixed on the targeting reticule. A ripped IV line drifted against his faceplate. Talon finally returned online, asking Runabout to cover her as she flew for the hangar.

One second more, then, the railgun's ready icon flashed green in his eyesight.

He fired again, targeting where the enclosed hangar's power coupling should be. It was a guess based on his naval experience and a correct one, since the hangar's exterior running lights winked out a second later. At least Nguyen's personnel wouldn't be able to escape, but the Runners would have to cut or blast through the hangar doors themselves.

Miss Cygni passed his starboard hull at nineteen meters, its docking claw already extended. With the bridge viewport gone, he could see *Cygni*'s bow.

"Good job Deadie, now keep me covered while my bots get inside and grab the goods," Talon said. "Fluxo, you've done great, but keep flying around the outpost, right? Have to keep MEC on their toes. Runnie, you finish off the docked corvette that Deadie boy damaged. Epsi, hell, keep on shooting at whatever moves. We've got this!"

"How are you gonna get in there, sing 'em a song?" Runabout asked. "Those doors are closed tighter than a preacher's credit case."

"My bots are cutting through now," Talon said in a buoyant tone. "You have to quit doubting me, Runnie. I plan for everything, all right?"

A proximity warning flashed in Deadeye's feed. A dozen small objects to port, speeding toward *Cygni* and its attached hangar.

"Did you plan for MEC drones?"

Deadeye tried targeting the robotic group with *Pohl*'s railgun, but they zipped past his field of fire too quickly.

"Shit, the pod, Cap'n; you've got anti-personnel drones, inbound to your—"

"I see them," Talon said. "Sending my bots after them now."

"Which means you'll have to cut into the hangar yourself?" Epsi sighed. "I was hoping to skip from this system by now."

"There will be MEC marines or drones waiting for you," Deadeye said. "You can't do that alone."

"Too late; I'm already doing it," Talon said. "But I need you to blast open the hangar door now. No time to cut it myself. Hurry, I'm almost to *Cygni*'s airlock."

It was madness; the outpost's defenders would be waiting for her... but Deadeye had little choice. If he didn't blast it open, all of this would have been for nothing, and the MEC drones might attack her while she waited for him to fire. At least the railgun's precise, non-explosive ammunition wouldn't damage her in an area of effect discharge, and any debris would be propelled through the hangar, away from her position. Yet they risked damaging their prize, which waited just beyond the barrier.

Deadeye squeezed the trigger twice. Both rounds sheared gaping holes in the hangar doors. Three seconds later, Talon jetted, via thrustpack, into the opening.

The others obeyed Talon's orders, and soon Outpost Nguyen lacked exterior defenses. The docked corvette was reduced to a wreck due to Runabout and Epsi's railguns, and Talon's bots managed to handle MEC's drones—though only two returned to *Cygni*. Yet Deadeye sweated in his suit, and his heart rate continued to rise. Talon was alone in that hangar, armed with a simple pistol, and MEC marines wielded .65 caliber recoilless caliber rifles capable of piercing the best combat armor. Regardless of her skill, she wouldn't stand a chance.

"Cap'n, you find the cargo ship?" he asked.

"I've just cut into its airlock, but I have some company," Talon said.

"Marines or bots?" Fluxman asked.

"MEC's finest jarheads," Talon said. "Well, fuck. I'm almost into the cargo ship."

Shit.

Deadeye thoughts raced, frustrated that he could only see through the UNS. If only he had a way to view what she saw—

"Tap me into your helmet's camera feed," Deadeye said.

"What good will that do?" Talon grunted and blew out a breath. "They have the gravity in Nguyen ramped up to 1.6Gs. Fuckers. They're not stopping me that easy."

"Just do it." Deadeye activated his targeting reticule. "Look at the marines."

"Fine, didn't know you had a fetish for watching people shoot me," Talon said. "*Heh*, I'm a little turned on right now."

"You two can smooch it up later," Runabout said. "Deadeye, whatcha doing? I can't play target practice with these assholes much longer."

Talon's helmet camera feed appeared as a rectangle in the upper right of his vision. The feed shook as Talon sought cover from rifle fire behind the cargo vessel's airlock frame, but he glimpsed enough to get his bearings. The familiar MEC outpost bulkheads, the hangar deck, figures in white armor aiming polished rifles....

"This."

Deadeye swiveled the railgun and fired.

His round punctured Nguyen's hull, flew across the hangar deck, and pulped three marines that had been standing too close together. The projectile continued through the rest of the outpost, damaging interior systems.

Talon laughed. "Whoa, Deadie boy, you're wanting a promotion!" Talon laughed.

"Look one more time, but then I can't help you," he said. "It's too risky."

"Got it."

Her helmet feed displayed the deck outside the cargo vessel again, just enough for him to target the other marines. Still unaware of what was happening, they grouped in squad formation, creeping toward Talon. The second round splattered two marines and severed through two others. Limbs and helmets scattered over the hangar, then floated along with countless red droplets—meaning Nguyen's gravity was gone.

"That one must have passed clean through to their centrifuge; the gravity just dropped to 0.1," Talon said. "Shit, I can breathe now. Here, Deadie, you keep watching."

"Huh?"

He gaped as the helmet feed lowered to her boots. It faced her, who wore a thin MPS mask. Talon grinned through the covering's compact faceplate, then the feed wheeled about and became stationary. The new position provided a view of the hangar from the cargo vessel's airlock ramp.

She'd removed her helmet and set it down, trusting her mechanical pressure mask instead. He could see the marines for one more shot before they closed with the cargo vessel. She'd have six minutes of air.

"What's happening over there?" Fluxman asked.

"Is Talon okay, Deadeye?" Epsi asked.

"She will be."

He fired a third time, but the marines had finally wised up to him and spread out. Initially, they must have thought the railgun fire was random volleys from the starship battle outside, but two precise shots weren't a coincidence. The round clipped only one marine, severing his legs from his body. The next instant, another marine aimed in the direction of the helmet, and the feed went dark.

Deadeye punched the pod's side, then forced himself to calm down. He could do nothing short of enfilading the entire hangar—and thus the cargo vessel, with Talon onboard. It was a waiting game, and he maintained radio silence since she didn't need distractions. He busied himself with a diagnostic on *Santo Pohl*'s shattered systems and watched the radar feed. The UNS flashed the information into his retinas at speeds unattainable with computer screens. So fast, the data was akin to his thoughts. So easy in such moments to think he was the UNS itself. Some pilots went mad like that, never seeing reality again; only the UNS feeds in their minds.

Movement on *Pohl*'s starboard scopes broke his reverie. Deadeye spotted Talon jetting back to *Miss Cygni*, tugging two large crates tethered to her belt. There was no nitrogen exhaust from her thrustpack; she'd expended its gases and now traveled on momentum alone. Meaning she'd not be able to escape the marines jetting from the hangar doors behind her.

Talon gestured behind her at the hangar. Maybe her mask's radio was damaged, or the marines had jammed her comm.

Deadeye swiveled his railgun as far to starboard as it would go, then activated a lateral thruster to reorient *Pohl*. His vessel experienced a power failure moment later—the shredders had maimed him worse than he'd thought. Auxiliary generators on the bridge kept him jacked in the UNS, powered his life support in the pod, and kept the railgun online since it was directly above him. The attempt still allowed him to fire just behind the marines, but he doubted the round killed any.

"Runabout, target Nguyen's hangar doors," Deadeye said. "Quick, do it!"

"Talon's still out there," Fluxman said.

"Somebody wants to be captain already," Epsi said. "I can make the shot."

Deadeye tasted sweat dripping over his lips.

"No, Runabout's the closest."

Deadeye tasted sweat dripping over his lips.

"Not the best gunner, done told you," Runabout said. "I need a better—"

"Take the shot!" Deadeye cried.

A round flew from *Annie Argent* on his radar. While it sped through the void, the marines jetted closer to Talon, who was near *Cygni*'s airlock with the crates. Two aimed their rifles. Talon grabbed the airlock lever.

The hangar doors buckled in. Debris flew. *Pohl*'s starboard scope went dead.

"Fuck!"

He squirmed in the pod as the UNS displayed the events on the radar. A debris field expanded from the hangar doors, overtaking the five blips closing in on *Miss Cygni*—the marines. Yet it swept over them and continued until it collided with *Cygni* itself and the three blips outside its airlock.

Deadeye yanked the jack out of his neck, tore away the remaining IV lines, and pushed himself from the piloting pod. Meter by grueling meter, he pulled himself through *Santo Pohl* until he reached its airlock chamber. Son of a bitch, they still hadn't put a thrustpack onboard. He'd have to go out there with nothing but the momentum of pushing off the hull.

If that's what it took, she might still be alive.

Within moments he was out in the black, limbs close to his body so he might avoid striking the small pieces of wreckage that now surrounded *Miss Cygni*. He wasn't going fast enough for the debris to be a danger, but he refused to take any chances. The crates drifted along with Cygni's bow across from his own vessel. Seventy meters away. A humanoid shape became briefly visible beneath the craft's running lights.

"Cap'n?" he called over the radio. "You hear me?"

Movement on his left, thirty meters away. It was a marine, switching their aim from the direction of *Cygni* to him. All Deadeye could do was wave. Without a thrustpack or surface to push off, he was on a doomed trajectory with the soldier.

The marine jerked and drifted away. Faceplate shards floated in their wake.

Deadeye continued past the corpse, only to encounter two more marines. Again, he waved, hoping *Cygni*'s running lights would reflect off him enough to distract them. Hoping Talon would fire. They glanced at him, and their lives were over a second later.

"Cap'n? I don't like hide and go seek."

He floated through tiny grains of debris and under a large hull fragment from Nguyen's hangar—then he saw her.

The joke sounded weaker than the hold Talon had on *Cygni*'s hull. Her other hand clasped the pistol. Twenty meters away, the two marines spun off into forever, a bullet hole in their faceplates. She looked around and, finally spotting him, aimed for his crotch.

"*Ha*, let's not play that either."

He bumped into *Cygni*'s hull and snatched a scope emplacement, stopping his momentum.

Talon arched an eyebrow and smiled, but she held her left arm close to her body. The MPS's inner liner had sealed, but red droplets still floated around a tear below her shoulder. They'd winged her.

"Hey, you find my *capità* yet?" Runabout asked as *Annie Argent* flew above the ruined hangar.

Its floodlights activated, bathing them in harsh white luminance.

"Yes, she's fine."

Deadeye offered his hand, then pulled them both along *Cygni*'s hull to its airlock.

"But I want my share spent on a thrustpack for every ship, okay?"

CHAPTER 11

"THIS MED BOT SAYS THE BULLET WENT CLEAN THROUGH."

Deadeye nudged the floating drone aside as he walked around Talon in *Miss Cygni*'s airlock chamber.

"Did it go to your brain? Why do you want to keep this from the others? After they risked so much?"

Talon slapped his chest with her MPS mask. "Lord Kattral wanted this haul for himself, right? Well, maybe I need some of this stuff. The others don't need to know, not yet. Remember the big score I mentioned?"

"The one you won't tell them about?"

He thumbed at *Annie Argent* outside the viewport, gradually closing in for an airlock link.

"Runabout will be here in a minute."

"The cargo bots have already sorted what I need from those crates."

Talon winced as the med bot suctioned excess blood from her wound and started tissue repair. Without the benefit of gravity, bleeding outside had prevented her injury from healing correctly. The blood had started clotting below a dome of plasma, where the liquid had maintained surface tension right above the wound. Now, under the influence of *Cygni*'s centrifuge, powered up to produce 0.8Gs, she could be stabilized.

"So you're shortchanging Kattral and lying to the crew," Deadeye said. "That's not good business, even for a pirate. Which you claim not to be."

Talon tried to holster her pistol, but her arm spasmed. He tried helping her, but she shrugged him off and secured the weapon on her belt.

"I'll tell that Lineage prick that this is all we found. The crew doesn't have to know, got me?"

She pushed back her sweaty bangs and grunted as the med bot continued.

"This new drive system MEC developed will fly faster and—*ouch!* Stupid bot."

"You can't continue keeping secrets. Not after we put our lives on the line."

Her eyes narrowed into dangerous slits.

"And you can't keep acting like I should listen to you just because we slept together, right? There's nothing between us, Deadie boy. Just the next job, the next mission, the next fucking haul, got it?"

"This isn't about us."

"Yeah, well, there's no us, either," she said.

Deadeye crossed his arms, she defiantly held his stare. Neither looked away.

The airlock warning alarm sounded, followed by a hiss of air.

"Yeah. I got it."

He turned and adopted an easy smile as Runabout entered *Miss Cygni.*

"See, you didn't blow us up out there. Good shooting."

"Hiya too, you crazy space devil. Lotsa fancy flying yourself."

Runabout gave him a friendly bump with her thigh, then looked at Talon.

"*Ooo,* you two must be fighting. Ain't wanting any part of that kinda battle, understand? So... did we get Kattral's shiny little MEC goodies?"

Talon grinned. "Hell yes we did. Talon grinned. Soon as we tow *Pohl* back to *Valkyrie,* we're jumping for Hartwell. Drinks are on me."

Deadeye headed for *Cygni*'s bridge. "I'll fly us to the others. The docking claw is secured, Runabout?"

Runabout answered, but he didn't pay attention. Lying came easily to him, too. It was part of the business. Yet Talon kept expecting him to remain silent about whatever project she was withholding from the rest of the crew. He felt used but knew she didn't owe him anything, not even another sleep cycle in her bunk. Flying through the void, jacked into the UNS—that's all that mattered, his typical mantra.

He tried repeating it himself as he slipped into the piloting pod. This time, the sentiment lacked conviction, but he didn't recall ever having such a thing anyway.

Talon's anger with him lasted less than a sleep cycle. Claiming to need the Sagittarii book again, she visited him in his bunk. There were no words between them, no arguing, only a flurry of discarded clothes and the creak of an overworked bed. Their lovemaking was desperate and demanding like they might die afterward. After the fury of orgasms relented, they held each other with satisfied smiles.

Over the next week, Deadeye slept in her bunk every cycle. It was another easy lie, claiming he was tending her gunshot wound. Though the round had gone clean through, and the med bot had replaced her muscle fibers with printed ones, circulation in her shoulder needed to be monitored for clots. His PTSD episodes had lessened—though once she had to wrestle him off the deck and make him swallow some melatonin. They had sex in every cabin aboard *Valkyrie*, even the engine room. It was more than just a rutting fixation; it was freedom—a physiological, psychological release.

Other times they worked out in *Valkyrie*'s tiny gym on resistance machines that were likely centuries sold. Fluxman crushed him at billiards, and he could not defeat Talon or Wizard at the chessboard. He danced with Runabout as she tried to show him her Catalonian jigs, while Epsi convinced him to accept a mud pack on his face. Talon snickered the whole time. One cycle, they honored Jhio and Perseus by ejecting their belongings in crates fitted with low-level beacons that broadcast their names in a perpetual downlink.

He made the mistake of taking on Wizard in a game of low G ping-pong, back in the hangar, with the gravity set to 0.4. The tentacles granted his opponent a serious advantage since they also stretched a few extra centimeters. Talon was the only one who bet on him and graciously paid the others after Wizard defeated him.

Yet the waking alarm on the final sol back to Hartwell signified that such leisure was over. A return to the reality of piracy, colonial strife, and the very real possibility that the next jump might cause him to forget all of the precious eternities he and Talon had shared during that time.

She offered him a cup of coffee as they awaited the others in *Valkyrie*'s galley, three hours out from Hartwell.

"Thanks."

He accepted the mug and sipped the caramel-like, bittersweetness.

"It's the last of my stores, so drink slowly."

She flashed him a smile, then returned her attention to the holo map on the galley table. She scrolled over its representation of the Spur, the swath of the galaxy that contained the legendary Sol system, the surrounding Golden Band, controlled by MEC and the Lineage, and the

Dust Systems—again, policed by MEC and exploited by the nobles. The Arcturus Ring was the great unknown, with some settlements dating back centuries and many others no one had ever heard from again.

There was Kapteyn, the origin of the stardrive, that had made light-speed expansion possible. He still marveled at how humanity had spread from the old systems within the Ross Boundary to other stars via simple fusion drives. Four light-years took a four-year journey; something they could now make in under nine sols with a Casimir Mark II.

Four years, though. It sounded like a fantasy. He gazed at Talon, wondering what such an expanse of time with her would be like.

"We don't have time for another," she muttered, catching his ogling.

"You could always accuse them of mutiny, then we throw them into the brig, and we make out in my bunk."

He sipped the coffee again. Butterscotch, she'd called it.

"We don't have a brig."

She grinned briefly, but it disappeared once Runabout and Epsi entered the room. The real question ate at him: would she keep their affair a secret from the crew? Part of him understood the need, but part of him wanted....

The coffee lost its taste, but he drained the mug anyway because the beans had not come from some world halfway across the Dust Systems, where some poor bastard probably harvested them with an antique thresher. It had come from her.

Epsi and Runabout looked at them, then gave each other a knowing glance.

Deadeye set the mug on the table and put his arms behind his head. "Did you two ladies have nice dreams?"

"Heh, looks like someone has, these past few cycles," Runabout said.

Epsi covered her smile and looked at the floor.

Talon cleared her throat. "Runnie, I know you just woke up, but I need you to give Valkyrie a full diagnostic check as soon as you've eaten."

"Haven't you two already done that?" Epsi asked. "I mean, you've been all over this carrier lately. All. Over. It."

Runabout stifled a chuckle.

"I'm not as good a troubleshooter as Runnie."

Talon drained her coffee mug without breaking eye contact with Epsi.

"She's awesome with hydraulics, though," Deadeye said. "Up, down, all around."

Epsi and Runabout burst out laughing.

Talon cringed, then laughed, too. "Okay, fuck that; I'm finished pretending to be mad, right? Yes, Deadie and I... we've been checking the ship regularly. And I was shot, okay, so I need constant attention. But I need a more experienced eye to make sure we didn't break anything."

"Ain't cleaning up any stains, oh no," Runabout said.

Epsi grimaced. "*Eww*. Epsi grimaced. You're worse than the last crew I flew with. Too much sex, not enough flying, and that's saying something for me. The Sadistos finally caught and enslaved them after I left, so I suppose they're happy little kinkers now. Somewhere near the Norsk Rom systems, around Ross 154."

"Norsk Rom? *Ha*." Talon leaned back. "Of all the heritage enclaves that make up MEC, they're the most fastidious. And punctual to a goddamn fault. One of them actually called me *fräulein* at a spaceport before trying to hire me for a job. That, and hitting on me. *Ugh*. I'm surprised they allowed anything like the Sadistos near their territory."

Epsi grinned. "The Norsk like some kink, too. Epsi grinned. So which enclave are you from? You speak like an educated brat that has spent too much time around scallywags and scuttlebutts. No offense."

Talon smiled. "None taken. Talon smiled. Let's just say I grew up in the shadow of rich assholes in the Band and leave it at that."

Epsi flashed the Runner's sign—two fingers pointed down, emulating a human running—and fist-bumped her.

"I can say the same, in a way. But it kills me how so many of the older enclaves got suckered into joining MEC when it formed. The Veld, the Tolteca, the Han, all the rest. So much for leaving Earth to find independence, eh?"

"Independence is a tall tale that always ends up with some tin can ninny getting spaced," Runabout said. "That's how it is for Dusters and Ringers."

"It was either band together or fracture into smaller powers, and then more people would have starved," Deadeye said. "MEC was about survival back then."

That earned him a flat stare from all three women.

He raised both hands. "That's what those books say, the ones Runabout got me."

"No, you ain't putting that shim sham on me," Runabout said.

Epsi crossed her arms and raised her brows. "And you believe that? Damn, I was starting to like you, Deadeye."

Leaning forward, Talon watched him carefully. Gauging his answer.

Deadeye shrugged. "It might have been true decades ago. But now? Hell no. They've taken on too much, too many systems, too many people, and don't want to admit it. Anyone that wants something else gets atomized or 'allowed' to settle the Arcturus Ring since nobody gives a shit about what happens out there. Not yet, anyway."

It felt good, remembering that much. The books had helped in more ways than simple factoids—they'd aided with memory retention. Since neuroscience wasn't his thing, he wasn't completely sure, but it felt right.

"The Runners need outfits out there, too," Talon said. "Imagine the possibilities. All of those worlds, and, come on, one of them has to be similar to Earth, right?"

"It's too far, a myth for all intents and purposes," Deadeye said. "Like crossing the Ross Boundary or finding a paradise planet at TRAPPIST-1. I prefer tangible goals, Cap'n—like fucking in every chamber aboard this ship."

Epsi and Runabout guffawed with laughter while Talon rolled her eyes, smirked, and blushed so fiercely he feared she might be holding her breath. She kicked him under the table, but he simply leaned back and whistled the melody he always liked.

"Speaking of expanding our horizons...when will we make some runs closer to Altair and Struve?" Epsi asked. "The last moot we attended, they said only one Runner outfit operated out that way, trailing to coreward. Why are we always going back to Hartwell?"

Talon stared at her empty mug. "It's our base, and I have a stash there.Talon stared at her empty mug. Some extra supplies, spare credit cases, shit like that, in a secure place."

Epsi laughed. "You mean that beat-up old trawler on Hartwell's lower docks? Epsi laughed. What's in that tin can, more coffee, or—"

Talon winked. "I'm going to fix it up when I retire." Talon winked.

"Oh, bullshit," Epsi said, laughing. "You'll never retire."

"Right?"

Talon's smile didn't fool Deadeye.

More secrets, or had Epsi intruded on something personal? He wanted to ask, but it would have to wait. He'd not ruin their pleasant moment, finding some release from the literal darkness around them, the cruel universe thatrefused to give them respite.

Hours later, he and Talon stood before Lord Kattral in the nobleman's posh cabin on Hartwell Station. Wizard had piloted the jump from the outpost, freeing Deadeye to come along, but Talon had avoided him the final hour before their arrival—until she'd asked him to accompany her for the meeting.

He'd not revealed her secret, so her returned aloofness confused him.

"We didn't find all of the cargo, m'lord," Talon said.

Kattral nodded as he tapped cards in his perpetual solitaire game. "You are stating the obvious, captain. I paid you partly in advance to take possession of that cargo—forty thousand then and forty thousand upon delivery. Double my initial offer, as agreed upon. Now you tell me that the cargo in question wasn't there? I want to know why. The honor of House Kattral has been impinged upon."

"The MEC outpost had already been attacked when my pilots arrived," Talon said. "The crew was all dead, and half of the cargo was taken. Whoever did it left too quickly, I suppose. We barely escaped a MEC patrol ourselves. Here's a vid of the damaged outpost and the—"

Kattral waved away her proffered mobile without looking up from his cards.

The guards watched Deadeye and Talon with more interest than last time. Though the noble houses of the Lineage weren't above dealing with pirates and such, they also weren't above eliminating them if betrayed. He hoped he wasn't sweating too much.

"How unfortunate."

Kattral placed a queen card over top a king of the same suit.

"You so-called 'Redshift Runners' are typically more dependable. You have my credits, of course? When you entered, I did not spot a credit case in your possession."

Talon's jaw tightened slightly. "We still delivered half of the cargo, m'lord."

"That was our old agreement... captain."

Kattral looked up at them, his eyes anything but friendly.

"I require twenty thousand back. The rest is sufficient for a job half-done."

"The Runners honor their contracts, m'lord." Talon flashed a polite smile. "We won't ask for the agreed-upon second payment of forty thousand since, sure, there's cargo missing. But we still made those jumps. You have something rather than nothing."

Deadeye kept his expression neutral, but he wanted to ask what she was doing. Money apparently wasn't her goal; it was starship engine parts like the Lalande mission. He doubted if other Runner outfits operated this way since they gained contracts based on reputation—and not completing a job soiled that reputation. It made her decisions all the more strange.

Lord Kattral drew a jack, frowned at the card, and reluctantly placed it atop the queen.

"You are suggesting that I feel satisfied with your subpar work? Perhaps you think you deserve those credits? Or have you spent the advance and cannot repay it?"

The guards inched a little closer, hands near their weapons. Talon looked like she would choke on the tension, but Deadeye smirked and waved a hand.

"Would you rather we'd not brought anything back? This is the risk of doing business, Lord Kattral."

Kattral tapped his chin, not looking at them. "I'd rather my advance be returned."

Before Talon could reply, Deadeye moved forward. The guards drew their pistols, but again, Kattral raised a hand. The man finally focused his cool stare on Deadeye.

"The mongrel wishes to speak?" Kattral asked.

"I think you missed this one."

Deadeye took a ten pip card from one of Kattral's draw piles and placed it atop the jack.

"That's what happens when you're not paying attention to what's right in front of you."

Kattral shut off the card holo game with a sharp gesture. "The Runners have fifty more captains who are just as capable of fulfilling my contracts without failure. No one will care if one goes missing here at Hartwell Station."

"You still don't see it, do you?" Deadeye laughed. "With that outpost inoperable, and MEC patrols seeking the perpetrators, the trade lanes will be more vulnerable, but only for a short time. The MEC navy will use secure drop-off points instead of the typical depots. I know where those are. I give you those; we call it even."

Talon's hands had become fists, and her left eye twitched. The guards maintained their aim until Kattral finally motioned for them to put away their weapons.

Kattral stood and walked around Deadeye, hands behind his back.

"How can I be sure of your data? Your Uzari brain might have corrupted it, or you could be lying."

"You could be wealthier for the next three orbits of this little station, too," Deadeye said. "What have you got to lose? These leads are useless to us, with MEC patrols in the area looking for a transponder matching ours. We both win here."

Talon kept looking from him to Kattral, a sliver of hope in her eyes, along with annoyance that he'd overtaken the negotiations. Deadeye could listen to her anger later. Right now, he wanted to keep her credits and get the hell out of Kattral's presence.

Kattral stopped pacing. "Very well. Meet my broker and his technician two levels down in an hour, and he will be waiting with a pilot pod so you can input those coordinates directly. This is to guarantee the veracity of what you say, of course. I cannot trust what you might provide with a handwritten or typed information set."

"We'll be there," Talon eased toward the door, tugging Deadeye by the arm.

"But of course." Kattral smiled.

Once outside, after the airlock hissed shut, Talon grabbed him by the collar. "Fuck. You don't have those sort of coordinates, do you?"

"No."

Deadeye pried her fingers loose. "Does your crew know you wanted starship engine parts instead of credits? No?"

Talon ushered him into a maintenance egress, where fewer lights shone.

"I swear by the void; I'll kill you myself if this doesn't work. Who the hell do you think you are?"

"The guy who just got you out of a shitty situation."

She leaned into him, and cupped his chin. "Lord Kattral isn't to be trifled with."

"But you did."

"I'm not to be trifled with, either, you hear me?" She kissed him.

"I'm hard of hearing."

He ran the tip of his finger down the front of her neck.

"Goddamn you, sometimes...."

Talon sucked on his finger, then kissed him again. "I don't like how you make me lose control like this. How you... *unravel* me, like some coiled-up tether trailing behind a dock drone. How you savor it when you do this."

"It's what hotshit flyboys do."

His finger drew little circles above her breasts.

She nipped at his earlobe. "Tell me how you'll fly out of this one."

"I give Kattral some bullshit coordinates; you give the crew their share, and no one knows what you're doing but me," he whispered in her ear. "But you need to trust me more, okay? Even if we don't have anything going on between us."

"As long as you understand that there's nothing between us."

Talon ran her fingers up into his hair, squeezed his rump, and continued kissing him. "Nothing at all."

Deadeye pulled her closer.

"He did what?" Fluxman glowered at Deadeye and chugged another beer.

"Sounds like Deadeye took the initiative."

Epsi spooned sugared protein mush into her mouth, dabbed her lips with a napkin, and swiped through the Hartwell media feed at their table.

"Why does that bother you?"

Wizard scooped more sugar cubes into his tea, the small white squares sliding off the tip of his tentacle.

"Because this Uzari bastard can't deliver, *ha*! Kattral once had a pirate from Fhava's outfit skinned alive for not coming through on an agreement."

Deadeye and Talon joined the rest in a café overlooking Hartwell Station's middle levels. The establishment granted a view of dozens of other spacers, merchants, hangars, Freelancer terminals, Homesteader recruits, and smuggler dens.

Runabout propped her feet on the table and ignited a Starrio tube. "Ain't Fhava the teeny tiny prick who went all piss crazy and flew into that cruiser at Kruger 60?"

Epsi high-fived Wizard and laughed. "Oh yes. Epsi high-fived Wizard and laughed. He was an asshole."

Deadeye reached for the can of berry carbo punch on the table.

"Sounds like you all should work with better people."

Talon snatched the can and elbowed him into a chair beside her. "Like you? Buy your own drink, Deadie boy."

She smirked and sipped the beverage.

Deadeye gazed up through the skylight above them, atop of the station. So many stars. It was impossible to enjoy such a panorama since his mind was so accustomed to the UNS. Pattern recognition, combined with star chart data, stole the view's beauty and replaced it with an ordered reality he sought escape from.

Epsi pushed her asparagus shake over to him. "You can have mine." Epsi pushed her asparagus shake over to him.

Deadeye tore his eyes from the skylight and smiled at her. "Thanks, but I have an asparagus allergy."

The corners of Epsi's eyes crinkled as she chuckled. "It's not bad, promise."

Talon laughed and swiped the feed for a carbo juice. "Fuck that shit;

it's bad. Talon laughed and swiped the feed for a carbo juice. Here, my treat for distracting those marines out in the void. To Deadie, everyone!"

Runabout sucked a hit of Starrio and waved with her pinky, Wizard raised his teacup, Epsi lifted her shake, and Talon hoisted her drink—but Fluxman crushed his beer can.

"Why are you being nice to him?" Fluxman burped and kept staring at Deadeye. "He'll get us all tossed outta the airlock. Kattral doesn't screw around."

Deadeye kept smiling as a drone waiter brought the juice.

"Neither do I."

Deadeye kept smiling as a drone waiter brought the juice.

Fluxman threw the can. Deadeye merely moved his head a centimeter to the left. The crumpled metal shot past his head and over the balcony.

Epsi gave Fluxman a scolding look. "Was that necessary?"

"*Santo Pohl* is shot to shit, and who has to fix it?"

Fluxman wagged a finger at Deadeye. "Not Uzari boy here. Who patched up that heap we still call *Princess*? Yours fucking truly. No way that we can keep this up. We're Runners, not a merc outfit!"

Deadeye kept his voice calm. "Who ate bullets from those shredders so Talon could get close to the outpost? Deadeye kept his voice calm. Who plastered those marines across Nguyen's hangar?"

Talon drank and leaned back in her chair. "Enough.Talon drank and leaned back in her chair. It's done; Kattral paid us, so we're good, all right? Do you have any coordinates that would be useful to him?"

"Maybe."

Deadeye took a drink, the carbonated juice bubbled on his tongue and sizzled down his throat. Its sweet, blueberry flavor bore the tartness of fruit grown in a cheap hydroponics lab. Like everything else, he'd forgotten the last time he'd drank the good stuff, but he did recall how it tasted.

"Dammit."

Fluxman started to rise. "I've had it with this—"

"Deadie saved our asses back there."

Talon eyed her drink as if it were the most interesting thing in the galaxy.

"If you want out, then go; you've got your share. I'll even split mine; you all can have it. Splurge a little while we're here. So no hard feelings, right? But I know you. What's the real issue, Fluxo?"

"Just tired of fixing all the shit afterward," Fluxman muttered.

Talon stood. "You think I don't appreciate what you do? Talon stood.

C'mon, you and me, we'll check Hartwell for some good repair bots and better beer. We'll be back in time for Deadie to give Kattral's people that info. Deal?"

"Yeah, sure."

Fluxman shot Deadeye a look and followed Talon from the café.

Runabout and Epsi snickered while Wizard rolled his eyes and stirred his tea.

"Why is he so angry?" Deadeye asked. "I thought Runners took risks, pissed people off, and rode the light-years without a care, that sort of thing. Fluxman is acting like a Homesteader banker that's lost his passcode and underwear."

"Hey there, don't be insulting my people like that."

Runabout sucked the Starrio tube via a slot in her helmet.

"Homesteaders ain't never wore underwear."

Wizard laughed. "I can vouch for that."

"You two, sometimes."

Grinning, Epsi shook her head and ordered another drink.

"So what is his problem, then?" Deadeye asked.

"Fluxo doesn't like battles," Wizard said. "I think his time as a magistrate left him mentally scarred or something. Poor sap can't sleep half the time because of it. That's why he's always walking *Valkyrie*'s corridors like some cryo ghost. He thinks all that beer will help him forget, but it doesn't. Hell, he doesn't listen to me, either."

"And here I thought it was the sex dolls," Epsi said.

"Hmm."

Deadeye drank his juice, trying not to think of his own PTSD. Sleeping without Talon had brought it back, but he'd never tell her he needed her for more than just sex. More than he wanted to admit, even to himself.

"Is that stuff any good?" Deadeye nodded at Runabout's tube.

"You're a pilot, and you've never had a hit of Starrio?" Wizard beckoned at Runabout. "Go on now, give that man a taste."

Runabout leaned over and placed the tube in Deadeye's mouth herself. "Here."

"Just pretend that's Talon's nipple," Epsi said.

They all chortled while Deadeye sucked on the slim plastic tube. The vapors entered his mouth, stinging his tongue and throat along the way to his lungs. Yet every stinging sensation ushered in a blissful, syrupy aftertaste that left him seeing many more stars than he'd spied through the skylight. Before he exhaled, Epsi turned his face toward her and gleefully opened her mouth to accept the Starrio smoke.

Wizard smiled. "Careful, Epsilon, if Talon catches you flirting with her boy...." Wizard smiled.

"I'm not from Epsilon, for the hundredth time."

Epsi patted Deadeye's cheek and leaned back into her seat. "And besides, Talon needs to share sometimes."

A sense of elation crept through Deadeye's body. Calming, yet alert. An odd, formless satisfaction overcame him, and he could focus on the conversation without his thoughts drifting to the UNS or star charts.

"Where are you from?" Deadeye asked Epsi. "Do you remember?"

Epsi stared at the fresh asparagus shake the drone set down.

"I have no idea. I know that House Traxe kept me as an indentured pilot for a year, and my family... shit, I suppose they're still there in the labor camp, but they must be old by now. Or dead. We travel the Spur in sols, but years pass for them. Got my callsign because of some guy I met there. He was from Epsilon Eridani. We had a fling, he promised to take me with him when he escaped, but he lied. My owners called me 'Epsi' as a joke afterward. Shit. The stuff we remember, right? It's always the worst memories."

Wizard grimaced. "House Traxe. Wizard grimaced. They don't call them the Blood Barons for nothing. Not even the Runners will deal with those cunts."

"Is that why you joined this outfit?" Deadeye asked. "To stop the Barons?"

"You might as well ask the galaxy to cease rotating," Epsi said. "But yes."

Wizard offered Epsi his tea, but she declined, mumbled something about gathering supplies, and left.

"Damn," Deadeye said. "Sorry I asked."

"Nah, don't be."

Runabout lay across the table and blew smoke at him from under her helmet rim.

"Epsi, she's a right elegant, go-getter pilot, but she won't ever forgive MEC for selling her and her kin to those stinky stanky nobles. If she liked women, I'd take off this helmet just to make her smile again; that's a right fact."

Deadeye smiled sadly as he watched Epsi enter a distant elevator. "I thought you liked men?"

Runabout sucked a long draw from the tube. "Reckon, I like everyone."

"You only like me when I leave lemon candy in your pod," Wizard said.

While Runabout rolled off the table and into Wizard's lap, Deadeye leaned close, the Starrio granting him clarity.

"What about you, Wizard?"

Wizard sucked on the Starrio tube, spanked Runabout, then set her back into her chair with both tentacles. His effortless strength impressed Deadeye; the man had just made a jump, with little sleep afterward.

"You're wanting everyone's story?" Wizard blew smoke from his nostrils. "Why? I have, what, maybe another year or two until I can't remember all this? Hybrids like you and me, we're likelier to forget all that shit than other pilots."

Deadeye leaned back and smirked. "And likelier to avoid the question."

As the smoke dissipated, Wizard studied him.

"Because we can't remember anything half the time, and we don't like to embarrass ourselves. But hey, you've earned our trust, I guess. I was a colony ship pilot for MEC, not far from the Ross Boundary."

"The Boundary?" Deadeye asked. "You flew near there?"

The Ross Boundary was anything within six light-years of Earth. Nav computers always became scrambled inside it, sending vessels far off course. No one had ever flown back out of it. Not alive, anyway. Derelict ships still drifted around the invisible, formless barrier, belonging to those who'd tried. It had become a legendary obstacle, with some claiming a divine being had created it to protect humanity's birthplace. Others said it was a remnant of a pre-MEC empire forbidding humanity's genetic offshoots from polluting their untainted worlds. A few mused that an accident had caused its creation, an explosion of fleets powered by alien drives. Deadeye didn't believe any of it.

"Only within a light-year or so, never close enough to get trapped in it," Wizard said. "It was good piloting in a MEC outfit for a while. Then they got all frightened of the Prestige's automated ships and had their little war at 82 Eri."

"I think I took part in that," Deadeye said.

The sparsest memories of combat versus unmanned vessels flickered in his thoughts. Yet if that were true, who were the people he'd strafed in his other recollections? He knew he'd killed humans in battle.

"You're what, ninth-generation Uzari, with that jack configuration in your neck?" Wizard asked. "I bet you did fly in that. Nasty little conflict. Fucking automated bastards hit us, zipping off the radar like a cloud of neutrinos from a nightmare. They're on you before any AOS blinks on your radar feed. MEC pressed me into service, but I escaped on a trade ship bound for... wait, bound for...."

Deadeye looked away while Wizard cleared his throat and sipped more tea. The humiliation of not remembering, the loss associated with it, never went away.

"Anyway." Wizard set the tea down. "I hooked up with the Runners sometime after. They called me 'Wizard' because I could do anything they needed: fly, repair, fight, fuck, whatever. Zyn, like me, we weren't needed by MEC any longer. The Lineage wanted us exterminated, and everyone else just saw tentacles instead of a human being."

"And Talon?" Deadeye asked.

Wizard shrugged. "I know Talon's demanding at times, and she's got one hell of a mean streak, but she took us on when no other outfit would. Even other Runner crews didn't want me or Runnie here because people hate where we came from. So I fly for Talon because it's my only game in the Spur now. Like you."

"Like me."

Deadeye stretched over the table, claimed the Starrio tube from Runabout, and finished it in one long draw.

"Hey now, your horny little mind will be all gunked to Dame knows where by the time we chat it up with Kattral's people," Runabout said.

"Relax, I know where I am."

Deadeye placed his hands behind his head and stared at the skylight again.

So many stars....

Runabout seized the spent tube and chuckled. "Yeah, and where's that?"

"Parallax."

It was the first word Deadeye thought of.

"Yeah, he's fucked up," Wizard said.

They all laughed, the Starrio smoke drifting high above them.

Chapter 12

The parlor where Kattral's 'broker' met with them was little more than a landing pad on the other side of Hartwell Station. The atmospheric turbines on the maintenance levels below fed the entire station its air supply in regular gusts. It almost felt like being in the wind, planetside, except for the oil and sweat reek.

Wind.

Deadeye blinked. Was that a recollection of him visiting a planet? There was nothing in his memories other than the wrecked beehive. Other spacers had told him how gravity tugged one down on certain worlds, almost gluing one's feet to the ground. It sounded confining, limiting. Maybe it was the Starrio affecting his brain.

Talon scolded him with a glance. "You smoked with Runnie, didn't you?" Talon scolded him with a glance.

She'd met back up with him while Wizard and Epsi returned to *Miss Cygni* with supplies.

"Don't be blaming me, now," Runabout said. "He was vaping madder than a Sadisto sucking salt off vinyl chaps."

"Great, another void-gaping junkie," Fluxman said. "You know beer's better?"

"I'm fine."

Deadeye sensed he was grinning too widely, too often, but he felt good.

"Seriously, I could fly us to Groombridge 34, no sweat."

"No coming back, either," Fluxman grunted. "This won't work, Talon."

"Let's just get this over with."

Talon led them into the parlor, where a line of piloting pods had been set up next to a station power coupling. The pods' IVs were clogged with sols-old nutrients. Stains marred the seats and terminals. Two other spacers were present, bearing the open-mouthed, dumbstruck expression of ones jacked into the UNS without actually traveling. Washed-up pilots often frequented such places, spending their last sols dreaming in navigational software.

Runabout clutched at her med-bandoleer. "This ain't looking healthy."

"Whatcha expect from a deal made with an Uzari flyboy?" Fluxman asked.

"I knew I should have brought my other gun," Talon muttered.

Deadeye stumbled into Runabout. "You won't need it. Deadeye stumbled into Runabout. Look, they have a chair ready for me and everything. Aren't they nice? Hugs and smiles, I'll bet."

Talon steadied him and sighed. "Definitely the Starrio talking."

The broker stood beside a pod at the end of the row with a hovering computer terminal. She kept her arms folded inside her black trenchcoat, her face covered in glowing line tattoos. A syncer, always online with whatever network was present. The technician looked more like a trawler mechanic than a UNS expert, with coveralls and unusually large, sharp tools for one of his alleged trade.

"An assassin and a bruiser," Talon murmured. "Kattral doesn't play."

"Hell with this, let's go," Fluxman whispered.

"At least try to look confident with me here, guys," Deadeye said.

Talon took him by the arm and leaned in close. "You fuck this up and I'll throw you off this pad myself, got it?"

Deadeye offered an easy smile. "Worrying causes wrinkles, you know."

"So does old age, which I'd like to see some sol," Talon said.

Deadeye grinned at the broker and sat inside the pod. "I'd rather actually live than live forever."

The broker loaded up a UNS nav dump on the terminal without a word, while the technician inserted a jack into the back of Deadeye's neck and strapped him down. From the corner of his eye, Deadeye saw that Talon started to step forward, but the broker warned her off with a glare.

"For his safety," the technician said.

Talon tapped her gun belt. "And this is for yours. Heh. You never know what my Deadie boy might do. I see any distress, or you touch him, we've got issues."

"Aw, Cap'n, thanks, but I've got this."

As soon as the UNS overlay appeared in his eyesight, Deadeye concentrated on five locations he could imprint into the dump to satisfy the agreement.

The technician flashed a cruel smile. "Do you need assistance?" The technician flashed a cruel smile.

"I might have to pee," Deadeye said. "Though my MPS doesn't have a zipper, help a guy out? You have such delicate hands."

The technician glowered. "You son of a—"

Talon coughed and tapped her gun belt.

Various star systems loaded across the UNS feeds in his vision. They appeared on the broker's terminal screen, one after another, faster and faster as he browsed through them: Sirius, Kapteyn's Star, Ross 614, L347-14. There: four systems, with four wild comet chases for Kattral's assholes to investigate.

Just one more....

"What the void is that all about?" the broker asked. "This is garbage."

"He's fulfilling the bargain."

Talon didn't sound as confident now.

Deadeye turned to see what they were talking about, but the UNS practically blinded him with more and more feeds. The overlay filled with detailed coordinate sets, so many that he was unable to focus on a single one. It was nothing; he could manage it.

"I've got this," he said, but his voice sounded weak, with the stifled ambiance of speaking while wearing a helmet.

Had the technician put one on him?

Stupid bastard....

Deadeye flew through the debris field with little effort. Drones had made it before the rebels put it up, but not with Casimir drives. The older Kapteyn light-speed engines would have taken many lifetimes to achieve the same goals. But not him. He was the best; the parent bots back at Uzari Corp had ensured that. Genetics was only a sliver of the pie. One needed training, discipline—and passion. The starving obsession with pushing the limits, then breaking those limits altogether. He smiled and activated the thrusters.

The UNS showed the light blue planet ahead, ringed in Stein warships. It was quite the gauntlet, flying through all of that until he—

"Wait, is he going into some kinda coma?" Fluxman asked.

"Dame Nyx, bring him through it," Runabout whispered.

"What the fuck did you do to him?" Talon asked.

"Is he still awake?" the broker asked.

"He will be."

It sounded like the technician reached for the wrench on his belt. Scuffling noises followed. Grunts, curses. Voices were raised. The broker told them to break it up.

Deadeye kept flying, trying to reach that planet, trying not to crash into....

"Fine, he's done. Now unstrap him, or I'll fill your asses full of holes."

It was Talon's voice. Deadeye opened his eyes as the UNS overlay faded from sight. The terminal screen flashed the logoff logo, and the broker snapped it shut and placed it into her coat. The technician, his nose bloodied, yanked the straps off Deadeye's hands and nudged him from the pilot pod.

Talon stood hand on her holstered pistol, while Fluxman clasped the technician's wrench. His knuckles were bloody. Runabout brandished a syringe in each hand, ready to fill Kattral's underlings with some dangerous cocktail.

Trying not to stagger, Deadeye pretended to dust off his shoulder and smiled.

"Nice doing, um, business with you. Give Kattral my regards."

"It's Lord Kattral," the broker said.

"Hey, I'm glad you're intelligent enough to know who your boss is, but I hope you have enough brain cells never to try that shit again, right?" Talon asked. "I told you not to touch him. Now, give me a copy of those coordinates. You heard me, that's Runner data, too, and I want a record of it."

The broker drew a memory chit from her terminal and flipped it at Talon, who caught it without flinching. Both of Kattral's underlings glared at them for a moment, then left the parlor for the nearest elevator.

"Let's have a drink sometime, eh?" Deadeye called after them, then wobbled into Fluxman.

"Hold me, big guy. I might need to puke."

"Get the hell off me."

Fluxman started to push him away, but Runabout laid a hand on Fluxman's arm and pushed a different syringe into Deadeye's neck.

"*Ow!* I thought you liked me, Runnie."

Deadeye fought drowsiness.

"Oh, I sure do."

She put away the syringe and chuckled.

"Stuck you with a detoxer. Reckon you can get to walking on your own now?"

Deadeye blew out a breath as the drowsiness faded.

"I always could; I just needed to see if you and Fluxman cared about me. I'm touched, big guy. Really. You were going to beat up that technician for me. That's sweet of you."

"Shut up, for void's sake," Fluxman said. "Starrio makes him a gabber, garden gnome. Don't let him smoke that shit again."

Talon pocketed the data chit and scanned the other elevators.

"We need to get to *Miss Cygni* right now. Kattral will send someone after us as soon as he realizes the data you gave him was nonsense."

"I hope it's the broker. She was kinda cute, in an assassin sort of way."

Deadeye rubbed his forehead and followed the others out of the parlor.

"How long did that take, anyway? It felt like I was in that pod for hours."

"A few seconds."

Talon found them a different elevator and hurriedly punched in their desired level.

"You looked like you would leap out of that chair and eat that technician, right? That's why he reached for his tools, and we had an, um, discussion about who had the deadlier tools at the moment."

"Really? Weird."

Deadeye didn't like the inquisitive look in Talon's eye. As far as he knew, he'd never lost control like that while jacked into the UNS.

The elevator door shut, and he had to crowd beside Talon as Runabout and Fluxman took up the rest of the space. The squeeze made him grimace.

"Fart, and I'll kill you," Fluxman said.

"Why would you say that?" Deadeye asked. "I don't have... oops."

"It's that damn detoxer; it gives you gas!"

Talon held her nose. "Shit, Runnie, you should have let him stagger back to the ship."

Fluxman pulled out a handkerchief and covered his nose. "I hate you all." Fluxman pulled out a handkerchief and covered his nose.

Runabout rapped the side of her helmet. "I'm good. Don't smell anything."

Half an hour later, they rejoined Wizard and Epsi at the landing platform where *Miss Cygni* was docked. As the others got on board and Talon checked her mobile for the next job. Deadeye loitered around her, wanting to speak, but unsure of what to say.

Talon put her mobile away and crossed her arms. "You're circling me like a crazed hawk, go on, talk."

"What's the next mission?"

"First, we need to help another Runner outfit deliver food through a MEC blockade, then pick up something from a Homesteader enclave. Both at Procyon."

"That system's, what, a light-year or so from here?" he asked.

"Yes. Then there's a Cepheid convoy transporting relics to their monastery at Denis 1048. We'll hit them at a refuel outpost before they get there."

Talon gave him the side-eye. "We're going to relieve them of their holy foodstuffs and give them to starving people. About five light-years away from Procyon, but that's not what you're really asking. Out with it, okay?"

"We're different people when we're in the UNS."

Deadeye looked from her to *Cygni*'s airlock, where the others watched.

"I hope this doesn't lower your confidence in me. What was I trying to do, attack Kattral's people?"

Talon shrugged and turned her back to the crew. "You were reaching for something. You said things about routes and coordinates, and then you lost it."

"Maybe we can examine that chit together once we've left here?"

"Is that a pathetic attempt to get me to visit your bunk later?" she asked.

"Did it work?"

"No."

Talon drew close, her lips near his ear. "This next job should be a simple little run, all right? So we go in like last time—you make the jump, I'll get you up a sol before, we... *study* that chit, and then you'll tell me about what you saw in the UNS."

He nodded. "Deal."

"Now get on board before the crew gossips anymore."

"Yes, Cap'n."

Talon had purchased an ancient flight simulator, much to everyone's surprise, while she and Fluxman gathered replacement parts for *Valkyrie*'s little fleet. Once they'd flown a safe distance from Hartwell

Station—if the Harpies wanted revenge or Kattral discovered their ruse—she urged them all to try it.

They drew lots from an old welding helmet, and Epsi won the first try. She slid into the tight seat, which was enclosed within a two-meter tall, rectangular frame.

"What is this?"

She fumbled with a single set of manuals that rose from between her legs.

"Is it broken?"

"It's called a joystick," Talon said. "Remember, this is a single-seater fighter craft. Sort of like the vessels the warlords used, pre-MEC, such as the Han's *Yīng*, or the Badawi's *Saeiqa*."

"Those little shitcans came apart at the touch of a micrometeorite," Fluxman said. "Took some serious balls to fly stuff like that."

"I don't need balls."

Epsi smiled like a kid in a gravity tumbler as the simulator began its routine.

"Look at these controls. How the hell did they use this many switches and knobs without the UNS? And an altimeter? Did they fly things like this planetside?"

"The ancients were supposed to."

Wizard leaned against the simulator's frame and laughed at Epsi's inept piloting.

"You'd never have flown on Earth; watch out for that mountain! Oops, oh shit. Well, too bad, Epsi girl. My turn!"

Epsi left the seat and smoothed her jumpsuit. "Mountains? I was robbed."

Lips pursed, Wizard flew the entire routine, only losing a few points when encountering turbulence.

"C'mon, no spacer has to deal with shit like that. Wind?"

"I flew transports in atmosphere, so let me show you how it's done."

Deadeye passed the routine, but the Starrio caused him to focus on the knobs and switches too much, and only on the third attempt did he land on the carrier at the end.

"Too bad, flyboy," Talon said. "Next!"

Fluxman shouldered past Deadeye as he left the seat.

"Landing something like that, on a ship floating on all that water? Fluxman shouldered past Deadeye as he left the seat. Gimme that joystick."

"A hundred credits says he crashes in ten seconds," Epsi said.

"Eat my ass; I got this," Fluxman said.

"Epsi, you're on!" Runabout giggled.

"Fluxo's good," Wizard said. "Steady, now, that joystick isn't my cock."

"You all wanna shut it for a second?" Fluxman wiped the sweat off his brow.

Deadeye stumbled into Talon, who brushed him away, her eyes glued to the simulator screen.

"Who did you buy this thing from? It's awesome."

"You're still high."

She playfully held him at arm's length as she continued watching Fluxman's attempt.

"Some merchant from the Golden Band. She was in trouble with the Vega Freelancers and in a hurry, so I got it for five hundred credits."

"A museum would pay at least two thousand for it," Epsi said. "But not if you beat on the console like that, Fluxman!"

After crashing into the carrier, Fluxman rose from the seat in a huff.

"Piece of shit. Nobody flies like that unless they're void-touched."

"*Ha!*" Epsi laughed. "Pay up!"

"Runnie, you're up," Talon said.

"*Hah*, flying is like dancing; you have to be moving and swooning and all that, and then some."

Runabout flew the routine to the end but ran out of fuel before reaching the carrier.

"Dame's toes and tits! This thing ain't fair at all."

Talon waited for Runabout to exit the simulator, then she slowly approached it, head slightly cocked.

"It's not like a starship; you can't hit the accelerator once and expect it to carry you the rest of the way. You went too hard, too fast."

Talon waited for Runabout to exit the simulator, then she slowly approached it, head slightly cocked.

"Okay, no need to be all dramatic," Wizard said.

"Show them how it's done." Epsi grinned.

"A hundred credits says she'll crash before the landing on the carrier," Deadeye said.

The others accepted his bet. Talon gave him a wry smile, then sat and started the routine. They all made a few jokes and jabs, but it was apparent Talon was faring better than any of them after a minute. She glided through the clouds, passed the mountains, cleared the turbulence, and landed on the carrier with the highest score of them all.

Talon stood and raised her brows at Deadeye. "Time to pay up, flyboy."

Deadeye grinned wide as he doled out one hundred credits to each of the others.

"Where did you learn to fly like that? You must have flown in atmosphere before."

Talon blew her fingertips as if they were on fire.

"Heh, just a natural pilot. I suppose I'm lucky like that."

Talon blew her fingertips as if they were on fire.

He gave her a sly look as Wizard and Epsi whooped and tossed their credit chits over everyone's heads.

"I don't believe in luck."

Talon caught a chit and tucked it into his belt. "Too bad."

Hours later, right before Deadeye plotted *Valkyrie*'s next jump; Talon paid him a visit on the bridge. The pod was crammed enough for one person, but they made it work: her riding atop him, the bridge's dim lights reflecting off her sweaty thighs, casting green highlights through her unbound hair. It floated above her head since all but the crew cabin centrifuges were deactivated during jumps. The lack of gravity granted their lovemaking a desperate quality; he had to grip her tight, so she wouldn't drift away. Her hands left marks on his skin where she refused to let nature pull her off him.

She squirmed, ground, and moaned until the unbearably hot release of orgasm took his breath and sent spasms along his legs. They lay still afterward, his hands cupping her buttocks, her fingers tangled in his hair. The ammonia stink of ejaculation mixed with the musky sweetness of their perspiration, grounding him in the reality of the moment far more than Starrio or the UNS could ever hope to manage.

"Is there still nothing between us?"

He twirled her floating locks into curlicues. The shocks of hair maintained their new shape in zero gravity.

"You have to do this now?"

He chuckled. "Nope. But when we exit this coming jump, this room will stink of some serious sex, and I need a good lie to tell the others. If I say it was their Captain Talon, they'd never believe me, not in a million light-years."

Talon lifted her head off his shoulder and nodded. "You're absolutely right, Deadie; they'd not believe that. Hmm. I'll say you got hold of that sex doll again."

"Works for me."

He kissed her.

"Right?" she whispered, then kissed him back.

"So, what the hell is a hawk?"

Talon laughed. "Cryoshit, are you kidding? It's a bird of prey. Like the raptor, the Harpies use for a mascot or whatever. They fly about and snatch vermin that aren't paying attention. Mice, rabbits, little furry shits like that."

"I've seen mice. MEC used them in their labs for tests sometimes."

He adjusted his knees, and she slid down beside him onto the seat.

"But not a rabbit or hawk, so...."

She stuck her pinky into his navel. "So?" She stuck her pinky into his navel.

"So, are you going to tell me where you're from? You obviously remember, unlike the rest of us. You have that provincial accent—which is a huge turn-on, I might add—and you've seen animals, like real animals on a planet, not the holo knockoffs or the ones the Lineage clones for their zoos. And no matter what you claimed earlier, you've flown in atmosphere, real atmosphere, with wind, turbulence, all of that."

"Apai, in Tau Ceti. It's a pretty little world. It even has trees, like real forests."

"I knew it! And the tattoos?"

"They're a representation of the Golden Band."

She leaned away from him a little so he could see the swirls along her body.

"Some artist on Eridani Prime did them. I figured maybe we'll get to expand the Band one sol, right? Make things nicer for everyone on this side of the Spur."

"I've heard Sadisto crews expect new members to get their genitals tattooed."

Talon rolled her eyes but grinned. "The things pilots remember."

Deadeye tried to smile.

"I'm sorry." She kissed him again. "I'm sorry.

I won't joke about that again."

"It's what we do." He held her closer. "It's what we do. We fly until we forget every damn thing."

They didn't speak for several moments, but their hands found each other.

"You remembered that stuff for Kattral's broker easily enough."

She rested her chin on her hand, studying him. "What's Parallax?"

"I have no idea."

"I think you're lying or avoiding the question—but you don't mean to, right?"

He stared up at the bridge ceiling. "I keep recalling strange things. Flying through a debris field, trying to reach some warships—old vessels, the ones you'd expect to have a Kapteyn engine inside. People are dying, and I'm... I cannot save them."

"I bet that's why you acted that way in the parlor pod." Talon eased herself back atop him and licked one of his nipples.

"More PTSD than a squad of MEC grunts."

He grinned. "I'm fine now that you're not sneaking into my cabin for that book. He grinned. Your turn, Cap'n—"

She placed a finger to his lips. "Don't call me that, not when we're like this."

"Then who are you when we're like this?" he asked.

"Whatever I need to be."

She roused his passions again, stroking, nibbling, licking until he dared not resist. He gave in to her, losing himself in her demanding touch, her hungry moans.

Yet later, when they were finally spent, Talon still hadn't answered his query about the book. It was a pleasant but obvious distraction, a veil she drew over his eyes like night falling over a planet. By the time she gently slid off him and placed his helmet back on, Deadeye was already entering the feed-filled dreams of the UNS.

"See you soon, Deadie boy."

His smile lasted for an entire light-year.

Chapter 13

"You want me to fly through that blockade after all, don't you," Deadeye asked. "After I made that jump. I really want that spacer's union now. With back pay."

Talon, already in her white armored suit, helped him from the piloting pod on *Valkyrie*'s bridge and smiled.

"It'll be a milk run, right? Besides, I need all hands for this op since some of us will be running as decoys to get MEC's attention."

He glanced at the red, winking woman's face on her suit's holo logo as he stood. "So is that the real 'Miss Cygni'?"

She blushed, and he started to laugh—what could embarrass a toughened spacer like her, after all—but then he caught himself.

"I'm sorry," he said.

Talon started to walk away, then she hesitated.

"My... *family*... they spent many credits on my education, training, my placement in their fleet."

She cinched on her comm cap while offering him a sideways glance, as if she hadn't told anyone that before.

"I was groomed for so much bullshit. Even in the fleet, others in the family dubbed me 'Miss Cygni.' After that stupid beauty pageant they run at 61 Cygni, right? Because they saw me as primped and perfect."

"This is your way of mocking that?"

Talon snorted. "Mocking? Hell no, I decided to claim it. Own it, like it's mine, so that wherever my frigate goes, or whoever sees this logo, they'll know what the real deal is. The person I want them to see, instead of that glitzy, fake nonsense."

Deadeye nodded. "Then where did you get your current callsign?"

She winked before snapping her helmet on. "Another story, another time."

An energy drink and glucose shot later, Deadeye met the others in *Valkyrie*'s hangar. They were all kitted out, helmets on, chatting over the radio as if they were heading for a joy ride. He fought to appear fit and ready, but he wanted a glass of juice and a warm bunk. Every few seconds, he spotted UNS numbers in his vision.

"You look like shit squeezed through a food processor," Fluxman said. "You're gonna fly out there with us, looking like that?"

"I might even make it back, too." Deadeye raised one brow and smirked.

"If I have to tow you back, it's coming out of your share." Epsi grinned. "Maybe your butt, too, if Talon ever looks the other way."

Runabout giggled. "Oh, *merda*." Runabout giggled.

Wizard laughed. "That hard-ass woman doesn't miss shit, she'd know."

"Damn right I would."

Talon stepped into *Miss Cygni*'s airlock and addressed them from the hatchway.

"We will meet up with another Runner carrier, *Wild Seed*, who will deposit a cache of supply crates they took from a MEC convoy bound for a military outpost. Their outfit has suffered a few losses lately, and they lack the vessels it'll take to make this work. We'll snatch those crates and make for the blockade around Procyon Prime, an industrial colony. This should be easy, but avoid engaging any bogies—get in and get out."

Wizard grunted. "Stealing food meant for the military? Won't those jarheads take it from someone else? Nah, this creates more problems for those we're helping."

Deadeye laughed. "Have you eaten that naval slop?Deadeye laughed. They'll probably thank us."

"That slop can feed many people," Talon said. "Wiz, I get what you're saying, but I'll leave that up to MEC's naval logisticians to work out. We have hungry men, women, and children six AU away."

"Right then, *capità*, what sort of blockade are we talking about?" Runabout asked.

"It's a standard naval blockade," Talon said. "According to *Seed*'s captain, MEC has four cruisers spaced around Procyon Prime at a distance of five hundred kilometers from the planet itself and six kilometers from each other. Then there's a screen of five corvettes one hundred and fifty kilometers from the colony, the edge of the mesosphere. They're thirty kilometers from each other."

"So that corvette screen is half a light-second from the cruisers," Deadeye said. "That's pretty tight. Blockades were a little looser when I was in the navy."

"They didn't have Runners flying circles around them then," Epsi said.

"Don't forget the destroyer patrolling the space between the cruisers and the screen," Talon said. "It could be anywhere in the vicinity."

"Who collects the food crates?" Deadeye asked.

Talon brought up a holo on her mobile, showing Procyon Prime and the ships orbiting it.

"Those of you with the crates will jettison them 1K from the munitions depot in orbit. Each crate is fitted with ECM and a small nitrogen thruster that will automatically fire five seconds after you drop it. One small burst, and it's on its way, as long as you are oriented toward the depot. The colonists have someone in place to gather the crates, but that ECM won't last long. But at that point, it's on the colonists, not us."

"Lotta effort to keep a colony starving," Fluxman said. "Do they still make munitions on that ball of rock?"

"Yes," Talon said. "Missiles, torpedoes, everything. It's one of MEC's key munitions suppliers this side of the Dust Systems."

Wizard wriggled a tentacle at Talon. "Then, even if we get those people the food, the blockade will be worse next time. MEC is vindictive enough to stick to those colonists' asses even more after this, especially if they're manufacturing important shit like that. How is this helping them?"

"So, what, we let them starve?" Talon asked.

"That's not happening; I joined the Runners for this sort of thing," Epsi said.

Wizard raised both tentacles in placation. "Epsi girl, I'm only saying that everything we do out here has consequences for all of those people planetside."

"We'll need another diversion," Deadeye said. "Something to make them think we're here for another reason."

"Why not threaten that there depot?" Runabout asked. "That'd scare the cold right out of their little black hearts."

Wizard scratched his goatee. "Not bad. Wizard scratched his goatee. I like this. MEC will assume we're here for armaments, those people get to eat, and there might be no repercussions."

"Good idea, Runnie." Talon smiled at her. "That's the plan, then.

After the crates are dropped, we'll rendezvous at these coordinates, twenty-seven AU out, spinward."

"Great, can we do this now?" Fluxman asked. "I have beer to drink."

———

Deadeye flew *Miss Cygni* toward the blockade, bearing half the food crates and *Valkyrie*'s shuttle, a tiny craft that lacked weapons, a jump drive, or even a Kapteyn engine. Runabout waited inside the shuttle's cockpit, strapped in, ready to risk herself in the ruse she'd suggested. The plan was to dispatch the shuttle once he neared the depot, make a 'demonstration'—in other words, attack—and then collect Runabout on the shuttle and blast away. In theory, MEC would believe that the shuttle was trying to dock with the depotand steal the munitions, and ignore the brief blip of the crates on their radar.

"You ready back there, Runabout?" Deadeye asked while waiting for an AOS on the blockade's corvette screen.

They were still two light-minutes from Procyon Prime, but he wanted to be ready.

"Ready as a fruit picker in harvest cycle," Runabout said. "Just make sure you're ready and rearing when I need you to pluck my farm girl rump out of that mess."

He chuckled. "I won't let MEC catch my favorite tater bug. You've still got many tater patches out there to enjoy."

Runabout laughed. "Ah, you slick talker, you."

"Ugh, don't make me puke in my helmet over here," Fluxman said from *Corsair*, flying off *Cygni*'s portside at a distance of thirty-five kilometers.

"You'd better get her, MEC boy, or it's your ass."

"It's my ass, flying this heap *Wild Seed* loaned us," Wizard said. "This shitcan doesn't even have aft scopes or cube ECMs. I'm fucked if MEC uses missiles."

Wizard was piloting *Drunken Deneb*, the only remaining vessel in Strike Group *Wild Seed*, a beat-up transport. The carrier's captain had lent it to them but requested its return upon completion of their mission. He flew thirty-five kilometers off *Cygni*'s starboard.

"Can we not with the bitching?" Epsi asked. "I'm the one lugging the other food crates over here on *Princess*. You and Fluxo have to get MEC's attention and make some noise. Or, you know, be yourselves."

"Stow the chatter, people; we're less than a light-minute out," Talon said from *Annie Argent*. It surprised Deadeye that she'd let him fly her favorite again, *Miss Cygni*, while she piloted Runabout's usual vessel. But the frigate would pose a more credible threat to the munitions depot than the other non-military vessels in their outfit.

With *Princess* twenty kilometers behind him and *Annie Argent* 92° above *Cygni*'s pitch axis at twenty-five kilometers, Deadeye felt like they had a chance. MEC would try to engage every target, and the corvettes would likely pursue his shipmates. The cruisers and the wandering destroyer were his real concerns since they'd have far more missiles, and each would converge more quickly on the depot's location.

A few seconds later, the corvette screen showed up on his radar feed.

Deadeye's destination was the depot, which currently orbited above Procyon Prime's eastern hemisphere—for him, 18° to starboard on his yaw axis. He glanced at his shipmates on the radar, sighed, and activated his rear thrusters in a short burn. He course-corrected with his portside thrusters and made straight for the depot a second later. His outfit had approached the planet on the system's ecliptic plane, and since Procyon Prime didn't have some weird elliptical orbit, they'd deployed with it dead ahead of them.

He wished he could offer some humor to them or even wish them good luck, which he usually found silly. But the need for radio silence prevented such niceties. He had warmed up to them, despite his arrogant, jockey demeanor. Deadeye hoped they made it. And Talon... he didn't know what he felt about her, but something was there between them, and he wanted it to continue.

Epsi followed his lead in *Princess*, taking the same trajectory toward the depot.

"Okay, we're two hundred and ninety kilometers from the screen, so get ready," Talon said. "They know we're here, so no more need for radio silence."

"I've got four missiles homing in on me already," Wizard said. "Those bastards deployed missile drones out here?"

"And here I thought this would be boring," Epsi said.

"We're too damned tight; we need to spread out more," Fluxman said.

"Right, Fluxo, everyone, spread out, make those corvettes come after you," Talon said. "Skim past, fire on them to get their attention. Deadie, Epsi, maintain the course."

"I fucking told you this can has no countermeasures!" Wizard cried. "They're still coming! *Shit, shit, shit.*"

"Roll out of it, make 'em burn up their fuel," Runabout said.

"Think I'm not trying?" Wizard asked.

Deadeye's instincts begged him to alter course and help his friends, but he dared not disobey Talon's orders this time. The depot was still two hundred and twenty kilometers out.

"Any sign of that destroyer?" Epsi asked.

"No, but they have two frigates we didn't account for," Fluxman said. "Fast little bastards, too. Just inside the screen."

"Hah ha!" Wizard laughed. "Those missiles are on their way to the Ring!"

"Good job, now engage that corvette that's creeping up, 38° on your pitch axis, trailing," Talon said. "Fluxman, spray those frigates if you can. Piss them off."

"I'm on it, but I'm gonna need help," Fluxman said.

"Sending help now," Talon said. "*Annie*'s railgun is out of range, but at least they know I have one now. I'll be there in five seconds. Deadie, Epsi, what's the situation?"

"We're still clear over here," Deadeye said.

"Yes, one hundred and eighty kilometers out from the depot," Epsi said.

"I've got this teeny tiny bird ready to fly," Runabout said.

"Good," Talon said. "I've got all five corvettes on radar now; the screen is tightening on our trio. This diversion is working. Keep at it, people."

Fluxman chuckled. "Goddamn, torpedoes? Fluxman chuckled. They think I'm gonna sit still out here? Captain, if you'd do the honors?"

"Don't mind if I do," Talon said. "*Ha!* Punked that bogey!"

"*Ooo*, nice shot, that one," Wizard said.

"Now for the icing on the cake," Fluxman said.

Deadeye watched *Annie Argent* and *Corsair* tear one of the frigates apart with railgun salvos on the radar.

That leaves the second frigate, I have a hunch....

"Cap'n, Fluxo, pull out now; your heatsink vents are putting out a lot of energy," Deadeye said. "I can detect it all the way over here."

"Shit, he's right," Wizard said. "Hold on; I'm coming."

"I don't see nothing," Fluxman said.

"There they are, goddamn it," Talon said. "Missiles, probably heat seekers. They waited until we overheated, the fuckers. Evasive, now!"

Helpless on his current trajectory, Deadeye could only watch as the blips engaged in the deadly interplay on his radar. The missiles streaked toward *Corsair* and *Annie Argent*—while *Drunken Deneb* flew right at the salvo.

"What the actual fuck is Wiz doing?" Epsi asked. "Is he void-touched?"

"Dame Nyx, guide them safely," Runabout whispered.

"Wiz, pull back!" Epsi cried.

"Leave him be; we have our duties," Deadeye said.

"He's going to commit suicide," Epsi said.

"He knows what he's doing."

Deadeye wasn't sure he believed his own words, but *Cygni* and *Princess* were ninety-two kilometers from the depot. The fate of their shipmates was out of his and Epsi's hands.

"Wiz, what are you doing?" Talon asked. "Wiz, damn it!"

"Take out that other frigate, captain; I'll get these little shits off your backs," Wizard said. "Fluxo, start spitting rail rounds!"

On the radar, *Drunken Deneb*'s signature flared with heat. Wizard was firing its railgun over and over, forcing the heatsinks to kick in and advertise his presence to the heat-seeking projectiles. Since he flew closer to them, they targeted *Deneb* instead. Laughing all the while, Wizard performed a series of rolls and quick, neck-breaking burns until the missiles expended their fuel and darted away on pointless, unending paths.

Corsair and *Annie Argent* dusted the remaining frigate with railgun fire, then sped closer to the planet, twenty kilometers out. *Drunken Deneb* followed, but Wizard sounded sluggish as he mumbled over the radio. Deadeye knew that sound; Wizard was nearing a blackout.

"Hit your adrenaline, Wiz," Talon said. "You risked too many Gs back there."

"I... I'm fine, just... a Zyn can handle..." Wizard's voice trailed off.

"Do it now, lieutenant; that's an order!" Talon yelled.

A second later, Wizard gasped over the comm, then chuckled dryly.

"Shit, captain, it's all good over here. What... what's next?"

"Those corvettes are bearing down on us serious and hot," Fluxman said.

"Deadie, Epsi, talk to me," Talon said.

"We're forty-nine kilometers out from the depot," Deadeye said.

"My crates are ready to go; got the ECM cubes ready," Epsi said.

"You should be good the rest of the way; we'll have our hands full with those corvettes," Talon said. "I have two cruisers on the radar now, too. *Ha.* This party is about to really start."

Deadeye didn't like it. That destroyer would have heard about the battle by now.

"Twenty-three kilometers, Deadeye, you want to do the honors first?" Epsi asked.

"No, you drop yours, then I'll release Runabout in the shuttle," Deadeye said. "That way, they'll think I'm going to hit the depot."

"I could fire a warning shot, make this charade more convincing," Epsi said.

"It's a munitions depot; you could ignite something and blow the whole thing," Deadeye said. "Remember, the people picking up these crates are waiting on that depot."

"You really think I'm that a bad a shot?" Epsi chuckled. "Wow, Deadeye. There goes your invite to my bunk."

"Do it, Epsi, but only one shot," Talon said. "Target their transponder; that way, they'll think we're trying to sever their communications before we raid the depot. Oh, and stop flirting with him; he's still just an ensign."

"That's not all he is," Epsi muttered playfully.

Talon laughed. "Shoot that transponder, and we might negotiate on him later."

"Don't I have a say in this?" Deadeye asked.

"No," Talon and Epsi said.

He smiled. "Whatever. Guess I'm irresistible, huh?"

"Oh, barf," Epsi said.

"Isn't that every hotshit jockey's fantasy?" Talon snorted. "Careful; we might strip you naked and then space you. There's no accounting for kink out here."

"Ouch," Deadeye said. "Come on; I'm not some piece of meat you can simply—"

A new blip appeared on his radar, coming over the planet's curved horizon.

"Son of a bitch," Deadeye said.

"The destroyer?" Talon asked.

"Yep, coming right at us," Runabout said.

"Targeting the transponder," Epsi said. "Firing!"

Princess's railgun clipped away the depot's transponder array in a single shot.

"Good, Epsi, now drop those crates and do a fast burn out there!" Talon shouted. "Deadie, you're up; make it look good for as long as you can!"

He glanced at the radar: *Annie Argent*, *Corsair*, and *Drunken Deneb* gave the corvettes and cruisers quite a chase right above the planet's stratosphere. The destroyer was less than five kilometers out from their position and closing fast.

"So, you still ready for this, Runabout?"

Deadeye opened *Miss Cygni*'s cargo bay, where the shuttle waited.

"Ain't telling you again." Runabout giggled and flew out of *Cygni*.

He maneuvered closer to the depot to give the impression he was about to fire upon them and board. MEC likely thought he had a complement of armed thugs onboard *Cygni* and were already sending marines to defend the depot's airlocks.

The destroyer was one kilometer away now. It hadn't launched missiles yet, which surprised him. He deposited the food crates and watched their nitrogen thrusters activate via radar—the collection of blips coursed toward the depot.

"Runnie, fly close and brash, make them think you're hauling Forever Girls in that thing," Talon said. "Deadie, you make the drop yet?"

That was good; it meant the ECM cubes had shielded the crates from Talon's radar—and thus MEC's.

"Yes, and I'm going to nab Runabout now," Deadeye said. "This destroyer is almost on top of me, though."

"Get the garden gnome and burn on outta there!" Fluxman yelled.

"Yes, everyone head for the rendezvous point; we're done here," Talon said. "Deadie, do you have her?"

"Almost."

Deadeye gritted his teeth as the destroyer passed four hundred and fifty meters from him, off to port. Runabout's shuttle was two hundred meters away, 220° on his pitch axis. Nearly right under him.

"What the hell are they playing at?" Wizard asked.

"I don't like it, either," Epsi said. "Should I circle back?"

"No, stick to the plan," Talon said.

As Deadeye flew *Cygni* near the shuttle, the destroyer released a trawler. It sped over to the crates, collected them, and traveled back into the larger vessel.

"Oh shit," Deadeye said.

"You're kidding," Talon said. "You're...."

"I'm back in *Cygni* girl, let's ride them there stars!" Runabout called out.

Deadeye reluctantly pulled away, staring in disbelief at the radar feed where the crates used to be.

While Talon cursed over the radio, Deadeye received an encrypted text.

"This will reach those who need it.
Thank you,
—A friend of the Runners."

"Hold on...our friend wasn't on the depot," Deadeye said. "They're on that destroyer."

"How can we know that?" Fluxman asked.

"Because they've not punked Deadie yet, that's how." Talon loosed a deep sigh. "Holy fuck. That was too close. Let's burn out of here."

Deadeye smiled as hee and his shipmates blasted away to the rendezvous point. At least there were others in MEC who cared. Others who wouldn't let families starve.

Chapter 14

Deadeye scratched the back of his head.

"So you're telling me we will purchase detachable crew berths from these people, but I have to wear these clothes? Does it at least come complete with homespun underwear, too?"

"If it does, you get to wear them," Talon said. "And nothing else."

The rest of the crew laughed as they exited *Miss Cygni* and entered Cap de Creus, a Homesteader outpost that orbited Procyon B, a white dwarf, at a distance of four AU. Though not as large as Hartwell Station, Creus had a pleasant gravity of 0.7, generated by five giant centrifuges that must have dated from the time of Kapteyn stardrives.

Deadeye chuckled. "Fine by me, but what's the deal?"

Talon paused as technicians scanned them for viruses or diseases.

"Your little deed, helping *Queen Ursula* against those Harpies? It got us a decent contact with these people, one that Runnie never could acquire. They have what we need, but cheaper."

Waggling a finger, Runabout shook her head. "Ain't taking the blame for that. I told you, ain't nothing my people want but this marriage contract on my helmet."

Fluxman scratched his crotch. "Easy, garden gnome, I'll keep them off you." Fluxman scratched his crotch.

"Ugh, I think I'll take my chances with a 'steader in chaps anytime," Epsi said. "And I fucking hate chaps because these people never shave their asses."

Fluxman grunted. "If I shave my ass, will you kiss it?"

"I'd have to get in linebehind all those sex dolls," Epsi said.

"Don't you talk shit about my ladies, now," Fluxman smirked. "I should've brought one of the gals, I might've gotten a good price for her here."

"Shut it, people; we're not here to get laid," Talon said. "Homesteaders play that game for keeps; just ask Runnie."

Runabout said nothing.

Wizard gestured at the homespun sleeves that wouldn't stay rolled up above his tentacles.

"Then why these fucking clothes, Talon?"

Wizard gestured at the homespun sleeves that wouldn't stay rolled up above his tentacles.

"Trust me; we need a disguise," Talon said.

They all wore brown jumpsuits and coveralls they'd gotten before leaving Hartwell. The garments were rough spun, as comfortable as having plastic fibers constantly raking one's skin. Probably machined in a cheap textile plant and unusually tight. Deadeye assumed it was to accentuate their figures since Homesteaders only seemed to have one thing on their minds other than colonizing every unclaimed rock between Altair and Sirius.

"Whatever this haul is that you're talking about?" Deadeye whispered in Talon's ear. "I want my share doubled after this."

"You don't look authentic enough."

Talon looked around, spotted a filthy plow motor on the dock, and touched its greasy cylinders. She wiped the black, oily substance on Deadeye's coveralls—then his face.

"Triple share now," he muttered.

Talon stuck out her tongue and winked.

"Here they come," Epsi said as the main airlock alarm beeped.

MEC soldiers exited, gave the crew a dismissive glance, and continued down the dock to a corvette.

"Well, shit, the cryopod," Fluxman said.

Deadeye and the others regarded Talon with questioning glares.

"MEC patrols it, and the only way we can make it through is to disguise ourselves," Talon said. "Homesteaders won't deal through a medium; they expect to meet their customers. Keep it down, keep it low profile, and this will be easy."

"Okay, fuck that," Wizard said.

Deadeye fought the urge to wipe the grease off his face. "What? It's just MEC."

Wizard snorted. "Just MEC? As soon as they see my tentacles, I'm headed for a slave vessel. Or get reported by these 'steaders, the racist fucks. No offense, Runnie."

"Not telling me nothing I don't already know," Runabout said.

Talon sighed. "I have a plan, come on, I'm not insane. If we go in as Homesteaders, then MEC will think we're going to colonize some little shit asteroid they designated as safe, and then we can be on our way, all right? These berths can hold lots of cargo, and we could start making drops like the Vega Freelancers."

Wizard's tentacles writhed into fists. "How will you make them believe that a frigate like *Miss Cygni* could colonize anything?"

"It'll be easy," Talon said. "Heh, have you seen the junk heaps these people fly? They'd ride a tin can attached to an engine if they had to and not worry about who died on the way. The real problem will be getting them to accept credits and not marriage."

"You don't have a plan for that part?" Epsi raised an eyebrow.

"I might have an idea," Talon said. "But we'll need two willing Homesteaders."

They all looked at Deadeye and Runabout.

"No," Runabout said. "Ain't no way; get that out of your mind box right now."

"Really?" Deadeye asked. "Damn it."

Talon grinned.

Cap de Creus held several expansive farms and gardens but bore an awful sulfur stink from the colonists' water. The water likely came from nearby Luyten B, the world Hartwell Station orbited. It was also known as Ubar Gamma—a desert planet with subterranean sulfur springs. Being Homesteaders, the people didn't seem to care, even though water treatments were available. It was typical behavior on their part; pragmatism taken to the extreme.

They were akin to a cult, hell-bent on colonizing the Spur at any cost, no matter what it took or, like Talon had inferred, how any died. As long as one person, or preferably a couple, made it to their planned destination —and procreated to spread humanity among the stars—they regarded it as a success.

Yet there was no denying their rugged ingenuity and skill. Deadeye had never seen such large tomato plants or chickens that roosted high above them without causing a ruckus, possibly due to Creus's cylindrical shape and the centrifuges' faux gravity. People waved as they passed, dressed in similar dirt-smudged coveralls.

"Runnie, no offense, but why the fixation on dirt?" Epsi asked.

Runabout proudly patted the ingrained soil on her MPS.

"Epsi darling, we right love the soil since it makes life possible. And there ain't much good soil in the Dust Systems, let me tell you. But you can't plant seeds if you ain't got dirt, and if you can't plant seeds, well, I reckon you snuff it out like a lonely Cetian spinster."

"That's why I need you and Deadie to play the couple, Runnie."

Talon sidestepped a mud patch in the middle of the path between the gardens.

"They're not going to sell to us unless they think we're, um, going to start a colony."

"You touch her, and I'll kill you," Fluxman said. "Runnie's a good gal."

"Aww, Fluxo, you big sweet sot." Runabout swatted Fluxman's rump.

"Calm down; I'm not going to do anything you wouldn't do." Deadeye held his nose as they passed a water trough. "So we're playing up to their little space fuck cult?"

"That shouldn't be a problem for you, should it?"

Talon rolled up her coveralls, showing more leg.

"Homesteaders believe in procreation. A *lot*. With you two love birds, they'll think we're one big happy family."

"You make it sound so scandalous."

Deadeye worried that the leather boots she'd given him weren't sealed; he didn't want sulfurous mud between his toes.

"Are you sure you weren't one of those Golden Chaplains that MEC has on every ship now? One at the academy always wanted me to eat wafers off her stomach and call me 'my son.'"

Talon snorted out a laugh. "I know you're lying. No, no Chaplain bullshit here. Though I may have to hire one since you and Runnie here are *soooo* in love."

"*Merda*," Runabout muttered.

Wizard nodded at a pair of MEC soldiers watching them from a guard post. "Hey, lover boy, you might want to act that part; we're drawing suspicion."

"Yes, at least hold hands," Talon said.

"Here, happy?" Deadeye clasped Runabout's right hand in his left.

"I'm not convinced," Epsi said. "A little affection goes light-years."

Deadeye smooched Runabout's tinted faceplate. "Good enough?"

"Yep, you're a dead man," Fluxman said.

"You left slippery slobber on my helmet," Runabout said.

"That's love for you," Deadeye said.

The community took on a more arboreal appearance the farther they went into Creus. Ferns, berry bushes, vineyards, and fruit-bearing orchards grew in former maintenance pits, now filled with loam and moss from generations of hydroponics engineering. Young couples performed what Runabout called a *sardana* among the foliage, an ancient dance their ancestors had brought from Earth. Dancing in a circle with interlinked arms, the group chanted phrases about seeds, sunlight, and fertility.

"Creepy," Wizard said.

"That's why I whisper my pretty little prayers to Dame Nyx," Runabout said. "She shows us spacers where to go and makes all that darkness out there a right comfort."

"Why do you say that, Wiz?" Epsi asked. "It's charming, in a way. I always wanted to be a dancer in the Ukumbi wa Nyota at 61 Cygni. Such beautiful masks and costumes. I felt like, if I were ever on that stage, then that meant I was worth something."

"You are worth something," Deadeye said. "You don't need a stage or applause to know it. Look at what you're doing for the Spur."

Epsi blushed, then elbowed Wizard. "Well, why is it creepy?"

Wizard kept his sleeves linked to hide his tentacles. "I mean, look at them. Wizard kept his sleeves linked to hide his tentacles. So intent on making more babies, growing more food, settling more worlds, all that 'steader shit, and why? What if someone doesn't want that sort of life? I sure as hell wouldn't."

"We ain't given a choice," Runabout said. "It's spread your legs, provide for the hubby or wifey, tend the squalling infants—or get right exiled and done with. Now you hangar scamps know why I wear this here helmet, with the marriage lettering and all, that I never will see through. Makes 'em think I'm still on the lookout for a mate. Only way I get to feel free, I reckon."

"Sorry, Runnie," Talon mumbled. "I shouldn't have asked you to do this."

"Not a thing to trouble over, *capità*," Runabout said.

Deadeye squeezed Runabout's hand, and they continued on.

Four people greeted them at the entrance to Creus's colony prep deck: two women and two men. They wore brown and green MPSs fitted with coveralls; each outfit bore an elegant "HS" insignia over the name patch and shoulder logos. The individuals themselves were clean, with several piercings in their ears. Long, braided hair flowed over their shoulders. They smiled in unison at the approach of Deadeye and his friends, already sizing the crew up as if they were interviewing for breeding exchanges.

Talon did the talking, speaking the easy, drawl-like dialect the Homesteaders used. She did it so well, that he suspected she might have been a spy or a linguist before becoming a pirate. Either that, or she had a weird fetish.

Runabout looked the most uncomfortable, looking at her boots or tugging his hand, which she held so tight he feared the circulation would cut off.

Once Talon convinced the four Homesteaders that he and Runabout had plans to 'colonize' a neighboring planetoid one AU away, they agreed to let *Valkyrie*'s crew enter. Moments later, Deadeye almost wished they'd been turned down.

A great mass of humanity milled about on the prep deck, awaiting passage on Homesteader ships to other worlds. Their lustful stares and dirty coveralls didn't alarm him anymore, but the weapons they carried did. They were more heavily armed than Dhavos's Forever Girls or any other merc gang he'd seen. A MEC platoon or a Lineage honor guard would have been hard-pressed to match them in terms of small arms. Pistols, rifles, SMGs, blades, bows, and other implements of death were strapped to belts or hung from shoulder slings and bandoleers.

The only exception was their children, corralled behind a railing where they played, argued, or cried for their parents. It chilled Deadeye, who recalled how Uzari were kept apart from other humans in certain spaceports. This case gave the appearance that their progeny were just another cargo to load on their colonization vessels.

"What a shit show," Fluxman said. "I didn't think anybody but MEC did this, with their little orphanages and such. Let's get this crap and get outta here."

Talon whispered as they walked along a muddy track toward a grounded cruiser wreathed in fruit vines and bushes.

"Stop staring; they'll get the wrong idea."

"What idea would that be, that I don't want to be a piece of meat?" Deadeye walked closer to Fluxman. "Quick, protect me with your breath, Fluxo."

Fluxman farted. "There you go, kiddo."

"Thanks."

Deadeye kept covering his nose.

"They're looking at me more than you two," Epsi muttered. "Why the fuck do these coveralls have to be so tight? Even your camel toe is show-ing, Fluxo."

"It's not easy being this sexy," Fluxman said.

"Play up to them a little bit longer," Talon said. "That's probably the only way we'll get the berths, right? Look at all these people. There might not be any berths left."

Talon led them past mobs who shouted, sang, cheered, or prayed while awaiting the next transport. A hangar beyond the cruiser held several shuttles; two lifted off and flew toward bright lights far overhead: orbiting starships. It dawned on Deadeye that some people were likely doing what he and his friends did: seeking something different. No doubt MEC wanted the would-be settlers gone, keeping lawlessness down since many would likely riot if they had to remain under such working conditions.

It still felt like a big lie, however, and he guessed that many of them were going to planets that would kill them within a few months due to poor atmosphere, lack of radiation shielding, or simply poor terraforming on the part of the Homesteaders themselves. It made the singing crowds, the partying mobs, and the horny people gazing and groping at him all the more depressing, and by the time they reached the mercantile center, Deadeye was ready to fly into a red giant to escape the clamor.

The charter certifier, a middle-aged man with an eye for Talon, spoke with them from the cruiser's airlock.

"Welcome to Homesteaders Mercantile Outpost 363 K, Procyon Chapter! Please know that our charters are MEC approved, granting you a full permit to settle any territory unclaimed by MEC and its subsidiaries. Oh, how lovely you all look, and we have a married couple, too? Aren't you excited to get started?"

"Yes, of course." Talon smiled sweetly at him.

"How many make up this gorgeous little family?"

The man beamed at Deadeye, then at Epsi.

"Me, these two, and our other husband back aboard our ship," Talon said.

"You have your own vessel? That allows me to present you with an upgraded charter, allowing you to claim other non-MEC affiliated communities that you may come into contact with. Remember, Home-steaders, create a home not only for themselves but for everyone! Do you have your fertility records and marriage licenses in order?"

Talon presented the man with a forged data chit. "Right here." Talon presented the man with a forged data chit.

The man loaded the chit on his terminal; Runabout grunted as it denoted her as 'extremely fertile' and Deadeye as 'belligerently virile.' Deadeye forced a polite smile while Epsi and Wizard shared amused glances. The man finished and grinned.

"Great, I'll be back with your certification and the transponder for your ship."

"Wait, before you do that, may we purchase a set of detachable crew berths?" Talon asked. "We want to get the settlement up and running as quickly as possible."

"*Ah*, great idea! Let me check."

After the man turned and went deeper into the cruiser, Deadeye leaned in behind Talon and whispered in her ear.

"Is this all that we have to do? Please say that it is."

"It should be, all right?" Talon rolled her eyes. "I've got this, so don't screw it up."

The man returned and granted them the certification, a beacon down-link that would make *Miss Cygni* recognizable to other Homesteader vessels—and a writ for the berths. Talon turned over a small credit case, still sporting the fake smile.

"*Oho*, wait there!"

The man shook a finger.

"I need proof of consummation for an expensive upgrade like that. Did your marriage licenser observe this?"

"*Holy shit*," Wizard whispered.

Epsi turned to hide her glower, and even Fluxman looked like he wanted to spit in the certifier's face. Now Runabout's nervousness made much more sense.

"*Er*... hang on...."

Talon gave Deadeye a helpless look.

Runabout squeezed his hand so hard he gasped in pain, but Deadeye thought fast.

"We're both virgins," Deadeye said. "We're not consummating our marriage until we actually settle the asteroid. It's part of the wedding gift, really, and—"

"That's highly unusual," the certifier said. "I don't typically allow this but hey, you already have your own ship and everything, and it'd be a shame to spoil your special moment. The berths will be delivered to your ship's docking platform. Anything else?"

They declined, thanked the man, and turned to leave, but the crowd jostled around and celebrated a news update on the screen outside the certifier's ship.

The crew stared in quiet disbelief. Runabout hung her head.

It showed Homesteaders violently claiming a moon in a neighboring system, where the original settlers, not being members of the faction, had been driven out by force. The sight of burning homes, bodies in ditches, stolen livestock, and smoke columns sobered Deadeye against making any further jokes. Talon tugged at his arm, and they hurriedly walked back to *Miss Cygni*. The rest of the Homesteaders cried in jubilation at another world 'rescued,' ready for them to repopulate it.

"I couldn't get out of there fast enough," Epsi said after they left the deck.

"May the suns bless your union!" a Homesteader called as the crew passed the orchards and vineyards.

Deadeye didn't bother smiling, unable to contain his revulsion.

"I hope these berths are right worth it," Runabout said.

Talon led them past the med bots to *Cygni*'s airlock.

"I swear, they are."

Wizard shook his head. "I feel dirty after dealing with these people. Shit, Deadeye, these are the types you saved from the Harpies back at Hartwell? Imagine how much we'd had to do if that little act hadn't gotten us this fucking contact."

"I'm trying not to," Fluxman said. "I just need a beer."

Talon turned and gave them a scathing look. "Yes, Homesteaders can be bad. Aren't we all? But this isn't all their fault, got me? Look at how the Spur is now. Even after those colonists escape this place and settle some other cesspit world or even kill other settlers for the claim, they'll still be poor, uneducated, angry, and heavily armed. They don't have much choice in these circumstances. It gives a MEC a way to clean them up, and the charter certifiers don't give a fuck as long as their claims in the outer systems remain valid. They both profit."

"Isn't that what we're doing, too?" Deadeye asked. "Stealing, profiting off all the strife and disagreements that plague the Spur? That's a choice, too."

"We're Runners, for void's sake," Talon said. "We all left something behind because this life offered us a choice."

"Yeah, whatever, can we get outta these 'steader duds now?" Fluxman asked. "I have beer to drink, dolls to screw, and billiards to shoot past your Uzari boyfriend."

"Yes, we're finished here. Get on board. We're leaving ASAP."

Talon jabbed a finger into Fluxman's chest. "And he's not my boyfriend. You got that?"

After Talon got onboard, Fluxman and Wizard looked at each other, glanced at Deadeye, and then snickered. Epsi smirked and boarded *Cygni*.

"What the hell, guys?" Deadeye remembered the grease on his face and wanted a shower. "I'm just a pilot—"

"Stow that crap."

Fluxman blew a raspberry. "Hell, I'm impressed, flyboy. She must really like you. You be good to her, or I'll kill you, you understand all that?"

"You threaten that a lot," Deadeye said.

"It's the only shit that worked back when I was a magistrate."

Fluxman sniffed, pinched Wizard on the bottom, and spat on the deck.

"That, or castration. People don't listen unless you draw the line, even if you gotta draw it on their ass with a knife."

"That's good to know," Deadeye said. "But Talon has nothing to worry about—"

But the others had already boarded, save for Runabout, who stared back across the deck at the orchards, the farms.

"Hey... I'm sorry."

He touched her shoulder.

"Want to help me?" She rubbed her arms as if she were cold.

"Sure, what can I—"

Runabout embraced him and wept.

Deadeye held her for several minutes, letting her expel the hurt and shame their trip had caused her. Guilt gnawed at him, a ravenous entity that made him embrace Runabout tighter and mumble the easy lie that everything would be okay.

Her whisper was muffled through her helmet speaker.

"Swear to me; you ain't never bringing me here again."

"I swear."

"That's why I gave myself this silly callsign," she said, helmet still buried against his chest.

"Runabout, 'cause I stayed one step ahead of this here craziness. 'Cause I always got away before they hitched me to a settler. They ain't never catching me, ain't never showing my face till somebody loves me for who I am, not what I can give them."

"Have you ever thought about changing it?" he asked. "This isn't your life now. You don't have to run anymore."

"Hell no. Going to wear this name with the Dame's pride. Like the dirt on this here suit I wear. Dirt, no matter how gritty filthy it is? Dirt is where life can grow."

She drew back, squeezed both his hands, and hurried into *Miss Cygni*.

Deadeye wished he could say something meaningful or supportive, but words weren't his specialty. All he could do was stare up through Creus's large viewport overhead, where more shuttles flew to the bright lights.

CHAPTER 15

The Cepheid monastery five light-years away was a former mining depot floating next to several old probes. Both had seen better times, with the depot bearing patched railgun holes and the probes covered in defunct logos that didn't glow anymore. Spacers often claimed waypoints by placing holographic designs on them, but most ignored them. Out there, ownership was nonexistent unless one could hold it in their hand.

"This is where the Cepheids set up a monastery?" Deadeye snorted. "What, are they bringing the Holy Variance to abandoned sites, too?"

"Just you keep that heading, right? I want to reach it before 05:00."

Talon prepared for their excursion in the corridor outside *Miss Cygni*'s bridge. They'd departed *Valkyrie* twenty minutes ago, with Runabout keeping watch at the carrier. Wizard trailed behind Deadeye in *Annie Argent*, Fluxman in *Corsair*, and Epsi in *Princess*. *Santo Pohl* was still too damaged to fly.

Deadeye checked the depot's stats on his overlay while Talon suited up outside the bridge. She stripped to her underwear without care for propriety; privacy wasn't even a secondary concern on a starship. She bore quite a few of the golden tattoos on the rest of her body: water and fire spirals curling into planets and star systems.

"I hope you're focused on your targeting feeds as much as you're staring at me."

She slipped into her red MPS, then donned her MEC suit's white, armored torso piece.

"I've never seen tattoos like those, and I've seen plenty."

Deadeye took his eyes off her and studied the overlay. *Miss Cygni's* radar and scopes revealed no other craft in their immediate vicinity.

"Those swirls on your body, becoming planets and other things... you said they represent the Golden Band but do those others lead to some long-lost pirate treasure? A favorite plush toy?"

Talon winked at him. "You've been watching too many of Wizard's sword and laser vids. You already know they lead to something good." Talon winked at him.

He smirked. "Well, yeah.He smirked. But it's weird how you hate MEC but wear their combat armor. You didn't even paint over the white plates; you just reprogrammed the logos. Now that's a soldier's kind of loyalty. Am I getting close?"

"*Ha*, you'll never get closer than you are now."

Talon pulled her hair into a ponytail, donned a comm cap, and snapped on her helmet.

"You still hear me?"

Deadeye mouthed words, pretending not to hear her. Talon sighed, leaned in close, and he flipped her off. She frowned and stubbed his boot with her own.

"You can be an asshole later," she said. "Can you hear me or not?"

"Yes, your suit comm is good," he said. "Why worry about your hair? Face recognition cams and voiceprint mics will still catalog and recognize you, regardless."

"Maybe I like to be someone else when I'm out there, okay? You could use a haircut yourself, Mister Man Bun."

"I have a man bun? Shit."

He smiled as she rolled her eyes.

"That's what annoys me about you, Deadie. You pretend to forget things. I can never know when you're being serious."

She strapped on a grappling gun, her pistol, and a bandoleer of flares. Icara floated behind her, ready to provide technical or mechanical support.

"I need you to be serious now, got me?"

Deadeye shrugged. "I've got you covered. But I don't like waiting for three kilometers to starboard while you rifle around in that shitcan over there."

Talon keyed in a command to the auxiliary cargo hatch. "This is a drop-off point, and I won have my girl be a sitting duck while I grab these priests' foodstuffs. You can take evasive action at that distance should MEC or whoever shows up."

"Airlock B ready," the computer voice said.

He yawned. "I thought Wizard and Epsi were covering us? He yawned. MEC's ambushed us once already, and their III Rimward Fleet patrols this region more often than a Ringer counts their food cans. How do we know this isn't a repeat?"

"They'll cover us after they take out those probes since they're probably disguised missile sites. I saw that trick once near Sirius. Nasty business."

Talon grinned and bumped his head with her thigh as she left.

"Besides, the Lalande job was a publicly advertised contract, but this doozy is from a private customer. Be a good little Uzari and stick to my plan. Okay?"

She exited the bridge, leaving Deadeye muttering and shaking his head. Who were the Runners feeding and supplying? There weren't any rebels that fought MEC anymore, at least not in significant numbers since the Stein Revolt. The cargo stolen and distributed by the Runners... such large amounts could supply entire colonies.

I'm still here for the thrill of flying, right?

The questions nibbled at his sanity. Once this mission was complete, he'd try to get some answers. Talon kept too many cards close to her chest. Too many gambles and too many jumps.

As he flew *Miss Cygni* closer to the depot, Deadeye studied the cam feed in Airlock B. Talon waited there in her armored spacesuit—with Icara and three gunbots. They floated before her, trapezoid shapes equipped with rotor engines and air jets. This allowed them to either hover in atmosphere or jet themselves across the vacuum. Each was fitted with a short 5mm minigun that swiveled 360°. If Deadeye recalled correctly, military issue, but a little out of date. They could be deadly little bastards in tight spaces, such as a crowded starship interior.

She had to be former military. Perhaps she'd received a dishonorable discharge and didn't want to talk about it. The only veterans he'd met who liked talking about their past service were those who'd never seen combat. Those who had usually avoided speaking of it since those experiences haunted their minds every waking cycle.

"I'm ready for a quick thruster burn to the telemetry Talon ordered," Fluxman said over the radio. "Those Cepheids should appear any second, and I've got the gun ready. We wait longer than a second, and their radar will pick us up. I hope you're awake over there, Deadeye. You snore louder than two Ceti pigs fucking."

Epsi laughed. "As long as he doesn't fly like that, we'll be fine."

"Don't do shit until we light up these probes," Wizard said.

Fluxman snorted. "Think I'm some kinda rookie over here? Fluxman snorted. "Soon as those holy fucks get here, I'm disabling their power router."

"Okay, Fluxo, but hold your fire until we take out the probes," Wizard said.

"You guys always have to get into a dick-wagging contest?" Epsi asked.

"I'm not the one you gotta worry about," Fluxman said. "Our Uzari hotshot will probably try to do it all himself, like last time. You copy that, Deadeye?"

"Sorry, I couldn't hear you over the sound of two Ceti pigs wallowing in oil back in my engine room," Deadeye said.

"I can hear all of you," Talon said. "Remember: no rules means no survival. Play nice while I'm gone; this should be quick. These priests never want to join with the Variance, no matter what they preach."

"It should be easy since there are no other ships around," Epsi said. "But be careful. They could have mercs or bots."

"You just worry about keeping Fluxman in line," Talon said. "Remember how he killed that Homesteader who stole his beer that time."

"Wow." Deadeye whistled. "The man really likes his beer."

"Fluxo didn't kill that woman; his nasty cock did," Epsi said.

"He didn't need to know that," Fluxman said. "I gotta reputation to uphold."

They all laughed. Mirth was often the best cure for the emptiness surrounding them, outside their hulls and inside their hearts—he wanted to fly away from that too.

A slight gravitational disturbance came over the sensors. Gravitational lensing blurred the stars in his scopes. Deadeye squared his jaw and took a deep breath.

A new blip appeared on the radar feed.

No one broke radio silence as the new craft drew alongside the depot. Deadeye's brow furrowed; whoever had made a jump that close to a physical destination was either highly skilled—or insane. Even the best pilots exited a wormhole at no less than ten kilometers from their actual coordinates. The craft's appearance in his scopes didn't make him feel any better, either.

The Cepheid vessel was an ancient colonial cruiser outfitted with Casimir engine cones. Faint yellow running lights glowed along the bridge and airlocks. Rust and grime caked the hull, hinting that the vessel landed on planets or entered terrestrial atmospheres. Only zealous missionaries would risk such maneuvers since most deep-space crafts weren't intended for planetside.

Wizard and Epsi opened fire on the probes. Sweating, Deadeye watched as the blips vanished off his radar feed. Three new blips appeared.

"Missiles!" Wizard shouted. "AOS, five kilometers out!"

"I knew those were a trap," Talon said. "Fluxo, disable the cruiser!"

"I'm letting 'em have it!" Fluxman's railgun round pierced the hull and struck the vessel's power router dead-on, disabling all major systems —an excellent shot. They'd need to hurry before the craft's auxiliary systems kicked in.

"Deadie, dock with that cruiser!" Talon called over the radio.

Moments later, Deadeye flew *Miss Cygni* alongside the other ship. It was two hundred meters longer than *Cygni*, with four times as many decks. No visible weapons.

"Missiles evaded; I'm covering their stern," Epsi said. "*Ha*, we got this!"

Deadeye fired *Cygni*'s forward thrusters in three quick bursts, slowing the frigate enough for its docking claw to latch onto the Cepheid vessel. Talon's gunbots flew over, cut into the other ship's portside airlock, and secured the chamber. Their separate video feeds popped up as square windows at the bottom of his vision.

"No resistance, Cap'n, you're a go!" he called.

"Right, I'm in."

Talon's voice grew fuzzy as soon as she left *Cygni*'s airlock for the opposite ship.

"Well, this is weird. They're just bowing to me as I pass or locking themselves in these dirty cabins. Shit, these people bathe less than Sadistos."

Talon's helmet cam showed the truth of her statement: numerous Cepheid priests, attired in white and yellow jumpsuits, begged for their lives or pulled themselves into other chambers and sealed the door. Some bowed and made the Cepheid Crucible gesture: hands out, thumbs touching, with index fingers up like an old sports goal.

The gunbots may have been a deterrent, but Cepheids were pacifists, despite condemning non-believers to suffer eternally in the Spur's black holes. Deadeye squinted at the feed, feeling the unnerving chill of familiarity. Their vessel was decorated with white curtains that stuck out at odd angles along the walls. Plates, cups, clothing, tablets, and other belongings drifted in every corridor. Cepheids never used centrifuges, believing that gravity held humanity back. As a result, many of them were tall, emaciated, with brittle bones that lay just beneath their thin skin. They seemed to be starving, which was made all the worse because they desired such an existence.

"This is why I could never be religious," Deadeye said. "Look at them."

"*Heh*, I'm trying not to, all right?" Talon whispered. "Icara, give me a second infrared scan. There, down the portside corridor."

"Shit, these people are creeping out," Wizard said. "Let's hurry this up."

"Almost there," Talon said.

Throughout the ship, yellow lamps flared in different luminosities at timed intervals, mimicking the stars their religion was based on. The Variance taught that people should also vary their feelings, their energies, and even their love so that it would not burn out and create more Darkness. At least that's what Deadeye remembered. He worried he might have believed that nonsense and had forgotten such faith.

Maybe losing memories wasn't always a bad thing.

A few plaintive radio messages came from the depot, where Cepheid monks awaited the delivery of the cruiser's relics: pieces of starship drives from vessels that had flown too close to solar flares. Since the nearest true Cepheid star was over eight hundred light-years away, the religion often sent its followers into solar disturbances to receive the Variance's blessing—resulting in highly radioactive wreckage.

"Okay, I had to jam that garbage," Wizard said.

"Thanks, I couldn't listen to that anymore," Epsi said.

Deadeye was glad for the radio silence, but he grew more nervous as he watched Talon's foray via her helmet cam.

So many people on that ship, begging for mercy....

"C'mon, get out of my way, people," Talon muttered. "Look at this craziness."

"They're blessing you as you're robbing them?" Epsi laughed. "Idiots."

"Go easy on them; they just don't want to die," Deadeye said. "Or get robbed."

Talon entered the nearest cargo bay, and even Deadeye's eyes widened.

"It's not theft when these bastards hoard food like this." Talon entered the nearest cargo bay, and even Deadeye's eyes widened.

Dozens of food and water crates lined the bay, stacked in neat, ordered rows. Far more food than the priests and their crew would ever require. Far more, even, than their cathedral ships could distribute in the name of so-called charity.

"Where do they get this stuff?" Deadeye asked. "Some of these crates have the fancy lettering of a Lineage warehouse. Is that why we hit this ship, Cap'n?"

Talon grunted as she pulled herself over several acolytes for leverage. They clung to the deck in fear. "Noble houses sell these supplies cheap to the Cepheids, which creates scarcity, which drives up food prices on MEC worlds. Which in turn causes riots and the shitty decisions that MEC makes, letting underperforming colonies starve."

"Why?" Deadeye shook his head. "Where're the advantages to that?"

"I'll explain later, but let's hurry up, right?" Talon asked.

"That could feed, what, a few thousand people?" Wizard asked.

"And starve a few thousand more," Fluxman said. "These Cepheids let that food get irradiated near a flare star and then donate it to hungry saps who believe the Variance's 'touch' will save them. I hate that sorta shit. Want me to shoot again?"

"No, you idiot," Talon said. "Here, Deadie, line up *Cygni*'s bay with this one, and I'll get the bots to send it over. Epsi, make sure no one leaves the depot; they can have their relics after we leave. The rest of you, stay sharp."

"Copy that," Epsi said.

"Whatever, just tell me when we're done." Wizard made a snoring noise.

Twenty minutes later, Deadeye waited as the gunbots funneled one crate after another into *Miss Cygni*'s cargo bay. Talon refused to leave the other vessel until the task was complete, her pistol aimed at the cowering priests on the deck. The other pilots bantered and argued, but he kept watching his feed and pondering what he believed, about the universe, about himself. He understood that some people needed such things to help them cope with reality, but there were no gods out there for him.

He only had faith in himself.

As the bots pushed over the last few crates, a new blip appeared on the radar, accompanied by a gravitational disturbance.

"We've got company," Deadeye said. "Friends of yours?"

"What?" Talon asked. "You always ask that. Of course not."

"I got them; they're coming in fast, starboard side of that cruiser," Wizard said.

Deadeye straightened in the pod. "Talon, you're a sitting target. Get out. *Now.*"

"Almost done," Talon said.

"Fuck that; there's no time!" Deadeye cried.

"Chain of command, Deadie boy," Talon said. "Now wait."

"I hope they're MEC," Epsi said. "Or Lineage mercs. I need the target practice."

"You're crazy," Fluxman said. "Captain, we outta here or what?"

"I'm coming over to *Cygni* now," Talon said. "You all get ready to—"

The comm went dead, and Deadeye sucked in a breath.

He flipped through the frequencies. "Anyone copy? *Princess? Corsair?* Talon, Wizard? *Son of a bitch.*"

He checked his radiation sensors, but they registered nothing unusual. At least that wasn't what was interfering with radio chatter. It could be signal noise from the depot, but he doubted it. The newly-arrived craft was jamming them.

Meeting another vessel this far out wasn't a coincidence.

New blips on the radar. Streaking toward the Cepheid ship....

"Missiles!" he cried.

Yet no one could hear him, it was already too late.

A short-lived fireball flared on his scopes. *Miss Cygni* rocked as the Cepheid cruiser split into two halves. Debris rained against the hull, creating the frightening, hellish noise of metal puncturing metal. The docking claw was ripped away.

Instinct took over. Deadeye closed the cargo bay hatch, jetted his portside thrusters and then the forward starboard ones. *Miss Cygni* pushed away from the wrecked vessel and spun counterclockwise on its axis. Yaw went from 12° to 260°.

On the radar, *Corsair* and *Princess* engaged the unknown ship, while *Annie Argent* neared the remnants of the Cepheid vessel's cargo bay. Deadeye wasn't sure if their radios were jammed, but he had to assume so.

Either way, he needed to reach Talon.

The enemy vessel was as large as the Cepheid cruiser and flew straight through the debris field between the two halves of the savaged transport. Scopes granted a glance of bodies flailing in the vacuum, only to go still with a terrible abruptness. Still, the other vessel came, the corpses striking its hull and flying off into eternity. Maybe his adversary had an armored hull and didn't care, but whatever the reason, it showed a flagrant disregard for their own safety. They sped for *Miss Cygni* as if to ram her.

Deadeye flew from the vessel's path and over its hull. The scopes gave him a glimpse of a large raptor insignia.

"Harpies," he muttered. "Goddamn it. Wizard, you copy? Do you have Talon?"

Nothing on the radio. Only him, the UNS feed, and the g-forces crushing him as he made another spinning maneuver to avoid the missiles exiting the enemy ship.

"Wizard, do you have the captain?"

He hated the desperation in his voice.

Hated worrying about someone who might already be dead.

He ejected what remained of the docking claw, then turned *Cygni* over in a barrel roll, so its railgun faced the other shipSqueezed the trigger. There was no satisfaction, only the need to do something. He fired again. A proximity warning flashed in his sight, and he corrected course. *Cygni* streaked mere meters above the ship's rear-engine cones.

A dark circle grew in his eyesight, blotting out the UNS. His lips trembled. Saliva leaked from his lips, splashed over his face, and rebounded off his faceplate. Hetried to keep *Cygni* on course. Tried to breathe.

Deadeye's eyelids flipped open, and he regained control of *Miss Cygni* as she spun away from the depot, now three kilometers behind him. He'd blacked out, and the pod's IVs had administered a dose of adrenaline. He shook with unspent energy, gasped so hard his chest hurt, gripped the manuals so tightly he no longer felt his hands.

"Deadeye, shit, do you copy?" Wizard asked. "They stopped jamming us."

"Yeah... I... where's Talon?"

He corrected his flightpath, spun about, and fired at the vessel again. One of its engine cones drifted away, severed by his railgun round.

"She's still inside that Cepheid cargo bay; we gotta get her!" Fluxman yelled.

"I'm on it!" Epsi said, then screamed.

On the UNS radar, *Princess* spun out of control.

"Epsi?" Wizard asked. "Epsi girl, you talk to me right now!"

"I... arm..." was all Epsi managed.

As he brought *Miss Cygni* back into the fray, Deadeye focused his portside scope on *Princess*. Its bridge had been breached with shredder fire.

The UNS feed once again blurred.

He fought the urge to pass out, remembering when that effect had disoriented him. The first time he'd experienced it as a pilot, flying in a MEC patrol. For a moment, he tried recalling other things. Simple things, like any family he might've had, despite not having live birth parents. He tried to remember his favorite color or favorite food.

"Deadie, I need a lift." Talon's calm request brought him back into the moment.

"Dammit, is he out of it?" Fluxman asked. "He's spinning again."

"No... I'm good."

Deadeye course-corrected again and flew for the back half of the Cepheid cruiser while Fluxman and Wizard tried to engage the Harpy vessel. They were woefully outgunned, having to evade another missile salvo.

"Three hundred meters out, better be ready for me, Cap'n," Deadeye said.

Ten seconds to the wreckage, then five. *Miss Cygni* swept alongside the broken cruiser. Deadeye blinked sweat from his eyes and opened his cargo bay. Wizard, Fluxman, and Epsi hadn't spoken over the comm, and the only sounds were the occasional alarm beeps in his helmet speakers.

He kept eying the feeds in his overlay. Waiting for the moment.

The sensors detected several tiny heat signatures around a slightly larger one—between *Cygni* and the wreckage.

Talon had fired her flares.

"You want to hurry it up, Cap'n?" He couldn't keep the joy from his voice.

"Miss me already?" Talon asked.

He swallowed and attempted to fight off the dizziness.

"I...."

Fifteen meters from Talon's position.

Almost....

Radar showed a small blip coming their way from the Harpy ship. A missile.

Deadeye had no choice but to fly through the Cepheid wreckage. Traveling so quickly, the missile was upon him in a second, but darting through the damaged ship's cramped interior paid off. The missile clipped a piece of shredded decking and exploded. The blast shook *Miss Cygni*. Multiple damage warnings lit up his feed. Teeth gritted, Deadeye flew out the other side of the wreckage.

"Do you have Talon?" Wizard asked. "Answer me. Do you have her?"

Deadeye grew cold in the pod. "No, I—"

"I'm on *Cygni*, but I need to puke now," Talon said.

He checked the cam feed in disbelief. Talon was there, just now manually closing the cargo bay hatch. The grappling gun was strapped to her belt, a cable extending from it to a piton-tipped round implanted in the bay wall. She must have gotten inside right before he evaded the missile and clung to the service ladder. Icara was attached to her belt via a tether. The gunbots and half of the food crates hadn't been so fortunate— they'd tumbled out during his maneuvers, jumbled by the missile's explosion.

Relief was short-lived as the radar showed *Princess* still spiraling away. The Harpy vessel jetted its lateral thrusters to reorient itself. He guessed they had railgun batteries at the ready and didn't plan to be around for that shit show.

"We need to get out of here," Deadeye said. "Epsi, you read us?"

No answer.

"We're not leaving her," Wizard said.

"Maybe she's gone, the Runner way," Fluxman said. "Sorry, man."

"Eat shit, Fluxo," Wizard said. "I've got a heat signature over there."

Deadeye sped toward *Princess*. "Epsi, you read me? I still want that hot pink MPS you promised me."

"We have to get the hell away from here," Talon said as she pulled herself into the bridge. "But if we can get her...."

"Talk to me, Epsi," Deadeye said. "If you can hear me, flash your landing lights."

Princess's landing lamps flicked on and off.

Deadeye smiled and slowed *Cygni* as they drew close to *Princess*.

"Okay, so I was wrong now what about these Harpy assholes?" Fluxman asked.

"They're in railgun range," Wizard said. "Hurry it up, Deadeye!"

"I see it on my overlay," Deadeye said. "I'm going to dive, then pull alongside *Princess*'s bridge. It'll be pretty damn close. You got me on this, Cap'n?"

"I've got you!" Talon cried as she hurried to the airlock.

"You idiots," Fluxman said. "There's no way we can pick her up before those Harpies open fire; we'll be—"

"Right there."

Deadeye fired the port thruster and opened the cargo bay hatch.

Talon was once again on the radar, no more than a pixelated blip glowing in his vision among the names of stars, nebulae, clusters, and the other craft in their vicinity. The Harpy vessel had a crew, too, and a pilot trying to outmaneuver, outfly, and outthink him. It was different from what terrestrial pilots must have experienced in Earth's past, of seeing one's opponent or a planetary horizon. Yet out there in the void, there was no up or down, no guiding landmarks. It was him and the UNS and what- ever data the sensors could fill his biological brain with. A machine could do it better, but the Casimir drives demanded a human pilot. Human triumph at the risk of human error.

He had to ensure his next move wasn't an error.

"Shit rounds coming in hot!" Fluxman yelled.

"Great, I lost my starboard thruster," Wizard said. "Any time now, Deadeye!"

No time to worry about them or that Harpy vessel. All energy had to be focused on those blips, on Talon and Epsi leaving that shattered, bullet-ridden bridge....

"I've got her; close the hatch!" Talon cried. "Fluxo, Wizard, punch it!"

Deadeye drew away from *Princess*, fired the rear thrusters, and left the depot, wrecked cruiser, and Harpy vessel far behind. Seconds later, Runabout was radioing them from *Valkyrie*, ready to jump as soon as they arrived.

A victorious smile came over his face before he blacked out again.

CHAPTER 16

"YOU REALLY ARE A STUBBORN SON OF A BITCH."

Deadeye moved his head toward the voice. His eyes opened, but it felt like a machine pried the eyelids up, not him. Soft white light made him squint. A slight ache in his right forearm told him that another IV had been plugged into his body. Hands dabbed his cheeks with a wet cloth, then cranked something on his left. The universe moved upward, and he went with it until the white light shone directly on his face.

Vestiges of the UNS overlay popped in and out of his vision. The coordinates weren't correct, he'd never reach that blue world.

Unless....

"I can fly through it," he mumbled. "Give me the manuals; I can do it."

His body twitched and jumped of its own volition.

"Nobody's giving you anything unless it's my boot up your ass."

That voice again, a woman. She sounded more amused than angry.

Boots. Ass. Boots on blue regolith. Troops outside the village had to fly around it, strafe those bastards, had to—

"Take it easy there, *capità*. He's going through some right serious hypnogogic jerks."

A different voice, softer. Feminine.

"A good shock isn't enough for him," a male voice said. "Now we have the Harpies trailing us. And we know why. All because of that mess at Hartwell."

"Listen here, you, he saved those Homesteaders, and not even the

Dame herself would deny it, so don't be waggling lies off that tongue," the second woman said.

"I'm just saying shit like that has consequences, Runabout," the man said.

"Wizard? Runabout?" Deadeye coughed as the overlay finally faded from his vision. The white light came into greater focus. It was a lamp in *Valkyrie*'s cramped med bay. The chamber stank more of alcohol than antiseptics.

Wizard shook his head and drank from a vodka bottle. Runabout waved at Deadeye and swayed her hips in what he assumed was her happy dance.

"You guys lived?" Deadeye laughed. "I told you that village wasn't...."

"See?" Wizard asked. "Poor bastard doesn't even know where he is."

"He's made a lot of jumps in the last few weeks."

Talon swept the cool, damp cloth over Deadeye's forehead, a relieved smirk on her face.

"*Heh*, I'm amazed he's even talking. Why the attitude, Wiz? He performed well out there. You all did."

"Look at what it cost us," Wizard said. "All for some goddamned food? Please."

"Say, can we argue at the moot? I like my med bay quiet, thank you." Epsi's calm tone made the others blanch and look away.

Deadeye glanced at her cot on his right.

Epsi's left arm was gone below the elbow, and the left side of her face was heavily bandaged. A med bot hovered above her, completing a diagnostic scan. Its report made Deadeye blanch. Epsi had suffered three broken ribs on her left side and a ruptured spleen. Though the shredder rounds had also destroyed one of her kidneys, she was stabilized. The printer could fabricate new organs, but an arm was another matter.

"I'm sorry," Deadeye said.

Epsi shrugged. "Don't be. The shipping data for those food crates have the merchant signature of House Traxe on them, so at least I stuck it to those assholes one last time. Good thing you sent Icara into that corridor to examine that terminal, Talon, or we'd not known who traded in that food."

"Yeah." Talon looked away. "At least now some colony will get to eat and spend their credits on better shielding or decent water purifiers, rather than over-priced food from MEC's merchants. That's how they keep people down."

"Looks like I'll be down for good," Epsi said.

"Screw that; you'll fly again; we can get you a cybernetic arm at the

Runners moot."

Wizard paced the chamber, swishing the remaining vodka in the bottle.

"Or we'll get you a single-handed stick like the old colonials used. But you're not out."

"She'll have to be confined to *Valkyrie* for a while," Talon said. "Listen, I know it sucks, Epsi, but you need to heal, right? Now I have to deal with Fluxman. He's saying he'll quit this outfit, but you know him and his bitching."

"He's the smart one." Wizard glanced at Deadeye and left with Talon.

"Ignore old Wiz; he's all puffed and pruned because Epsi got shot up," Runabout said. "People will eat now, and that's nothing to fret and frown about."

As Runabout exited the med bay, Deadeye rose from the adjustable cot.

"I, um, need a drink," he said.

Epsi smiled sadly. "No pilot likes to be around an injured shipmate. It's a reminder that the same can happen to you. I understand."

He paused, then faced her. "You're staying in the Runners after this?"

"What else am I supposed to do? Would you quit?"

"Hell no."

They shared a smile.

"Now you know why I waste my credits on vanity nonsense or getting laid, or spas and the like."

Epsi winced as she shifted on the cot.

"I never had any of those things when Traxe owned me, and I'll be damned if I'll not have them now. Not when each flight might be my last. Shit, you know this already. You're a pilot; you get it."

Deadeye smiled. "It's okay. But don't you wonder what drives Talon? She spends her share on the crew or our ships; she doesn't talk about a family or ever settling—"

"She's got you," Epsi said. "Or am I misreading what's between you two?"

"I'm not even sure what's between us," he mumbled.

Epsi sipped from a water dispenser near her head. "That's what makes it exciting. Epsi sipped from a water dispenser near her head. Who cares what drives her? This is life. This is who we are. Just accept it."

"Maybe it's those old books I read, asking questions like that."

She snorted. "Still droll. I see the captain milling around out there in the corridor. Never keep a woman waiting, flyboy. Besides, I want to sleep awhile."

Talon waited outside the med bay, back in her red fatigues. She looked him up and down, rubbed her temples, then touched his shoulder.

"Okay, then, Mister Hotshit, how do you really feel?" she asked. "I know you're too proud to say much in front of the others."

He ran a hand through her ponytail. "You've never blacked out during some high-thrust maneuvers?" He ran a hand through her ponytail.

She playfully slapped his hand away, then frowned.

"I'm serious, all right?"

Deadeye started to answer, but the recollections of the village he was supposed to strafe had gone. Who was he talking to, again? The evacuation boats had departed, and he'd been left with the task of jumping from the system with the remainder of the colony staff.

No, wait. Was this the med bay aboard Santo Pohl? Wow, the physician had gotten much more attractive. Maybe I need to pass out in the pod more often....

"Hey... so how do you feel?" Talon's question was softer as she tapped his hand. "You're worrying me, Deadie boy. And I don't have time for worrying."

"I'm good."

Deadeye flexed his fingers and blinked a few times.

Damn.

The overlay finally vanished, he had been disconnected from the UNS.

"Need me to make another jump? We're looking for a relic left by that Kattral prick, right?"

Talon flashed a concerned glower.

Deadeye laughed. "Gotcha! I'm good, really. We still took plenty of those food crates, I hope? Sorry about your gunbots. Now I don't have any competition."

Some tension left Talon's face. "I'm not into bots, hadron brain. Sure, we have half of those crates left, which is better than nothing. The Harpies wanted that haul, too. They were going to ram *Cygni*; I watched it all from what was left of that Cepheid cruiser. That's a Harpy for you—they'll try anything, take any risk."

"Like us?"

She frowned. "Nothing like us."

"That was pretty convenient, the Harpies showing up at that monastery."

He searched her face for the slightest crack in her façade.

"Suspicious, even."

Talon said nothing, but she stared holes through the hull.

"Cap'n... the coincidences of that are almost nil."

"I was a Harpy before joining the Runners," she said. "My first pirate outfit, and heh, my last. They're very cruel, and you can't trust any of them. So I left."

"Is that why you didn't want me firing on them when I saved those Homesteaders at Hartwell? If they're assholes, why care?"

"They're more vindictive than you realize, Deadie. They probably have been tracking us ever since that happened. Many other spacers saw us dock on Kattral's level at Hartwell, so it's not hard. Besides, this haul I've got has been in the planning for a long time. You're going to back out on me now because you're scared of a few psychos in a stolen MEC cruiser?"

"A cruiser armed with missiles and railguns," he said.

Talon massaged her forehead. "Please not now, okay? I still feel like total shit after getting Runnie to do that thing back at Creus, and now Epsi is... *goddamn*, I keep doing this to all of you, and I can't...."

He hugged her.

Embracing him right back, her shuddering breaths heated his neck as she leaned into him. "I shouldn't be your captain. I shouldn't involve you at all...."

"We all chose to be here."

He stroked her ponytail.

"But... I know something's eating at you. Driving you. It's not credits, or the crew's problems, either. Is it?"

"Will you leave it alone? Come on. I need you."

She walked down the corridor.

Deadeye let it go and followed. He'd hoped to get the truth out of her, but Talon's deflections bore an angry veneer disguising something else, pain. She was guilty of something. The entire enterprise wasn't just about landing a big haul—it was personal. Like all personal endeavors, once you let another person in, it becomes something else. The more people knew about it, the heavier the responsibility. For that reason alone, he understood why she didn't want to tell him. But he and the crew were risking their lives for her to deal with that guilt. There was an emotional deferential there, and he didn't want to be on the negative side.

"We're going to a Runner moot at Sirius," she called over her shoulder. "Closer to the Ross Boundary than I like, but we can get this food to people who need it through those channels."

"That's what, about five light-years?"

Deadeye struggled to catch up. Still weak from the jumps and still too stubborn to admit it.

"Something like that."

She walked faster, driven by that internal obsession.

"So what goes on at these moots? Do I finally get my own red jump-suit and golden tattoos? Maybe I can drink Fluxman under the table at the Runners' flesh club?"

"There's no flesh clubs at a moot."

Talon stopped at the hangar bay door and gave him a disapproving look.

"Not that you'd participate in such activities, right?"

"Certainly not, Cap'n."

"We're not married, Deadie. We're not even in a relationship contract, the way. Homesteaders do it. You can fuck anyone you want."

"That's not what I want."

She bit her lower lip and stared over the hangar. "Will you help me with *Santo Pohl*? The bots have fixed most of the damage MEC dealt it, but there's more we need to do. The others need a rest, and Wizard is probably giving Fluxman a pity fuck right now so that drunk will stay with us."

"Sure. What do you need me to do?"

He wouldn't dare let on that he'd seen her display even the slightest shred of vulnerability—or that it made him feel naked, too, unshielded by his usual bullshit. Yet, at that moment, he wanted to be around her more than flying, and he didn't recall ever feeling that way about someone before.

Like Epsi had said, this was life, this was who he was, at least while his mind lasted, and he should accept it. Savor it.

For the next several hours, with the aid of repair bots, Deadeye and Talon modded *Pohl*'s Casimir drive. First, the parts they were supposed to have delivered to Kattral, then the elements she had pilfered from *Happy Maui*. *Pohl* still needed a refurbished hull and a better pod, but by the time they'd finished, the ship had the potential to travel faster than anything else in *Valkyrie*'s hangar. Its improved hadron compensator would push it to the level of a Mark III, making voyages in one-third of the time it took a Mark II.

Casimir Mark III. The fastest device humans had ever created.

"Where did you learn to put all these components together?"

He tugged off his work gloves and leaned against *Pohl*'s engine room hatch.

"Surely Wizard could have provided better help than me or Fluxman.

Hell, I'm not even good at holding a wrench."

Talon undid the kerchief wrapped around her brow and tossed it into a laundry bin.

"I told you, this has to be kept a secret for now. I trust the others, but a Casimir Mark III? That could test anyone's loyalty—shit, especially credit-hungry pirates. Do you have any idea what this thing would be worth? Ha. But no one will expect this sort of engine on a little shitcan like *Santo Pohl*."

He smirked. "How do you know I won't make off with it and sell it at Hartwell or some crazy spacer who wants to settle the Ring?" He smirked.

"Because you're my Deadie boy," she said. "Plus, I'm promoting you to lieutenant, and you're getting plenty of hush totty from me in my bunk."

"I wasn't aware that was a transaction."

She undid her ponytail and loosened her collar. "It isn't. When it does, that's when it stops. Got me?"

Deadeye walked around the fusion core housing, admiring how polished it was compared to the rest of the chamber's grunginess—admiring how she had deflected him.

"You still haven't answered my question."

She stared at him. "Does it matter where or how I learned to get this rig ready?" She stared at him.

He drank from a water bottle. "Not everything has to be a secret. He drank from a water bottle. It's a simple question. I'm not MEC customs, Talon. I'm only curious."

She walked around the engine, occasionally touching or tapping it like someone who had achieved a goal but was uncertain about how to proceed.

"I used blueprints I acquired from a Lineage server. Not many ships in the Spur have this technology, save for the nobility's personal vessels or MEC's top-of-the-line warships. Mark IIIs are riskier to use, and they eat hadrons like candy."

"Are you trying to have the fastest vessel in your little Runner armada? Or is this to help us land that massive haul you keep hinting at, the job to end all jobs?"

Talon studied the engine with satisfaction. "Speed means more than profit."

"Freedom, then?"

He set the repair bots into rest mode.

"For some," she said with a too brief smile.

Afterward, they sat before the hangar viewport, sharing a beer, her sitting in his lap. He toyed with the hairs along the back of her neck while they stargazed.

"How many do you think you've visited?" he asked.

"Every star on this end of the Spur, out to twenty-two light-years or so."

She undid his man bun and braided it into a facsimile of her ponytail.

"And you?"

He sipped the beer. "Lots of them."

"Yeah."

A brief sadness passed in her eyes, then she feigned a smile.

"Don't feel sorry for me, Talon. Now, or ever. Promise me that."

Her hands lingered on his braid. "Never." Her hands lingered on his braid.

"Is that book still in my cabin?"

He tilted the beer to her lips, and she drank deep.

"Oh shit, here we again with your precious little book."

She burped, then laughed.

"You're obsessed with that old Earth cult. But everybody needs a hobby—"

"Hobby? It's educational, flyboy. Did you know that the earliest spacefarers wore water-cooled undies beneath their suits so they'd not get overheated? They didn't have the heat dissipaters we have now. Maybe that's what you need, to keep your crotch rocket in line."

He chuckled. "Yeah, but one look at you naked, and I could heat your coffee."

"You're damn right."

She kissed him.

"So, the Earth cult? Come on; you're not distracting me that easily."

"Okay, here's one thing that catches my curiosity about the Sagittarii, right? All these stars and we've found none, absolutely zero, that have a planetary system like Earth's. What I mean is a moon like Earth was supposed to have. That old story about their moon being at the right distance and size so that it occulted Sol?"

He pinched her bottom. "Occulted? He pinched her bottom. Now you sound like a Badawi scholar."

She kissed his cheek. "Oh fuck off. She kissed his cheek. But seriously, right? They called it a solar eclipse. Some say it scared the hell out of primitive humans, who didn't even know what their sun really was, much less why it became dark suddenly. The Sagittarii still keep track of those events with all sorts of calculations and mark them as holidays."

"Is this one of those holidays?" he asked.

"It can be."

She gently pushed him onto the deck and straddled him.

Later, while she snoozed beside him atop their clothes, Deadeye kept staring out the viewport. A moon that made a sun disappear. It sounded like a children's story, of having one celestial body so perfect in size, in relation to another, that it defied coincidence. He shook the empty beer bottle and sighed. Fantasy and its comfortable lies were the greatest drugs of all. But that was how the human mind worked: always refusing to believe what was right before it.

Just like he refused to believe he could ever forget about Talon.

The next five sols passed in the typical UNS fugue state for Deadeye. Talon relieved him from piloting as *Valkyrie* stopped to refuel at a spaceport set on an asteroid, a little floating shithole called Grand Nero. The merchants wanted extra for the few hadrons they had on hand, and the presence of Thule Freelancers guaranteed that any piratical raids would be costly. *Valkyrie* jumped another three light-years afterward, with Wizard in the pod, but Deadeye spent that time recovering in his bunk.

No drinking, no holo billiards, no Starrio... no time with Talon.

The nightmares and cold sweats returned. Once, he was able to sleep on his bunk for a few hours, but he used the floor again the rest of the time. No one came to comfort him or offer melatonin tabs when he awoke, cursing, swinging. He'd not realized how important it was to have someone who could help. Who cared.

Talon busied herself modifying *Santo Pohl* every waking cycle—adding the detachable berths, installing a small complement of missiles taken from *Valkyrie*'s magazine—but she always brought his final meals at 18:00. And she always asked random questions before kissing him and leaving. The questions were tests, checking his memory. He didn't blame her, but it depressed him all the same. The second sol, he tried watching a few sword and laser vids that Wizard recommended, but the tales of shirtless heroes blasting diabolical villains on Mars, Eridani Prime, or the drifting space tombs of the Tolteca bored him.

The tits and titans feeds were as simple and pornographic as he'd suspected, but he quit watching them after one actress reminded him of someone. It was doubtful he knew the person, but the illusion of memory and its tricks on him robbed such trifles of their entertainment value.

He read the books Runabout had bought for him—especially the

Sagittarii one. The cult believed that Earth's ancient cultures should be preserved across the stars, which might have accounted for some of the earlier colony names, like New Ypres or Tashkent Beta. They also reviled the Prestige and any sort of machine intelligence and frowned upon human genetic variants—such as himself.

They considered themselves guardians of humanity's destiny and had several saints. Key among them was Pietist Bester. The book showed a picture of her in shell-like silver armor, standing atop a heap of smoldering Prestige drones. He wasn't sure if it were a myth, religious propaganda, or both.

Why Talon was obsessed with the Sagittarii, he couldn't fathom.

On the sixth sol, *Valkyrie* shuddered as it exited the wormhole, but Deadeye was already awake. The chronometer read 09:00. Back in the navy, he'd have already been up for several hours, manning his station, waiting for the klaxon noise of general quarters, which called the crew to ready for battle.

The village. The Stein Revolt. That's when he'd fired on those people.

His cabin door swished open, interrupting his revelation.

"You have twenty minutes, so get cleaned up."

Talon wore a finely-tooled vinyl jumpsuit dyed dark purple.

"C'mon, Deadie boy, wakey wakey and all that crap. You need to impress these other Runners, and it'll take more than cheesy flirting and boasting. Can you manage that?"

He smiled and rolled off the bunk. "Does a Homesteader shit in a crater?"

"Good."

Talon watched him for a moment longer, then left, calling over her shoulder.

"First, we'll deliver part of the food we took from the Cepheids; it shouldn't take long if our contacts follow the rendezvous. Then we'll be on *Xīng Huā*, a Runner carrier that plies the lanes around LHS 288. Their gravity is set to 1.1, so be ready."

"I'm always ready, Cap'n."

His magnetic soles clipped to the deck since Talon had already powered off *Valkyrie*'s centrifuges to save energy while they attended the moot. He glanced at the books on the way out and wondered if all that reading had helped him remember the Stein fiasco.

Maybe that was why Talon kept reading them.

CHAPTER 17

THE FOOD DROP-OFF POINT WAS A SMALL FLEET OF MERCHANT vessels bound for a colony deeper in the Sirius system. Talon allowed one of their shuttles to ferry the food crates back and forth to the other ships outside *Valkyrie* while she kept a close eye on the proceedings. One never knew when MEC might infiltrate such a group, and the merchants would be disguised, armed jarheads instead. If any assailants tried to board the carrier, Talon had two gunbots guarding the hangar.

Deadeye leaned against *Miss Cygni*'s hull while Talon stood nearby, arms crossed, frowning. He sipped water from a bottle, the last of their stores, until they resupplied at the moot.

"They're moving as fast as they can," he said.

"They're still taking too long." Talon took the bottle and drank.

"Not everyone can go like you can, Cap'n."

She arched an eyebrow and passed the bottle back to him. "What's that supposed to mean?"

He shrugged. "Look at how this outfit operates. From one mission to the next, with little to no rest between. You push us more than a naval crew in wartime."

"Aren't we at war, against letting people suffer... lieutenant?"

"I wonder if you're at war with yourself, too."

He offered a polite smile.

Talon gave him an annoyed glance. "You can handle it, Mister Hot-shit. So can the others. Talon gave him an annoyed glance. "What's your real point?"

Deadeye eyed the remaining water in the bottle. "I don't know. Maybe this sort of thing is easier if it's not based on revenge? Or hate?"

She neared him and slowly uncrossed her arms. "You think that's how it is?"

"You're driven, so damned driven, Cap'n. You've been avoiding me, and that's fine; I know there's no obligation in what we have with each other. But you're obsessed with *Santo Pohl,* and you haven't spoken much to anyone else since the Cepheid op. I can tell when someone's being eaten from the inside—because that's how I feel sometimes."

"You're just a lieutenant, a pilot." She snorted. "Not a psychiatrist."

"I care about you. That's all the credentials I need."

"But you don't know what I need," she said.

He stared at her in puzzlement. "I'm trying—"

Voices carried across the hangar. Deadeye and Talon faced the merchant shuttle.

An older man tried to shush and hold back a group of children, but the kids hurried toward Talon. Each wore ragged jumpsuits or patched overhauls that practically hung off their emaciated frames. They had sunken cheeks and swollen bellies.

"I am so very sorry for their rudeness; they do not understand," the man said. "They have never seen a Runner up close. I couldn't leave them on the ship, you see...."

"Are you a Runner?" a little boy asked. "A real Runner?"

"Wow, an Uzari, too?" a girl asked. "You're so tall!"

Another girl stared up at Talon in awe. "You're so pretty. Are all Runners as pretty as you are? You're like Nyx herself."

The old man shoed the children away. "I apologize; they slipped past me out the airlock; I will get them back aboard."

Talon smiled at the children. "No, it's okay. Talon smiled at the children. Yes, we're Runners. I hope you're ready for what we brought you: cantaloupes, squash, pasta, sweet gherkins, oranges, beans, and maybe some chocolate, too. Do you like chocolate?"

"I've never had it," the boy said.

"Is it brown, like poop?" the first girl asked. "I heard it's brown."

Deadeye laughed. "Yes, but it tastes great. Here. Make sure you share this."

He pulled a can of orange juice from his belt and handed it over—his last one. The children eagerly accepted it, joking about who would get to drink it first.

"Please, we must go, but thank you so much."

The old man started to bow to her, but Talon grabbed his hand and shook her head.

Talon grinned. "You are very welcome. All of you." Talon grinned.

The third girl turned and spoke as the man led the kids away.

"Could I be like you one sol? A pretty Runner, in a pretty uniform like yours?"

"Of course, you can," Talon said. "*A les estrelles!*"

The children repeated the phrase, boarded the shuttle with the old man, and left the hangar. Talon watched them go with the saddest expression he'd ever seen on her.

"Hey, they'll be fine," he said. "That's a lot of food, and—"

She shut her eyes and sighed. "He tried to bow to me." She shut her eyes, sighed, and opened them.

He smiled, hoping to cheer her up. "It's that accent; maybe he thought you were nobility. You did say you came from a rich family."

"And no matter how hard I try, I can never get away from it."

She walked to the bridge elevator, leaving him alone in the hangar.

Deadeye regarded her receding form with an uncertain yearning, finished the water, and watched the merchants' vessels disappear into the blackness.

Though the moot was a gathering of ships fifteen AU from Sirius A, the binary system's white dwarf, the captains met on *Xīng Huā*, situated in the center of the gathering. It was an older carrier than *Valkyrie*, with smaller hangars—but more of them and bearing larger engine cones, some the size of *Miss Cygni*. Lighted viewports dotted it, a city adrift in the void, where life and possibilities might meet.

Or, Deadeye hoped, some easy credits—and easier answers. Talon still hadn't told the rest of the crew about her grand haul or the true nature of her modifications to *Santo Pohl*. Keeping a secret wasn't a difficulty for him.

Watching that secret exploit others...that was another matter.

Once Talon's crew passed through the joined airlocks, Deadeye squinted. A crimson, diffuse haze lit the first chamber, and he realized it came from a series of red paper lanterns installed in the ceiling. Once his eyes adjusted, he found it quite lovely, casting everything in rosy shades. Two bots hovered over, offering cups of tea on lacquered trays. Talon urged everyone to drink with a commanding glance; he assumed it was social etiquette and would be rude to refuse. The tea possessed a slight sweetness.

"*Ooo*, they're treating us with honeyed tea."

Runabout set her empty cup back onto the bot's tray.

"Reckon, this oughta be a pretty pickle show."

Talon downed her tea in one gulp. "Just keep that swagger to yourself; there's lots who will lure you with a marriage contract. Talon downed her tea in one gulp. I need my Runnie, okay?"

The two women shared a long look, and they squeezed hands. It lifted a weight on Deadeye's heart; maybe they'd reconciled over what had happened at Cap de Creus.

Runabout elbowed Talon and continued. "*Hah*, ain't going nowhere."

"Why the tea?"

Deadeye kept pace alongside Talon, but the higher gravity made his joints ache.

"An ancient Earth custom meant to make them look hospitable," Talon said.

"And are they?" he asked.

"We're all flying for the same cause, but there are lots of pirates, mercs, and outlaws in these outfits," Talon said. "Wait here, let me log us into the manifest."

As Talon walked over to a terminal, the rest of the crew waited, fidgeting, checking their mobiles. Deadeye was calm. Since he'd been expecting a rowdy group of privateers, their respectful reception so far surprised him.

"And dying just the same," Fluxman muttered, wearing his magistrate fatigues. "I'm not for this team bullshit. Nobody is here for that, except to make some credits."

Epsi winked. "Are you going to be a downer on this trip? Epsi winked. You don't see me complaining, Fluxo."

"No... guess not."

Fluxman glanced at the hoverchair Epsi sat in, cleared his throat, and nodded. Until her internal injuries fully healed, she'd not be able to walk, but she had refused to be left aboard *Valkyrie*.

"Easy, Fluxo, we'll get some drinks, then you'll be fine," Wizard said.

Though he never left Epsi's side and regarded their surroundings cautiously.

"Should we be worried?" Deadeye asked in a low voice. "You're spiffed up for a person going to a meet with other pirates."

In his black and silver jumpsuit, Wizard glowered for a moment and squeezed his tentacles together.

"I hate it. Talon always talks us into doing this because image is everything to spacers, especially Runners on this end of the Spur. But I don't live this life to impress anybody."

"Then why do it?"

Deadeye gestured at the Runner carriers outside the viewport. "You don't seem like the pirate type to me. You speak in complete sentences; you actually practice hygiene, you don't engage in affairs with sex dolls...."

"Eat shit, Uzari boy," Fluxman said. "Touch my girls again; you're dead."

Wizard and the others laughed, then he sighed.

"Talon doesn't need Fluxman, Runabout, or Epsi. She could do all of this shit with bots, except for you and me, because she needs an Uzari or a Zyn for the jumps."

Epsi looked down at her lap. Runabout's shoulders slumped, and she gazed out the viewport. Fluxman's typical frown deepened.

"Oh, come on." Deadeye shook his head. "That's not true; we're all good pilots."

Wizard gave the Runner armada a forlorn look. "Some pirate crews are all bots now, with the captain and pilot being the only humans. Talon gave us home on *Valkyrie* like I told you. She gave us a chance to be something we can't be out there, at least not right now. Yep, there it is. You and that goddamn smirk."

Deadeye waved a hand in deflection. "I'm smiling because that's great. Not many people out there would care enough to do something like that. Talon's treated me better than I have any right to. Even though I've saved your asses... I've lost count."

Despite his joking demeanor, he wondered how many jumps Talon had made in the pilot pod. How much she had placed onto others instead of doing it herself.

"That's it; I've had it with this outfit." Fluxman groped his crotch.

Wizard stalked over to Fluxman, tentacles clenched. "You really going to stay on, or will you find another crew at the moot? Wizard stalked over to Fluxman, tentacles clenched. Because you'd better fucking not. Talon doesn't make friends easily. Neither do I. You think about that too, Deadeye."

"I'm staying; get off my ass," Fluxman said.

Deadeye raised both hands. "Hey, loyalty, I get it. I plan to stay on, too. Unless some cutie captain seduces me with Vegan wine and a ship all to myself."

"The hell you will." Talon rejoined them. "Who else would have you?"

"Sadisto keloid artists?" Deadeye asked.

"Let's find out."

Talon led them through the next hatch once *Xīng Huā*'s techs completed their scans. A cold or stomach virus on one ship could prove fatal to the crew of another, and MEC lacked enough vaccines, which was the one thing they gave freely.

The air inside the next chamber smelled of old plastic and human sweat. Even though one grew accustomed to the smells of one's crew-mates, whenever encountering the aroma of other outfits, it came as an olfactory shock. Deadeye had heard it was due to the confined spaces aboard starships and the human nose's tendency to highlight strange scents. Whatever the reason, he forced himself not to hold his nose.

The strains of plucked zheng carried across the chamber, adding to the veneer of calm discourse. Other Runner gangs milled about tables and refreshment stands that held a variety of food and drink from across the Spur. The spicy jalapeño scents of Tolteca cuisine mixed with the briny, sweet aromas of soy-covered vegetables from Han gardens. Some tables had bowls filled with oranges, apples, mangoes, and pineapples—rare fruits grown only in the best hydroponics labs. More paper lanterns hung overhead in a collection of colors that went from dark red to light yellow, granting a brightening effect the farther one walked into the room.

The other Runners numbered less than fifty, with some groups consisting of just the captain and pilot—underlining Wizard's comment about automated crews. All wore varying degrees of pomp and finery, with one woman decorated in feathers and gold and a man outfitted in an ancient Kevlar suit complete with laced boots. Yet for all the lively conversation, the musicians performing in the corner, and a few gambling on a *pai gow* match, the crews regarded each other with guarded glances.

One table housed several thin individuals in piloting fatigues. Some stared into space, open-mouthed, while others chatted to themselves about jumps and distances.

Deadeye's skin chilled despite his suit.

They were Uzari. They'd flown so many jumps by all appearances that the UNS dominated their minds, even when not connected to a pod. The other Runners either pointedly ignored that table or snickered at those Uzaris' mentally-defunct states.

"Easy, Deadie," Talon whispered. "I swear, we're not all like that, right?"

"What a happy gathering," Deadeye muttered.

"This is the happiest I've ever seen a moot," Epsi said. "The last two ended in violence between two rival outfits. I still got laid, though. Twice."

"The Harpies aren't part of the Runners now, nor are those assholes from the spinward Ring worlds," Talon said. "This should be peaceful, okay?"

Epsi eyed the pistol on Talon's hip. "You wore that in here, though." Epsi eyed the pistol on Talon's hip.

"It's for show; I've never drawn at a moot," Talon whispered.

"First time for everything." Deadeye nodded to a crew approaching theirs.

"Fuck, here we go," Fluxman muttered.

In matching black bag suits that miners wore in the pre-MEC trading wars, seven people came over and blocked *Valkyrie*'s crew from the refreshments. Upon their arrival, the other Runners quieted. The musicians stopped playing and stared at *Valkyrie*'s crew as if Talon had requested they play a Homesteader breeding ditty.

"So you're back, and with new faces, too," a voice called across the chamber. "You don't even follow the Runners' code anymore, bringing whomever you please."

Deadeye and the others turned. Talon wheeled about slowly as if she had all the time in the galaxy—while keeping a hand near her holstered pistol.

A short, muscular man in black fatigues walked over and stood with the bag suit crew. Wushu tattoos lined his temples and chin, accentuating his stiff, military bearing. Indeed, anyone who had earned the markings of that ancient art was formidable.

"You stand this guy up on a spacewalk date or something?" Deadeye muttered.

Talon poked him in the ribs without taking her eyes off the other captain.

Talon grinned politely. "You've kept *Xīng Huā* in excellent shape, Jiàn. I can't even see those railgun holes you earned at Eridani. And, hey, these new lanterns are a nice touch. Sort of posh and comfortable."

The other Runners either snickered or bristled at that comment; Deadeye knew it was a criticism, inferring that Jiàn and his crew hadn't been flying the space lanes lately or had grown soft. Pilots kept their reputation through deeds as well as personality.

Jiàn's smile was cool, patient. "No Runners in this sector can be comfortable after you've broken our truce with the Harpies, bungled a Lineage contract, and got ambushed by a MEC patrol. Fewer people are hiring us now, which means more families in the Dust Systems are starving. Unless you have something special up those purple sleeves, I'm challenging your captaincy."

"Hey there, we drank the welcoming tea," Runabout muttered. "That means we have hospitality rights and all that—"

"Not now, garden gnome," Fluxman whispered.

"*Ha*, we never should have made a truce with those Harpy pieces of shit."

Talon examined her gloves with disinterest.

"But I see word travels fast for those who have nothing better to do. Or do the colonists at LHS 288 have better homes now? The last I heard, the storms left them living in the mud."

Jiàn's face hardened more if that were possible. "That has nothing—"

"These lanterns couldn't have been cheap," Talon said. "How many housing modules would all this bullshit have bought on the Freelancer market?"

"I've lost eight people in the past month," Jiàn said. "Maybe you should ask them. These lanterns you keep criticizing? At a higher price, I bought them from colonists so MEC wouldn't get too suspicious as to how those same colonists managed to purchase more rations this season. No one is slacking here, Talon."

"Good, because we haven't been, either."

Talon tapped her mobile, and a holographic readout flashed above it.

"I've got enough food left to feed at least, oh, eight thousand colonists. It's from House Traxe, traded to the Cepheids. So challenge all you like. And my new people? They made that happen, so screw the initiation stuff."

An air of respect descended on the gathered crews. Some nodded in approval. Jiàn gestured, and one of the bag suit guards displayed a holo on their mobile. It showed where the food would be headed—several colonies as far out as Ross 882, abandoned by MEC. Some were blockaded by Lineage ships to pry goods from the people in a food racket. A Runner outfit would fly that blockade and deliver the food.

For the first time, Deadeye felt good about what he had accomplished with *Valkyrie's* crew. With Talon. He shot her a congratulatory grin, which she returned.

"Ah, then I have another challenge."

Jiàn dropped his attempt to boot Talon from the Runners all too quickly; that was a lot of food, probably more than any of the crews had stolen in some time. Diplomatic as well as opportunistic.

"Name it." Talon crossed her arms, looking bored.

"I finally have a lead on the Tombs."

Jiàn flashed a victorious smile, a genuine display that bore no sarcasm. "They are real. Not a legend."

The other crews gaped and whispered amongst themselves. The rest of Talon's shipmates shared incredulous looks, but Deadeye frowned in confused ignorance. Talon herself stared at Jiàn with an unassailable focus.

"You'd better not be joking," Talon said.

Jiàn held up a hand. "Wait. Jiàn held up a hand. The only issue: we need a highly-skilled pilot and a crew that can handle such a find."

"What's the matter? Nobody here can manage it?" Wizard asked.

"Two of my pilots have died trying." Jiàn frowned again. "One was a Zyn. The route is tricky, full of wreckage, false beacons, and volatile fusion drives that explode at the slightest disturbance. The UNS can't always be trusted to navigate it."

Talon smirked and nudged Deadeye forward. "Then here you go. My Uzari flyboy will get us to the Tombs."

Deadeye blinked. "The Tombs?"

Jiàn chuckled. "You present this pilot as your best, and he doesn't even know what the Tombs are? Jiàn chuckled. I think you're lying to us again, Talon. Like you lied to that rich bastard from House Kattral. This isn't one you can skip through."

Talon sauntered over to Jiàn, ignoring the guards in the bag suits. "Okay, then. Test Deadeye in the navigation simulator. When he proves you wrong, I'll leave right away. Unless you have something better to offer?"

Jiàn looked at the other crews and finally smiled: a thin, humorless look that underlined the warning in his eyes.

"This is one of the most important finds in decades, and we need to get there first. Everything we've been flying for—dying for—this might make it worth it. Be ready to jump a sol from now, Talon. That should give your hotshot here plenty of time to rest. If he passes the simulator test, that is."

Talon returned the smile, the two captains nodded at each other, and the musicians started playing again. Crews returned to their drinks, carousing and laughing.

"There goes all the drinking and whoring I planned on doing," Fluxman said.

Wizard snorted. "I can make that flight, Talon. You know I can."

Epsi sighed. "This was the shortest moot I've attended."

Runabout danced to the music. "Reckon we all got dressed up for nothing." Runabout danced to the music.

"You're still wearing the same suit and helmet, garden gnome," Fluxman said. "And I say let Deadeye do it, Wiz. It's suicide, anyway."

"Everybody shut up and have fun, all right?"

Talon motioned them over to an empty table. "I need to sort this out."

"So, where am I taking us?" Deadeye whispered as he sat beside Talon.

"The Tombs is a ship graveyard a few light-years from here, between star systems," Talon replied in a low voice. "There's plenty to salvage and loot, as long as you can find the place. Most pilots fail to fly through the debris and wreckage fields, as it's hard to pinpoint the best jump coordinates since the fleet is constantly drifting through space, and the numerous beacons are all giving false positions and whatnot."

"So... what can I expect to fly through?" Deadeye asked. "I want details."

Talon took one of the oranges on the table and held it up.

"Am I supposed to get flight prep from a citrus fruit?" Deadeye asked.

"Imagine this is the region around the Tombs, right?" Talon pried apart the orange, revealing the white lining and the moist slices inside. "There's a treasure in there, but you've got to go through all this first. The peeling, the inner liner, the seeds, the slim core. That's what flying into that place will be like. You'll jump to the coordinates, but you can't use the UNS to navigate all the anomalies and wreckage."

He plucked one of the orange slices and pried the white liner off it. "Simple."

Talon snatched the orange slice from him and ate it. "*Ha*, nope. Not at all."

"Okay, so what's there that is so special to the Runners?"

He took a beer from a server bot, but Talon yanked the bottle out of his hand.

"Nope, I need you sober. See, Deadie boy, the Tombs were a bunch of colony ships that never reached their destination. There should be preserved food, frozen water, spare parts, and even whole engines and hadron cores. The Runners could really use such a haul. We must get to it before anybody else."

His eyebrows raised. "Okay, but what's so special about this lost fleet to you?"

"It might have something we need."

She chugged the beer.

"We all need something," Epsi said. "Seriously, what would you do, captain, with more wealth than your bots could count?"

Talon set down the bottle. "I'd have better beer, for sure. Talon set down the bottle. Jiàn gets the best tea this end of the Spur, but this swill would make a Sadisto gag. He's getting cheap."

"What is it with you and Jiàn, anyway?" Deadeye asked.

Talon toyed with the empty bottle. "I'll need another beer for that." Talon toyed with the empty bottle.

"Ah, *capità*, that was a nice little fairy tale," Runabout said. "Deadeye, Jiàn got Talon here into the Runners, see, and I reckon he regrets that now, sure enough. But you shoulda s seen them two, like a pair of doves in a gilded heart cage!"

"Shut it, Runnie," Talon muttered.

"You were Jiàn's lover?" Deadeye smirked. "That explains everything."

"Love ain't the word for what those two got down to." Runabout giggled.

Talon kicked Runabout under the table but gave him a sweet smile. "Jealous?"

"Me?" Deadeye asked. "I can't remember how to be jealous."

They all laughed, had a few more drinks—save for Deadeye—and pretended they might not die trying to navigate the Tombs. Deadeye might be the lead pilot, but the others would follow his path to maximize their haul. The crew told wide-eyed dreams about lost treasures, impossibly fast stardrives, preserved celebrities in cryopods, or forgotten technologies that might change the Spur. Spacer's tales that covered their uncertainty with silly hopes of what might be found in the ancient fleet.

A few faint recollections of similar gatherings passed in Deadeye's mind. The barest memory of faces in a galley, where other MEC personnel bragged and told outrageous stories about their actions and how far they'd traveled. Boastful lies that were meant to cover the mental strain of killing other human beings or deal with the long jumps that became an ever-widening gulf between a spacer and their families.

A starship crew became the real family, the people one lived and eventually died with. There was no physical or emotional connection to parents, siblings, or homeworlds. One had to find those things where they could, be it another pilot or a battered frigate.

"So why are you picking Deadeye over me?" Wizard opened a beer and sipped it. It smelled like fermented piss ran through a dirty pipe.

Talon laughed. "You haven't forgotten how to be jealous, I see. Talon laughed. That chit I got from Kattral's data broker on Hartwell? I loaded it up, and went through all those coordinates Deadie gave them. They're bullshit leads, but his mind raced from one coordinate set to another without mixing them up. That takes some serious mental processing. No one else in the crew can manage that, or in any of these other outfits, I'll bet."

Fluxman grunted. "If he's so good, why didn't the MEC navy keep him?"

The others lowered their drinks and regarded Deadeye with curious stares.

Deadeye looked back at them, hiding nothing. "I wish I knew." Deadeye looked back at them, hiding nothing.

"No one that good gets demoted to flying a damn cargo ship," Wizard said.

"I want to know as much as you do," Deadeye said. "But I don't."

Wizard took a long drink. Fluxman shook his head and mumbled.

Talon rapped the table. "*Pohl*'s manifest just listed him as an Uzari navy veteran, but I know he can do this; that's all I need to know. So that's why Wiz. Let's get Deadie to that simulator; then we can make the jump. If Jiàn has found the Tombs, someone else might have, too, or will soon. Let's make this happen; you got me?"

Deadeye stood, as much to get things going as to avoid further questions about his past. "I got you, Cap'n."

CHAPTER 18

The journey to the Tombs took thirteen sols. Though Deadeye passed the simulator test, Jiàn had been reluctant to turn over the fleet's actual location. Only the promise of much-needed supplies gleaned from the derelicts changed his mind. Talon talked her former lover out of enough hadrons to get *Valkyrie* to the Tombs, which didn't sit well with the other strike group captains. The exotic matter wasn't easy to come by, and Talon promised great rewards for such an investment.

So his outfit was running on momentum, as old spacers liked to say. Yet he knew Talon had more engine fuel than she let on—and he suspected it was on *Santo Pohl.*

Deadeye made the first jump, and then Wizard, which granted Deadeye a few sols with the rest of the crew before they reached their destination. But that precious time was spent mending *Santo Pohl* with Talon—in secret. They patched its hull and sealed the bridge breach. Wizard was in the pod, Epsi still needed rest, Fluxman repaired *Princess,* and Runabout kept *Valkyrie* in working order. They all thought he and Talon were languishing in a bunk and never asked otherwise.

He wasn't sure what they really were doing, or why he was helping Talon. The obsession burning within her was like a different sort of star he was trying to reach, only it remained distant, elusive. If he got too close, it might incinerate him.

On sol five, *Valkyrie* had to exit its jump due to navigational obstacles. Since Wizard remained unconscious in the pod, Deadeye rushed along with the others as the alarm announced a call to general quarters. Recollections of his naval service haunted him as he ran with the others to the bridge. Battle stations. Had to suit up, make sure his helmet was connected to the oxygen tank correctly, don't say anything to hinder morale....

What they found left him unable to sleep for a cycle afterward.

A merchant fleet had been blown to pieces, its wrecked vessels clogging the space lane where most pilots plotted their wormholes in that sector. The damage to the hulls was familiar to Deadeye. He'd seen it before. Up close and personal.

"This is one helluva scavenger haul," Fluxman said.

Epsi glowered at Fluxman. "*Fuck*, read the room." Epsi glowered at Fluxman.

"Hey, I'm only saying," Fluxman said. "Those people out there don't need any of those things now. Don't moralize that shit with me."

"Dame Nyx, take them home, deep through darkness and grand through the stars," Runabout whispered.

Deadeye rubbed his face. The Tombs felt more daunting now.

Talon glanced at him. "Shit. Look at all this. What are you thinking, Deadie?"

"It's the Prestige."

He pointed at one of *Valkyrie*'s scope screens, which magnified debris that was one thousand two hundred kilometers away.

"See the blast damage on that one's bow? It's from a Prestige fusion torpedo. Hard as hell to outrun those, and countermeasures aren't worth a damn. And when it hits, it practically melts through the hull. Armor plating doesn't mean dick. That's what MEC created shredders for, I think, to shoot those things down."

"And that's if the shits don't hack every bot on your ship afterward," Fluxman said. "I hate bots. Never know when they might turn on you."

Icara flew a circle around Fluxman's head, but he shooed her away.

"You too, even if you have been helping me with Princess," Fluxman said.

"Runnie, any life signs out there?" Talon asked. "Heat signatures?"

"No, *capità*," Runabout said. "Ain't detecting nothing but dead fusion cores."

"Why would those automated assholes strike a merchant convoy this far from the Boundary?" Epsi asked. "I thought their drones concentrated near there, after the war."

Deadeye shook his head. "Not unless there's something their hive mind ordered them to protect out here. Like the Tombs?"

The others grew silent, staring at the wreckage via the scopes.

"We're getting back on course regardless," Talon said. "We can't stop now."

"We going to scavenge anything?" Fluxman asked. "Hey, it needed asking."

"No, we don't have the time," Talon said. "If there were life signs, I'd risk it."

"Fuck, what happened? Who are you, people?"

Wizard turned in the pod, blinking away fugue stupor.

"Easy there, Wiz." Talon patted his shoulder. "Just some... debris, that's all. Can you re-coordinate the jump? We have to get going, for the Runners, right?"

Deadeye exited the bridge, no longer wanting to see through those scopes.

Sols later, while *Valkyrie* waited outside the fleet's debris field, Deadeye flew out in *Miss Cygni*, with Talon onboard. Runabout followed in *Annie Argent* and Fluxman in *Corsair*. Epsi kept Wizard company back on the carrier, though he could tell she hated it. A grounded pilot felt they were more useless than wings on a deep-space freighter.

Not as useless as he'd feel if they ran into that Prestige fleet. Nothing in the Runners' arsenal could deal with them.

Deadeye sucked in a breath once *Miss Cygni* entered the Tombs' debris field. The UNS overlay filled with a cacophony of data, much of it contradictory: stardrive signatures appeared a few kilometers to port, then the same signatures reappeared a mere four hundred meters off to starboard. Transponders that advertised their vessels as battleships, while the actual craft was a cargo transport. Radar sweeps came back as clogged feeds after they'd passed a few kilometers into the field since there was so much wreckage. It forced him to depend on scopes, which had a much more limited range.

It was like flying blind.

He wanted to wipe his moist brow but couldn't due to his faceplate. Talon sat beside him in the captain's chair, wearing her spacesuit. One hull puncture would rob them of atmosphere and pressure, and the suits allowed them to save on life support. She didn't look at him as she checked the computer console's readout.

Minutes of tense silence passed. Runabout and Fluxman followed less than two hundred meters between each Runner vessel in his wake. One piece of wreckage drifting out of synch with the debris field could take them all out. The ancient fleet possessed its own rotational cycle, like a rogue celestial body cast adrift between star systems. Deadeye had to obey that rotation in his flight path, even as he kept course-correcting to avoid the scattered, dead colony ships.

Talon gaped through one of *Cygni*'s scopes. "All these people... Makes you wonder what the hell happened to them, you know? Who might have punked them."

"Don't... have a... clue," he muttered, trying to pass between two jagged hulks that might have been starships once.

The UNS showed them as giant shapes that flickered in and out of existence, while the scopes granted a horrific, all-too close view of a snapped leviathan that might atomize him.

Talon leaned back from her console. "Phew, fucking finally.Talon leaned back from her console. You did well; we bypassed the outer layer of hulks and wreckage. Engine economy is at 18%. That's... better than I expected."

Deadeye coughed and drank from his helmet's water tube. "We've still got all these ships to navigate around. *Ugh.* Brain freeze."

Talon turned in her seat and offered a slight smile. "Thirsty?"

"It's this pod of yours. I told you, it needs larger nutrient canisters."

"Then drink up because I need you to be ready," she said. "Fly to that vessel, the one 23° to starboard, 48° roll axis. There, I highlighted it on my console. It looks less damaged than the others we've passed."

He laughed dryly. "Ready for what? A surprise inspection? The Prestige?"

"You better hope not." Talon stood and paced the bridge. "Runnie? Fluxo? We're heading for that intact colony ship, 23° starboard, 48° roll A. Get ready."

Deadeye brought *Miss Cygni* along the vessel's portside hull, where a large, rectangular depression led deeper into the craft's interior. A hangar.

"Cap'n?" he asked. "You sound like you might know. Ready for what?"

"Anything." Talon headed for the airlock.

Talon headed for the airlock.

He whistled a few notes of the old Homesteader song and sighed. While Talon prepped several bots to guard *Cygni* and their comrades brought their ships alongside, he peered through the scopes.

The intact derelict was a large ship, at least two kilometers long. It preceded the current era, dating before even the Ross Boundary itself. He grimaced; it was an ugly cylinder with more cargo berths than thrusters, meaning it was intended for a one-way voyage. He'd heard stories that ancient colonists utilized their starships to create their new homes, living in the same damn eggshell they'd spent years traveling in.

"We'll need to access this ship's nav system ASAP."

Talon narrowed her eyes at the camera in *Cygni*'s airlock chamber, knowing he watched her through it.

"I know you've just flown us here, and your mind is tired, but if I could connect your feed to this ship's computer?"

"I'm not a hacker, Cap'n."

She grinned at the camera. "If you could navigate that system, it could pinpoint what I'm looking for better than Icara. No hacking, just browsing.She grinned at the camera. All right?"

"How did you get this sorta info, anyway?" Fluxman asked, his voice filled with static. "You've never mentioned anything like this to us."

"I'll explain later," Talon said. "Let's get it done, okay?"

Deadeye loaded up their helmet cam feeds in the UNS. "I'll try, but these older ships don't have a UNS. I'm not sure how much help I'll be."

He jetted the thrusters for a split second and eased *Miss Cygni* right beside the large hangar.

"I know I'm asking a lot... but this is important."

Talon urged him on with her slate-grey eyes. Once again, asking him for something while she promised more ambiguities.

"Enough to buy better beer? Sure, Cap'n. I'm in."

The smile she flashed was all he wanted.

"But you'll have to enter this behemoth with us," Talon said. "I'm picking up radio interference as soon as I near this hangar, and you'll lose connection with us as soon as we traipse inside. You can't do this from your comfy little pod."

"Shit." He raised his brows and chuckled. "I don't want to be a liability in there—"

"You won't be; I'll have you." Talon winked. "See you down here in five."

Less than five minutes later, Deadeye stood in *Cygni*'s airlock chamber. Runabout and Fluxman had already jetted over from their ships.

Runabout examined Deadeye's suit and grunted in approval.

"So you do know how to wear one of these, that's right and true, a good thing. Thrustpack looks good."

"And here I thought Uzari always lived in those stupid little pods," Fluxman said.

Deadeye smiled, but Fluxman shoved him through the airlock.

"Sometimes we get to go on vacation." Deadeye smiled, but Fluxman shoved him through the airlock.

"Hey, go easy now; a stray piece of debris out there will zip right through these fucking suits," Talon said. "Besides, I wanted to do that."

"Thanks," Deadeye said.

The movement sent him spiraling across the space between *Miss Cygni* and the derelict. It would have been a foolish act in any other situation, but *Cygni* was less than twenty meters from the ship's hangar. Deadeye didn't even have to correct his trajectory with his thrustpack and enjoyed the view. Stars and ships rolled across his vision as if he were traveling through a tunnel. Cracked hulls and engine cones, hundreds of meters distant, were visible due to the sparse illumination offered by *Cygni*'s running lights. Some stars vanished at regular intervals, eclipsed by wreckage in the darkness.

"Something is keeping all this scrap close together, a source of gravity," Deadeye said. "Do you think it's an even larger ship?"

Talon jetted over to him, followed by Runabout. "It could be.Talon jetted over to him, followed by Runabout. Or it might be a collapsed wormhole drive that made the tiniest of black holes instead."

"That bullshit's a myth," Fluxman said.

"These here Tombs ain't," Runabout said.

"Head for that hatch on your right," Talon's voice grew patchy over the connection. "If these old schematics I have are correct, it should lead to an egress that ends in the ship's main concourse."

"Since it's the only one I see, sure."

Deadeye's thrustpack jetted a burst of nitrogen, and he veered toward the hatch.

"Why am I the first one? Talon has the gun, Runabout has the dance moves, Icara has the tools, and Fluxman has those burps."

"I'm staying on *Cygni* with Icara," Fluxman said. "Rule number one about being a pirate: never leave your ship unmanned."

"Good advice."

Deadeye grasped the hatch's handrail as he drifted near it. It struck him that he was likely touching a centuries-old vessel.

What it must have been like, flying one of these....

Flying into that trap where the Stein ships had shot down his comrades, one by one. Their marines, boarding his craft, trying to force their way into the bridge....

Deadeye blinked and shook his head. The memory faded.

Talon and Runabout appeared beside him, their boots touching the vessel. The hull's absorption of their momentum sent a slight tremor over the metal surface, which he felt on the handrail.

"You're not going to zone out on me, are you?"

Talon extended her torch and started cutting into the hatch.

"You weren't answering us on the radio."

"It's probably signal disturbance from all these wrecks."

Deadeye didn't look at her. He'd been trying to remember, to summon those fuzzy realities from his brain that had seen too much UNS use. Too many stars but not enough light.

"Sure."

Talon's faceplate tinted as she deftly cut around the hatch's edges.

"So much for preserving the past," he said. "Why not have Icara do that?"

"These older ships have tricky dickey security systems that target bots."

Runabout helped pry the hatch open where the vacuum had cooled the seared metal.

"If we'd brought a bot along, it'd set off whatever nasty alert system haunts this here vessel. I ain't much liking the idea of cutting through every single hatch in there if there's a lockdown."

"Ah, the Prestige again," he said. "Great. And that's assuming the ship's computer is still operational. Easy, those slag pellets might puncture this thin suit. I've seen thicker tissue paper."

"You're alive, aren't you?" Talon asked.

She, with Runabout's aid, pulled the hatch free. It drifted away into the void. She winced and cradled her wounded shoulder.

"I'd like to stay that way. You go easy on that shoulder, Cap'n. Hey, wait... what do you mean, security systems? It's a colony ship. With cryopods."

He followed them in as his helmet lamp activated.

"Frozen people shouldn't need security."

Runabout tugged him along by the arm to keep pace with Talon, who had jetted her thrustpack to speed down the hatch's access shaft.

"Earthers were a weird lot, they must have been running from something awful rather than settling all these fine worlds just to spread humanity across the stars and all."

"They hated bots," Talon said. "Maybe it had something to do with the Prestige, even back then, who knows? Just don't touch anything."

"Kind of takes the romance out of it, doesn't it?"

Deadeye glanced at the intact bulkheads they passed, the lack of grime. "At least the place looks clean."

"*Heh*, let's hope it's not picked clean," Talon said.

"So... what's here to be picked, anyway?"

Deadeye hoped to cajole a hint out of her regarding their excursion.

"That's where you come in, my daring Deadie."

Talon exited the shaft first and caught herself on a railing outside, waiting for them. Runabout came next, with Deadeye last. The shaft terminated in a vast, circular chamber filled with floating crates and tools. A single body in an ancient IVA suit drifted past, clutching the utility knife they'd used to sever the crates from their tethers along the walls. The IVA bore a patch that read "SAG" in large blue letters.

The rest of the ship's interior was a bedlam of mashed bulkheads, burnt walls, crumpled ramps, crushed terminals, and savaged walkways. A few gaping holes here and there hinted at what had happened to any wreckage and bodies. They'd been suctioned out into the debris field outside upon the vessel's exposure to vacuum.

"This must have been one hell of a battle," Deadeye said. "The breaches are directed outward—maybe someone set off grenades or charges inside?"

"Prestige?" Talon asked.

"Maybe."

He gazed around, fighting the urge to jet back to *Cygni*.

"Okay, this got butt-biting creepy real fast," Runabout said.

"Stay close to me; I'll protect you with—oh, that's right, I wasn't given anything to protect myself with."

He shot her a mocking grin.

Talon jetted among the crates, examining each one. "What's wrong now?" Talon jetted among the crates, examining each one.

"Only one dead guy in a suit."

Deadeye pushed through the crates to the other side of the chamber.

"We're fine, don't worry."

"*Pshaw*, the only thing worrying me is no Fluxo on my radio."

Runabout held up three fingers to the corpse, the sign of Dame Nyx.

"Ain't even static from him, *ha*."

"Our connection is getting more static," he said. "A jamming device?"

"This isn't what we're looking for anyway, so let's keep moving," Talon said. "And stop worrying about the Prestige, Deadie; you're stifling morale. My schematic says we should make a left at this corridor."

Runabout patted Deadeye's shoulder and used the crates to push herself to Talon.

"Careful, now. This ain't nothing like that wreck we scavenged at Luyten's."

"This next hatch leads into the main concourse," Talon said. "Shit. I wish this were as easy as that run at Luyten's. If there's a security system still active...."

Deadeye took the utility knife from the corpse. It looked as perfect as the sol it'd been fabricated, printed on one of the ship's machines. Only MEC offered a titanium alloy blade with a tungsten edge in its best fabbers. He was surprised the two women had passed it up—until a red light flared above them.

Talon and Runabout shot him a look.

Talon pointed at his hand. "Goddamn it, flyboy!Talon pointed at his hand. Drop that damn knife!"

"*Huh?*"

He did so, and the light continued to flash. Deadeye pushed off the dead body and spun around—then he spotted it.

A fine laser tripwire beam. It had been set right on the corpse, and his taking the knife had disturbed it. He'd wondered why someone had cut the crates free... they were supply containers labeled for food, tools, and oxygen. A theft that the bots had been waiting for? That meant any other provisions on the ship would be trapped, too.

"Well, shit."

"Come on!"

Talon motioned him and Runabout to follow her through the next hatch onto the concourse.

"What'd he do?" Runabout asked.

"Flyboy just fucked up everything, that's what," Talon said. "Cut off your suit's heat dissipaters and CO_2 vents, both of you. Their heat sensors might not find us. Don't radio, don't jet, don't fucking move."

"It'll get hot in these suits," Deadeye said. "And we'll be breathing carbon dioxide after about a few minutes."

"Better that than dead in thirty seconds," Talon said.

Runabout was the first out the hatch, then she pushed herself backward and waved for them to stay back. She pointed at her neck and made a cutting gesture. Cursing, Talon drew her pistol. A moment later, Deadeye saw why.

Three floating forms moved about outside the hatch on a wide concourse lined with cryopods. Red security lights flashed above them, reflecting off their silver, trapezoid bodies. Each was outfitted with a gun pylon that swiveled 360°.

They looked like Prestige security drones.

Runabout started to crawl backward, but Talon held her in place and steadied her with a calm look. Deadeye didn't move as a cool resolve washed over him.

Several minutes passed as the mechanical guardians surveyed the concourse and made a sweep of all connecting hatches and corridors. Deadeye's exhalations increased, and he felt slightly disoriented. Dizzy, even. It was the unfiltered carbon dioxide inside his helmet. Sweat slid down his earlobes, onto his cheeks, and pooled around his collar.

His faceplate fogged up. The temperature inside his MPS had increased from 20° Celsius to 26°. His forehead throbbed with a headache.

As one bot flew near the hatch Deadeye and his shipmates had almost exited, Talon went limp and allowed herself to float in place. Runabout did the same, and Deadeye followed suit, imitating the dead body they'd encountered a few minutes earlier. It was a risky ruse; if the bots possessed adequate sensors, they would know Deadeye and the others were alive.

One bot paused near the hatch. Its gun pylon swiveled, and multiple camera eyes installed over its body panned in various directions. Deadeye got a better look at its weapon: a rapid-fire needle gun, likely equipped with toxic flechettes that wouldn't pierce a starship's hull. The dead person had probably died quickly.

What was so special about the Tombs that the Prestige guarded them?

The drone jetted away across the concourse and entered a cubicle inset into the ceiling. A small hatch closed back over it, hiding the cubicle from view.

Talon, her ownfaceplate fogged over nodded and waved at him and Runabout. They spent the next minute purging the excess CO_2 from their helmets and allowing their heat dissipaters to lower their suits' temperatures. Deadeye gasped and shivered in relief.

Talon sighed and hung her head. "Motherfucker. That was close."

"It's gone for now."

Deadeye clambered past them and pointed at the concourse ceiling. The red lights had been deactivated.

"Sorry about that, Cap'n. Won't happen again."

"Yeah, that makes me feel safe," Talon said.

Deadeye smiled. "At least we know we're not alone in this hulk. After you?"

He gestured out of the hatch.

"That was still stupid, just so you know," Talon said. "I'm hurting you later."

"What in the void did you want with that knife, anyway?" Runabout asked.

Deadeye grunted. "To cut to the chase? Deadeye grunted. Listen, with fabbers that can make tools like that, and Prestige drones with toxic needle guns... I think it's time you leveled with us, Cap'n. What's in here? You have schematics for an ancient colony ship, and you knew these people loathed bots. Anything else you think we should know?"

"I think it's time for you to connect to the nav system on this wreck... then I'll tell you."

Talon looked at him, then at Runabout.

"Listen, let's get what we need to find the real haul we're looking for. Before those shitcans wake up again."

Deadeye wanted to say more, but she was right. They'd need to act fast because he suspected, the security protocols would reactivate once he accessed the nav system.

The concourse was lined with dozens of cryopods inset into the walls. All of them were attached to a life monitor; each one featured a glowing red square, indicating that the frozen occupant was dead. He glanced at the faces still visible through the lightly-frosted cryopod covers. Men, women. No children, since the ancients had sent only adult colonists at first.

Now, even infants were transported with ease across the dark expanses across the Spur. He wondered if they had dreamed until the end of their lives, forever awaiting a new life just beyond the unconscious walls of stasis, much like his own existence. Just another dream, another memory, another recollection, and he might know who he was, where he'd come from, or his real name.

But he was still alive, unlike these corpses in frozen repose. Still capable of forging some sort of destiny across the stars. Even if it was for a pirate captain who seemed more concerned with secrets than riches, secrets lasted longer.

They finally reached a terminal at the end of the concourse, one hundred and twenty meters deeper into the vessel. Communicating via hand signals, they maintained radio silence. Talon nodded at the terminal, tapped her helmet, and pointed at him.

After taking a breath, he nodded back and ran the connection cables from his helmet to the terminal. They were already attached to the jack in the back of his neck. Talon watched anxiously as he booted the ship's nav system and accessed a login screen. He glanced at her, waiting for the required credentials to allow access.

Runabout frowned at Talon and tapped her arm. Talon shook her head.

His excitement waned. *No password?*

The login screen flickered, then an overlay appeared before his eyes. An older version of the Uzari Navigational System, rudimentary and straightforward. It worried him that he'd been given automatic access until he loaded up what the ship contained in its databanks. Coordinates and numbers scrolled down the overlay.

"Holy shit," he breathed, breaking the silence.

CHAPTER 19

The first thing that came across Deadeye's overlay was the
ship's name: *Unrelenting Mercy*. A strange title, hinting at a savage determination to do what someone thought was best for humanity. As he
scrolled down the overlay's feed, his eye movements guiding the interface,
that resolve became apparent: the vessel had traveled many light-years to
reach what was now called Vegaspace, around the Vega star system—but
it had flown off-course and drifted across the space lanes ever since.

The reason: a mutiny had happened on board *Mercy*. One led by a
faction that didn't want the ship to reach its destination. They were the
fleet's security forces: an elite military branch called the Sagittarii.

The corpse in the IVA with the SAG patch....

Deadeye kept scrolling through the report. It was biased, written by
the ship's chief security officer, who'd sided against the mutineers. Still,
one thing was clear: the Sagittarii believed that humans should try to
reclaim Earth instead. Yet it was forbidden to do so. There was no
definitive reason given other than some great calamity. To combat the
mutiny, *Mercy*'s leaders had deployed the Prestige Protocol.

His body chilled. The Prestige had been built by ancient humans and
replicated themselves into deadly fleets; that was common knowledge—
but he'd never heard of a colony ship using them against their own people.
The act backfired, and the drone ships destroyed most of the colony fleet,
scrambling transponders, and beacons to ward off any other mutineers
and prevent their escape.

The Sagittarii who'd survived the mutiny departed the fleet in a
stolen shuttle while the remaining colonists journeyed on to their doom,

adrift between star systems without proper power or caretakers. Thousands of people in stasis never woke again. The Prestige had pursued the Sagittarii across the Spur, leaving only the security bots behind. All of that, centuries in the past now.

He'd never heard of the Prestige being constructed for such a purpose, but he recalled battling its automated vessels and how, once MEC gave up on the Boundary, the Prestige ceased its attacks. The Stein Revolt had transpired shortly afterward since people still wanted new worlds to settle, despite MEC's defeat. That's when the calculated abandonment of colonies had started—the deliberate weakening of the Spur's civilization in a twisted effort to hold it together.

It was still ongoing. The very reason the Runners existed.

But all of that mattered little compared to where *Unrelenting Mercy* had been. Drifting through the Dust Systems for centuries, the vessel's nav computer had recorded those trajectories and coordinates, granting access to alternate routes across the space lanes that could prove valuable to MEC, the Lineage, the Homesteaders—and pirates. Even routes leading deep into the Arcturus Ring, sometimes as much as sixty light-years out from the Golden Band. Such knowledge could lead to new habitable worlds and end the Spur's strife.

"Is this why we came here?" Deadeye uploaded the data into a drive installed in his suit.

"More Sagittarii legends? There's stuff in here about the Prestige protecting Earth from... MEC? From all of us?"

Talon's eyes widened. "So it is in there! Hell yes, we've got this, we can—"

"This wasn't for the Runners at all... was it?"

He turned from the terminal. "No food, water, supplies, forgotten technology—just this."

"You saw those supply crates back; they're all set with tripwires, I'll bet," Talon said. "There's nothing else to salvage here—"

"Cap'n..." Deadeye said.

They stared at each other, then she waved her hand dismissively and smirked.

"Now you ask me something like that?" Talon asked. "Hurry it up, okay? We need a flight report written by Ensign Tasha Bester. I hope to the void it's on this ship."

"Pietist Bester, the armored, saint-like woman from that book?" he asked.

Runabout shot Talon a look. "That's why we trekked to these Tombs?

A dead woman's report? Here now, something stinks here, and it ain't last week's space diapers."

"We're already dead in this line of work, but some of us like to live a little before admitting it."

Talon tapped his shoulder. "C'mon, flyboy, continue. Don't make me shove my boot up your ass. I know an Uzari can do this faster than—"

"Did you treat Jhio this way?" Deadeye asked. "How many times did you tell him an Uzari could get it done quicker or could fly better?"

"What the fuck did you just say?"

The breathless anger in Talon's voice seemed to fill the entire concourse, but he didn't back down.

"Did you treat Jhio this way?" Deadeye held her gaze.

"You bastard!" Talon grabbed him by the collar. "I never asked him—"

Deadeye snorted. "What he wanted? Deadeye snorted. The Lalande job, the Kattral contract, those Cepheid monks—all these missions for your secret project. You keep doing this, again and again."

"Doing what, keeping us all alive?" Talon asked. "You got somewhere better to be then go. We're making a real difference out here; we'll change the Spur—"

"For who?" he asked. "You're pissed because you feel guilty, am I—"

"Just get it done."

Talon's reply bore an edge to it, but he didn't care. He wasn't another tool to use and discard like she might have used Jhio. Runabout was right to be concerned. The crew, and the rest of the Runners, were expecting a large haul from this endeavor, and what Talon was doing was beyond suspicious now.

He wouldn't be able to lie for her anymore after this—but he wanted to know.

After resuming the connection, Deadeye searched *Mercy*'s manifest, then cross-referenced that with the fleet's crew complement. Such ancient armadas usually kept a record of everyone involved in the mission, on each ship, in the event the other vessels were lost. He'd heard tales of how some older fleets kept the DNA of all its crew frozen on every ship in the event that if one perished, another could be recreated. It was a laughable concept, but it was a familiar hubris. Colonizing other planets where humans shouldn't be... they'd all been modified somehow, just to survive out there.

And the Sagittarii had demanded a return to Earth—and been denied.

The datafile appeared in his overlay: Tasha Bester. Ensign aboard a small cruiser that accompanied the colony fleet. He scrolled down the feed, then loaded a catalog enumerating all the vessels in *Mercy*'s little caravan. Sure enough, Bester's ship was among them—along with its logs, shared across the fleet's network. He downloaded the file, wondering how much of it he'd remember after a few more jumps. After a few more jumps, he downloaded the file, wondering how much of it he'd remember.

Or if Talon would still need him afterward.

The familiar knot formed in his gut, and he tried to whistle the Homesteader ditty to calm himself. The radio silence between them echoed with the screams of those he'd heard on the radio, begging for their lives in the Stein Revolt. Begging him not to kill them.

"You're whistling Bolero?" Runabout asked.

"That's what it's called?"

He tried to smile, but Talon's hurt glare prevented it.

"Oh yes, it's an old Homesteader lullaby, a right good one," Runabout said.

Lullaby... strafing those people....

He sucked in a breath as if he'd been punched in the gut.

During the battle on the blue planet—if it could be called a battle—he'd heard a mother whistling that over the radio. Trying to comfort her children before he destroyed their village. The one he kept recalling.

"What is it now?" Talon sounded like she wanted to say more.

The regretful undertone in her voice only angered him further.

"Deadie?"

Deadeye squeezed his hands into painful fists, swallowed bile, and nodded.

"It's done. Now we should leave, so you can explain why we need her flight log—Cap'n." Deadeye disconnected from the computer terminal.

"I swear to you both; this is more important than treasure or posturing in the Runners."

Talon patted his arm. "Sorry, Deadie, I got carried away, right?"

He nodded again, unable to get that damn tune out of his mind.

"Ain't never seen you like this," Runabout said. "Why're this dead woman's words so important? You really taking us to a big hefty haul, something kept secret from Jiàn?"

"I'll explain everything soon."

Talon faced the hatch they'd just exited across the concourse.

"Just please trust me. We need to get back on *Cygni* as soon as possible."

"At least we agree on that."

Deadeye joined the other two as they jetted their thrustpacks. The trio traveled back over the concourse at a slow but steady speed. His heart pounded with the need to get off *Unrelenting Mercy* as quickly as possible. Talon had even more to answer for, and he felt... used? Guilty? So much stabbed into his heart at once, like dying a thousand times in those few seconds.

Out of habit, he started to whistle the tune, then bit his tongue until it bled.

"You freaking out on me, Deadie?" Talon asked. "I said I would explain—"

Runabout jerked and careened off to their left, leaving a trail of red globules.

"Shit!" Talon drew her pistol and fired into the hatch they were floating toward. "Shit!"

The security bots had reactivated.

Talon fired again. "Why the fuck are they back? Talon fired again. Runnie, you okay? *Runnie!*"

Deadeye ignored the shapes coming through the hatch and jetted after Runabout. They must have shot her, the round violently interrupting her trajectory and rupturing her suit. There wasn't a group med feed on his faceplate, so he had no idea if she were still alive, and there was nothing from her on the radio. It was filled with Talon's curses. Runabout spiraled off across the concourse, a lonely, spinning asteroid.

Since Runabout's thrustpack wasn't firing, he reached her in seconds. He grabbed her left ankle, lost his grip, then snatched for her belt. His fingers locked onto the stiff fabric, and he pulled her close. A seemingly weightless, broken doll that would have been more at home on a peaceful farm colony than in a pirate gang.

The same type of farm he'd destroyed for MEC.

As he turned Runabout over, red globules floated around them, and he spotted the entrance wound: she'd been shot in the right leg, in the quadricep. A flechette.

Deadeye had to get her on *Cygni* and drain the wound before the toxins killed her.

"Go, I cleared the hatch!"

Talon jetted away from two other bots, who had exited their cubicles.

As the thrustpack sent him and Runabout to the other side of the concourse, he yanked sealant tape from his belt and patched up the rupture on her leg. Didn't think about how quickly the toxin might work or how much blood she'd lost; all attention focused on the hatch Talon had indicated.

"Runnie, can you hear me?"

He held her steady as they neared the hatch. Something shimmered a few centimeters past his right hand—another flechette.

"These pieces of shit," Talon said. "Keep going, Deadie!"

Runabout started shaking, and she coughed over the connection. "I...."

Talon barked a relieved laugh. "Holy void, she's alive!" Talon barked a relieved laugh.

"I've got you; we're getting out of here, okay? I've got you."

Deadeye jetted to the right, left, and then right again to confuse the bots if they fired again. He didn't turn to see how Talon was doing, even though he no longer heard her over the radio. Either she was dead or had opted for silence once more to elude their enemies.

Two seconds later, they reached the hatch. He gently pushed Runabout through the opening, gripped the railing for leverage, and turned around.

"Are you okay?" he asked.

"Must have been... a tranquilizer... so sleepy," Runabout mumbled.

He nudged her again, setting Runabout on a course with *Miss Cygni*, who waited outside the colony ship.

"Fluxman, you read me? Got a cute little package for you."

"Do you have eyes on my *capità*?" Runabout asked, her voice faint.

Deadeye pushed off the railing and floated over the concourse. "Not yet." Deadeye pushed off the railing and floated over the concourse.

"You're just as crazy as mad hogs in grazing season," Runabout said.

"Fluxman, if you read me, get off your ass over there and get Runnie to the med bay," Deadeye said. "I'm going back for Talon."

Talon could be dead or pinned down by the bots, and they didn't look like the types interested in quality conversation aboard a derelict ship filled with dead, frozen people. He had fetishes, but nothing that specific.

Another body now floated with the other corpse they'd seen earlier.

Deadeye stilled himself. All of his anger at Talon evaporated in an instant.

A few more meters, and he saw it was another colonist, not Talon. He didn't express his relief on the radio or use his suit's heat sensors to seek her out. Anything he did electronically could be detected by those bots; if he so much as farted over the frequencies, they'd know it. He set his thrustpack commands on manual to prevent that from showing up on their instruments, too.

With each meter he drifted, Deadeye kept telling himself that Talon was worth it, that she had a good reason for leading them into this grave- yard. Or that she had their interests in mind, too, not only hers, and he should have held his temper....

Drifting over the cryopods didn't elicit any recollections, and for a moment, he was saddened. He could remember those colony ships at Scobee Station, but not what their interiors looked like? Maybe he'd never been aboard one. The answer could be anything when one couldn't identify truth from convenient self-delusion.

But the woman whistling to her children....

It was he who wasn't worth it, not Talon. He was a murderer. Such a tiny, sharp revelation urged him to bury his self-loathing for the moment and find her.

He kept watch for any signs of struggle, floating debris, or ruptured bot shells.

Fifty meters later, still floating above the concourse, Deadeye spotted them. Three bots clustered above a railing that housed a row of cryopods. One of the mechanical guardians had cut into a pod, its cover floating away along with cooled slag pellets.

Deadeye's heart threatened to push out of his chest.

Talon lay inside the pod, trying to defend herself with her pistol. They had her cornered. The gun wouldn't be enough to handle all of them.

Deadeye slipped off his oxygen tank, then his thrustpack. Tied them together with his belt, pointed the pack in the bots' direction, and ignited its jets. Bursts of nitrogen sent the bundle over the concourse. The bots didn't detect him until he broke radio silence.

"Hey, Cap'n. Peekaboo."

The bots wheeled about and aimed at him as Talon spotted the pack and fired. The bullet pierced the oxygen tank and ignited the flammable gas inside.

The resulting explosion ripped over the bots in a brief, beautiful fireball.

Talon jetted from the cryopod into him, flinging them back to the hatch he'd pushed Runabout through.

"Drinks are on me."

Deadeye grinned at Talon, their faceplates touching.

Talon held him tight. "That pack's coming out of your share." Talon held him tight.

"Drinks are on you, then. And, oh, I have maybe six minutes of air."

She shook her head, but a faint smile parted her lips—until they exited the hatch.

Runabout floated outside *Miss Cygni*'s airlock, along with several security bots' remains. Talon's gunbots also drifted in the void, savaged and burnt. Icara barely floated about, one of her thrusters sparking.

One more shape drifted between the ships, limbs outstretched, faceplate smashed.

"Fluxman?"

Talon jetted to their comrade. "Fluxo, answer me!"

Runabout sobbed. "The colony ship bots... they got him, they sure did.." Runabout sobbed.

CHAPTER 20

"The security bots must have checked the airlock when you tripped that laser," Talon said. "And Fluxman... he was waiting for us right outside...."

Deadeye, back on *Miss Cygni* and flying away from *Unrelenting Mercy*, cleared his throat.

"You're saying his death was my fault?"

"He's gone now; it doesn't matter."

Talon's voice sounded patchy; she flew *Corsair* behind him while Runabout piloted *Annie Argent*.

"Fluxo mattered to me; he mattered a right much to this outfit."

Another sob interrupted Runabout, then she continued.

"He ain't space junk, he's—"

"Gone," Talon said. "I'm sorry, Runnie."

Deadeye said nothing, still thinking about the flechettes that had broken through Fluxman's faceplate. Though the tiny projectiles were indeed tipped with a sleep-inducing toxin—based on the med bot's analysis—the breach had robbed Fluxman of his air supply. Maybe the poor bastard had asphyxiated before the loss of air pressure had caused the water in his skin and eyes to boil away.

Which end was worse, Deadeye couldn't fathom.

He flew back through the Tombs' debris field; the overlay feeds in his vision scrolling with a never-ending stream of numbers. After the recollection he'd just experienced, he wanted the UNS to wipe his mind.

Clear away such events as if they had never happened. He struggled with which was more evil: the deed itself or its erasure.

Yet once he exited the Tombs, Deadeye slid into the other reality that was the UNS. Even as Talon urged him on over the radio right before the jump, he didn't need to hurry. Every motion and action was second-nature and required no mental energy.

Mechanical, just like the very things humanity had tried to escape from.

Why would the Prestige want to keep humans from returning to Earth?

He thought another memory was surfacing, but the Casimir drive activated, and a wormhole coalesced into existence, then *Miss Cygni* zipped across the light-years.

For Deadeye, it felt like a single, long session of lying in an isolation tank, the ones they'd trained him in during his time at the naval academy. Bees flew above him....

Bees.

A swarm of them buzzing around the wrecked apiary in the Homesteader encampment. His dropship had been forced to land due to damage from the battle. The higher gravity on the planet's surface had caused his joints to ache for several sols afterward. Yet those bees, they'd flown above their destroyed home with ease.

As if gravity wasn't holding them down.

He smiled, unsure why that sounded like a beautiful thing.

Several landed on his gloved hand, their stingers impotently failing to puncture the suit's thick lining. Or had it been another crewmember's hand? Memories didn't always tell the truth—unless they hurt.

He shook himself awake as the jack left his neck socket. The UNS overlay vanished from his eyesight. It was always there, a transparent entity that partially obscured the rest of his reality, and he missed it instantly. He stared around at the tight, packed bridge, wondering where he was.

A split second of fear suffocated him, stealing his breath, his very thoughts, and he gripped the sides of the pod. The uncertainty of who, or where, he was, his name... it was unbearable.

Wait. He was a pilot, a damn good one. One deep breath, then two. This had happened to him before; the fear would pass.

I was onboard

Miss... Miss....

The rest of the name wouldn't come to him.

Ah well. He leaned back in the pod and stared out the viewport at the countless stars. Their sight always comforted him, for he never forgot their positions, their names. He recalled the damaged life support system on that scout ship near Epsilon Eridani, and, while the rest of the crew else fought to keep calm, he'd maintained his composure by keeping the stars in view. It was a simple mental exercise, like an infant gazing up at a mobile above its crib. That's what a pilot in an Uzari pod was—

He blinked. Had he ever actually been in a crib?

"Finally. You're awake."

A woman's voice with a crisp accent. The words lingered in the air before the speaker showed herself. She wore red fatigues, hair tied back in a ponytail with the bangs hugging her eyebrows. The UNS jack was in her hand. He smiled up at her.

"To what do I owe this pleasure?"

He had no idea where he was, who she might be, or why she expected him to stop sleeping—but he savored how she looked at him. Like he was important, and she needed him for something.

"Um... you owe me a new thrustpack after that stunt you pulled on that colony ship."

She sat in the captain's seat beside the pod and leaned toward him.

"*Ha*, I know that look. Do you remember my name?"

He smiled. "I... well, I don't know how I'd ever forget your name, but it seems I have?"

"I'm Talon. You remember what ship you're on, right?"

She stirred something into mugs on a tray. The bitter, rich smell of coffee reached his nose.

"I remember stashing those coffee crates under my bunk when I flew to Groombridge."

He smirked. "But I'm guessing this isn't that ship?"

"No."

She handed him a steaming mug but didn't drink hers. Just held it, letting the heated vapors waft up into her face as if she were cold and sought warmth.

The UNS overlay. It had stated his callsign right before she'd disconnected him.

"My name's Deadeye."

He nodded to reassure himself. "Sounds right."

Her fingertips grew white on the mug, and her lower lip trembled.

"Oh, come on, don't fret. You ever played these little memory games with Jhia? Wait... Jhio? Was that their name?"

Talon stirred her coffee without taking her eyes off him. "His name was Jhio."

Deadeye dropped the smirk. "You liked him."

"Yes. He was my friend. For a time."

"Friend... hey, did her leg heal up? The cute helmet girl?"

Talon rolled her eyes but laughed. "She'd kick your ass for calling her that... but yeah, Runnie—Runabout, I mean—she's good, right?"

Deadeye sipped the coffee and sat up straight in the pod. "And that guy. Oh shit. He's dead, isn't he?"

"Yep."

Talon stared out the viewport as the stars gave way to a hangar door. He must have flown into the carrier they used before Talon entered the bridge. *Valkyrie*, that's what they called it.

He drank the coffee. It was a little too hot for his taste, but he sensed she wanted to share it with him.

"Flux... something? That was his callsign?"

"Fluxman," Talon mumbled.

Watching him, she sipped the coffee, gently tracing her finger over the mug's ceramic brim.

"Well?" Deadeye asked.

"Well, what?"

Talon sipped again, then kept her lips on the brim as she eyed him.

"Is Epsi okay? And Wizard? That's his name, right?"

Talon snapped a finger and straightened.

"So you do recall their names. Good, Deadie. Now, what's mine?"

"*Miss Cygni?*"

"Smartass."

Talon downed the coffee and stood.

"I mean, you just told me your name. Do you think us Uzari forget shit that quickly?" he asked. "Give me the benefit of the doubt here. So when are we jumping back to... where is it?"

"We're already back at Sirius, ready to meet with Jiàn and the other Runners."

There was a resentful undertone in her voice.

"But I just saw the hangar door close through the viewport."

He tried to smile, but a chilling confusion swept over him.

"How long have I been in this pod?"

"The whole time, from the Tombs, all the way back here. Thirteen sols, Deadie."

"You didn't wake me? Why wait until now to pull the damn jack out?"

Her eyes hardened. "You were in a goddamn UNS coma. Wiz said if we disconnected you, it might fry your brain, all right? So we left you in here. I checked on you all the time and kept these nutrient canisters full. You're welcome."

He stared out the viewport at the closed hangar door, feeling that other mental portals had likewise closed. Doorways to things best left forgotten.

"You kept mumbling some shit about bees," Talon said.

"I'm good, Cap'n. I'm just a little tired, that's all."

He wanted to puke.

Talon sighed and set the cup aside. "You've made too many jumps in a short amount of time. Navigating the Tombs, well, that did something to you. It's my fault, really, if you've forgotten anything."

He stood from the pod and stretched. "I remember that you promised to tell us all this has been for, all these missions, the secrecy. They still don't know about the new drive on *Santo Pohl*, do they?"

"You and your fucking memory."

She moved to kiss him, but he held up a hand.

"Not yet," he said. "Not until you tell us what the hell is going on."

"Be that way, then."

She stalked toward the exit.

He barred the door with his arm. "When, Talon? I don't know what you're doing or why, but you don't have to do it alone."

Talon gave him a playful smile but firmly moved his arm from her path.

"You'd just forget it if I told you, right? See you in twenty minutes, in *Valkyrie*'s main airlock with the others. Get cleaned up and look sharp because Jiàn's going to have lots of questions. Got it, lieutenant?"

He watched her leave, her shoulders tense, thumbs thrust into her gun belt. She still didn't want to tell him—or the others—what was so important about the Sagittarii.

There was no tea when they met with Jiàn aboard *Xīng Huā*. His bag suit guards wore pistols this time, and *Valkyrie*'s crew wasn't allowed past the other carrier's airlock chamber. The red paper lanterns had been darkened, and only the room's running lights offered illumination. Deadeye and the others waited while she and Jiàn argued.

"I got you pretty detailed data on coordinates that circle the diameter of the entire Dust Systems," Talon said. "Sometimes even into the Arcturus Ring. That's worth a shitload more than obsolete engine parts, or frozen food that dead colonists didn't eat. Shit, Jiàn. Those vessels used

Kapteyn engines, for fuck's sake. The Runners can't use that, but these routes—"

"We had an agreement."

Jiàn was a statue of restrained anger, hands behind his back like a Han naval officer.

"Those hadrons I supplied you with could have fueled several smaller vessels on far more lucrative runs. These coordinates are useless if we don't have the supplies or the ships to reach them."

Talon threw up her hands. "Then what are we doing all this for? We're keeping people out there from starving, we make sure children have water purifiers and medicine, and we steal all of that precious shit from MEC, the Lineage, whoever, right? We can't steal forever, and you know that. People need new homes, like the Homesteaders or the Tolteca are out there searching for. Food isn't enough—they need hope."

The passion in her voice commanded Deadeye's attention in a way it hadn't before. It wasn't petty Runner politics or deflection. She believed her own words.

"If we openly try to settle the Dust Systems or any worlds beyond it, such as the Ring, MEC will see that as an act of war."

Jiàn's nostrils flared, but his voice remained calm.

"Remember the Stein Revolt? I do. The Han joined MEC beforehand because it thought things would change, that order would be established on the frontier after we survived the Prestige's attacks. Yet that fiasco was simply more targeted genocides, more 'unlawful' settlements eliminated. We stick to the shadows, Talon. We make them think we're simple pirates and thieves, or else they will—"

"MEC will come after us anyway," Deadeye said. "They've already ambushed us once. It's only a matter of time before they seek out every Runner outfit and—"

"And we need that time!"

Jiàn's eyes widened, and he bared his teeth with the frustration of one who had fought impossible odds for many years—then he assumed his calculated demeanor once more.

"If we blatantly flaunt their established laws, MEC will crush us, and the Lineage, the Sadistos, the Homesteaders—none of them will lift a finger to help us. If we continue as is, we can save some people. If we fail, far more will die."

"Then the Runners are already dead, too."

Talon tossed Jiàn a data chit; he caught it without flinching.

"That's a copy of the coordinate sets from *Unrelenting Mercy*. Do what you want with it. I'm taking my strike group back to Hartwell, and we'll do what it takes to make a real difference."

Jiàn shook his head. "You'll lose your captaincy.Jiàn shook his head. You're one of our best, but you're driven by the same inner demons when you were in my crew. A real difference? How many times have I heard you say that? When does it end?"

"We all have to be driven by something."

Talon walked back through the joined airlocks to *Valkyrie*.

Deadeye glanced at the others. Wizard sighed and followed Talon, Runabout gave Jiàn an apologetic shrug and left, but Epsi lingered as if she were having second thoughts.

"You don't have to travel down that path with her," Jiàn told Epsi, his voice soft. "I know your record. Your dedication and skills. You are welcome to join *Xīng Huā*'s roster at any time."

"I need to see where this goes... but thank you."

Epsi nodded to Jiàn and left.

The friendliness left Jiàn's tone, and his eyes narrowed. "And what about you? Talon goes through Uzari like a shredder goes through bullets."

Deadeye snorted. "Like you offer anything better. Deadeye snorted. I saw the Uzari among your other crews the last time we were here. You all use us until we can't remember anything but star charts and coordinates. Maybe that's on purpose, so we don't complain?"

Jiàn stepped closer. The bag suit guards started to follow, but he raised a hand, and they stayed in place.

"During the Stein revolt, one of the settlements the Han fleet was ordered to bombard was an Uzari academy that had gone independent. Uzari Corp's representatives had been displaced, and the Uzari there established their own little government. It worked for a time."

Deadeye smirked with all the humor of a spent railgun. "Until you destroyed it?"

The pain of remembered horrors passed in Jiàn's eyes.

"No. I disobeyed orders, spaced my captain and crew, and flew my corvette out of the system—with as many Uzari from that academy who would come. The remainder surrendered to MEC, but their Han fleet incinerated that place anyway. Among those I rescued, most joined the Runners when we created the organization. Most of them aren't with us any longer, and those that are you saw earlier, their minds all but gone. They are little more than human computers now, but I still treat them with dignity."

"I don't need pity masked as dignity," Deadeye said. "I need to keep flying."

"Flying wasn't an escape for them, either."

Jiàn studied Deadeye for a long moment. "I don't know what Talon is trying to escape from... but there is no reason you should burn yourself out while she tries to deal with it. You're a brilliant pilot. One of the best, I must admit, to have navigated the Tombs. Don't let her take you down with her."

"It's all I've got now," Deadeye said and returned to *Valkyrie*.

CHAPTER 21

TALON GATHERED EVERYONE IN *VALKYRIE*'S REC ROOM ONCE THEY'D flown a short distance from the Runner fleet. There were no smiles, no sipping of beers, or vaping on Starrio. Wizard, Runabout, and Epsi all watched Talon with resentful expectation. Like Jiàn, they'd been promised a major haul. Something to make them wealthy, or at least comfortable for a while. The loss of Fluxman only heightened that bitterness.

Deadeye sensed the anxiety within Talon. The way she kept looking to him for support. But she needed to come clean, once and for all.

"Okay, *capità*, let's hear it," Runabout said.

"Right."

Talon gestured at Icara, who displayed a holographic map.

"Ensign Tasha Bester was one of the last people to fly out of the Ross Boundary, making sure all the other vessels in the colony fleet were accounted for. Once those colonists left the Sol system, nobody has flown through the Boundary since—and lived."

"Let me guess: Bester was one of those Sagittarii?" Wizard asked.

"No, but they had a fragment of her report, passed down over the centuries. Some of them must have escaped that colony fleet after all, and saved the fragment ever since. They revere her like some sort of saint now."

Talon loaded the document on Icara's holo.

"Their mythology claimed that their founders knew how to fly through the Boundary, right? This Bester flight report confirms it. A way to get past all the false gravity signatures, the neutron stars that telescopes show aren't there, but the UNS detects. A map through a maze. A way to fly past the Prestige fleets just inside the Boundary."

"Okay, so?" Epsi asked. "Fluxman died for some dead woman's report?"

"The report gives a clue on how to navigate through the Boundary."

Talon gauged their reactions and upon receiving no enthusiasm, shook her head.

"That doesn't interest anyone? Holy void, do you know what this shit means?"

"It means we don't have enough credits to buy more hadrons," Wizard said. "Or food, water, or even the fucking air we're wasting discussing this."

Talon looked at her feet, then made eye contact with them.

"With this report, I can fly some... clients through the Boundary."

Runabout stiffened, and Epsi gaped. Mumbling, Wizard paced the room. Even Deadeye stared at her in shock.

Runabout's arms fell at her sides. Runabout's arms fell at her sides. "Huh? By the Dame herself, what for?"

There was more than a bit of frustration in Epsi's voice. "Is this the haul you've been telling us about? Who the hell is it, rich Lineage assholes?"

Talon stared at the holo map instead of meeting their glares. "This has taken me years to get together; you got me? The least you can do is try to understand—"

"The least you can do is tell us the starry blue truth," Runabout said in a low voice. "We're your friends, supporting you across all them stars out there. Your right loyal crew. We've backed you on so many ventures, punked MEC and all, and risked our void-damned lives. Why ain't you trusting us?"

The realization washed over Deadeye like ice from a water trawler.

"Because this isn't her first time trying to assemble all of this information, or these circumstances... is it, Cap'n?" Deadeye asked.

Talon looked away. "No. It isn't."

Epsi's expression darkened by the second. Runabout kept shaking her head while Wizard kicked aside an empty beer bottle.

Deadeye continued.

"I'm guessing the reason the Harpies despise us and keep turning up...is because you made them the same promises of a great haul, of awesome wealth, but you didn't follow through because you didn't have everything you needed. Before you ever joined the Runners, before you flew for Jiàn—back when you were a Harpy. Back when you earned the callsign 'Talon,' related to their bird of prey fixation. Am I right?"

"What the actual fuck?"

Wizard flipped over the chessboard, his tentacles flailing about. Though the pieces were magnetic, the force tossed several over the room.

"Why didn't they stick with you?" Epsi asked. "Because you lied to them, or—"

"They didn't give me enough time!" Talon yelled, visibly shaking as something within her finally gave way.

The sudden expulsion of emotion made the others step back, their magnetic soles snapping over the metal deck.

Deadeye drew closer to her as if proximity would help him understand.

"Okay.... well, you have the things you need now. That means you can tell us."

Talon sucked in a breath, swiped away Icara's holographic map, and booted up another one. It showed the Ross Boundary and the systems contained within it. Sol, Alpha Centauri, Barnard's Star, Luhman 16. A mere handful of stars.

"I have a contract to transport Sagittarii pilgrims across the Boundary," Talon said. "They're trying to return to Earth. Like their ancestors, right?"

Deadeye gripped the back of the chair. Memories of the blue planet....

"How much does this 'contract' pay?" Epsi asked.

"Nothing," Talon said. "The credits aren't the point."

Wizard's expression contorted as if someone had shoved a spike into his ear, then he laughed.

"You can't be fucking serious."

Epsi shook her head. "Even MEC can't cross the Boundary. No pilot can navigate all the bullshit data that clogs the UNS as soon as you cross over—and that's if the Prestige doesn't blow you to dust. The Cepheids claim we're not supposed to return to Sol, that we were cast out. Maybe they're right?"

"And you believe that dung drivel?" Runabout snorted. "The reason ain't no matter to me, but that Boundary sure is. There's no way we can fly into that—"

Talon looked at each of them in turn. "You're not going. Talon looked at each of them in turn. Only me."

Deadeye's brow furrowed, and heat rose in his chest.

"Are you insane? You're not an Uzari or a Zyn; that's a death wish for anyone else. And *Santo Pohl*."

"I knew you were refitting that shitcan," Wizard said. "But not for this craziness."

"You needed me for the Tombs...but not this?" Deadeye asked.

Talon didn't look at him. "I needed you for Parallax." Talon didn't look at him.

Wizard's brow lowered in puzzled rage. "Huh? Wizard's brow lowered in puzzled rage. That weird shit Deadeye mentions sometimes?"

"Parallax is the name of the defense system that creates the Ross Boundary," Talon said. "It's right there, in Bester's report: a navigator's nightmare. Only, she didn't know how it worked. I... think I do. Deadie, the stuff he gave Kattral, and the way he flew through the Tombs, he knows some of it—"

"Then why not let me fly the mission?" Deadeye asked.

"Because you've already forgotten bits of it."

Talon swallowed and pushed the bangs from her eyes.

"I've tested you now and then, little things in the UNS that show your mental state. You're not reliable, all right? You'd never make it through."

"How do I know anything about Parallax at all?" Deadeye asked.

"MEC installs that shit in every UNS, embedded deep in the software," Talon said. "But they don't have the entire sequence. Uzari minds were cultivated for that shit; it's why people like you exist. They took over Uzari Corp, put Zyn-Tro out of business, and started breeding people... like you."

"So they could eventually crack the Boundary," Deadeye said.

Talon nodded.

"Did you do this to Jhio or all the other Uzari that Jiàn told me you've used up?"

Deadeye trembled, his skin so hot it might ignite his suit.

"Did you, goddamn it?"

"No!"

Talon stared at the ceiling, then faced him. "Not...not at first. You've outperformed the others that have been in my crew. You completed the sequence."

It finally hit him. The secrecy. The affection she'd shown him until she'd finally gotten what she wanted from him. That didn't hurt as much as she probably thought he'd simply forget her anyway.

Runabout's voice shook. "Why?" Runabout's voice shook.

"I have to do this," Talon said. "I don't expect any of you to understand...."

Deadeye kept staring at her, having no words.

Wizard stomped forward. "Then tell us!"

"I'm a member of House Traxe," Talon said.

"The Blood Barons?" Runabout asked.

Epsi glared at Talon. "House Traxe, one of the largest slave traders in the Spur? Epsi glared at Talon. The same people who forced me and my family into that labor camp? The same bastards who—"

She turned away, jaw so tight it could have cracked a diamond.

"Goddamn it, I'm not part of the family anymore, you got that?" Talon shouted. "I'm just a distant cousin of that piece of shit household. They disowned me after I set Sagittarii captives free on Apai. Sol after sol, I had to watch those horrors since I was the labor camps' officer in charge. The way they tortured those people, worked thousands of them to death... the baron got me discharged from the MEC navy—"

"Shit, I knew you were former military," Wizard muttered.

Thousands worked to death. How many thousands had Deadeye killed in the Stein Revolt? He had no right to be angry with her, despite her deeds. At least she had a purpose, a reason to fly and risk everything—unlike him. He ignored the rest of their accusations and angry reminders as he touched Talon's shoulder.

She turned to lash out, saw his sad smile, and calmed.

The others fell silent.

"Did it work? His anger was already evaporating. Did you free anyone?" His anger was already evaporating.

Talon searched his eyes. "I only got thirty-eight of them out. Talon searched his eyes with hers. Twelve of those were recaptured. But the others made it. I've made raids since then, saving others. I'd do it all again, all right? Fuck them all, Deadie; I'd do every bit of it again."

Deadeye nodded. "Then that's what matters to me. Fuck the rest."

Runabout sighed deeply, then shrugged. "Nyx curse me, then. Fuck the rest."

"It's not that easy," Wizard said.

Epsi shook her head. "Damn right, Wiz. It's not that easy for me, either. I can't just forget that you're one of them, Talon. I fucking can't. I lost an arm for you!"

Talon blinked and backed away.

"That's not her fault, and you know it," Wizard said.

"Sure thing Epsi, you joined up, knowing the risks," Runabout said.

"So, what, I'm supposed to forget it happened?" Epsi asked. "Fuck that."

"I'm not asking for forgiveness," Talon said. "But those Sagittarii saved others of their kind, almost two hundred more that House Traxe enslaved. I've funneled funds and weapons toward their freedom, but now they need a place to live. And they won't be safe anywhere else in the Spur because MEC observes the Barons' slave laws. The Homesteaders hate Sagittarii—no, Runnie, you know it's true—and there's little chance they'll make it on the outlying worlds in the Dust Systems. This is their only shot, right?"

"Your only shot to assuage that guilty conscious of yours," Epsi muttered.

Talon hugged herself and stared at the deck.

"But the Boundary is a death sentence," Deadeye said. "I get what you're trying to do... what you think you need to do... but this is crazy. Let us help you."

Runabout nodded. Wizard sighed and shrugged in acquiescence.

"No," Epsi said. "I'm out. I'm not helping someone from House Traxe."

Talon looked hurt, then assumed a stony expression. "We'll head to Hartwell Station. That's where the Sagittarii is waiting, in my old trawler docked in the lower levels. You three can remain behind on *Valkyrie*, go your separate ways, go back to Jiàn and the rest of the Runners, whatever you want, got it? I'm sorry it came to this, but I've made up my mind, and if I can save these people... then I'll do it."

"You're a real savior, all right." Epsi stormed from the room.

"Rethink this," Wizard said. "I'll fly into the Boundary; the hell with it; I've got nothing out there anymore anyway—"

"No," Talon said. "This is on me. I have to do this."

"It will kill you," Deadeye said.

"That's not certain," Talon said. "The Boundary has only a six light-year radius, and with the Casimir Mark III that we souped-up on *Pohl*—"

"You don't have the jump experience, the flight time, or the mind for that much UNS fugue," Deadeye said. "Talon... don't throw your life away."

"Like you have?"

Talon's face flushed with instant regret.

He started to turn away as she raised her voice.

"It's mine to do with as I please, right? Like the rest of you. I've used you all enough, so you deserve better. The rest isn't up for discussion. Let's jump to Hartwell."

"*Capità....*"

Runabout extended a hand, but Talon left for her quarters.

Deadeye remained in the rec room long after the others left, staring at the Boundary map. Talon had used them all but for a noble—if foolish—

cause. He paced the room, around the chairs and couches where they'd all ate, drank, laughed, and sometimes made love. The holo billiard table, where Fluxman kicked his ass every time, or the overturned chessboard, where Talon had asked him back to her bunk.

The black king lay on the deck, where it had fallen after Wizard's outburst. It was carved in the shape of an old Martian monarch, with a visored helmet and an excavator's pick, symbolizing the conquest of the legendary red planet. Deadeye took the piece, stared around the room one last time, and put the king into his pocket.

"Checkmate," he whispered.

An hour later, Deadeye entered *Valkyrie*'s piloting pod and set coordinates for Hartwell Station. It felt like a defeat rather than a victory.

Talon finished putting her hair up in a more intricate ponytail as if she were trying to remake herself. She didn't look at him.

"Once we get to Hartwell, I'll be looking for another crew," he said.

Talon tapped her terminal screen. "That's fine."

He wanted to say more, but anything else would be lies, or things they already knew and didn't need to speak aloud. Some connections were weakened once spoken of, an old spacer proverb went. Once admitted, those connections could be destroyed. Maybe if he kept them close to his heart, they would remain there, even if he forgot about them after the jump. Memory and emotion might be two different things after all, and if he couldn't have one, maybe he could still possess the other.

The pod felt colder than usual. The jack port in his neck number than he'd expected. Maybe it was a survival mechanism, something to focus his perceptions so he wouldn't let emotion take over. But emotion had driven humanity across the stars in the first place, and without it, nothing else mattered. He wanted to tell Talon that, tell her anything, but she kept staring forward, stiff in that seat, angry that she'd been forced to reveal her past. He surmised she was angrier with herself than with any of them, and forgiving oneself was the hardest thing of all.

He started to whistle the Homesteader tune out of habit, then stopped.

Yes. The hardest thing of all.

"How are we back there, Runabout?' he asked since Talon wasn't going through the typical jump sequence.

"Everything's tip-top, we're good to go," Runabout said.

"Epsi?" Deadeye asked. "Wizard?"

"Good to go." Epsi's voice was still tight with antipathy.

"Sure, let's do it." Wizard sounded despondent.

"Cap'n... you ready?"

"Waiting on you," Talon said.

Deadeye glanced at her. It might be the last time he could see her in such a frame of mind, with those feelings. Those memories. She still didn't look at him.

The UNS overlay filled his sight, and he faced forward. He initiated the jump and closed his eyes, letting the link with his mind do the rest.

Maybe seeing her wouldn't hurt so much when he opened them again.

CHAPTER 22

Hartwell Station appeared with the immediacy of an illusion in Deadeye's overlay, as if it hadn't existed a moment before and now filled his reality with all its immenseness and countless occupants. A few more ships were docked to its lower ports than usual: bulky cargo transports from surrounding mining unions.

One thing that wasn't an illusion was how Talon looked at him right before rising from the captain's chair. Those grey eyes held remorse yet determination. So proud, so stubborn. He couldn't help but admire her for it. But she was tired instead of angry, and such a mindset often proved terminal in the void.

Their silence was more than a personal disagreement. If Talon was successful, it would change the Spur. A new race among the Spur's powers would begin, each trying to pass through it themselves and take whatever happened to remain on the other side. The Prestige would likely attack humanity again. People would die—but some would die free.

Was she ready for all of that? MEC would never stop chasing her afterward.

Part of him wanted to see what was past the Boundary, too. In his memory, those colony ships around Scobee Station were the one recollection that never went away. He could forget people's names, their faces, his relation to them, even the name of the ship he was on, but that memory refused to die, like Parallax.

He wanted to tell Talon this, but she had already left the bridge. It was like they'd never had a relationship, never enjoyed all that sex in her bunk, never talked about their fears and dreams before the hangar viewport. Unfortunately, such personal attachments came and went, but she at least remembered them and likelier better than he ever could.

After making the jump from Sirius, she'd not even scolded him for not immediately going to sleep in his bunk. He was thirsty, hungry, and still quivering from UNS fugue, but he couldn't sleep. Not now.

Docking permissions with the station took extra time, as most of the hangars were full, and the exterior docks demanded higher rental fees. Deadeye brought *Valkyrie* into orbit around Hartwell, ready for Talon to leave in *Santo Pohl*. Once she was gone, he might join Jiàn's crew or seek employment with the Thule Freelancers.

He'd find something.

Seconds later, *Princess* departed *Valkyrie*'s hangar.

"Good luck out there, Epsi," he said.

A long moment passed.

"Sure... hey... you too, Deadeye," Epsi finally said. "Wizard, say a prayer to the Red Buddha for me. And Runnie? *A les estrelles*, you sexy thing."

"*A les estrelles*," Runabout said.

"Give them hell, wherever you go," Wizard said.

The smile was evident in Epsi's voice. "You know it."

Talon offered her no goodbye.

A gravitational disturbance registered on the UNS in less than a minute, and *Princess* was gone. Pilots flew across nothing and expected nothing in return.

"Those Freelancer scamps ain't answering our comms," Runabout said over *Valkyrie*'s radio. "What're they playing at? There are docks open for us down there."

"Just hold; I almost have *Pohl* ready to go," Talon said.

Wizard grunted. "Oh, it's like that, huh? Wizard grunted. Leaving without even telling me to kiss your fancy Cetian ass. At least tell us who's going to be the next captain."

"You'll figure it out."

Talon's voice sounded stiff. She was distancing herself already.

"*Heh*, that's it?" Runabout asked.

"The Runners will find you, someone, *Miss Cygni* is a good ship, and...." Talon paused, and Deadeye checked the hangar cam.

She was leaning against the wall, helmet in hand. Shaking. Wiping her eyes.

He switched off the cam, granting her privacy.

A pre-recorded message gave them permission to dock on the lower levels, where Talon had said the Sagittarii waited in a transport. It was an old, pre-MEC trawler with one too many patches in its hull. One railgun shot would reduce it to dust.

A new voice came over the radio.

"May we come aboard *Valkyrie*, Captain Talon?"

A man with a harmonious accent he'd never heard before.

Talon cleared her throat. "Yes, Overseer Sereda. Bring your people over to our carrier. The transport is ready; my bot Icara will guide you to the hangar."

"Coming around now," Deadeye said.

Minutes later, as the Sagittarii hurried through the linked airlocks, a second, familiar voice filled their comms.

"Captain Talon, you are ever the intrepid yet reckless pirate," Lord Kattral said. "A pity that your career should end here and not in some romantic skirmish in the void."

Deadeye tensed in the pod. Checked the radar, and the scopes. Expecting an ambush.

"Kattral?" Talon asked. "What the hell do you want?"

"Restitution," Kattral said. "Or, rather, the closest thing to it. House Kattral will be compensated for the nonsensical data your Uzari delivered and the theft of those MEC engine parts. They have come in person to reclaim them."

"Deadie, what's out there?" Talon asked.

The UNS radar feed made Deadeye curse.

The bulky mining transports undocked from the level below them and changed their transponder designations from mining union craft to MEC military vessels. On *Valkyrie*'s aft scopes, Deadeye made out compartments opening on the ships' hulls, revealing weapon emplacements. They were one thousand six hundred meters away—a death trap.

"We're under attack!"

No sooner had Deadeye spoken than a barrage of railgun fire ripped through *Valkyrie*. The carrier shook, warning alarms blared, Talon shouted orders, and the Sagittarii screamed for help.

The airlock tube, joining the two ships, had been shot away. A few small forms floated off into the darkness. *Valkyrie*'s rear thrusters were gone, its portside thrusters were leaking, and the central centrifuge had ceased rotating.

Deadeye knew the carrier was doomed. Their only chance was to board the smaller craft in the hangar and escape. He set *Valkyrie*'s auto docking procedure to keep Hartwell and MEC busy, then left his pod.

Weakened from the recent jump, it took all of his strength to pull himself from the bridge and down the corridor. Tools and beer bottles floated in his path. He brushed them aside, fighting post-jump stupor.

"Runnie? Wizard?"

He reached for a handle along the wall, only to recoil as a railgun round sheared the entire bulkhead away on his right. The puncture was clean, nonexplosive, and meant to disable, not destroy. MEC wanted them alive.

"I'm heading for the hangar now!" Wizard called.

"The Sagittarii are loaded on *Pohl*; I need you all to get out there and grant me some cover!" Talon cried. "Please, you'll do that, right? These people need us!"

Deadeye passed the airlock chamber, grabbed a thrustpack, and put it on.

"Sure thing, Cap'n. We've got you."

He jetted the rest of the way through *Valkyrie*.

Several cabins had been blasted open, and the crew's belongings drifted around him. Wizard's Buddha charms, Runabout's soil collection. Fluxman's magistrate service award plaque. The books Runabout had bought him. Epsi's lipstick. His red-grey MPS.

Talon's butterscotch-flavored coffee packets.

"So this is goodbye, huh?" Runabout said. "I'm boarding *Argent*, so I reckon I'll help. Better not waste any tricky ticky time, *capità*. Get them out of here."

"Who knows, you might see me again," Talon said. "Have a little confidence in me, at least?"

"I'm almost to *Corsair*," Wizard said. "Shit, there's debris all over the hangar."

Valkyrie's corridors changed orientation as the carrier absorbed more gunfire. Lengths of hull tore away, revealing the eternal blackness outside. A few more hits would send the vessel into a spin. By now, the auto docking procedure would have terminated, but he hoped it had gotten them close enough to Hartwell Station. MEC would have to cease fire to avoid hitting the station, which meant a boarding action would follow.

Deadeye jetted the thrustpack again and finally reached the hangar.

Floating shrapnel, tools, spare parts, bots, crates, and even two unfortunate Sagittarii littered the chamber. *Annie Argent* flew out the hangar doors, only to be clipped by a railgun round. *Argent* spun away from the carrier, out of his line of sight.

"I took a right shitty hit, but I'll get this bird flying!" Runabout cried.

Deadeye headed for *Miss Cygni*, which was docked across from *Santo Pohl*. "Hartwell's right there; eject if you have to! Don't die in that can!"

Another large shape lifted off the hangar deck and made for the exit: *Corsair*.

"I'm coming out hot!" Wizard yelled. "Suck on this, assholes!"

Corsair's railgun dispensed death at something out there, but again, not connected to the UNS; Deadeye had no idea if the round had connected.

A moment later, two shots pierced *Corsair*'s hull, not far from its power router. *Corsair* kept going, its brief thruster blast still enough to clear *Valkyrie*'s hangar door.

"I can still punk them, Talon," Wizard said. "Get your ass going, girl!"

Deadeye pushed aside pieces of drifting, crumpled hull and spotted Talon near *Miss Cygni*. She was floating toward *Pohl*, where a Sagittarii in a blue spacesuit beckoned her from its airlock. The ship was online, ready to go, as was *Cygni*.

Talon had taken the time to prep the frigate for him.

"Get the hell out of here, Deadie!" Talon shouted.

"Almost there, Cap'n—"

Five figures landed on the lip of *Valkyrie*'s hangar door. White armor. Rifles.

"Go back!" Deadeye cried.

The MEC marines opened fire. The Sagittarii in *Pohl*'s airlock jerked and spun across the hangar, trailing crimson globules.

"Fuck!" Talon drew her gun and fired—but the recoil pushed her back to *Cygni*.

One marine's helmet exploded in red mush. Another spun out of the hangar, gripping their chest. The other three took cover behind a drifting tool crate.

"I'm right dead in the void out here; I can't move!" Runabout cried.

"Wait, there goes that one's bridge," Wizard said. "*Ha*, you bastards. I'm targeting their next ship. Hang on, garden gnome!"

"I leave you assholes for a minute, and you're already in trouble?" Epsi asked.

Wizard whooped and laughed. "You came back, Epsi girl?" Wizard whooped and laughed.

"The Dame herself sent us an angel!" Runabout cried.

"Epsi," Talon said. "I...."

"We're good; get those people away from here, captain," Epsi said. "Go, I'm already taking fire!"

Two more marines jetted into the hangar. They were cutting off Talon from *Pohl.*

Deadeye looked at *Santo Pohl,* then at Talon.

"Don't you dare," she breathed. "No, Deadie boy, I mean it—"

He used the remainder of his thrustpack fuel to reach *Pohl's* airlock.

As she screamed at him, Talon continued firing. A third marine ate vacuum.

The need to help those people on *Pohl,* to do something with his life, drove Deadeye on. Just like his need to keep Talon alive. Not because she might serve a higher purpose; she'd likely continue being a pirate if she were successful. But the look in her eyes when he'd said he'd still support her, even fly the cultists into the Boundary, despite all she'd done... he'd brave a hundred solar flares to be looked at that way again.

Plus... he was just another space jockey. Life was cheap in the Orion Spur, and people like him were even cheaper. Grown by corporations or the military, corralled away from the other humans, or used to ruination, like the Uzari at the Runner moot. At least now, he might be helping someone for once.

"Wizard, Epsi, can you cover me, too?"

Deadeye gripped *Pohl's* airlock railing, but his weak fingers were like strands of jelly in his gloves.

A hand reached out and grabbed him—another person in a blue suit. The name patch read "Overseer Sereda." Soon Deadeye was onboard *Cygni.* Multiple hands from eager, frightened passengers ushered him to the bridge—the oldest form of propulsion.

One of the Sagittarii pilgrims was a kid.

The heaviness of what he was about to do hit him. They were taking their children along with them. No wonder Talon had been so adamant. She'd never forgive him.

He'd never forgive himself if he didn't try.

"I'm doing my best out here," Wizard said. "Who's flying them out of *Valkyrie?*"

"Yes, punked another one!" Epsi shouted. "Hurry, my heatsinks are too slow!"

"Damn it, flyboy; I said no!" Talon yelled. "This was for me to do, not you! This was on me to fix, my mistake to correct, not some fucking glory ride for you to—"

"Runnie?" He smiled and slid into *Pohl's* pod. "Runnie? Do me one favor, will you?"

"Anything."

She sounded like she was crying. He wasn't worth any tears, but it made him feel something in his chest anyway.

"Make sure Talon doesn't follow me," he said.

"I... I will, Deadeye. May the Dame grant you swift passage."

It was an old parting phrase uttered by superstitious Homesteaders. Predicated on the ancient belief that divine powers watched over spacers and allowed them to fly between the stars. Deadeye knew it was nonsense, but the sentiment was appreciated.

"Our rules mean our survival. Goodbye, everyone."

He cut the connection.

Santo Pohl exited *Valkyrie*'s hangar. A burst of thruster gas flung the marines out into the void and sent him across the airless expanse. All around him, Hartwell's other starships were also fleeing since most of them were criminals. People lived in those vessels as de facto dwellings since a spacer's only real home was the vacuum. People that no one wanted or needed. People that had decided to forge their destiny, quaint or grand, at the whims of physics and a technology that most still didn't understand.

People like him bred and spliced from millions of different genetic databases to create humans capable of surviving the dark frontier. In these so-called heavens, ancient humans thought their gods lived. Gods and paradises did indeed thrive in that darkness, but not of the sort humans fully understood or appreciated. They were ephemeral entities that came and went with each spacer who encountered them. Like the memories he had built, stored, and then forgotten in his quest to touch the infinite, the unattainable.

Now he would do that one final time. He wasn't even nervous or excited.

A second later, the MEC ships blew *Princess* apart. There was no message from Epsi. No way of surviving such an abrupt end. He gripped the manuals tighter.

The MEC vessels targeted him next, sparing *Wizard* and *Runabout* for a moment. He didn't squander it. In a flurry of small thruster blasts, he reoriented *Pohl*, darted a hundred meters to starboard, oriented 55° to port, then jetted for another sixty meters.

Several minor blips passed on the UNS radar feed. Railgun projectiles, flying through the locations he'd just occupied. The ships closed in, less than nine hundred meters now, hoping to bar him from escaping.

Sweat dappled his brow as he started to orient *Pohl* again. The other ships would rip him apart in a few seconds, too, unless—

Something else appeared on the radar, and the bridge of one MEC ship exploded.

It was *Miss Cygni*. Covering him with its single railgun.

Deadeye blasted away from Hartwell Station. Soon it was six kilometers behind him, then thirty. He minimized the radar feed. The others might make it, but he had to focus on his adopted mission, not the fate of *Valkyrie* and his shipmates.

In the corridor outside the bridge, the Sagittarii waved at him. He turned in the pod and raised a hand in greeting, the old human method of signaling that he did not intend violence but peace and trade. An empty hand, free of tools or weapons, bereft of hidden devices or trickery. Such a simple thing to emote, but the smiles on those children's faces made him grin back.

Deadeye removed his helmet after *Pohl* filled with air. Though their current system, Luyten's Star, was just over six light-years from the Boundary, Talon had loaded plenty of life support, food, and water. No wonder she had kept and refitted the cargo ship. He checked his pod IVs, enjoyed the taste of fresh air, and put his helmet back on. The jump coordinates popped up on his overlay. The voyage would take at least four sols —more, depending on where the pilgrims wanted to go inside the Boundary.

The Casimir Mark III he and Talon had installed made that possible. A Mark II would lengthen the journey to thirteen sols.

The Sagittarii elder, Overseer Sereda, entered the bridge. He was an older man with constellations tattooed on each cheek.

"Captain Talon was our original pilot, but I will trust you, for I saw how you helped her. Thank you for saving us from MEC."

"We're about to make the jump, so get your people ready," Deadeye said. "Ignore all outside communications and requests, we're not clear yet."

Sereda nodded. "You have the coordinates? You look sick, my friend."

Deadeye nodded back. "I'm fine. I'll get you there."

Smiling, Sereda hurried back into the corridor, bringing forth a chorus of happy voices. Deadeye activated the Casimir drive. Its familiar thrum vibrated the deck.

The coordinates were set, and the UNS overlay filled his vision with wormhole trajectories. He eased into the drifting sensation of the connection, even as it might destroy the memory of what he was currently experiencing. A small price to pay for what others would gain. It didn't make him a hero or even a player on the galactic stage.

It made him feel human, if only for a moment.

Santo Pohl jumped.

CHAPTER 23

An alarm blared in Deadeye's ears. He loaded up *Santo Pohl*'s configuration stats and checked the status of the passengers. They were enjoying a sleep cycle. Icara hovered around him, ensuring his nutrient canisters were functioning.

They were one sol out from Luyten's Star. Everything was in good working order. The wormhole's integrity held steady at 83%, and though a Mark III had a collapse rate of 15%, he wasn't worried. Gravitational lensing caused by the engine made the stars outside the viewport warp, bend, blur, and diffuse into a random series of shapes.

For a moment, he saw familiar faces or places in them. Pattern recognition seemed even more magical out there, far from all the actual people and locations.

Once, a MEC engineer had tried to explain the wormhole effect to him, of being outside of spacetime but still part of it. Yet words could never do justice to the visual.

He started to lift the mug to his lips, but his hand was empty. Frowning, he wondered if he'd been drinking anything at all. Then he realized his helmet was still on.

A dry laugh escaped his lips, morphing into a cackle.

The mirth lasted but a moment; as the next instant, all of *Pohl*'s systems went offline. He only had the UNS overlay, haunting his sight with useless information that was likely several seconds old. He reached for the manual interface, but the ship shook and creaked, and he opened his mouth to cry out as a burning sensation traveled up his legs to his torso and into his skull—

Deadeye coughed. Opened his eyes.

The ship's systems were operating normally.

Sixteen more hours had passed.

All was quiet. Deadeye stared around, wondering what kept breaking his fugue state. The rich smell of coffee made him lick his lips. Hopefully, Talon had saved him some. He kept glancing at the bridge hatch, expecting to see her walk through at any moment in her underwear, holding two mugs and that mischievous smirk that meant she'd pounce on him before he could finish the drink. He waited, and waited....

The empty coffee mug hovered above Talon's head as she slept beside him in the pod. He'd not wanted to make love in it again, afraid their jostling would damage the components, but it made it easier to sit in afterward, knowing she'd sweated all over—

The alarm. Again.

He shivered; it was so damn cold.

The heating system must be damaged.

Santo Pohl had never been much of a ship, but MEC had kept it in running condition. Shit, he doubted he could make this next jump to Vegaspace, let alone the tiny asteroid they were supposed to deliver the seeds to.

Ah well. That's on me.

Taking a Homesteader contract on the open market as an Uzari free-lancer with nothing to his name but debt.

Have I ever traveled with Talon to Vegaspace?

Something felt wrong.

A buzzing noise woke him. Deadeye stirred in the seat, his limbs so weak it felt like prying them out of industrial glue. The UNS overlay flickered in his vision, barely maintaining the connection with his brain and thus the ship's engine. If the link were lost for more than five seconds, the vessel would exit its jump early, and *Pohl* would be stuck light hears from nowhere. Rebooting the UNS after something like that usually had a low chance of success, often taking hours—if not sols. And that was if one had the right coordinates to continue the jump, make trajectory corrections....

Wait. The coordinates. The ones Talon had gotten from Sereda and the dead ensign's flight report.

He scrolled through the feeds, not believing his eyes.

These coordinates were different.

Deadeye checked the trajectory history. The coordinates weren't only different; they had changed in mid-jump. The chronometer revealed that nearly three more sols had passed.

He'd already flown into the Ross Boundary.

Now he'd have to make a second jump to continue the voyage. He had no idea if he could manage such a demanding pace; it took him two minutes to replace the first nutrient canister beside the pod and only then, with Icara's help. The ship was getting colder, and the air stuffier.

The air?

Deadeye thrashed in the pod, feeling for his faceplate, the rest of his helmet... there, he'd not taken it off. Damn, he'd nearly pissed himself. There were stories of Uzari or Aquarii who'd removed their helmets during fugue and suffocated due to the bridge's life support not being on. Yet his pod's air supply needed changing.

He blinked and found himself leaning over the pod's side, fingers a few centimeters from the oxygen canister. The overlay's chronometer showed that an hour had passed. He cursed and tried to sit up. The air tasted worse, like rotted paper books.

An hour. Fuck.

An hour could cost these people their lives, where every second of life support counted in the passenger cabins. The coordinates must enter the rest of the sequence, make the next jump....

The sequence. Numbers. Coordinates... but they led nowhere. The Ross Boundary was filled with objects that prevented any further travel. Three neutron stars and a collection of nebulae filled with super-hot gases that would melt the hull. An asteroid belt a hundred AU from every star, as thick as a planetesimal disk.

He laughed. That many celestial objects and phenomena in a six light-year radius were ridiculous. Yet there it was, clogging the UNS with a maze of impossibilities.

"You believe this sit?" he asked Icara, but the bot lacked a personality AI and responded with a status report on the wormhole integrity.

They were holding at 76%. 1% more, and the wormhole would collapse.

If he made two more jumps after the next one, those numbers could lead through the Boundary. Or was it just one jump? He wasn't sure anymore, the overlay was more liar than aid, and his body was failing him by the second.

She'd been right; he wouldn't make it... the woman with the coffee, the ponytail... Epsa? Runner? Jhia? One of those had been her name; he was sure of it.

Certainty wasn't a given between the stars. Between the realities of his past, his present, and whatever future awaited an Uzari whose mind was slowly being eaten by the very purpose he was created for.

That was the corporate bioengineers talking. Uzari had free will; they didn't have to throw their lives away as pilots for the Spur's powers, they didn't have to sacrifice themselves as many did in the pre-MEC era, just to travel from star to star....

Sacrifice.

Isn't that he'd done to prevent her from dying on this same voyage?

Deadeye crawled from the pod, changed the oxygen canister, and lay on the deck for some time. The jack cord in his neck grew taut, being so far from the pod. The overlay trembled in his sight as if the UNS was barely linked with his mind.

He wanted to puke.

Wait. How many times had that happened?

Such a weak connection might mean they'd been flung off course. They could be halfway across the Spur by now, thousands of light-years distant. Grunting, he struggled with his right glove. He had to see his skin, check it for liver spots, and examine it for wrinkles. Whether or not he could see the veins underneath the thin, aging flesh.

Shit, the cryopod; I'm probably an old man now....

Deadeye caught himself as a glimmer of sanity crept back into his consciousness. The bridge was sealed to preserve the air in the passenger cabins, and its temperature would be well below freezing. Exposing his hand to that would expel the pressure in his suit, then the oxygen in his blood would boil, his hand would freeze, and he'd die. Painfully.

"You could be more help, you know," he told Icara.

Icara maintained her hover distance as if waiting for him to fuck up.

The deck grew comfortable. He was accustomed to sleeping on it, not a bunk. At least if he woke up on the floor, he could simply stand and escape, but the bunk might trip him up. He'd meant to explain that to Talon when she'd woken him that time.

Talon! That was her name.

He laughed again, not caring if it caused him to vomit in his helmet. It was a thrilling, alien sensation, recalling details after traversing the seemingly infinite distances between rotating spheres of rock and gas.

"Talon."

Saying her name grounded him more than gravity ever could.

Slowly, he pulled himself back to the pod. The urge to vomit faded. His old traumatized impulse to sleep on the deck was easier to resist. The déjà vu of thinking the ship was off course vanished. Lips pursed, he whistled Bolero without shame. It was his way of keeping that woman alive, even if he eventually forgot why she'd mattered altogether.

Tears streamed down his face, but he wasn't sure why—

No.

They reminded him that he was still alive. He got back into the pod.

He studied the overlay again. At first, the coordinates looked like nonsense, impossible trajectories through what the nav system considered impassable regions. But the more he ran the calculations through the UNS, the more apparent it was that the neutron stars, nebulae, and asteroids were ships.

Like the Tombs, it was flying blind—with the UNS claiming he could see.

"Parallax," he muttered.

Again and again, he ran the calculations, with 18 and then 46 individual feeds open in his overlay—an overload of information that normal human brains couldn't process at once. Yet the price for such abilities drifted like a specter in the back of his mind. Each calculation likely eliminated a small, insignificant memory until the cumulative effect was a total loss of recollection, like those Uzari on *Xīng Huā*.

A ship broadcasting the false navigational data. Then another ship was performing the same function. They were spaced four light-years apart, at regular intervals within the Boundary. They were guaranteeing that any vessels approaching the cradle of humanity would be stopped by the erroneous information. Observational data that stated the truth—that there were no neutron stars in the Boundary—mattered little; the UNS detected what was there implied or otherwise.

He wasn't certain which star system the Sagittarii expected him to deliver them to. He'd need to wake them and ask. He still had to get these people to whatever paradise they imagined awaited them. It reminded him of some ancient myth, of a boatman ferrying the dead to their afterlife. It was a silly notion, shuttling the dead across a river to a better place, but no sillier than the idea of a human soul, which sounded more like Cepheid propaganda than the truth.

Yet the Boundary was a lie. A barrier that might as well be a bludgeon in the hands of MEC and the Lineage. The Prestige.

He touched his pocket; the chess piece was still there.

"Checkmate, motherfuckers."

Deadeye took a deep breath, did his best to recall the taste of that butterscotch coffee, and made the next jump.

Chapter 24

Though *Santo Pohl*'s warning alarms sounded, Deadeye maintained course. The Parallax coordinates allowed him to bypass a set of energy signatures emanated from four sources within the Boundary. Solar flares, gravitational waves, and in one case, a supernova. It was the same ships but broadcasting different information. Traveling via a wormhole demanded accuracy, and such navigational phantoms threatened to pull him from the jump. He recalled Epsi's warning about flights through the virtual barrier failing. Not even MEC's best crews had managed it.

He wondered how many Uzari, Aquarii, and Zyn had been forced to make the attempt.

Considering that the ships were light-years apart and the literal years it took for the signals from each vessel to travel the void, he surmised that each broadcast a continually evolving set of navigational quandaries to fool any who ventured into the Boundary. It was ingenious in its own annoying way.

Deadeye wanted to know why.

The bridge hatch slid open, but he didn't turn around. He'd watched the anxious Sagittarii on the security cam feed for the past half hour; they were concerned. Most expected to have reached their destination by now. And with *Pohl* shaking due to wormhole integrity of 78% and the alarms eating away at their eardrums, they wanted to know what was happening. The children in the passenger berths still played their games, oblivious to the genuine dangers awaiting mere centimeters past the ship's hull.

Sereda walked up to the pod and stared down at Deadeye.

"What has occurred? My people, they think the ship might come apart at any time. Are we in jeopardy?"

"Not exactly."

Deadeye studied the UNS's central feed. Seven hundred kilometers to go.

"Then what are you doing?" Sereda's voice lowered. "Talon promised that we would be able to return to our ancestral home in less than a week."

"Keeping us alive."

Deadeye didn't look at the man, his gaze transfixed on the overlay. Five hundred kilometers until he exited the jump.

More warning alarms. *Pohl* shuddered as the Casimir drive tried to maintain course through the wormhole, confused by the jumbled navigational data.

"You'll fly us apart! This isn't what we contracted you for!"

The rest of Sereda's words became lost in the mental jumble now invading Deadeye's thoughts. The human mind wasn't a computer, nor was it meant to be. It wasn't good at running data in a conscious effort but rather in the background, via instinctual controls and subconscious reactions to stimuli. It worked best on a savanna, chasing antelopes while armed with a spear; it worked magnificently while copulating with abandon in the night; it reached its apex when it could set aside hatred, hunger, fear, and selfishness to save others. That was what he was attempting now, even as he acted as a conduit between the UNS and *Santo Pohl.*

Wormhole integrity fell below 75%, and *Pohl* exited the rift in spacetime.

Just like Deadeye had planned.

The ship waited fifty-four kilometers ahead. A blip on the UNS, broadcasting far larger shapes. Its beacon was barely detectable through the false data on radiation and flares. For Deadeye, being so close to the very thing broadcasting the errors meant to deter anyone from navigating a path through the Boundary....

Wait. There was something else. Chillingly familiar.

The UNS radar revealed other shapes that did not flicker and transform into navigational viragos. Rectangular entities that measured five hundred meters long, spaced in ring-like formations around the broadcasting vessel.

They were Prestige ships.

A half-smile stole over his face as Deadeye remembered. He'd flown into a hive of such craft at 82Eri. His naval commanders had projected victory over the automated enemies that refused to let MEC ships near the Boundary. Half of the fleet had been lost in that battle, but the Prestige had withdrawn. Celebrations had been short-lived, as the Stein Revolt came soon after. That's why he recalled it.

Son of a bitch.

That's why he remembered strafing the village—because afterward, he'd disobeyed a direct order to finish the deed. The navy had discharged him, but being an Uzari, he'd still gotten contracts to fly MEC's merchant transports...

There were no orders now—no chain of command. Parallax had allowed him to do what MEC had tried—fly past the Boundary and evade the bulk of the Prestige fleets.

He still wanted to know why—

The Prestige ships reoriented themselves and set course for his position.

He readied the small complement of missiles he and Talon had installed on *Pohl.*

"Oh, holy Nyx," Sereda breathed. "Is this it, at long last?"

"What... is it?" Deadeye gritted his teeth against the flow of UNS data.

A sphere lurked just under four hundred thousand kilometers from the broadcast ship and Prestige vessels. He'd been so focused on the automated craft; Deadeye hadn't noticed. Typical sensors masked its presence due to the false nav information.

A hidden planet.

Sereda held onto the captain's chair, though his magnetic soles kept him rooted to the deck.

"The birthplace of our species. The planet of tall, green trees and wide, deep, blue oceans. Clouds that transform shapes as the winds toss them across the sky. And the animals, the wildlife—so many they cannot be counted, my friend. So many species and subspecies that it feels like another universe, rather than a single world."

Deadeye glanced up at him and recognized that crazed smile, the glazed look in Sereda's eyes as he stared out the viewport, where only stars stared back. It was the look of the true believer, one who could never be dissuaded from their convictions no matter what befell them—or proved them false.

"You really think that's true?" Deadeye asked.

Sereda smiled sadly, no doubt having heard such questions before.

"You are right to question, but I have seen vids and images. I have heard the stories. Many of them are fantastical or meant to lead others to a line of thought or an agenda, but we simply wish to return home. Our original home."

"What if it's no longer there? Or poisoned by radiation or pollution? Or these Prestige bastards have conquered it?"

He was glad Sereda couldn't see what was happeningout there, not being connected to the UNS. Let the old man enjoy some calm after all that hiding.

Sereda straightened. "So be it. We knew the risks before setting out, even before preparing so this journey. There is nothing for the Sagittarii in the Merged Earth Colonies or the other regions guarded by the Prestige's automated fleets. Our species built those unmanned craft, but their purpose is no longer necessary. That is what my people have long believed since Pietist Bester proved that the Boundary was a ruse. Why did you bring us if you don't believe it yourself? That is the real question."

A targeting reticule appeared in the overlay. Deadeye smiled.

"I'm no philosopher. I just fly the ships."

"A philosophy of action instead of thought—but a philosophy all the same," Sereda said. "What would you do, young man, if you found your original home?"

Deadeye almost cursed him since Uzari were unlikely to recall such a thing. Or even have a home in the traditional human sense, since so many came from MEC labs now, based on Uzari Corp's genetic templates. Yet there was no ignorance or malice in Sereda's question, only a simple curiosity, and that was something Deadeye could appreciate. He indulged curiosity every time he made a jump.

The reticule locked onto the broadcasting ship. The Prestige craft closed in.

"I'd give it to someone else," Deadeye said.

Sereda grunted in surprise. "Truly? Whatever for?"

"Someone else could make better use of it. Someone who might make it a home—for themselves and maybe other people too, I don't know. I do know that I'd probably ruin it. Let someone else have it."

"What a charitable thing to say," Sereda said. "I wish more people in the Spur thought as you do. Yet MEC and the Lineage keep so many under their heel, and the Homesteaders promise a new beginning without any thought to the risks. This is the only option for the Sagittarii, and we must...."

The rest of Sereda's words faded in the background as Deadeye flew closer to the other vessel. Now less than twenty thousand kilometers away, *Pohl*'s scopes granted a few visual details of the craft. The images chilled him to the bone—and a new wave of UNS readings took his breath.

The vessel was an ancient colony ship, similar to those in the Tombs. It transmitted distress signals that had become mixed with Parallax's navigational trap—creating the Ross Boundary. A barrier that prevented humans from using their greatest engineering achievement—wormhole travel—to pass through. Initially, he'd thought Parallax might be some insidious design meant to protect or hide something.

The ship, and its three counterparts, warned people to stay out of the Boundary not because of some sacred site, an alien presence, or any other conspiracy theory. They had been put into place to spare others from the same fate.

Deadeye blasted past the Prestige ships. They'd be upon him within minutes.

"What... what is this?" Sereda asked with trepidation.

Hundreds of similar colony vessels appeared on the radar, undetectable until now due to Parallax. They all drifted in sluggish orbit about the planet—a blue-green planet. *Pohl*'s spectrometers revealed no activity on the ships, not even fusion core signatures—meaning the scattered fleet was effectively another graveyard, like the Tombs. The sensors did pick up an inordinate amount of radiation on each craft.

"Your home," Deadeye said. "Or what's left of it."

"*This* is the Earth?"

There was no joy in Sereda's voice.

Deadeye checked activity on the system's parent star. A yellow main sequence sun with an unusual amount of solar flares. He leaned back in the pod and sighed.

"Tell me, what is it?" Sereda asked. "Why do you appear so downcast?"

"I'm guessing this is why our species left Sol in the first place, in such large numbers," Deadeye said. "This sun was too dangerous to live near, at least when these colony ships worked. Those flares? They must have disabled all these vessels I'm picking up on radar and scopes. Maybe this was Earth's last colony fleet, trying to leave but caught by the radiation? It shorted out their systems, even their reactors, stranding them to a slow death. Damn."

"No!"

Sereda stomped to the viewport as if he could push the derelicts from their path.

"If that is true, then Earth... oh, blessed Nyx, please, not after we've come so far!"

"The Sagittarii was the security arm of the old colonists," Deadeye said. "That's what that ensign's report was about, then. It was a warning, not a map. The rest must not have believed her and wanted to turn back."

Sereda shook his head. "No..."

"I guess the Prestige was built by whoever put the Boundary in place," Deadeye said. "Meant to keep all of us out, for our own good. Only now, those damn AI keep replicating themselves, spreading over the Spur. So much for that plan."

Sereda glared at him. "My people have not been living a lie, damn you. Sereda glared at him. We have suffered too much, for too long—"

"Welcome to the universe," Deadeye said.

Sereda closed his eyes, took a deep breath, and calmed himself. "Very well. I cannot deny the logic of your assumptions. But I also cannot deny my people. Will you take us into orbit above that planet?"

"You're serious? There's Prestige everywhere—you still want to do this?"

"If we are to perish, let it be here, on Terran soil," Sereda said.

Moments passed as Deadeye checked and double-checked his feeds. Sure enough, the automated vessels were still on course to intercept *Pohl* in thirty seconds.

"It's your choice," Deadeye finally said. "The radiation might have mutated everything down there, all those trees and oceans you mentioned. Or maybe it's still beautiful. I hope it is. I also hope you brought shelters, hydroponics labs—"

"We have all that we need."

Sereda stared at the sphere through the viewport , then nodded.

"Thank you. I will get my people ready."

"First... let me do this."

Deadeye loosed *Pohl*'s missiles.

Sereda gaped. "What in the void was that for? There is no enemy out there—"

"That's right, there isn't," Deadeye said.

Less than seven seconds later, the missiles destroyed the vessel broadcasting Parallax. The false anomalies and objects in the UNS vanished. A mental weight lifted from Deadeye, and he relaxed for a moment. Though three other Parallax craft remained in the Boundary, destroying one gave him some immediate respite.

The Prestige craft jetted braking thrusters and remained in place. No more than inert blips on his radar feed. He considered using the rest of *Pohl*'s missiles on them, but no. Parallax controlled them, too, at least within the Boundary—and if it wasn't broadcasting a warning message, perhaps the Prestige didn't see him as a threat.

A plan formed in his tired mind.

"I hope you don't mind sharing Earth, Overseer, because soon, everybody will be able to return."

Deadeye gave him a tired smile.

"Now, you might want to buckle up in those berths. Get your people ready. I hear reentry is one hell of a ride."

Santo Pohl orbited four hundred kilometers above the blue-green planet's surface. The world's thermosphere was filled with numerous satellites, stations, and space junk, but Deadeye easily navigated it. *Pohl*'s sensors detected no unusual amounts of radiation, so perhaps the Sagittarii would be fine after all.

Other sensor scans fueled his fantasies of what it must be like, planetside: Earth had a gravity of 1.0, a 24-hour sol, and was twelve thousand and seven hundred kilometers in diameter. There were various biomes, ranging from slim ice caps to deserts, to great green swaths he took to be a jungle.

It also had bodies of water. Clouds that drifted and changed shape before his eyes.

He wished *Valkyrie*'s crew could see it. Wished Talon was there with him.

He watched the Sagittarii weep, cheer, embrace, and sing songs on the security cams. As he started the berths' release sequence, their excitement gave way to hushed whispers, nervous looks, and ecstatic smiles. Parents held up their children to see through the tiny viewports. Some murmured prayers or shook hands in congratulations.

Just before he detached the berths, Deadeye spotted Sereda on one of the feeds, holding a hand to the camera. A sign of peace and trade, of civilization.

"Right back at you."

Deadeye jettisoned the berths.

He watched the armored, curved shapes streak down into Earth's atmosphere for several minutes, each a brilliant star of hope and promise. Sereda had asked him to jettison them over a continent shaped like a horn, with a massive desert leading to lush green forests and turquoise-rimmed coastlines.

He observed the glorious blue-green sphere for hours, making a complete orbit every ninety-three minutes. So much water, more than any other planet he'd heard of in the Dust Systems, the Arcturus Ring, or even the Golden Band. Scopes made out grey-brown patches here and there, particularly along the coasts. Cities, he assumed. He'd heard that ancient peoples had dwelled near great bodies of water to facilitate sea-going voyages. They'd used the stars to navigate, too.

Such a small expanse to explore—yet full of mystery and possibility.

Finally, he set course for the next Parallax ship he'd detected. *Santo Pohl* had enough hadrons for eight more light-years. Though he could escape the Boundary and perhaps find an outpost in the Golden Band, he had no reason to return. His friends might be dead or had already forgotten him. And Talon....

Deadeye slept a cycle, ate what little food remained in the galley, and jumped.

Debris from the second Parallax ship scattered across his radar, but Deadeye barely noticed. That last jump had taken a toll; he'd vomited for an hour afterward and had to sleep half a cycle. *Pohl*'s air was getting thinner, and he forced himself not to puke again since he'd have to remove his helmet.

And he was out of missiles, with two more Parallax vessels yet to be eliminated.

"What do you think, huh?"

He snickered as Icara hovered above his helmet.

Maybe he'd ram the next one. With only enough hadrons for three light-years, he'd have to make up the difference in distance with *Pohl*'s fusion engine, which barely made light-speed. There wasn't enough air or nutrients left on the ship to sustain him for that voyage. *Pohl* only had supplies for twenty-three more sols.

No matter. He'd chosen this end.

He crawled back into the pod. Set the coordinates and plotted the trajectory.

Santo Pohl exited the jump after a mere five seconds.

The wormhole integrity refused to go above the required 75%, which was still dangerous. He was stuck out there. Drifting a few light-years from Earth.

He chuckled and blew out a breath.

"*Ha*, you son of a bitch."

He chuckled and blew out a breath.

After staring aimlessly at the now inactive feeds, Deadeye disconnected from the UNS. He left the pod and put on a thicker spacesuit, one of the IVA sets Talon had left onboard. He could try to jump again, but that risked causing the Casimir drive to detonate before traveling a few AU. He was drifting past Alpha Centauri at a distance of one point four light-years. It was a trinary system that was the closest to Earth. Such a strange name for a place. He wondered what it meant.

If he used *Santo Pohl*'s fusion engine, he could reach it in one point four years, making him laugh again until he examined the power routers. The ones leading from the reactor to the Casimir drive and the conventional engine had fried during his failed jump.

"Well, damn. Looks like you'll be captain soon, Icara."

Deadeye allowed himself to float back through *Pohl*'s corridors. Limbs spread out, eyes closed. Trying to navigate his final ocean.

Maybe the Prestige ships would find him after all and end it....

Six hours later, he was still floating on the ship. Maybe if he set his air tanks to leak until he asphyxiated slowly....

Three more hours until he grew nervous, licking his lips. The temptation to jack back into the UNS and make the jump any damn way was overpowering. Six times he paused outside the bridge, unable to fling his atomized body across the cosmos just yet.

Two sols later, he eyed the utility blades in the tool locker outside the airlock chamber. One quick cut, the blood would balloon in the wound due to the lack of gravity, his air pressure would vanish, and it would be over.

Three more sols. Or was it five?

Suicide was a constant afterthought as he floated back and forth through the corridors. He might have slept; he wasn't certain. Thoughts of the Sagittarii occupied him for a while. Wondering what they would name their new colony. Probably some crazy cult title. He laughed, thinking about them erecting a statue to him, the fool who had brought them there. He rather liked being remembered as a jester deity, a spacer trickster who's saved them in their hour of need.

All the while, Icara followed him. The crazy little bot probably still wanted to shoot him. He couldn't recall why, but it made him smile.

Sometimes he whistled that weird tune. Every now and then, he stuck the king chess piece on the wall, its magnetic bottom holding the miniature potentate in place. He laughed for hours while staring at it but didn't understand why it was humorous. Often, he floated into the crew cabins and touched the bunks. He'd slept in one with somebody; they'd had very warm, smooth skin and smelled of cocoa butter soap....

More sols passed—too many. The food in the nutrient canisters ran out first, then the water. Though, they still had oxygen as if some vengeful space god wanted to keep him alive to suffer. Icara kept refilling his air canister since he was too weak to try.

"Why don't you lemme die?" he mumbled. "Gonna make the Cap'n mad...."

Icara's holoprojector displayed a woman's image, with the title 'captain' beneath it. Dark brown hair, grey eyes, a crisp military uniform... it was a naval ID pic.

The name displayed was "Lieutenant Commander Miranda Traxe."

He laughed. "That's not the Cap'n, that's... my Miss Cygni. Look at her. Wow."

Deadeye closed his eyes and continued drifting through the ship. His breathing and the latent static of an empty radiofrequency were the only sounds.

Other sounds passed in his memories. A woman whistling a lullaby or the creak of a hull as projectiles sheared through it. The commands of a naval officer, demanding he finish off the village or engage those damned robotic vessels. It was all noise in the end.

He kept imagining the woman from Icara's holo with a ponytail. Ah, that MEC uniform. How smart she'd appeared, how hopeful and determined she must have felt when they snapped that image. She would have wanted him to stay alive.

"Can't displease the Cap'n, now... gimme some more air, then."

He smiled at Icara, who obeyed. "Not the air... from *Valkyrie*, either...."

Valkyrie... the ship I'd served on? No, wait....

He didn't know why, but he recalled an old military salute and delivered it as if he could see the woman right before him, a ghost cast across the light-years, an illusion his mind mercifully delivered to him, even as *Santo Pohl* delivered him to eternity.

As he drifted past the airlock viewport, bright white light shone. He smiled.

"Deadie boy?"

A voice. Ha. The goddamn ship was playing tricks on me. Or Icara. Damn bot.

"Deadie, you read me in there?"

"Poor bastard's probably dead, Talon," another voice said. "Look at *Pohl*'s hull. Did he fly through an atmosphere or some shit?"

"The berths are gone, and with that scoring on the hull, heh, it means he got those people home," the first voice said. "Come on, get *Cygni* closer, right?"

Deadeye tried to speak, but only a croak escaped his dry lips.

"Hey there, Wizard, did you plant a nasty fart in that pod?" a third voice asked.

"No, Runnie, that noise wasn't from our ship," the first voice said. "Here, the airlock! Shine that floodlight again!"

The bright light appeared once more. He squinted. Tried to shield his eyes.

Something clasped at his hand.

"Deadie? Oh fuck. Runnie, hurry with that med bot! Icara, you sweet girl, keep that air canister handy!"

Deadeye's fingers came to life, then his palm, then his wrist. Life returned to the rest of his body in short order. He flexed his fingers. Their gloved tips connected with something tangible. Soft, yet firm. Whatever it was gripped his fingers back, so tight it hurt. It was a glorious pain—the pain of being alive.

He floated up against something as the light through the airlock settled on him. The hatch was open, exposing him to the abject nothingness of vacuum. But there was something in there with him, and his gaze slowly roved up a pair of legs, a waist, torso, all of it wrapped in a white armor panoply. A faceplate came next, and there was a visage behind it, past his reflection therein. Framed in a comm cap, beaming with emotion.

He grinned so wide it hurt his freezing face.

"Deadie? You know who I am?" she asked.

"I...."

He touched her faceplate, uncertain. "How... you here?"

"I snatched up Runnie and Wizard before we left Hartwell. Epsi... she's a hero, she gave us time to... but she's gone. Then all those Free-lancer ships got in MEC's way, the hadron brains. Thank the void for spacers who shit their pants in a fight. Had to leave *Valkyrie*, *Annie Argent*, and *Corsair*, but... well, then we followed your trajectory, and the Boundary was... *gone*. The Prestige let us pass."

"Reckon you had anything to with that?" Runabout asked.

Deadeye smiled and tried to shrug. "I... punked them all."

Talon grinned, holding him closer. "Yeah, we could travel after you pretty safely. Word will spread since those Sagittarii are broadcasting a message to the rest of the Spur. You've started something, right? I hope it's good. For business and all."

She told him other things, but Deadeye simply watched her eyes dart back and forth, her lips move, her expressions change from excitement to gratitude to relief.

"Cap'n Talon," he managed to say. "Hey... I remembered... this time."

"You did; you sure as hell did."

Her hand rested on his chest.

"Captain, we need to get him and get the hell on out," Wizard said. "*Pohl*'s reactor has been compromised. He must have made a bum jump."

"Send the repair bots over and get the Casimir drive first," Talon said. "His vitals are still decent but a little weak if that sensor in his suit isn't screwy. Thank the void for Icara; he'd probably be dead if not for her."

"That's..." Deadeye coughed. "That's why you... followed me? The... drive?"

"Oh fuck off. I'll show you why later, all right?"

She smiled, though her eyes misted over.

"You got me?"

"I got you."

He clasped her hand as she jetted them back through the airlock to *Miss Cygni*.

The story continues in Dying Suns.

Thank you for reading Parallax

We hope you enjoyed it as much as we enjoyed bringing it to you. We just wanted to take a moment to encourage you to review the book. Follow this link: **Parallax** to be directed to the book's Amazon product page to leave your review.

Every review helps further the author's reach and, ultimately, helps them continue writing fantastic books for us all to enjoy.

You can also join our non-spam mailing list by visiting www.subscribepage.com/AethonReadersGroup and never miss out on future releases. You'll also receive three full books completely Free as our thanks to you.

Facebook | Instagram | Twitter | Website

Want to discuss our books with other readers and even the authors? Join our Discord server today and be a part of the Aethon community.

ALSO IN THE SERIES

You just read: Parallax
Up next: Drying Suns
Then: Termination Vector

Looking for more great Science Fiction?

A daring rescue. Interstellar war. Reality-shattering conspiracy...

In the midst of fighting a reignited war with the deadly Nimic, Lt. Commander Johnny Rangers of the Confederation of Aligned Planets is dragged into a rescue mission by mysterious agent Koya Nyrus.

With his best friend's life at stake, he finds himself on a restricted world full of secrets that could alter the course of the war.

Meanwhile, Rangers' father, Inspector Frank Branza of the Gravity City Police Force, sets out to uncover a vast conspiracy with plans to affect the very fabric of reality.

Little do the estranged father and son realize they're on the same deadly path that will change the galaxy forever.

. . .

Don't miss the start of the Gravity City series by CJ Valin and Artie Cabrera. Space will never be the same after this rip-roaring adventure across the stars!

Get Thieves of Destiny Now!

Kyle Washaki 'Wash' Williams thought his life couldn't get any more complicated. Then the aliens showed up...

After his mom died from cancer, Wash gave up his girlfriend and his dream of being a career Army officer to stay home and take care of his father, a former Special Forces soldier stricken with PTSD. Wash works three jobs just to pay the bills, and one of them is at the ranch of the man who's engaged to his ex-girlfriend, Jimmy Bonner.

Sound rough? He thought so too...until a portal to a hell-world of giant, insectoid aliens opens behind the ranch house, sucking Wash and Jimmy into the nightmare domain of the Hive Mind, a monstrous, underground blob of brain tissue that stretches across multiple planets through the Gate System.

It exists only to spread itself across the universe. And its next target is Earth.

Will Wash be able to defend the planet from conquest by a swarm of giant alien insects? And will Jimmy be able to put aside his rivalry with Wash to fight for Earth, or will he decide that an alien horde is the perfect tool to dispose of his old enemy?

The answer lies on the other side...of the Gates of Hell.

Get Gates of Hell Now!

They fight the wars nobody else wants to.

The Frontier Corps are the Terran Empire's repository for failures, malcontents, criminals, and other people with nothing left to lose but to sign their names on the dotted line of a ten year long contract for another shot at life.

But flung across the stars to face horriying enemies, it may as well be a death sentence.

Pari Petrosyan is a grizzled veteran of the Corps. With only a few months left of her contract, she has her mind on her discharge papers. Her easy path on her way to freedom is interrupted when a new commander arrives, ready to launch a large-scale military offensive to finally end the conflict she had spent her entire career fighting.

Caught between the grinding war machines of the empire and the inhuman monstrosities known as the Resh, Pari has to try to survive if she ever hopes to be free.

Get Frontier Corps

For all our Sci-Fi books, visit our website.

that it was a bad gun— it was a damn fine gun— it just wasn't his. It wasn't the Dragoon. It was an 1860 Colt Army revolver converted to take metal cartridges, and the man who'd last owned it was lying dead in Bette's Creek with a bullet through his skull. The only name Balum had known him by was Fletcher, and if he had placed his bullet six inches to the right, Balum would be lying face-up on an empty barroom floor in Bette's Creek. But Fletcher had missed. His bullet had struck the barrel of the Dragoon, rendering it useless. And so for the first time since the age of seventeen, Balum found himself with a new gun. The Colt Army was lighter than the Dragoon, slightly smaller, easier to load, and it fired true. He should count himself lucky to have it, he knew that. Lucky, yes, but it didn't change the fact that he missed his old revolver.

The fog had cleared. A treeless landscape emerged, full of sand, grass, a few stray tumbleweeds. Balum unholstered the Colt and held it to the morning light and drew the hammer back. The cylinder rotated. A soft click. A new chamber. He dropped the gun into his holster and picked out an agave plant growing some sixty yards out, then drew and fired.

If anyone was around to see it they might have thought some trick had been played on them. Some slight-of-hand, a bit of witchery. His fingers had hung motionless beside the leather holster, and then the gun was bucking in his palm and the agave was vibrating from the smack of bullets. The faintest blur of motion was the only giveaway, and not many an eye would have caught it.

He holstered the Colt and walked out to the agave and

squatted beside it. Two leaves, two holes. He stood and walked back to where he'd started from and did it all over again. Hand beside the gun, palm to the butt, the swoosh as the barrel cleared leather, thumb raking back the hammer as he brought it level, the sharp recoil of the shot.

The agave shook. Two new holes appeared below the first.

"Did that agave have a wanted poster out on it?"

Balum turned. Joe stood with his thumbs hooked over his belt, a smile across his face. His black hair lay over his shoulders, halfway down his chest.

"You can't help but sneak up on a man, can you?" said Balum.

"Blame it on the Apache in me," said Joe. He glanced at the plant and narrowed his eyes. "That's some fine shooting. And I'm not just talking about the speed, I'm talking about placement. You can put those bullets anywhere you want."

"It's not so hard when nobody's shooting back."

"I've seen them shoot back at you and it's no different." Joe unhooked a thumb from his belt and motioned to the Colt Army. "What do you think?"

"It's alright."

"Just alright?"

Balum holstered it. He looked off across the flatlands and snorted. "It's no Dragoon."

"I'd say that's a good thing. How long would it take you to load that Dragoon? Fastest time possible."

Balum thought about it. The truth was that it took too long; measuring out the powder, inserting the wad, then the bullet, ramming it all down the chamber, repeating it six times